Past encounters

DAVINA BLAKE

Davina Blake

ISBN-13: 978-1499568257

ISBN-10: 1499568258

Also by Davina Blake

writing as Deborah Swift

The Lady's Slipper

The Gilded Lily

A Divided Inheritance

Rhoda

I'd seen *Brief Encounter* fourteen times, but today the picture house was half-empty. I sat at the back and lit a cigarette as the auditorium dimmed, and for the first time the titles struck me as old-fashioned – too square and bold. I exhaled and watched a curl of smoke drift into the slant of light coming from behind me.

Over my shoulder I caught a glimpse of the flickering square of the projection booth, a reminder that what seemed real was just smoke and light, an illusion repeating the same thing over and over. I crushed my cigarette into the brass half-moon ashtray.

He's not here, I thought. *No matter how many times I watch it, I'll never find him here.*

Unsteadily, I found my way towards the slit of brightness round the door. Outside, life was rushing forwards. I put my hand on the door plate, took a deep breath.

Peter

Peter knew he should go; leave Archie and Helen to have their last moments alone. He squeezed Archie's hand and it felt dry and flimsy, like a bag of rattling bones. He could not say the word 'goodbye', could not imagine him gone.

'Count with me,' he said, through tears, 'like we used to.'

Archie's breath faltered. His throat was closing to life and he was lost in a blizzard of morphine and pain. Peter let go of Archie's hand, counted for him, 'One, two, three …,' and kept on, even as he found his way to the door and drove away.

1

1955 Rhoda

I SAW HIM do it. Put his fist through the window of our back door. The blurred shadow at the window, then the crack as his white knuckles burst through. I was coming downstairs with a batch of laundry and my first thought was that it was a burglar. But then I saw Peter's white face as the splatter of glass fell away.

I dropped the clothes and rushed through the kitchen, calling, 'Are you all right?' Only afterwards did I have time to think, what a ridiculous question. My husband had just put his fist through a door. On purpose. Of course he wasn't all right.

As I got to the bottom of the stairs he was pushing his way inside. 'An accident,' he said, not looking at me. Glass chinked as the door scraped over the mat.

'What in blazes were you doing?' I glared at him, waited for an explanation.

'I've made a bit of a mess,' he said. He wiped his cheek with the back of his hand and a smear of blood appeared there. It was only then that I became aware his eyes were wet. Peter was crying. I'd never seen him cry. I didn't know what to do.

'You've got blood on your cheek,' I said.

'Oh, heck.' He tilted his head to wipe his cheek on the shoulder of his jacket.

'Don't do that! It'll stain. What a stupid thing to do!' I tried to bring him inside, but he would not move. 'Let me look at your hand.'

'No, it's nothing. It's all right.' He did not want me to see, but I insisted. It was only a small cut, but it was deep, and I could hear him breathing heavily as if he'd just run up a hill. It shocked me, to see the brightness of his blood.

I patted him on the sleeve. I needed to get back to normality. 'We've got Elastoplast in the kitchen drawer, let's get you fixed up. Don't want to be late, do you?'

'No,' he said, but his blank expression showed he wasn't really hearing me. I walked backwards into the kitchen, my feet crunching on bits of stray glass, but he didn't come. I turned to see him still standing motionless by the open door, looking out over the garden, over the clumps of papery daffodils. It was then that I noticed the letter held tightly in his left hand. As I watched, he folded it in half, trying not to get blood on it, and put it in his jacket pocket.

When he did eventually come in, the blood had spotted his white cuff so that I had to hold it over the sink and scrub at it with the carbolic. It wouldn't do for the new headmaster of St Cuthbert's to have blood on his shirt. I did not dare ask him what had got into him; it raised far too many questions for that time in the morning, only ten minutes before he had to leave for work.

At twenty to nine, I handed him his briefcase of books and he pressed his familiar dry lips briefly to mine. The blare of the wireless behind me assured me it was a 'good morning, Britain'. I watched his back as he walked up the road. It put me in mind of an empty suit walking. As if he was just putting one foot in front of the other. He crossed the road without even looking. *Be careful!* The thought was too late, a car swerved and a horn blasted.

He had been odd for the last few weeks, distracted somehow. I knew something was wrong, but whenever I'd asked him what was the matter, he'd brushed me off. Two letters had come today. One was obviously a bill in a long brown envelope, and the other handwritten, though I hadn't paid it much attention until now, because he got that sort of letter quite often, from grateful parents.

Summer or winter, he took the day's post and his morning coffee out into the garden for a few quiet moments before setting off for work. Usually he sauntered in when he'd read the post and left his cup with its cold dregs on the worktop. But today the window in the door was a gaping hole, and the glass glinted on the step. I hoped the neighbours next door hadn't seen him, or what would they think? His cup was still there on the bench, the milky coffee half-drunk.

Later, as I piled his cup and saucer into the bowl and aimed the rubber nozzle at them, the image niggled me. Peter standing there on the doormat, his face ashen, holding on to his fingers with the blood dripping on to the lino. It was unlike him. Had he gone mad? I had never been able to get that much reaction from him over anything, even when we argued.

On the stairs a pile of Peter's shirts and underwear straggled where I'd dropped them. I gathered up the white work shirts, the checked weekend shirts with the frayed collars where his stubble had worn the fabric thin. I stared down at them. I probably knew more about the shirts than I knew about the man.

The incident with the door jolted me. I felt something, and I realised I hadn't felt a flicker of anything for Peter – not for a very long time. When love dropped into my lap ten

3

years ago, it was like an incendiary, consuming everything around it.

But then I lost Matthew. And I thought the fire in me had gone out for good, that I would never feel anything worth feeling again.

Before Peter came home from work, I put on lipstick, wore my new skirt with the stiff petticoat.

'Are we going out?' he asked.

'No, I just thought I'd make a bit more of an effort, that's all.'

'That's good. I've got stacks of reports to do.' He dumped the briefcase on the dining table with a thud.

'How's your hand?' I asked.

'It was only a scratch.'

'But I saw you do it. You just broke the window yourself. Was there something in those letters that—'

'Just leave it, okay? I'll get the bloody window fixed.'

I pushed the cottage pie round the plate with a fork. I didn't feel like eating any more. I stood to take the plates.

'You're not going to waste that, are you?'

'I'm not hungry.'

'Give it to me then. Why serve yourself so much if you can't eat it?'

I left him at the table. What had happened to us? I felt old beyond my thirty-four years. The future stretched ahead like a dark tunnel. We would be sixty, maybe seventy before we died, and I was to have another thirty years of this. I had an urge to fling open the door and run, keep on running until my soles wore out, like in that film, *The Red Shoes*.

I thought back to my eighteen-year-old self and wondered what she would have thought of me. But she would have been yelling at me to run too.

2

1955 Rhoda

WHENEVER I WENT in and out of the back door I saw the new window. Not a patterned glass one like we had before, but a new frosted one. The door would not let me forget. I took more notice of Peter's mail now. He often had letters with the same rounded handwriting, postmarked Lancaster. I'd already let it go on for a few months. When I asked him about them, he said they were from a teacher at another school, asking his advice. But since the door incident, I did not believe him.

I couldn't find the letters in the house and wondered if he threw them away or took them to his office at school. I became obsessed with them, watching for his reaction whenever one came.

Finally I could not resist. I monitored the post until another of those letters dropped through. I snatched it up and hid it in my dressing gown pocket, made Peter's coffee as usual, and then let him collect the remaining mail from the mat. When he'd gone to work I tried to steam open the letter.

In novels it was always quite straightforward, this steaming business. But the flap was stuck well down, and the letter got damper and damper, until the ink on the front began to blur. Damn, damn. Eventually I resorted to a kitchen knife and managed to ease the flap open.

The envelope contained a single sheet of paper.

> *14 Bygrove Street*
>
> *Lancaster*
>
> *15th April*

Dear Peter,

So lovely of you to send me flowers, I was really touched. Looking forward to seeing you next week at the usual time.

Much love,

Helen x

The usual time. The words were like a fist in the stomach but I fought the urge to rip the paper in two. I fetched some gum from the drawer, sealed up the envelope again and the following morning replaced it on the mat with the rest of the bills. At the breakfast table there was no sign of it, so that was proof enough.

Two days later I got on a train.

Whoever she was, I had an address for Helen. I had never once had flowers from Peter in my whole life. Anger swamped me in waves. Now he infuriated me, behaving just the same way as he always did, coming in and wanting his evening meal ready on the table, or leaving his half-empty cup on the bench outside and expecting me to collect it. I knew our marriage wasn't perfect, but that he should have someone else made me want to hit him, even though I, of all people, had no right to be angry.

Several times I nearly asked him who Helen was, but I was scared to. What if I was wrong and she really was just another teacher? I'd feel such a fool. I needed some proof, needed to know first if it was true. So today I was on my way to Bygrove Street, Lancaster.

The landscape rushed by in a blur of rain, diagonal rivulets of water streaming off the carriage windows. Peter thought I was going shopping with my friend Jean and then to her house for tea. I'd told him I'd be back late. The lie had stuck in my throat but gave me a sting of satisfaction; that I could do to him what he must have been doing to me for — how long? Years, probably.

I walked around the town aimlessly until it grew dark and I could go to the address on Bygrove Street. If this woman was really a teacher, she might be in, if I waited until after six. I asked someone directions, but the closer I got, the more nervous I became. The houses shrank from large stone-built Georgian terraces to smaller brick-built ones, all crammed together, their front doors almost touching.

Bygrove Street was neat and tidy, but uninspiring. The houses had yellowing net curtains and dustbins in the front yards. Slowly, I walked down the row, handbag over my arm, looking for number fourteen. At number sixteen I hesitated. It seemed melodramatic, this idea of confronting Peter's mistress. Even the word. There wasn't a sensible adult word for what she was. I stood a moment, flustered. Should I go back? There would be a bus into town from the main road. It would be much easier to do what Peter and I had always done — sweep our difficulties so deep under the carpet they never resurfaced.

I brushed down the jacket of my best Dior-style navy

suit. I'd buttoned it up tight and added an expensive checked silk scarf at the neck. It made me look a little intimidating, not really like flighty me at all, but I wanted Helen to see me as a serious person, someone to be reckoned with.

Number fourteen had a paved front path and shrubs in the tiny front garden. Weeds poked up from the gaps in the flagstones. So not a gardener then – not like Peter; he loved his plants.

I steeled myself. I had to do it, had to confront it. I was over thirty, for God's sake! Too old to be putting up with these things. Yet even though I was in the right, inside I felt like a nervous teenager again, all fingers and thumbs and awkward corners. Strange, because when I was eighteen I felt as though an older woman lived inside me. I straightened the scarf, ran a hand through my unruly hair.

There was a knocker in the shape of a brass urn in the middle of the front door, not a bell. I rapped and the noise of it gave me a jolt. Through the frosted glass panel on the door I saw a hall light come on and then the glass darken as somebody approached. My stomach dropped. So she was in. The door opened and a small, neat woman of about my own age stood there, eyebrows raised in question.

My mouth was dry. 'Are you Helen?'

She was more ordinary than I had expected. 'Yes,' she said brightly, evidently unaware of why I was there.

'I believe you know my husband, Peter.'

I waited for her flustered reaction but instead she looked puzzled.

'Peter Middleton. I'm his wife.'

Her eyes flashed wide in surprise. 'Good heavens, are you Rhoda? Oh, please, come in.' She was opening the door wide. 'Where's Peter?'

I was momentarily at a loss. I'd expected her to be

shocked, to make excuses. Even to be apologetic. But she'd surprised me; she knew my name, who I was. She was looking up the path as if to see Peter behind me. 'No. He's not with me,' I said curtly, as with a stab of envy I took in her trim figure, her tiny waist. 'I came on my own.'

'Oh.' She paused, frowned as if trying to work something out, then turned and went down the hall, expecting me to follow. 'Well, it's lovely to meet you at last. Come along in.' She stopped suddenly and looked back over her shoulder. 'Is something the matter? He's all right, isn't he?'

'Yes, he's fine,' I said automatically, annoyed with myself for being unprepared for this small talk. The hallway smelt of fresh coffee. A wireless was talking in the background. It was lovely and calm, and homely. For some reason this made my eyes well up, but I swallowed and quashed it.

She led me into the front room which was furnished with a modern beige suite with circular cushions neatly arranged. Lots of ornaments, figurines of shepherdesses, polished horse-brasses above a glowing gas fire. A paperback crime thriller lay open, face down, on a pointy-legged side table. It was all very tidy and ordered, so much so that I had a sense of things unravelling, of my breath coming sharp and fast.

'I'll get coffee,' she called, as she bustled away to the kitchen. 'I was just making some. I'll be back in a minute, you just make yourself at home. Who'd have thought it, after all this time!'

I sat on the edge of the sofa, my knees clamped together, my handbag still over my shoulder. This wasn't what I had imagined. Something wasn't adding up. I'd come expecting to find some sort of femme fatale, someone I could confront with all the anger and hurt I'd been chewing over for the last few months. I reminded myself of why I'd come. Why was Peter sending her flowers? What was going on?

I stared round the room looking for any clue. But there were no photographs, just a tasteful pair of landscape prints in the alcoves on either side of the fireplace. There was a gramophone and next to it a rack with a selection of records. Some were lying on the floor and I recognised some big band favourites, Big Bill Broonzy and Glenn Miller, but also newer ones – Eartha Kitt and Nat King Cole.

Helen came in with a tray of coffee and biscuits and set it down on the low table. I took in her roundish face, her blonde hair waved into artful curls. I noticed she'd put lipstick on since going in the kitchen.

She dropped herself into an armchair and leaned over to pick up the coffee pot. 'Sorry, it's only Nescafé I'm afraid, but these biscuits are a bit of a treat – chocolate wafers. So, tell me what brings you over,' she said, then smiled at me as she poured.

I swallowed, couldn't think of how to put it.

'It is nice to meet you at last,' she said. 'I thought it would never happen. Milk?'

My voice burst out harsh and accusing. 'I want to know why Peter sends you flowers. I want to know what's going on between you.'

She paused with the jug halfway tilted. Then she rested it back down. 'What?' Now she did look shocked. 'I think there's been some sort of misunderstanding. I don't know what you're accusing me of, but Peter is Archie's friend, not mine.'

'Archie? Who's Archie? I don't know who you mean.'

Her eyebrows knitted together in puzzlement. 'My husband. You surely didn't think—'

'I'm sorry, the name means nothing to me.'

The atmosphere in the room thickened, the smell of coffee suddenly cloying. 'What do you mean, you don't know Archie?' She gave a nervous laugh. 'You must. Peter must have told you. Archie died of cancer, March this year. I wrote to tell you.' She was looking at me as if I had lost my mind.

I let this sink in. I couldn't find the words to say sorry, I was still trying to work it all out.

'You're Peter Middleton's wife, right?' Helen was leaning forward in her chair willing me to remember, but it was as if my mind was wading through mud. Nothing came. Helen prompted me: 'They were in a prisoner of war camp together. Don't tell me he never mentioned Archie Foster!'

'No. No, my husband never talks about the war.' I heard the words 'my husband' come out in a slightly proprietorial way. 'I think Peter wants to forget all that.'

Helen looked incredulous. 'But he must have done. They met up every week for lunch. It was one of the reasons we moved up here, for God's sake, so Archie could be near you and Peter. Only you were always too snobbish to show your face.'

I shook my head, dumbfounded.

'And he visited Archie every week, sat right where you are with his milky coffee … You mean Peter never told you anything? Never mentioned Archie's name?'

Milky coffee. Yes, Peter always had his coffee like that. Helen's mouth had turned down. She looked as if she did not believe me.

'Sorry, but truly, I've never heard of him.'

She stood up, her face blotched red. 'Then you're not welcome in my house. I don't know what you want, coming here accusing me of all sorts. You're crazy, pretending you don't know who Archie is.'

I leapt to my feet. 'Well, why are you writing to Peter? Why did he send you flowers?'

'Because it was my birthday! He was just being kind. Because he knew Archie always used to ... and now ...' Her face crumpled into tears. 'Archie's gone, and only Peter understands.'

She was telling the truth. It hit me like a blow to the ribs. 'Oh God, I'm sorry. I'll go. I didn't mean to upset you. I didn't know about your husband. Honestly.'

Her shoulders heaved and she slumped back into the cushions, took a handkerchief from her sleeve. I hovered, uncertain what to do. It was my fault she was crying, I couldn't just leave her like that.

She blew her nose hard. 'Is that true? Peter never told you about us?' She was tearful, indignant.

I shook my head. 'I feel terrible. I'm just as confused as you are. Look, shall I pour that coffee now, and we'll try to get to the bottom of it?'

'Archie would have been devastated. I can't believe it.' She was staring at me with an expression of accusation.

I poured the coffee and I think both of us were relieved that English politeness had taken over, something safer, for which we both knew the rules. The coffee was hot and strong and I added two spoons of sugar. The taste of the sweetness in my mouth revived me.

Helen wiped her nose again. 'Hang on a mo'. You drink that, and I'll be back.' She hurried out of the room and I heard the sound of her stockinged feet pad upstairs followed by cupboard doors opening and closing. When she got back she had a photograph in her hand. 'Look.' She sat next to me on the sofa and held it up for me to see.

'Oh!' I recognised it. I had one just like it, but I hadn't even thought about it for years. She was looking to me for a reaction. I said, 'I've got the same one. Peter sent me the photo from the camp. It's in the wardrobe at home. But I didn't know he was still in touch with anyone in it.'

'There's Peter, in the back row,' she said, pointing him out with a well-manicured nail. 'And here in front, that's Archie, see those pale shoelaces? They couldn't get new ones in the camp so his were made out of string.'

The photograph was silvery-brown and smaller than I remembered; the man in the front row was smiling, but I didn't recognise him. I looked harder at this enigma, hoping it might jog some memory, something Peter might have said. Still nothing. The clock on the mantelpiece chimed the hour.

Helen pointed again. 'And here – Nebs and Harry,' she said. 'Neither of them survived. It was taken at the work camp in Poland. Archie and Peter were lucky, they stayed together all through the war, right from the beginning, right to the Great March at the end. Archie used to say that apart from me Peter was the only person who really knew him. But he never mentioned Archie?'

It was as if Peter had insulted her. She kept asking, but I could not change it to the reply she wanted.

'It's not a great picture. It was much worse conditions than this photograph makes out. Really rough. They made them pose and smile as if it was some sort of holiday camp.'

She let go of the picture, leaving it in my hands, and moved over to fetch her coffee, but she didn't sit. 'You know, Peter came to Archie's funeral,' she said. 'Stood up and spoke about him too. A lovely speech. Very moving.'

'I had no idea.' *When?* I was thinking, *when did he come to a funeral?*

'He said you were unwell. It was a few months ago now. He said … you would have been there but you were in bed with … flu, I think it was. The weather was terrible. Rain

13

coming down in stair rods. But Peter came. Surely he told you about that?'

'Oh, yes. Yes, I seem to remember something.' I didn't. I knew nothing about it. But I couldn't have known nothing about them for my whole marriage, could I? Maybe I'd forgotten, denied it somehow. But no, I was sure Peter had never said a thing.

Then it dawned on me. March. The door. That was when he'd put his fist through the door. I took another sip of coffee and the cup rattled when I placed it back on the saucer. Everything seemed to be crumbling and I was trying to shore it up, put it back together, build some sort of defences.

Helen tried to be sympathetic, 'Well, it was an upsetting time. They were like brothers. Perhaps Peter didn't want to talk about it.'

Now she was making excuses for my husband too. There was an uncomfortable silence. All at once I couldn't bear it. I put my cup and saucer down on the tray and stood. 'I didn't mean to barge in on you like this,' I said. 'You must think me a terrible clot. I'll be going now. I made a mistake. I'm sorry.'

I hitched my bag on to my shoulder, blundered towards the door.

'But what about Peter? Don't go.' Helen stood up, uncertain whether to stop me or not.

'I must, I'm sorry.' I couldn't look at her; I'd been such an idiot. And I was so angry with Peter for not telling me that I was close to tears myself.

'Will you tell Peter you called?' Helen asked, and the words hit me like a small bomb. He'd be mortified.

'No,' I said, more harshly than I intended. 'Much better not. Just forget I ever came. It was silly, and …' I tailed off, found my way into the hall, wrestled with the Yale lock on the front door. Helen followed me, helped me as I fumbled with the latch, desperate to get out of there. We did not even exchange goodbyes. I turned briefly and raised my hand, saw her silhouetted in the doorway, her eyebrows creased in concern, her pale flyaway hair like a halo.

When I got home Peter had already gone out again to a meeting at school. There was a note.

> *Sandwich in pantry if you're hungry.*
>
> *Your mother dropped by, all okay.*
>
> *See you later. P x*

All wasn't okay. I felt as though I'd been kicked in the chest. And my mother, that was all I needed. She had such hopes for Peter and me, for our future. But we'd disappointed her – no bouncing babies for her to coo over, and I didn't know how to tell her that we didn't ... well, that there'd be no chance of that.

Helen had no children either by the look of it. The vision of the shapely Helen and her navy slacks was still in the forefront of my mind. Replaying our meeting made me blush with embarrassment even now, hours later. She would think I had a screw loose. Why hadn't Peter told me about Archie? I couldn't understand it. Was it because he was ashamed of him? No, Peter had never been a snob. But why on earth didn't he want me to know?

Ten years of our marriage, for heaven's sake. According to Helen, he'd kept Archie Foster a secret from me since the war. Even more bizarre was the fact that he'd deliberately stopped me from meeting them, by making excuses for me

– like at the poor man's funeral. I couldn't fathom it. Peter had always been a quiet man, but this? This was a mystery.

I opened the pantry door and lifted the plate that Peter had used to cover the egg sandwich, but lowered it again. I had no appetite. I couldn't settle; it was as if the dust had been disturbed and now there was nothing to weigh the past down. Facts and dates flew into my mind from all directions. Perhaps he had mentioned Archie after all, and I'd forgotten? One thing I did remember – there was a box of Peter's wartime stuff upstairs; maybe that would hold some clues. I hurried upstairs.

When I reached to the back of the wardrobe, the only thing I could find was a small bundle of envelopes tied up with gardening twine. They looked a bit the worse for wear and were obviously donkey's years old, but then I realised – they were my letters to Peter. The ones I'd sent to him when he was a prisoner of war. How sweet that he'd still kept them. But they made me feel uncomfortable. I feared he would be able to read something between the lines, that my memories of Matthew would be stuck there like flies between the pages. As if love lingered like an invisible perfume.

A few years ago I'd told him to throw the letters out, but he wouldn't. 'I kept them all across Czechoslovakia and Germany,' he'd said, 'even when I'd lost everything else. So I'm not going to let go of them now.'

I had to use scissors to get the twine open. I spread the letters on the counterpane. My own youthful confident handwriting burst from the page, the blue-black ink still fresh-looking. It took me aback. I had forgotten the younger me completely.

But I remembered sending them. The early ones were cheerful and full of jokes. There were fewer of the later ones, after the film crew had been to Carnforth, and I remember filling the pen and blotting it, wondering how to finish. 'Yours?' – well, I wasn't sure I was really his. Not then. 'With love?' Did I love him any more? It was complicated. In the end I had signed them all with my name and a single x.

It set me thinking about the letters he wrote to me. I knew where they were – in a tin behind the sewing box. I hadn't done much sewing lately, couldn't afford the material. Not now the fashion was for tiny waists and billowing dirndl skirts. But that photo was in there too – the one that was the same as Helen Foster's. I dragged down the cigar tin amid a sprinkling of dust and fluff. I had to rifle through a lot of old birthday cards before I found them, but I recognised the letters from Peter because of the censor's marks.

I inhaled the faint scent of cigars from the inside of the tin as I unfolded Peter's letters one by one and read:

Dear Rhoda, we are well. Hope your pa has managed to get his beans planted.

Cold today, but Red Cross parcels arrived yesterday.

Absolutely the tops. Good to have English [crossed out] Tea.

All fine here. Tell Mother I miss her mince.

In my mind's eye I saw my younger self reading them, my rayon-clad legs lounging on the slippery burgundy quilt of my bed. I remembered fiddling with the buttons on my cardigan as I read. Thinking back, I don't know what I imagined life in a prisoner-of-war camp could have been like, but I suppose I'd always believed the Red Cross propaganda and taken Peter's cheery words at face value. So it had surprised me when Helen Foster had said they'd had a rough time.

Once no letters came for more than two years, and then a big batch arrived all at once. I was so naive; why didn't I think to read between the lines? I should have, because my letters to him were just as opaque. Like steamy windows, if you rubbed the surface a whole different view awaited you. I told Peter so little of my life when he was gone. But then that wasn't surprising – my story had nothing to admire, whereas he at least was some kind of returning hero.

I pulled out the photo that was identical to Helen's. Helen had been proud of Archie, I could tell by her voice. I examined Peter's smooth, young face; he hadn't changed much. He was smiling stiffly in his uniform. Why was I not proud of Peter? Helen seemed to know all about his time as a prisoner of war, and yet I barely knew a thing. It was a panicky feeling, to try to grasp after him, as if I was chasing a moving train and could never quite catch up.

I looked at him again. Was this the same person who would come back later and ask if I'd had that sandwich he'd left in the pantry? It didn't seem possible that the Peter then could be the same person as the Peter now. Time seemed to crumple and fold in on itself.

At the bottom of the tin were some old photographs and souvenirs.

I picked up one of the scraps from the bottom of the tin. Tickets. For the cinema. The old Roxy that was now the Co-op supermarket. Our first date, that had nearly not been a date at all. As the room darkened I sat and remembered.

3

1939 Rhoda

THE MINUTE HAND juddered forward a notch again. Still no sign of him. I wished I'd dressed for warmth instead of vanity, now I'd been waiting on this draughty platform for nearly twenty minutes. August, and it looked like rain again. Shivering, I buttoned my raincoat across my thin summer blouse and knotted the ends of the belt tight to keep out the wind. I looked up at the station clock. Another minute clicked by.

A freight train whistled past with its load of coal, and dust blew into my eyes. I rubbed at them, blinked, hoped my mascara hadn't run. I stepped from foot to foot. Should I wait any longer? My stomach seemed to contain not just butterflies but a whole swarm of birds. Peter Middleton wouldn't stand me up, would he?

He was four years older than me and actually quite good-looking, though he didn't seem to know it. He was long and lanky, with lively brown eyes and a nice smile, when he used it – which wasn't often because mostly he was serious. My brother Andrew said Peter always looked as if he was trying to work out a complicated crossword puzzle.

I'd met him at the practices for the Carnforth Brass Band; Pa was a trombone player and I often went down to listen to the music and help with the teas. So I knew Peter was the new teacher at the boy's school – St Cuthbert's, where the posh boys went, the ones with smart blue blazers and polished satchels. I imagined them all calling him 'Mr Middleton', or 'sir,' and it gave me a sense of pride to think of it. Truth be told, I was intimidated by him a little because he kept himself apart from the other men and asked deep questions about the music that confused the conductor and my father.

'I was wondering, do you go out much?' he'd said, balancing a cup and saucer that looked far too small in his large hands. At first I didn't know what to say because nobody had ever invited me on a date before, and I wasn't really clear what he was asking. So I just stood there. 'I mean, would you walk out with me?'

He flushed bright red, but I was flattered despite his obvious embarrassment, and my stomach had given a great swoop, so I said, 'I'd love to,' before he could change his mind and before Pa or Mr Grainger could notice my red face.

He'd given me one of his rare smiles, and I felt my face grow hot.

After that I looked at my feet and he suggested meeting under the clock, so here I was. I looked up at it for the umpteenth time.

On the other platform a goods train came in with a screech of whistle and a hiss of steam as it trundled by. The stationmaster glanced over at me. He must think me a complete idiot. He'd guess I'd been stood up and he'd tell my father and it would be all over the marshalling yard and Carnforth Station. And I'd told Patty Howarth I was meeting Peter too, and now I was wishing I hadn't.

'Peter Middleton?' she'd said. 'Mr Smartypants?'

'What do you mean?'

'Well, he's got degrees and everything. And he lives in those new houses at Crag Bank.'

'He's nice,' I'd said defensively.

She pursed her lips. Everyone knew that the only time Patty ever kept her mouth shut was as a sign of disapproval. Now I wished I hadn't told her anything. And heaven help poor Peter Middleton if he let me down and my pa ever found out.

I sighed, got ready to open my umbrella, and turned to go. I wasn't sure I even liked Peter Middleton now, with his fancy manners and university tie. I marched though the double doors of the booking hall with my head held high, heels clacking on the tiled floor. I'd walk a while. I certainly couldn't go home yet; Mother would be full of awkward questions.

'Rhoda!'

I turned. Peter was running towards me, wet trench coat flapping. A clap of thunder sounded outside. My heart gave a nervous flip. I stopped, tried not to look too eager, made my face neutral.

'Wait!' he said. 'Oh Lord, you've not changed your mind, have you?'

'I thought you weren't coming.'

'Half-past seven it was. We said half-past seven.'

'No, seven o'clock. I'm sure you said seven—'

'Well, never mind, we're here now. Sorry if I got it mixed up. Gosh! It's a bit wet for walking, come on, let's go across the road to the Kinema.'

'It's called the Roxy now. They've done it up.' I was frosty because I was still trying to work out whether I had got the time wrong, or whether he had. 'If you like. What's on?'

'Something called *Goodbye Mr Chips*.'

'I've read the book. And Patty said the film made her cry. It's about a schoolmaster at a boy's school. It sounds good.'

He curled his lip and stuck his hands in his pockets. 'Oh no. It's not, is it? I didn't know that. I get quite enough of school in the daytime without going to see a film about it at night.'

I moved to the side. I was aware of people frowning as they shook out their umbrellas and tried to pass us, in a hurry for their train. 'I didn't mean to put you off. Patty really enjoyed it. What time does it start?'

'Twenty to.'

'It's nearly that now,'

'We'd better run then, it's pelting down.' He grabbed my hand and we hared across the road, heads ducked down to avoid the rain.

The Roxy was busy, and smelled of damp coats and cigarette smoke, but we squeezed through a row of people to find seats at the back corner. Thank goodness the film was easy to follow – for what I remember most is the stillness of Peter's profile as he became absorbed in the film, the slight Roman bump in his nose, the curve at the back of his head and the bristly bare part where the barber had shaved down to the nape of his neck. And later the touch of his warm fingers as they found mine, right at the end of the film, just when I wanted to reach into my sleeve for my hanky.

4

1939 Peter

PETER DREADED TAKING Rhoda home to meet his parents. When he was a child, and went to other friends' houses, he used to find the ready laughter and tears confusing, but as he'd grown up he had seen that the eerie quietness at home was unique to his house, and not at all how everyone else lived.

He suspected that Rhoda might find his parents cold and unwelcoming, but he hoped not, because she was the first girl he'd ever met who was on his wavelength – good fun without being giggly or over-flirtatious like other girls. She'd listened to his plans for starting a school brass band, and said it was a wizard idea, and he had been ridiculously pleased.

Before Rhoda he'd always been rather useless with girls. And Rhoda looked so pretty he thought she might be out of his league. He knew his mother would think her too young for him, but Rhoda seemed older than her years; she was self-contained in some understated way. He thought back to the other times he'd asked girls out, when meeting his parents had been a disaster, with the girl dumping him and it all being a bit of a let-down.

So today he was bringing Rhoda over to meet his parents and Mother was insistent they should do the whole

'English tea' thing which was rather excruciating, with doilies and napkins and a fork to eat cake. A fork, for heaven's sake.

They'd hardly even sat down before his mother asked Rhoda, 'What does your father do?' – as if that wasn't a loaded question.

Rhoda answered her straight. 'He works for the Railway. As a driver.'

'Oh. That must be interesting.'

'It takes a lot of study,' Rhoda said, obviously feeling the pressure.

'Does it? I'd no idea. Still, I expect he sees a lot of different places.' Peter's mother smiled brightly, as if to compensate for her obvious disappointment.

His father grunted, said, 'I suppose he must.' He shook out his napkin. 'And I believe he plays in the band with Peter. Is your mother musical?'

Rhoda finished chewing her sandwich. 'Not a bit. My mother's tone deaf I think. She enjoys listening to the radio and she says she likes to listen to the birds, but that's about it. Mrs Middleton, these sandwiches are really good.'

'Yes, I love my wireless. There was a wonderful recording of Rachmaninov this morning. Did either of you hear it?' Father asked.

'I don't think so. I was at work and Mother went to do some shopping in Morecambe,' Rhoda said.

'Do you like Rachmaninov?'

Peter saw the trap in the split second before Rhoda answered. If she said yes, she was damned as a philistine who should really prefer Tchaikovsky. If she said no, Father could lecture her on why she should. There was a pause whilst Rhoda put down the sandwich,

'It's all right. But I love the brass band music. That's

why I go down to the band practice to help with the teas. I like the big bands – Tommy Dorsey, Glenn Miller.'

Father's face closed down like a shutter on a shop. Peter knew what he was thinking. How could she not like the classics? Father's collection of treasured 78's in their stiff cardboard sleeves took up several shelves in the place his family called simply 'the room'. 'The room' was at the front of the house and reserved for Father or special guests. It housed a highly polished upright piano Father no longer played, and it seemed to Peter to exude a permanent air of gloom. There, Father would listen to his music for hours on end, do his *Times* crossword puzzle, and avoid the rest of the family.

The fact that Rhoda had not been invited into 'the room' but only into the kitchen was already an insult. And poor Rhoda, she did not know that to admit that you did not like classical music was tantamount to stamping 'outsider' for ever on your forehead. At least in his father's books.

Mother shot Father one of her looks, which Peter interpreted as meaning, 'Oh dear, she'll never do.'

This made Rhoda seem to him all the more endearing, sitting there like an innocent with her napkin demurely on her lap, and her face flushed pink. She looked over to him with an appeal in her grey-green eyes, but before he could say anything his father said, 'Peter used to play the piano, but he gave it up. It's a shame. He was really quite good, could have made a concert pianist if he'd wanted to.'

'That was when I was about eight,' Peter said. 'And I hated it. You know I did. That's why I gave it up. I much prefer the cornet. And anyway, not everyone has to enjoy the same sort of music. Now Handel – you saw us playing for the *Messiah* at Christmas. That was glorious, wasn't it?'

'Oh yes,' Rhoda said, brightening, 'I loved that. The whole atmosphere in the Church at Warton was so beautiful with those gorgeous Victorian windows, and the place all lit up with candles.'

'It was lovely, very nice,' Mother said, as if to dismiss a child. 'More tea?'

'Rachmaninov has a wonderful concerto for two cornets,' Father said.

Peter cringed. His father just would not give up.

They ate and drank politely. Father fetched in Mother's speciality, a beautifully decorated trifle, topped with glacé cherries, in a cut-glass bowl. Once they had finished it Father begged to be excused from the table. On his way out he gave Peter more room than usual, walking around him as if he did not want to enter his air-space. From this and his heavy sigh, Peter knew he'd met with disapproval and that his father was disappointed with Rhoda. His heart sank. What must she think of them?

When he walked Rhoda back to the bus stop, she said gloomily, 'I don't think they liked me.'

'Of course they did,' he lied. He slipped his hand into hers. 'It's only that … well, my father's a bit awkward with younger people. He's got his own funny little ways. And he can be a touch old-fashioned – not accepting of new things. He doesn't like change, for him everything has to be in a routine.' This much was true at least. 'Like, he has to write down all his journeys. If he was you, he'd already be working out which bus he was getting and taking his pencil out. Whenever he goes anywhere he makes a note of what time he set off, what time he arrived, whether it was a bus or train and how much it cost. Can you believe it? He used to do it even when he biked to work.'

'What an odd thing to do. Why?'

Peter wished he hadn't mentioned it now, it felt disloyal to his father. 'I know. Crazy, isn't it? Even now, if he walks anywhere he carries a notebook and writes it down. He's got dozens of ledgers in the spare room upstairs with his journeys all mapped out with the tickets glued in and everything.'

'What about if he just goes to the corner shop?'

'He has his own little rules about what constitutes a journey. He gets bad-tempered if we don't leave him to get on with writing it down when he gets back. He says he needs to get it all straight. Mother says it's since the last war, he had a pretty bad time of it in the trenches. He got shell shock and by all accounts he had to make notes in his head to keep himself sane. Now he can't be separated from his glasses and his pencil.'

'That's awful. But it does make more sense when you know why.'

They'd reached the bus stop where there were three other people waiting, their shoulders hunched against the wind.

Peter put his arm around Rhoda's shoulders, pulled her close. 'Cold, isn't it,' he said, as an excuse.

She put her arm around his waist. It felt good. 'My father would never do that,' she said. 'He's never still long enough. He hardly ever sits down. He must always be doing, doing, doing. It drives Mother to distraction. She spends ages cooking, then he's barely sat down two minutes and he must be up and out again. Often he folds up his bread and butter and dashes off with it in his hand rather than sit there at the table with the rest of us.'

'My mother would never stand for that – she's a stickler for proper table manners.' He said it as a fact but it sounded like a criticism of Rhoda's mother, so he lapsed into silence. Rhoda frowned and pulled away from him, stood at the edge of the kerb and looked down the road, watching for signs of the bus. He thought how trim and attractive she looked in her belted green raincoat and jaunty little hat. His chest constricted. 'Will you be all right?' he asked.

'I should think so. Unless the bus driver's Dr Crippen.' She said it deadpan, but the twitch at the corner of her mouth betrayed her.

They laughed, and it felt so good. There might still be a chance for him; she'd met his parents and was still smiling. The other people began to shuffle closer to the edge of the road as the headlights of the bus slewed round the corner. Rhoda put her arm out for it to stop. 'Thank your parents for me,' she said. 'It was a lovely tea.'

Now was his chance to kiss her goodbye. He moved towards her, but she was already preparing to get on the bus and had turned away. Should he ask her?

'Rhoda?' he said as the bus slowed in a crunch of brakes. She turned to face him, but he couldn't get up the nerve. Not in front of a whole busload of people.

'Goodbye then, go safely,' he said awkwardly. 'I'll see you Monday at band practice.' She smiled and waved. Did he catch disappointment in her face? It was hard to say.

A moment later the bus pulled away and he was alone at the stop, kicking himself.

5

1939 Rhoda

PETER WAS WELCOMED into my family with barely disguised relief. Mother told me he was 'quite a catch' and I knew she approved because she tidied her hair before opening the door to him. She and Pa had been worried about another war coming, but we were young and carefree and even though the radio was full of predictions of a conflict with Germany, Peter and I ignored it. It would all blow over. We could not believe that a war could come again so soon, convinced with the optimism of youth that in the 'war to end all wars', lessons would have been learned.

So when September came and war was actually announced, it shook us both. Even then, I did not really know what it would mean, not until I saw the recruitment centre in Carnforth with long queues of excited men waiting outside. Suddenly we had hard evidence that not everyone shared our pacifist views.

'Whatever happens, Peter will be exempt,' Mother said, as she ran the iron over one of Pa's shirts. 'Schoolteaching's a reserved occupation.'

The kitchen was full of steam from the iron and the smell of hot starch. I ducked under the flex hanging from the light fitting, folded the shirt that Mother had just finished and added it to the growing pile on the sideboard.

She continued talking as she slid the iron back and forth. 'Though I heard them say on the news that they need officer material like him.' She passed me a blouse, and the iron hissed as she crashed it down on another piece of damp fabric.

I grimaced. 'I can't see him in the army. Though I have to say, there's something about a man in uniform.' I winked at Mother who raised her eyebrows. 'Except for him it's always going to be the band uniform. He's happy where he is; they need him in school. We've talked about it, and he doesn't see the point. Everyone says it will be over soon.'

Christmas came and went, and like other northerners we read the papers and listened to the wireless, trying to feel as if we were a part of this great event, and slightly jealous to be so far away from the action, despite the frightening propaganda about gas attacks and bombs. The 'phoney war', that's what people were calling it. We just carried on as usual, until June, when Mrs Edwards from next door came to tell us that Johnnie, her only son, had been lost at sea.

Johnnie had been on the aircraft carrier HMS *Glorious* which had been sunk somewhere off Orkney. We'd all heard radio reports of it and imagined the hollow darkness of those cold salt waters. I took one look at Mrs Edwards's face and went to make tea, leaving Mother to comfort her as best she could. When I brought in the tray, Mrs Edwards's eyes were streaming, her hands clinging to my mother as if she could claw her son back from the waves.

Johnnie used to sit next to Peter in the cornet section and now the empty chair spoke to us in a way no news report ever could. Mr Grainger struggled through a trite speech about what a wonderful player he was, what a great sacrifice he'd made, and how much he'd be missed. His words failed to conjure up the Johnnie we knew, the Johnnie with his habit of rubbing his mouth with the back of his hand before playing, the Johnnie whose coat always slid off his chair to the floor.

'Come back with me,' Peter said, after the practice had finished. 'You can stay for tea. I need to talk to you.'

I had my bicycle with me so we took turns to push as we walked. Peter was morose, and when I said, 'What's wrong?' he said, 'Just thinking about Johnnie, that's all.'

Peter's parents lived in a newish semi-detached in a row of other identical houses. Mrs Middleton took our coats, but Peter almost dragged me away from the hall and into their gloomy front room. It was hardly ever used, and was stuffy and airless. The curtains were already closed on the big bay window; presumably they hadn't been opened all day.

'Shall we have some music?' I said, putting off the moment when Peter would tell me he was going to enlist. I noticed an aspidistra wilting on the sideboard.

I went over to the gramophone, which was a recent model, but the rack of records it contained were all classical. One after one, I put back the Prokofiev and Rachmaninov, ghastly old-fashioned Russian stuff – his father's choice, I presumed. No jazz or swing or anything modern. I resigned myself to a Beethoven piano concerto. Better to ask him straight, I thought. 'You're thinking of joining up, aren't you?'

Peter sighed and sat down on the hard leather sofa. I knelt on the rug at his feet and tried to take hold of his hands in mine, but he leaned away from me. 'Beethoven. Long time since I heard this.' He lay back on the sofa and deliberately looked at the ceiling. 'They're asking for drivers and navigators. And that's one thing I can do. I can speak French and a little German and read a map.' After a pause he sat up, took hold of my shoulder. 'I've got to do something. I can't walk down the street and look Johnnie's mother in the face any more.'

'But what about your job?' I said. 'Boys have got to be educated. Someone's got to teach them Latin and Greek.'

He let go of me, and flopped back. 'The boys are all war-mad. They can't talk of anything else but shooting and blowing up Germans. I'm forever confiscating the *Beano* with pictures of soldiers and airmen and cartoons of Hitler. Everything's black or white with them. All Germans have moustaches, all Englishmen are heroes. And the older boys stare at me with that look, the one that means I'm not worth their time. The look that is almost a sneer, as if I'm too weak to be of any use. They despise me because I'm not out there fighting for my country like their fathers or brothers.' Peter got up, went to turn up the volume on the music.

'But it can't be any good you going out there and wasting yourself on something that might only last a few more months.' I had to raise my voice over the crashing chords of Beethoven. 'Those boys will remember you their whole lives.'

'Like Mr Chips?'

'No. I mean, you aren't exactly cut out for it.' I saw a hurt look cross his face, and his expression shut down. I tried to recover myself. 'I mean, there must be men more suited for it, men with less education …' I tailed off, knowing I'd made it worse. 'Can you turn it down a bit? I feel like I'm shouting.' I reached out towards his knees, tried to make contact.

He lowered the volume and sat down again out of reach. 'So it's all right to send people out there who aren't as lucky as we are, is it?' he said tersely. 'Men who haven't had a grammar school education? My grandfather half-killed himself working seven days a week in the ironworks to put my father through school and university. But you're saying it's all right for men like him to be cannon fodder but not me? You know that's not right.' He let out a long, ragged breath. 'It can never be right.'

I got the feeling he meant the world in general.

'Don't let's argue,' I said. 'You know I agree with you. I'm just upset. I know you miss Johnnie, but I don't want you to go. I'm scared of what will happen.'

But he wasn't listening, he was intent on his own thoughts and the sharp words between us had lodged like a splinter that could not be withdrawn.

He got up, ignoring me, and went to fetch the tea from the kitchen. His mother always put the kettle on when I came to see him and provided us with hard inedible biscuits. I heard his mother's voice say, 'All right, dear?' and he did not reply.

I looked across at the photographs on the side table. Peter in a perambulator with the hood squashed down, wearing a lopsided bobble hat. Peter standing, flag in hand, behind a sand castle, his shorts hitched up to his chest, squinting at the sun. And one in a silver frame of an older Peter standing side-on to the camera, dressed in a cap and gown with an embarrassed-looking smile.

There were no photographs like this at our house – Mother was always too busy to take any. There were the school snaps, that was all. I wondered fleetingly what it must be like to be the only child, to be solely responsible for fulfilling all his parents' hopes and dreams, and I was suddenly stifled. I stood up and went to the window. I parted the curtains with a finger and a cut-glass vase wobbled precariously. The sliver of daylight from outside swung over the furniture in the room like a needle.

The creak of the door behind me made me drop the curtain back guiltily. Peter avoided my eyes but pulled out a table from the nest of tables and placed the tea tray down. There were sandwiches and malted loaf and a pot with jam, more than we ever got for tea at my house, as if to impress me that they could still maintain proper standards, despite the war.

Peter carried on talking as if we were already in a conversation. He often did this, halfway through a dialogue with himself. I always had to catch up to get on to the tail end of his thoughts.

'I know. I'm still not sure.' He poured milk carefully into the cups. 'But I've been reading and rereading anything I can about it, to help me decide. We shouldn't be at war at all. It was lack of foresight on behalf of the government. And up here we're away from it so it doesn't seem so pressing. But men like Johnnie are dying and I can't help thinking that it's easier to talk and make excuses than it is to screw your courage to the sticking place and join up.'

'What do you mean, "sticking place"?'

'Shakespeare. Lady Macbeth. "Screw your courage to the sticking place and we'll not fail." Oh, never mind.' He looked at me as though I was a disappointment.

'Are you sure you're not being pressurised into it?' I asked.

'Of course I'm being pressurised! It's ghastly. Such a waste. I keep remembering Johnnie's face when we played our Whitsun concert last year.' He knelt to pour the tea through the tea-strainer, put the pot back under the knitted cosy. 'Even young Graham Garside from the grocery has volunteered.'

'He can't have done. He's too young, surely?'

He put his tea on the top of the piano, and hovered in

the middle of the room. 'I remember teaching him the first year I went to St Cuthbert's. He was in his last year at school, one of those who work and work and still can't seem to grasp the first thing. Sad, really. But when I went in the grocer's the other day to collect Mother's shopping Mr Garside just stared at me and said, 'When are you signing up, sir? Our Graham's gone, scraped his way in, even though he's only just turned seventeen.' It was him calling me sir. I suddenly felt he shouldn't be calling me sir. Not if Graham Garside was out there and I wasn't. That – and he had such a look of accusation on his face.'

I felt my stomach tighten and my mouth struggle with the words. They came from my lips even though a part of me was standing shaking my head at their futility.

'But surely that's the point,' I said. 'There will always be people trying to get you to fight. The hard thing is to stand up for what you believe in. Pa fought in the last war and I know enough from him to know that the other man is just a man, like us. They're not Germans – they're just people. I don't understand what's changed. Are you telling me you could stand there and kill another man?'

'Don't be melodramatic. What am I supposed to do? I can't object to the war – it's too late to object. It's already happening, and men like Johnnie are dying. But I can drive. That's what I'm saying I'll do, drive and read maps.'

'But we agreed. Pacifism is the only way forward.' I was struggling, losing my own battle, knowing that it was not just words that were at stake. I couldn't believe it, after all we'd said to each other about solving conflict in better ways. He'd betrayed me.

'Come on, Rhoda, I'm not joining the army to fight.'

I let the words hang so he could see how stupid they were.

He dropped his head. I knew I was browbeating him too and I could see him squirm, caught between his old ideals and his new convictions. All at once I couldn't see him suffer like this, couldn't bear the tightness it gave me in my chest.

'Sorry,' I said, 'Sorry. I'm being a pig. I'm just worried, that's all.'

He looked away from me as he passed me my cup and saucer. 'Have your tea whilst it's hot.'

I took a gulp but it was scalding and burned my tongue. I set the cup down beside me on the floor where the tea slopped into the saucer. We both knew that what he said was nonsense – that battlefields were battlefields, whatever you set out to do. But I didn't say anything because war was a man's thing, and girls could do nothing; nothing except watch.

The room felt more airless than ever. I peeled off my cardigan and pretended to ignore him when I heard the squeak of leather as he sat down next to me.

He took my face in his hot, damp hands. 'You're the best thing that's ever happened to me. I've never met another girl like you. Please, don't be like this. A chap needs people at home. Wait for me, Rhoda.'

He was serious. This was the sort of thing people said in films when they went off to war. It was really happening. He would really go.

'Don't be silly,' I said, squeezing his hand. 'Of course I will. They said it would be over by Christmas, and now it's summer. It can't go on much longer.'

I let him hold me tightly. Under my hands I could feel his shirt was stuck to his back.

'I love you,' he said. The words were like an electric

current running through me. He leaned in towards me and his lips rested gently on mine.

I was still reeling from his words when the door creaked open and Peter pulled abruptly away.

'Oh,' said his mother, eyebrows knitted in disapproval. 'I've just come for the tray.' She wiped her hands on her waist apron as though we were dirty. 'You've not eaten much, and you know I can't abide waste.'

'Sorry, Mrs Middleton.'

'Rhoda, it's time you were going.' I glanced at the old grandfather clock in the corner. Six-fifteen, it said, still early.

'But Mother—' Peter tried to interrupt.

'No, it's time. Your father wants to talk to you this evening, and you still have all that marking to do, remember?'

I waited for him to argue with her, but he didn't, just caved in. I stood and gave Peter a polite hug, under his mother's watchful eye, before cycling home. Afterwards I replayed his words, I love you. *I love you.* A thrill of wonder went through my heart.

6
1955 Rhoda

'OH, HELLO,' HELEN said, but I could hear the surprise and a certain wariness even in those two words. She held the door half-open between us and waited to hear what I had to say.

'Look, Peter still doesn't know I came to see you, and I still would rather keep it between us, but I wondered, could I take you for lunch?'

'Not today, I mean, I don't think—'

'Then another day. Please. I want to know more about Archie. I feel terrible about last week. I was hoping you'd be able to tell me a bit more about him, and about Peter. About the war—'

She cut in, 'I'm not sure … if Peter doesn't want you to know, perhaps we should respect that. He dropped by last week for a chat and it was awkward not to tell him I'd seen you.' She did not invite me in.

'He's still coming round to see you?' My voice sounded more annoyed than I wanted.

She let out a sigh. 'Only out of habit, I think. He comes on Fridays like he always has. We talk about Archie, I ask him how his school cricket team are doing, what he's growing in the garden. Honestly, I swear there's nothing more to it.'

I flinched. He always told me he had a staff meeting on Fridays. I pressed on regardless. 'I know. I do know there's nothing going on. Please, let me take you for lunch. We don't have to talk about the past if you don't want to. I was terribly rude and I'm sorry. I'm apologising and I'd like to make it up to you.'

'I'm not much of a person for fancy lunches, and you really don't need to—'

'Please say yes. We could meet in Lewis's in town. Just for an hour.'

The door opened a little further. 'Well, all right.' I could feel her reluctance, but she was too polite to say no. 'When?' she asked.

'How about Wednesday?'

'Wednesday's okay. But I have a dentist's appointment at two-thirty, so it will have to be short.'

'I'll meet you at half-past twelve then, upstairs in the restaurant.'

'Sorry you can't come in,' she said, still keeping me at bay. 'I'm going out in a few minutes.' I didn't believe her, but I pretended I had another appointment too and after taking her telephone number, I went. But I hoped she'd come on Wednesday and wouldn't make an excuse. I was curious about them, about why Peter had kept them a secret.

On the train I pondered it. Peter hadn't many other male friends, in fact not many friends at all, so this Archie must have been something special. Peter was different when he came back from Germany; he had no interest in music any more, wouldn't listen to records or play his cornet. And he'd never talk to me, except about mundane things. It was almost as if he was scared of talking.

Often I'd see him reading his *Gardener's World* magazine and wonder what went on in his head. Where had the man who thrived on politics and history gone? Was he really thinking of bulbs and planters and grafting trees, or was there something else behind it? If there was, he never let me know. Our conversations were all practical – 'Have you put the rubbish out?' 'Shall I get another pint of milk?' 'Where's my green jumper?'

What did he find to talk about with Archie? Helen had said gardening. But it sounded so dull, and Helen couldn't have any interest in plants, her garden was more paving slab than flowers.

I looked out of the window at the dark blur of rain over the estuary as it bled away. Seeing the picture of Peter all those years ago had made me realise how we used to be before war came and changed everything. Softer somehow, more fluid. Still able to dream without the limitation of time; the newness of the world was still with us. During the war we lost all that, became fixed and hard in our ways. I hadn't given Peter a chance when he came home. I had always compared him to someone else, blamed him for my own unhappiness. And we had settled into a routine of wary distance.

Now I wanted more. I was jealous, I realised, jealous of Helen and worse, jealous of Archie, a dead man, who'd had a relationship with Peter that Peter didn't want to share with me. My marriage was failing. I'd known it for years, but hadn't truly grasped that unless I did something, this would be it. My life would be *this*. This empty shell. But now there was a chance. If I could only be a friend to him like Archie, I reasoned, then maybe the old Peter would come back, and cease to be just a memory, a memory that was slowly fading away like that old brown photograph.

7

1940 Peter

SEVENTEEN HOURS' TRAINING was not enough, he knew that much. The truck rattled along the pitted road, the noise of its eight-hundredweight engine a roar in his ears. The roads were mercifully straight, which was a godsend because the steering was creaky as hell. Next to him Private Jardine had the map out and was turning it this way and that trying to make sense of it. Nobody had thought to give them military map training, with targets and positions. This map was nothing like a conventional road map, and took some working out. Mind you, even the training in using their rifles had been laughably rudimentary.

He couldn't help Jardine with the map, and drive at the same time, and Jardine was clueless, having left school at fourteen years old to be a brewer. Of course there were no road signs, all uprooted to confuse the enemy. Peter gritted his teeth as the truck hit another pothole.

'Bloody hell, Middleton.' Jardine shot up into the air. They were told to avoid craters in case of detonating the cargo.

'Sorry,' Peter yelled, dragging the steering back on course, though there was nothing he could do about the state of the road.

Behind him the rest of the trucks were following.

Like Peter's, they were full of ammo and petrol. There were rumours of mass evacuations, of shrinking front-lines. Something big was happening, that was all he knew. It didn't seem possible here in this peaceful countryside with the mist gradually burning off the fields in the morning sunshine. To the sides of them, beyond the occasional avenue of limes, the landscape spread flat as pastry in all directions.

When he came to a crossroads he paused, unsure which way to go, and the engine cut out. He let it rest and Jardine passed him the map while he tried to work out where they were by looking at the landscape and aligning it to the features on the paper. Right. It had to be. The farmhouse over there needed to be on their left. The quiet in the truck allowed him to hear distant rumbling and the 'ba-da-da-da' of gunfire. Jardine shifted uneasily in his seat.

Braithwaite from the truck behind came panting up, 'Keep moving, can't you. We're sitting ducks for planes here in the open.'

'Sorry, it stalled. And we were just checking our bearings. Here, have a look.' Peter thrust the map out at Braithwaite who turned it this way and that.

'Left,' he said. 'The road to the coast's that way. Pretty sure it's not right.' Cochrane, his co-driver, had arrived by this time.

'What's up, what's the hold-up?'

'Lost. But I've put them right.' Braithwaite chucked the map back in through the window and strode away.

Peter raised his eyebrows at Jardine who grinned. 'Bet he doesn't know any more than us. What do you reckon, boss?'

'Left. Or we'll just have him on our backs. If it's wrong we'll turn round at the next junction.'

They laughed. There was no way he could turn that

convoy around. He twisted the key and the engine spluttered back into life.

The grind of the engine and rattle of the cargo drowned out everything else, which is why they didn't hear the German tanks close in behind, not until there was a large boom and the ground literally shook.

It was a reflex reaction to stop. Peter turned round to look. The truck behind them blazed orange beneath clouds of black smoke, and another explosion peppered them with a rain of fiery shrapnel.

They had to get out of there. He turned the key to restart the truck.

Jardine jammed on his helmet and turned his head to look out of the open side window. 'Oh Christ.'

Peter followed his stare. The whole field alongside wavered with the ragged lines of dark uniforms. Too late he heard the strafe of machine-gun fire.

'Out!' he yelled at Jardine. Jardine yanked at the door handle and dived for cover.

Peter scrambled out of his side and hurled himself flat in the shallow ditch next to the road. Under the truck undercarriage he saw Jardine lying on his belly. A spray of bullets spat up puffs of dust from the road. Peter covered his head with his hands.

When the noise stopped he raised his nose an inch from the dirt. A stripe of a wound had burst open Jardine's back like a kapok pillow, the dark blood pooled under him. He lay still. Peter's first thought was, *we should have turned right*. His second thought was that this was probably it, and how convenient it was he was already in a ditch for burial. He pressed his face into the yellow soil, waiting for the sensation of bullets in his back.

8

1940 Rhoda

'HEY, GIVE US a kiss, you can make my tea any time!' The dark-haired lad winked as he caught my eye. I couldn't help smiling at him as I looped the string handles of the jam jars over my arm. The air was full of the piecing sound of wolf-whistles, but of course the whistles weren't really for me, not me properly. Just for any woman in a skirt who would smile at them as though it was any other morning.

The guard blew his whistle, as if to assert his superiority, a long piercing blast. 'Quick! Pass them over,' I shouted. The men leaning from the carriage drained their dregs of tea, stretched the jars out of the window so I could collect them in. The train pumped steam ready to depart, and the early-morning light shone weakly through it, as if we were standing knee deep in clouds.

'Marvellous cuppa, that!' came a voice over the scraping of coal and the hiss of steam. A young man grinned at me over the window of the door as he passed me his jar, taking hold of my wrist and squeezing it hard.

'Two sugars next time! I'm Philip. What's your name?'
'Rhoda.'

'Nice name. Be sure and remember.' The train shunted sharply back, causing him to stagger and let go. His face lurched against the other men crammed into the doorway. 'Two sugars!'

'He'll be lucky. What does he think it is? The Ritz? Can't remember the last time I had any sugar in my tea,' yelled my companion, Patty, over the speeding wheels and whoosh of wind of the departing train.

The train snaked away, taking with it the smell of hot metal, the bright eyes and banter of the men. I watched the tailgate round the bend southwards before stacking the last few jam jars with their milky slops of tea into the crate. The platform fell silent beneath drifting wreaths of steam. A seagull squawked somewhere overhead. Patty shook her head silently, arms folded. We both knew some of those men would not be returning from France for a second cup.

'None broken?' Patty asked.

'No. Don't think so.'

'Good.' She glanced up at the clock. 'Next train's at fifteen minutes past, so we'll have to be quick.'

I picked up the first crate and trotted down the slope towards the WVS canteen, a small room that had been set up with a gas burner next door to the refreshment room. Carnforth station prided itself on providing tea for the troops at any time of the day or night. Patty's footsteps echoed behind me. Her voice was boomy in the underpass as we headed for the platform. 'Any news?'

'No.'

'Guess that's good then.'

I did not answer her. Whenever anyone asked after Peter, a part of me banged tight shut like a stove door. Especially if it was Patty. Her husband Frank had registered as a conscientious objector and been assigned to farm labouring. It still rankled me that Peter hadn't done the same.

I thought back to Peter's flurry of letters, one every day. He'd told me to be kind to soldiers on the station, because whatever they looked like, however much bravado they pretended, inside they were all scared as hell before they got on the boat to France, not knowing what they were going to. Any one of those men I served with tea could have been Peter. Even the one with the sweaty palms and the leer.

But suddenly Peter's letters had stopped.

'No news is good news,' said Patty, putting an arm around my waist. 'He'll be all right.'

I pressed my lips together in a rueful half-smile, but was grateful for Patty's sympathy. War had thrown us together, and now I counted her as a friend.

'Hey, do you want to know a secret? I wasn't going to tell anyone yet, but you look like you need cheering up.'

'What?' I stopped with my hand on the brass handle of the door to the refreshment room.

Patty's eyes shone. 'I'm expecting.'

Her announcement was like a drench of cold water. I reached out to give her a hug, heard the words come out of my mouth: 'Oh Patty, how marvellous! When's it due?'

'I guess October-time. Frank's over the moon. Of course it's not ideal right now, what with rationing and everything, but we'll manage. I'm glad he's still here, though I know he finds it hard. People aren't always kind. We get a lot of support from the other Quakers though, so it's not so bad.'

'He's standing up for what he believes in. I'd be proud of him. And a baby, that's wonderful news.' At the same time, I thought, *but she's far too young. It will change everything.*

'Oh Rhoda, thanks. You don't know how much it means to have a friend I can talk to, like you.'

I hid my mixed feelings. And I couldn't help the feeling

that if Peter had stayed at home that could have been us, celebrating a new baby. Patty's news only made me more frustrated and fearful.

I lowered the jam jars in the sink and set to the washing. I sent my thoughts to Peter, willed him to be alive. His parents had promised they would tell me straight away if they heard anything, but so far no letter had come. I had not realised that waiting for news could be so hard, that it would weigh on me with a physical pressure like a stone. That every time the telegram boy went up the road on his bike, I had to quell the urge to run after him for news. Did he hate his job, this boy, now that he was carrying life and death in his satchel?

In the morning I leaned on the scullery door, a slice of toast and dripping in my hand, watching Mother wind the mangle. Our daily help had gone off to be a nurse, so now everything had fallen on Mother's shoulders. The mangle creaked from lack of oil, and her arms were scrawny and white as they pushed the handle round. She looked dead beat.

'Is Mr Illingworth still working with you?' she asked.

'Mother, I told you. He's had to go away, something hush-hush. Essential war work. There's only me and Mrs Illingworth on the bookstall now, remember. Has Pa gone out to the Home Guard?' I asked, licking my fingers of the remains of the toast crumbs.

'Yes. Out at the crack as usual,' Mother said. 'And there was a letter from school this morning to say Andrew's been in trouble.'

'Nothing from Peter?'

'No, love, sorry. Just the letter from the deputy head about Andrew.'

I tried to hide my disappointment. 'What's he done?'

'Truanting. I thought he skipped off early this morning. I bet he knew the letter was coming. Read it for yourself.' She slapped the typed sheet on the top of the cupboard, hoisted the laundry basket on her hips and ducked outside to the washing line.

I scanned the letter, and shook my head. Four absences with no note. I worried about my brother. He was miserable most days. Nothing seemed to interest him any more; he'd stopped going fishing, never got out his stamp albums. All he seemed to want to do was ride round the alleys on his bike. He'd got to that awkward stage an eleven-year-old gets to when he wants to stop being a child but doesn't know how.

Mother came back with the empty laundry basket. 'Will you have a word with your father, love, about Andrew? He'll listen to you.'

'I'll have a go. But you know what he's like.' I put the letter back in its envelope.

'I know. But I've tried and tried with Andrew and he just cheeks me, won't listen to a word I say. Maybe his father can drill some sense into him, that's if he's in the house long enough to do it.'

I said nothing, because just like Mother, I was frightened of Pa. When he was at home the house shrank Gulliver-like, the rooms too flimsy to contain his temper, and I couldn't see him listening to a tale of Andrew playing truant without wanting to give him the back of his hand. I stood the letter on the kitchen table where Pa would see it, and wished that I was married like Patty, with a baby on the way and no need to be subject to Pa's moods.

9

1940 Peter

THE SCRUBBY GRASS prickled his cheek, but Peter pressed himself down into the earth.

'*Hoch! Hände hoch.*' Peter knew enough German to understand. Just that was a relief, something familiar. He did not dare move, but a prod of metal in the ribs made him gasp and sit up, flinging his hands above his head in the gesture of surrender. It never occurred to him to fight. He had no gun, no weapons at all.

Smoke from the burning truck billowed blackly around him; the stench of burning rubber made him cough.

Above him the German soldier stood like a solid wall, neat, clean, tidy, his bulk compressed by sturdy serge and brass buttons. '*Stehen Sie auf.*' Peter stood shakily and the German searched him cursorily with one hand. Thank God to be unarmed. It gave Peter a strange feeling to be so close to a German soldier. He was just a man after all, this enemy; Peter could see the sweat where his helmet met his forehead.

'You walk,' the soldier said in English, pointing down the road. Peter looked and saw two more khaki uniforms limping on the dirt track. His heart raced. So he wasn't the only survivor. He was almost elated and set off after them, hunched, trying to make himself small, afraid in case another German should take a potshot.

Finally he caught up with the two men in front. One of them was injured, blood dripping from his arm leaving a trail of spots on the road. He avoided standing on them as he walked, pushed by a haze of fear and adrenalin. After half a mile they came to a roadblock and a town where more armed soldiers escorted them to the local French prison.

Five men were in the same cell, none of them men Peter knew.

'*Qu'est-ce qu'ils vont faire?*' a nervous young French soldier asked him. What are they going to do? They'd all heard lurid and unlikely stories of executions, but another man said, 'We'll be prisoners of war. They'll have to keep us in good condition. Camps, likely. It's the Geneva Convention.'

Peter clung to that thought. When he looked round the cell everyone was glazed, blank. Like him, maybe they hadn't been prepared for the shock of war, the sheer indiscriminate nature of who lived and who died. When Peter chose which direction the truck went in, he had never truly considered his responsibility to the rest of the men – the decision was over in a moment. He hadn't known the consequences of what he was deciding. Braithwaite, Connaught, Whiteley. Most of those he'd led in that convoy were dead.

He'd had to leave Private Jardine on the road without even looking back. Jammy Jardine, he used to call him. Not so jammy now. Jardine's family back home would not even know he was gone. When Peter said goodbye to his parents, his father pressed on him a copy of *The Times* to read on the train. Peter remembered his tight dry handshake, more urgent than usual, his mother's frantic waving as if the speed of the wave bore some relationship to how much she cared.

And Rhoda. Her disbelieving face when he told her he was going to join up. Would anyone let them know?

Peter sat and smoked to ease his frayed nerves. He held out the pack — it was the only thing he could do to help his cellmates, to offer something, and the Frenchman accepted with a nod, blowing smoke rings which the men watched float and fade. One of them stuck his finger through the hole of one of the rings and laughed nervously. Nobody joined him. Peter found the coarseness of the joke offensive.

He was still clinging to his civilian mentality. When he'd driven out earlier that morning with the birds trilling the dawn chorus, the world hung quietly in the mist, beautiful and pleasant still, almost drowsy. But not any more. He'd woken up, he'd become something that was no longer himself; a soldier, an enemy, as if he'd stepped out of his own story. Around him, his cellmates were equally restless. Legs twitched, fingers tapped. There was no putting any of them back to sleep now.

Peter and the others emerged blinking into the grey light. The prison must have been one of many billets because by the time they were ordered to march, breakfastless and hungry, a long thin stream of khaki stretched ahead and behind. They walked continuously for a whole day, often not on the roads, but beside them — in fields bogged into mud by feet tramping in front of them. The roads themselves were left free for military vehicles and convoys of trucks.

'Ours,' the short stocky man next to him said, pointing at a field dotted with white headstones. 'One of the Somme cemeteries.'

The Germans slowed them on purpose as they walked by, and passing it brought a melancholy that leached the fire from their hearts and filled them with the smell of defeat.

Just to see the place where the fallen of their fathers' generation lay. A memory jutting out of the earth in white marble, the dead grouped in fives, or threes, just as they were walking now, three abreast. Would Jammy Jardine be given a grave in a long row like these, Peter wondered?

That night they slept in the open. The guards were well organised, with Sten guns trained on them from the perimeters of the field. The ground sweated with damp and there was no space to move for there were so many prisoners. Above, the moon was visible only as a grey blur behind slow-moving cloud. Somewhere in England, Peter thought, Rhoda might be looking at the same moon. A pang of nostalgia ran through him, with a pain so sharp it made him catch his breath.

He shifted and rolled, unable to adjust to the hard ground. His hipbones seemed too big, they were resting on stones. Sleep was in fits and bursts with frequent attacks of panic when he woke up and realised where he was. The next morning he queued for a pale watery soup which could have been hot once, but was no longer. Globules of yellowish grease floated on its surface. But as it hit his stomach the sensation of fullness was such a relief that he smiled down at his companion, the stocky man with the thick dark eyebrows and crinkly hair. 'Shame they forgot the bread,' Peter said.

'And the soup.'

'It's probably their washing-up water.'

'Better keep our eyes open for food on the way,' the other man said. 'If we're expected to survive on this muck we'll need anything we can lay our hands on.' His voice had a slightly whining tone, his accent from somewhere in the south of England. 'I'm Harold Tyson. People call me Harry.' He didn't give his rank or his number.

Peter held out his hand. 'Middleton. Peter.'

Harry looked surprised at the hand, but shook it vigorously with a grin. When the order came to form up, they fell into step together. It was comforting to have someone walking alongside him who had chosen to be there. Harry looked to be in good shape; he was striding out, almost strutting, unlike some of the others who had the dazed look of sheep, or limped because of badly fitting boots.

When they got to the town of Trier on the German border, he could only stare. It was seething with German soldiers. Red bunting and banners with swastikas hung from every upstairs window. Another knot of fear formed like gristle in his stomach. In the face of this show of strength and propaganda, he pitied England with its soft green fields, its stubborn little hill farms. They'd be no match for this.

Harry seemed to pick up on his thoughts. He said matter-of-factly, 'I can't see the Brits caving in like the French.'

A voice from just behind said, 'Hear hear.' Peter turned to see a young lad, a round-faced recruit with nervous blue eyes. 'I say, do you know where we're going?'

Harry walked backwards to talk to him. 'No idea, pal. I don't care as long as we get fed soon.'

'My name's Foster,' the young lad said.

'*Stumm!* No talk.' A German guard put an end to the conversation, and Peter was glad. It was too much of an effort to be civil and pleasant. He needed all his strength for marching.

At the railway station they lined up in front of a rusting goods train, but there were far too few wagons for the number of men.

'They'll bring another train, won't they?' Foster was pale, his eyes darted from side to side. Something about his face reminded Peter of Graham Garside, the grocer's son. He gave Foster a brief reassuring smile.

Two German orderlies ran along the train heaving open the doors with a scrape of metal and wood. '*Auf! Schnell!*' came the shout. They were to be transported like livestock.

'I can't. I can't go in there.' Foster eyed the end truck where two Germans with Schmeiser machine guns were bullying men through the open door.

The prisoners tripped and trampled over each other in their haste to get on board. More than fifty men were squashed in before a soldier slammed the door and shunted the iron bar home. Fifty men in the space for four horses.

'I can't,' repeated Foster.

'Don't be dumb,' Harry whispered. 'We've no choice. It's that or be shot.'

'We'll get in together.' Peter took hold of Foster's sleeve to pull him forward.

'No, let's wait.' Foster had trouble getting the words out. 'Wait for another train.' He had gone grey, perspiration shone on his forehead. He rubbed his hands over his cheeks, as if he was washing.

In the panic to avoid the machine gunners, Harry Tyson got separated from them and corralled into a different wagon. Foster moaned, pulled, his boots scuffling as he tried to follow Harry and move in the other direction. Peter propelled him forwards, thrusting him ahead of him, shoving his sweat-soaked jacket. Behind him more men pressed at his back. *The lad's crazy*, he thought.

There was no room for Peter or Foster to sit or to lie down, nothing to cling on to except each other. The light cut off as the door slid shut, and Peter heard the sound of a bolt shunt home. *Please God, let the journey be short.*

'Let me off!' Foster's face was wild, his arms flailed, he clawed and pummelled at the men around him.

'Calm down,' Peter said, 'Just calm down. You're all right.' But Foster carried on yelling. The other men covered their heads or turned their backs against him like a wall, until Peter called, 'Get him to some air!' and they all had to shuffle to let him get close to the door where a little breeze came in through the vents at the top.

Foster struggled towards the air vent. 'Claustrophobic,' he mumbled. A moment later Peter saw his eyes roll upwards and his knees give way. He slumped and would have fallen over but for the fact that there was nowhere to fall. The men next to him pushed him upright. Peter watched him come around, looking groggy before he vomited over his own boots. The men looked away, tried to breathe different air. No one did anything, there was no room.

The rattle of the wagon jolted Peter's teeth and a draught whistled in through the slit in the top of the wagon that was too small an opening for anyone to crawl through. But as the long hours stretched out and the train did not slow, it became obvious they were going further than they'd hoped. Someone spotted a hole in the floor near where he was standing that they could use for latrine purposes. Every so often Peter shifted politely to allow someone to make use of it, but not everyone could aim straight on a moving train and soon he was standing in a puddle. Some men who could not move used their helmets to do the necessary, stowing them afterwards in the corners.

Nobody could sleep, and if one of the men started to fall the others would prod him back to alertness. Those at the edge of the carriage fared best. Being in the middle, all Peter could do was close his eyes and try to keep his mind busy. He played through all the pieces of music he knew in his head. Sometimes they fitted with the rhythm of the train, sometimes they didn't, but it gave him a grim satisfaction to be imagining these quintessentially English tunes. When that failed he tried reciting Latin: *amo, amas, amat, amamus, amatis, amant.* I love, you love, he loves.

Once or twice he opened his eyes to see Foster's pale terrified face staring at him as if to weigh him up. He smiled at him with fake reassurance. Pins and needles made Peter's legs shake, then stiffen. Lack of sleep blurred his eyes.

'Sorry,' Foster said to him. 'I'm all right now.'

Peter nodded, closed his eyes again. He was desperate for something to drink. Some men tried to light up, and it made the air even drier and his eyes watered from their smoke.

Hours later the train ground to a halt and buckets of water and husks of stale bread were thrown in. For a moment the door was left open and unguarded and Peter made out the name 'Leipzig' on the signal box. The French soldier stuck his head around the door, looked left and right, then leapt down to run for it across the tracks, sprinting towards the cover of another goods train. The cacophony of fire was instant. Nazi snipers were positioned on the roof of the station. The soldier jerked, ran another step or two and fell. It probably only took one bullet to kill him but at least forty strafed his body to make it kick and twitch even after he was splayed face down on the tracks.

In the truck there was a moment of horrified stillness, before the whole body of men pressed further back inside the carriage. At the rear, men flattened themselves against the walls. Foster screamed and pushed back. 'Please, we can't breathe!' The door slammed shut and the train stuttered on the rails before picking up speed. Peter glanced to

Foster. A stain at the front of his trousers showed he had pissed his pants.

Poor bugger. His teeth were chattering. Peter judged him to be no more than eighteen. There had been no chance to mourn the French soldier. That man's only legacy to his countrymen and their allies was a little more breathing space. Meanwhile Peter had plenty of time to contemplate the rapidity of the German response to escaped prisoners.

For days they stood, legs barely supporting them. They were finally unloaded at a small station with a single-track line; when the doors opened they revealed a tangle of barbed-wire fences surrounding crumbling rows of barracks. Tall sentry posts on stilts, like stiff-legged creatures, rose up at the corners, with their ominous slits for gunners. All around the siding where the train stopped were discarded helmets full of human excrement.

Foster bent double, his hands to his knees. His legs were trembling. Peter clung on to his arm, helped him up. He wanted to make sure they weren't separated. They lined up with the rest in an open courtyard with a muddy surface that squelched under their dragging feet. 'Stick with me and keep your head down,' Peter said.

Foster didn't answer but he did stay close.

'Where are we?' Peter whispered to another man walking ahead of him towards the wire gates.

'Hell by the look of it.' He gave a wry smile. 'Take no notice. From the distance and direction my guess is Silesia, Poland.'

10

1955 Rhoda

HELEN WAS WAITING, this time more obviously dressed up for the occasion, with pink lipstick and a gold chain and a chiffon scarf around her neck. I'd made an effort to be less forbidding, and wore stretch slacks and a scarlet lambswool jersey which I thought looked rather dashing.

After we'd ordered I asked Helen how she was and apologised again for my odd behaviour when I'd come to her house. She brushed it away and we made small talk about the news – the inquest into the dreadful train disaster at Sutton Coldfield, and how it had made me wary of train travel ever since. Helen told me she and Archie had often travelled by train and by boat abroad – France, Belgium. I asked her if she'd known Archie before the war.

'Oh no,' she said, shrugging off her coat, and hanging it over the back of the chair. 'We met afterwards. I was working in the shop on the corner where he lived with his mother. He used to come in for his ciggies and we just hit it off. He was so handsome – pale blonde hair, blue eyes, a real dish.' She shook her head. 'It was throat cancer, you know, that killed him in the end. Thank God it was so quick. They couldn't do anything. I had to just watch him die. So sad. He wasn't even old.' She looked up at me, and her eyes were glistening. 'Near the end that was why I took to speaking to Peter – because Archie couldn't.' The words hung between us.

I swallowed. 'It must have been terrible.'

'You just have to carry on. And of course I miss him like mad. I keep thinking I should move house, now he's gone, to be nearer my sister and her children, but it would be like leaving him behind. You know, the handle he fixed on the kitchen cupboard, the shelves he put up under the stairs. Memories of better times. Sorry, I sound morbid.'

'No, it's natural, I think.'

'He was a lovely person. Gentle. A bit of a dreamer. Frustratingly so at times.'

'Did he take to army life then?'

She twiddled the ends of her scarf. 'I don't think that's easy to answer. Yes and no. War must have been a terrible shock for a seventeen-year-old. I don't think we women have any idea. Peter saved him. That's what Archie said, that he wouldn't be here at all if it hadn't been for him.'

We sat a moment whilst she realised afresh that Archie was no longer here, he was gone. I saw her blink, and then fumble in her handbag.

Helen took out a hanky and blew her nose. 'Oh dear. It just catches me sometimes. When I'm out here I forget, then I'll get on the bus and go home to my empty house and I have to realise it all over again.'

'I once lost someone I was close to and I remember that feeling.'

Helen did not seem to hear me. But I thought to myself how when someone dies, people insist on telling you that time is a healer and you'll get over it. But it wasn't like that for me at all. I just got better at hiding it, the gaping hole where someone once was. Now I didn't know who I'd be without it.

The arrival of the food made me aware I'd been miles

away, and we ate our vegetable soup and rolls politely. I asked Helen whether she worked and she explained that she had retrained after the war to be a part-time community nurse. 'That was why they let Archie stay at home,' she said.

Where my husband could send you flowers. I pushed this bitter thought away, and was silent while we ate. When I'd finished I picked up the menu, said brightly, 'I'm going to have a cake, how about you?'

'No thanks,' Helen said, 'I won't. That soup was very filling.'

I went to the counter and picked out an éclair, feeling guilty. Perhaps I should be watching my weight. Helen was so trim and petite, I felt like a carthorse next to her.

When I was halfway though eating it and still trying to stop cream oozing through my fingers, she said, 'Will you tell Peter we've met?'

'I don't think so. It's too embarrassing.' I put the remains of the éclair down and wiped my fingers on the napkin. 'If he'd wanted me to know about you and Archie, I think he would have told me. But he's deliberately hidden it, I don't know why. I thought something must have happened to him in the war that meant he didn't want to talk about it. He used to say, "Let's not dwell on the past. We can't change it so there's no point."'

'Isn't that strange? I suppose the war took people differently. Archie never stopped talking about it. At first it used to bore me rigid, but I just got used to it. And he took an interest in anything to do with it – we went back to see the war graves, the D-Day landing sites, all that. He'd have even gone to Dresden if they'd have let us. Wartime memorabilia. It was part of him, so I had to like it or lump it. Deeply unfashionable, I know. But in the end I quite enjoyed it, picking up things at auction, looking out for souvenirs for him.'

'What did he do, I mean before he was in the camp with Peter?'

'Just an infantryman.'

'An officer?'

'God, no. Nothing special. Though his father had been some kind of big shot in the first war. But they didn't get on, Archie and him, and Archie hated all that army bravado. "I'm no hero," he used to say. Just to survive it, he said, that was the thing. Funny though, I think he missed it in an odd kind of way, the structure, the routine. He started collecting things. He was worried people were forgetting. The first thing he collected was an army first-aid kit, but later he got books, magazines, papers, maps, medals. I think he thought by reconstructing it he'd be able to come to terms with it.'

'What will you do with it all now?'

'I haven't had the heart to get rid of it. I did think other collectors might like it, but I hate to break it up. I think Archie thought he'd write a book about it one day, but then he got ill and the book never happened.'

'What a shame. I would have loved to read it. Would you show me his things?'

Her face brightened. Then it fell. She'd remembered Peter. I saw the argument pass across her features, before she said, 'Actually, you're the first person who's ever asked. Everyone else I know would think him funny in the head collecting all that stuff. But do you know what? I think he was sort of doing it for Peter.'

'Why?'

'Oh, I don't know. Some sort of odd way of thanking him maybe, to make a record of it. But whenever Peter came he just used to want to get Archie away from the house and all that stuff, and down to the King's Arms. To be honest, I think Archie was a bit disappointed that Peter would never show any interest. Maybe now Archie's gone you'll be able to persuade him.'

'Maybe one day,' I said. 'But he doesn't know I've arranged to meet you. Don't tell him, will you?'

'It feels so strange. I don't know why he kept you away from us.'

I stared at her. It was the first time I'd thought of it that way. That perhaps Peter was ashamed of me.

I swallowed, covered my embarrassment. 'I just need a little more time. I'll try talking to him about the war a bit first, see if I can get him to open up to me.'

'Good idea. You could tell him a bit about your war, share some of your memories.'

But something inside me resisted this. I knew that if the door on my memories opened then it would be hard to force it closed again. It was one thing to find out Peter's past, but I wasn't sure I was ready to revisit my own.

11

1940 Rhoda

I TOOK THE post office telegram out of Mrs Middleton's hand. I knew it was not good news even before I got to Crag Bank, by the look in Mother's eyes when she told me I'd better cycle over. But there was something different about seeing the typed words myself. The intensity of those full stops.

DEEPLY REGRET TO INFORM YOU
42387 P/O PJ MIDDLETON HAS BEEN REPORTED
MISSING IN ACTION. ANY FURTHER
INFORMATION WILL BE PROMPTLY RELATED.
OP EVANS

From the next room I could hear the strains of piano music, discordant and clashing. I wondered how Peter's mother stood it. I reread the telegram with unseeing eyes.

'Of course I know he's not dead,' Mrs Middleton said, when I finally looked up. Her eyes were already red-rimmed, the lump of a handkerchief bulged in her cardigan sleeve. 'I'd know if he was. A mother knows these things. But we just have to wait for news, that's all.'

I did not like her confidence that she would know if anything had happened to him. At the same time I did want to believe her, that he was alive. I took a deep breath. 'When did you last hear from him?'

'Not since before France. He wrote to us just before he left, telling us he was sailing the next day, but nothing since.'

'Me neither. I brought his last letter in case you'd like to see it. He sounds very jolly, very ...' I could not finish. The enormity of what was happening to us had suddenly hit me. I put the letter down on the table, pushed it towards her.

She looked at it as though it might bite her. 'I don't think I will, right now.' Her eyes were glassy. 'Shall we have tea?' It was her answer for everything, a way to pretend things were normal. She began to fill the kettle. I watched her stiff back, the crossed straps of her frilled apron.

I steeled myself to sit at her kitchen table, endure more conversation over the cruet, when really all I wanted to do was run out of there, get some privacy. It was daunting, the thought of having to tell people Peter was missing, to bear their sympathetic looks. It was easier to do what Mrs Middleton was doing, to pretend he would come home, rather than confront the bigger terror that he might not.

Mrs Middleton handed me a cup of weak tea, and sat down.

I took hold of the saucer, and the spoon tinkled. I saw Mrs Middleton's eyes fix on my hand, and the slight rise of her well-plucked eyebrows. 'I see you are wearing a ring.'

I put the saucer down and withdrew my hand hurriedly into my lap. 'Yes. Peter gave it to me on the day he left. At the station. It was all such a rush. There wasn't time for him to ask Pa's permission properly, so we couldn't make any sort of announcement.' I was blushing under her intense scrutiny.

'Well, then.' She paused, and I saw her come to some sort of decision. 'He couldn't possibly object. Not to some-one like Peter.' The implication was that Peter was higher class than my family. I squirmed, as her eyes took in my old skirt and jersey. I hadn't thought to change, just biked over as quickly as I could when the message came.

'Let me look at the ring, dear,' she said.

I held out my hand, seeing with shame that there was bicycle-chain oil on my fingers.

'A diamond. Very nice,' she said. 'I hope you'll look after it. We'll help, if it's necessary,' she said. 'With the wedding, I mean.' She got up, took the hanky from her sleeve and dabbed her eyes. 'I know times are hard for everyone, it being wartime, and we'd want the best—'

'I don't think Pa would—'

She cut me off. 'It will have to be in St Oswald's,' she said, her voice breaking. 'We'll start making plans. Oh, just wait till I tell Gerald. He'll be so surprised – we never guessed, you know. I mean, we knew you were fond of each other, but … well. He must have saved his wages months for that. So like him, such a generous boy …' She ran out of breath. A sob erupted from her throat but she turned away to hide it. 'We'll have to get material,' she said. She wiped her eyes, began pacing up and down. 'And it's hard to get silk now they need it for parachutes … and it should be a June wedding, sunshine, roses in the church—'

I could bear it no longer. 'Stop it.' My voice was louder and angrier than I intended. 'He's missing, Mrs Middleton. There might not be a wedding. And if there is, then my father will pay, and I'll decide where it is and what to wear.'

Mrs Middleton opened her mouth as if to speak, but then sat down heavily on the kitchen chair, head bowed into the handkerchief, shoulders shaking. I reached out and took her hand. 'Sorry, Mrs Middleton. I didn't mean to upset you. It's just—'

'I know,' she said. 'He can't be gone, can he? Not our Peter?'

I shook my head, 'Like you said, we'll just have to wait for news. Keep hoping, that's all.'

At that point Mr Middleton emerged from the other room. Mrs Middleton braced herself, dabbed her nose. 'Rhoda's here.'

'Yes,' he said, looking uncomfortably at his wife's tear-stained face. He turned to me. 'I expect they'll let us know when they hear anything.'

'She and Peter are engaged.'

'Say again?'

'Engaged. To be married.' Mrs Middleton put her hand on his arm, but he twitched it off as if it was not welcome.

'Damn fool boy. Why did he do that when he knew he was going to war?'

I might as well have been invisible. It was as if my feelings didn't count at all.

Mrs Middleton put on a soothing voice, 'Well, dear, I expect he thought it would make sure Rhoda waited for him, I mean—'

'Of course I'll wait for him,' I said hotly. 'I don't need a ring to make me wait for him. I promised him.'

Mr Middleton looked me up and down with an expression bordering on distaste. 'Oh. Well, he must have thought you did. And I don't know why you encouraged him. I might have known something like this would happen.' He slid the paper off the table and without a word retreated into the other room.

I wasn't sure if he was blaming me for Peter joining up or for him being missing. What was clear from his manner was that whichever it was, it was somehow my fault.

12

1940 Peter

THE QUEUE TRAILED right the way around the perimeter of the yard and then up past the first row of barracks. After a few months at Lamsdorf, Peter had got used to the fact that queuing was to occupy most of his waking hours. That, and standing to attention for '*Appell*' or roll call.

Soup was doled out twice in a day, once in the morning and once at night, and if you were near the front you got bread and if you were near the back you often didn't. So the lines formed hours early with all the men wrangling to get to the top of the queue. He imagined that from above it must be like watching scum collecting in a river. Nobody moved fast – they had not enough energy for that – but they gravitated towards the blockage, the food creating the only stopping point in the endless drift around the barracks.

Foster was just behind him as usual. Since their arrival he had followed Peter like a servant, always a few steps behind, close on his heels. Peter was not sure whether he liked this or not. On the one hand it was comforting to see a familiar face, on the other hand he was beginning to feel responsible for him and he was not sure that was a good idea. However, Foster seemed to want to keep him always in view. When they first arrived the sight of so many men in one place was awe-inspiring – just the sheer volume of uniformed men. It seemed to send Foster into a panic; he kept looking behind him, as if they might all suddenly close in on him.

'I never knew there were this many men in England,' he said.

There had been no sign of Harry Tyson, though he might be there somewhere, but every day more trains arrived with more prisoners, and the numbers in the camp swelled into thousands. Peter gave up looking in the end; he supposed his mind just could not process all that information and he learned to discount everyone but Foster. He couldn't lose Foster, anyway, he stuck to him like flypaper. Over time he learned that he'd joined up straight from school, and that his first name was Archie.

Gradually summer turned to autumn and then to a bitter winter with no let-up in the routine. The rumour was that Lamsdorf was just a holding camp and they'd soon be transferred to other camps, but as the months went on and the camp seemed to fill but never empty, Peter forgot.

One particular day he was at the tail end of the queue for food, his greatcoat collar buttoned up to his chin, when a clap on the shoulder made him turn to see a German guard behind him.

'*Kommen Sie mitt*,' the guard said. He was a short square man with small heavy-lidded eyes behind spectacles. To be singled out set the hackles up on the back of Peter's neck and he couldn't help but glance around searching for Archie. There he was, about thirty yards away, dawdling along after him at his usual shuffle, eyes looking downwards like always.

'*Was ist los?*' Peter asked loudly in German, hoping Archie would hear his voice and look up.

'*Arbeit.*' So that was it, work. The guard marched him

over towards the wire where a bored-looking sergeant stood by a waiting truck. Six other trucks were up ahead of it and this was the last one in the line. Through the open back he could see it was filled with men.

Peter was conscious of Archie behind him, but didn't dare turn. The guard was counting and there were now seven men including himself.

'*Nein, acht*,' said the second guard. They needed eight.

By this time Archie had seen what was happening and was almost trotting over, his eyes fixed on Peter. Peter gave a slight shake of his head, frowned at him and did not call out. Archie faltered. He looked the way a dog does when you call out 'Stay'. Peter did not want to be responsible for taking Archie wherever they were going. He hadn't been asked to fetch his kit, so what if the word 'work' was some kind of euphemism for something worse?

Meanwhile the bespectacled guard was motioning Peter to climb into the truck, where other expressionless prisoners sat waiting, and he had no option but to obey. Archie stood a little way off, hands dangling loosely from his greatcoat sleeves, eyes wide with worry, unsure whether to come nearer the wire. Men avoided getting too close to the holding wire in case the snipers on what they called the goon towers thought they were going to try an escape.

'*Du!*'

Archie stared.

'*Schnell! Kommen Sie hier!*'

Archie hurried over, almost stumbling over his own feet. The guards did not even bother to tell him where he was going, just loaded him into the truck. Peter caught his eye and saw his expression change from panic to relief.

'Do you know where we're going?' Archie asked.

'Nope. Work, they said.'

'Oh.' He paused, and then turned to look at Peter. 'I hope that's what they really mean.'

Peter heard the undertow of fear in his voice, but he tried to be bracing. 'We'll be all right. Food can't be worse where we're going anyway.'

The searchlights of the compound lit up the horizon with an eerie glow long before they arrived, the only patch of light in utter darkness. Peter sagged as the truck drove through the gate between concrete stanchions and another ten-foot barbed-wire fence. A panic assailed him, the instinct of an animal to run for its burrow, its territory. Except he had no territory; he was adrift in an alien place with no landmarks except the wire.

They were deposited before a row of brick-and-timber barracks. The next day they were issued with filthy over-alls labelled on the back, *Oehringen Werks E22,* and caps and gloves black with coal dust. Peter looked down on them in dismay. A mine. How would Archie cope, if the work was underground?

It was a quarter-mile walk to the Hermann Goering Werks coal mine in a wind so sharp it would have shaved them if it could. They marched in rows of three with a German *Unteroffizier* with each group of twelve. Theirs was a man with a lantern jaw and permanently dour expression. Even after this short walk they were out of breath, and deaf from the wind. It might be a relief after all, to be in the mine out of the bitter weather, Peter thought, glancing back at Archie who was wearing only an army-issue forage cap. His nose was running and his fair fluffy hair did nothing to protect his ears which were red with cold. Pull your cap further down, he wanted to say, but Archie couldn't have heard him, not in this wind.

The work for their party was building a railway track. At first he didn't see how they could do it, eight weak men – shift railway sleepers and carry rails. The weather was sleeting and the sleepers and rails were slippery and heavy. But there was of course no choice. One man went on each end of the rails and at each end of the sleepers.

Peter and his partner were equally matched, strength-wise. Neb was a tall rangy Cornishman with large fleshy hands, whose big nose had given him his nickname. Peter worked steadily despite the cold and rain. The ground was frozen into ruts and slippery with ice and wet. He felt his back muscles swell and throb. After only a few minutes he realised he was in trouble. This was backbreaking hard labour.

Peter saw Archie's breath puff out in white clouds with the effort of supporting the weight of the track and trying not to lose his footing. His knees buckled and his thin white hands in their army mittens could hardly get a grip on the rails to heave them off the ground. Archie's partner, a dogged, terrier-like Scot called Brodie, became frustrated. 'Lift the bloody thing, can't you,' Brodie said. 'I can't hold it on my own.'

Peter gave up watching Archie as icy rain dripped down his forehead and mixed with sweat so it stung his eyes. Each journey got longer as the track lengthened.

A clang and a yell. Peter's head whipped round. Brodie and Archie were down. Brodie was on his back groaning, the rail across his shin pinning him to the ground. German guards appeared like a swarm of flies.

Brodie flailed his arms, trying to stand. 'Get it off!'

Peter and Neb put their sleeper down where they were and rushed to help. Between them they heaved the rail to the side. It was obvious Brodie's leg was smashed. It rested at a peculiar angle and there was a deep gash where bone was showing. Blood oozed from the wound. Archie's face was the colour of the grey sky; he'd moved back, away from the redness of the blood.

The guard with the lantern jaw summoned a truck and they shoved Brodie, still bawling, into it.

'*Stumm!*' said one of the guards, pointing his gun at him. Brodie stopped his noise and fell silent, but Peter did not miss the look of accusation he threw at Archie.

The truck drove away. When the engine noise faded Neb said, 'Poor bugger.'

'I don't know what happened. I tripped and it just sort of slid out of my hands.' Archie was white, his eyes looking fearfully from Peter to Neb. 'I didn't mean to. It was so slippery.'

Neb looked at Archie as if to say he was an idiot, and shook his head.

'His leg looks pretty bad,' Peter said. 'I hope they've got a good hospital.'

Archie screwed up his face as though he might cry. 'Don't look at me like that. I've said I didn't mean to.'

They were not allowed to stop working. Another prisoner was brought almost immediately to partner Archie. A British soldier called Williams with his forage cap turned right down over his ears and a muffler up to his nose. By lunchtime Archie was weeping with the effort, and swaying on his feet. There was nothing anyone could do to help him and the German guard who came periodically to check their progress laughed at him.

'Too hard, *Fräulein*?' he said. 'The English army are all soft. No wonder you run away like rabbits. With men like you, no wonder you lose the war.'

There was nothing anyone could say back to him. After all, they were prisoners, so the German army had beaten them, no matter what was happening in England. When they were allowed a five-minute break, they limped gratefully to the concrete loading platform.

'We need to do it differently,' Peter said, 'more efficiently. Or we'll not last. I'm just not fit enough for this. And on their lousy rations—'

'No, not more efficiently. That's what they want. We don't want to help them, do we? We'll do it as slow as we can,' Neb said.

'What I meant is, we need to conserve energy. None of us are used to this sort of work.'

'What did you do before?' asked Neb.

'Teacher. How about you?'

'Bus conductor.' Neb laughed wheezily, and coughed. 'Course they trained us, but there wasn't time to get properly fit.'

'I only had three weeks' training, then I was posted,' Archie said. 'It was just bullying, all that screaming and shouting at us as if we were stupid.'

'They have to do that. They have to change your mentality. Otherwise you wouldn't be able to take it,' Peter said.

'Wish we were out there fighting, instead of in here,' Neb said.

'I don't.' Archie pulled a face.

'Why did you join up then?' Neb said.

'I needed a job.' The way Archie said it, it sounded as though he'd applied for work in a shoe shop. Peter raised his eyebrows. Seeing their scrutiny, Archie went on: 'I needed somewhere to live and I didn't want to go home.'

Neb began to laugh. It was infectious and soon Peter was laughing too.

'What? What are you laughing at?' Archie said.

'You. Well, you've got a live-in job now. Bleeding hell-fire,' said Neb, 'what a useless crew.'

When Big Jaw had gone for a smoke they worked out a more efficient system whereby they'd carry the rail between four of them, swapping so that the end people got to go in the middle, the easiest place, every now and then. Peter knew their efficiency helped the German war effort, and it grated inside, but he gritted his teeth. They needed to survive.

Twelve hours of shifting sleepers made the fifteen-minute walk back to camp a torture. By then it was snowing. The swirling flakes made him feel as if his feet were made of clay and the rest of his body was floating somewhere above cloud level. As a child he'd been sentimental about snow, thought it magical; sledging down Warton slopes in his red hat and mitts, and scrounging lumps of coal from Mother to make eyes for the snowman in the front garden. But now, the snow was just something else to make their lives hell.

'You all right?' Peter asked Archie as they stood in the yard shaking the sludge from their shoulders for the evening roll call.

Archie did not answer except with a flicker of his eyes. Perhaps he did not have the energy. When his number was called, his voice had a desperate edge. Thank God he and Archie had been wearing their greatcoats when they were called up at Lamsdorf. All Peter's valuable things lived in its deep pockets; his letters from Rhoda and his mother, his first-aid kit, string and other useful bits and pieces, army-issue gloves. And in these arctic conditions, without their coats and extra gloves they'd have been in a sorry mess.

Back in the hut, none of those who had arrived on the truck the day before had the will to queue for food, but just collapsed on their wood-shaving mattresses unable to move.

On the call 'Raus!' at 5 a.m. Peter could hardly stand; his legs and shoulders were cramped rigid. He washed under a dribble of water from the freezing tap and limped over to where he saw the queue at the canteen door for coffee and bread, with Archie at his heels as usual. Peter suppressed a quiver of irritation; he wished Archie would find someone else to talk to for a change. Above them men were manning the gantry and the pit-head machinery was already creaking into motion.

That morning they had a small piece of sausage with the bread so Peter was heavily engrossed in wiping his mug out with the bread when a voice behind him said, 'Middleton, isn't it?' It made him jump, as if someone was calling his name across a street, or in a pub at home.

He turned to see the dark stocky man he'd marched with to the train, looking at him with his calculating bird-like eyes. 'I don't suppose you remember me? You shook my hand on the march through Trier.'

A quick scan showed him that the man looked thinner, darker around the eyes, but otherwise healthy.

'Hello,' he said, responding in the same polite way. 'I never thought I'd come across you again. Are you working in the mine?'

'No. The surface, towing trucks to the wagons. Tyson, Harry, remember? Where you billeted?'

'Number five, over there.' Peter pointed. 'And Archie Foster too. Do you remember him?' He nodded his head towards Archie who was squatting to rest his legs, his bread still in his hand.

Harry looked over to him. 'Foster, yes.'

Archie stood and pressed his lips together in an almost-smile, but did not join them.

'I'm in five too,' Harry said. He stood up taller, flexed his muscles. Peter was aware of him sizing him up, the way men do if they're going to fight. 'I guess you've just arrived,' Harry went on. 'You'll get used to it.'

'Suppose so. We only got here the day before yesterday.'

'God knows how anyone can think to call this stuff coffee.' Harry swallowed the luke-warm liquid from his mug, looking over its rim at Peter the whole time. 'If you need anything, just tip me the wink. I can get most stuff – for a price.'

Peter gulped at his coffee. The liquid was bitter and grainy.

'It's cushier here than at Lamsdorf,' Harry said. 'Better rations and better billets. We get parcels sometimes. Though without the Red Cross I think we'd soon be goners.' He glanced over to Archie who was still just holding his bread and not eating it. 'Is he all right?'

'Think so. We've to lug sleepers and rails for the new track, to carry coal out of the mine. It's tough going.'

Harry gave Archie a dismissive look. 'Looks bomb-blasted. I saw quite a few like that in Lamsdorf. Usually deaf too. Is he deaf?'

'No. He's fine, just tired I think.' Why was he defending Archie? It was something about Harry, an edgy quality about him that made Peter shrink from his attention. He covered his discomfort by saying, 'Any news from England?' He was really asking if there was any sign the war would be over, how long he'd have to be stuck in the camp.

'Zilch.' Harry lit a cigarette and inhaled deeply. He blew the smoke downwards away from Peter. 'Just Jerry propaganda about how England will fall like France. They dole out those sorts of reports if there's any trouble. To put a hole in our morale. I wish I was still fighting. I only saw a bit of action. Here, have a drag.'

Peter took the cigarette and took a deep draw on it before handing it back. The buzz of nicotine loosened his tongue, relaxed him. 'I never got that far. I joined as a driver but never even made it as far as the front.' He squirmed inwardly, realising too late this might sound cowardly.

'You not see any fighting?'

The implication was clear. Peter bristled. 'I've got skills in mapreading. It was where I'd be most useful.' Why had he said that? The irony made him wince. Harry was half-smiling, as if he didn't believe him. Peter hurried on. 'We were on our way to Dunkirk, but we were ambushed, they blew up our convoy. I was lucky, we lost quite a few. What about you, how did you get taken?' He said this to remind Harry that they were both in the same boat now.

Harry whistled through his teeth. 'Sheesh, you are new, aren't you? You don't ask that. You can ask anything, but you don't ask that. It's just not done.'

'I didn't mean to offend.'

'None taken.' Harry smiled at him in a condescending way. 'You want to relax a bit. Here, have another drag.'

Peter inhaled again, held the smoke in his lungs, felt the fizz rush through his veins. He hadn't had a cigarette since France. People kept impressing on him to save them, so he could barter with the Germans for food. He tried to make a joke, to lighten the atmosphere. 'Thanks. The best way to finish a meal, hey.'

'Except for the other.' Harry winked and then cackled, before saying, 'I'm off, going to chat up Big Jaw, give him a fag, see if I can get the pick of the jobs.' He leaned in towards Peter. 'Guess I'll see you later. Keep an eye on your friend. If he stops eating then he's had it.' Harry's breath smelt of smoke and decay. 'And he's got that look about him.'

Peter raised his eyebrows in question.

'Doolally,' mouthed Harry, before he strode away, hands in his pockets.

'He was talking about me, wasn't he?' Archie appeared at his side.

'No, he was telling me not to ask about how people got here. Says it isn't done. Want a smoke?'

'I don't. Filthy habit.' They walked over to lean against the barrack wall. After a moment he said, 'On second thoughts, maybe I'll try it, seeing as everyone else does.'

Peter passed him the tab end. Archie took a drag and his eyes watered as he tried to inhale the smoke.

Archie coughed, 'I bet he doesn't want you to know how he got here because he can't admit he made a mistake. Like all of us. All of us who've ended up here. Anyhow, I wouldn't mind you asking me.'

Peter took the cigarette back. He waited, watched Archie take a swig of the foul coffee, knew he was going to tell him even if he didn't ask.

'All that overblown talk you hear at home – our brave boys this, our brave boys that –' Archie put the tab to his lips again, sucked. 'Nonsense. All of it.' He looked up to check Peter was still listening. 'All I know is, when the time came we charged at them and they charged at us and most of us shot over each other's heads. They waved their guns like they didn't know what to do with them. Like kids. Most looked in worse shape than us – overweight, or wearing spectacles, panting, just plain bloody terrified. Nobody wanted to kill anyone.' He shook his head in a shudder. 'Even the British army knows that. Why do you think they issue us with so many bullets – way more bullets than we need?'

'I don't know.'

Archie gave a short laugh. 'Because everyone does it. Them, us – we all fire to miss, that's why. How stupid is that?'

'Christ,' Peter said.

'There's no hate, no anger with people you don't know. How can there be? Why would you want to kill another man for no reason? Two armies blundering about France with the big nobs yelling at us, trying to get us to hate each other. I suppose I might kill in anger or passion, but they can't pump that into us, no matter what they do.' Archie paused to let people past them into the hut. 'Give us another drag.'

'Here.'

Archie held the smoking cigarette in front of him; he spoke to it, not to Peter. Peter watched his face darken. 'Those few seconds before you go in, they're the worst. You've been jumping out of your skin from the noise of shelling and there's fire in your blood so you think you'll explode if you don't do something soon. You just want to run, run any-where. So you're hopping from foot to foot, your heart beat-ing out of your chest. You wonder what you're doing there, what it's all about. It doesn't seem real. But it's too late to turn round and go home. After that, it all happens so quickly.' His eyes came up to meet Peter's. 'One minute I was stood there, then the shout came and I was running. I tripped over a leg, someone's body. My rifle flew out of my hands. I fell. Lucky really.'

'Then what?'

'When I got up, Jerry was standing over me with his gun at my chest, and he just looked at me, as if to say, "I wish we weren't doing this. I wish we could go somewhere else, have a nice cold beer." I flung my arms up – I didn't know what else to do with them. Soon as I lost my gun I'd had it. As if a number three Lee-Enfield was all I was.'

Peter nodded, waited a few seconds in case there was more, but Archie had gone somewhere in his mind, some-where he couldn't follow. Peter said, 'I felt the same when they took me on the road. I'd no pistol, no knife, nothing. I was useless. But I bet the German holding the rifle thought he was brave.'

Archie coughed, a hacking hollow sound. Peter clapped him on the back.

'Sorry, Pete. I feel sick. The smoke's got to me.'

Or maybe the thought of another day laying track, Peter thought. Archie thrust the cigarette back to Peter, who pinched out the end with his fingers and pocketed the stub. The loudspeaker crackled to life with the call for the work parties to assemble.

'Oh God. Time,' Archie said.

'Come on, I'll give you another smoking lesson later.'

13

1940 Peter

WEEKS PASSED. PETER had no more energy to look out for Archie. Pushing his body to the limit every day in the freezing November weather meant he could barely think about himself, let alone Archie.

The track was longer now and it was further to go with the sleepers. They had been supplied with creaking iron trucks to ferry the sleepers down the track. The truck had a tailgate that was permanently down to allow them to load and unload.

'Hey, Pete!' Harry Tyson was on their team that morning. Peter asked where the other soldier was, who worked with Archie. 'Sick,' Harry said. 'Too weak to work. Dysentery they're saying.'

'Morning, Harry,' Archie said.

Harry frowned at the idea of Archie as his partner. Archie was gaunt and thin now, with a desperate hangdog look. None of them were fed enough to build more muscle and the guards had taken to calling Archie *'Fräulein'* and taunting him with insults. Archie tried to ignore it but Peter knew it ground him down, and it made him angry to watch Archie grow more lacklustre every day.

Peter and Neb had to heave the sleepers out of the truck

at one end and lay them. Two other men were levelling the ground for them to lay them on. When the truck was empty it had to be pushed back to the loading platform where the crew at the other end loaded up more rough timbers. Even that was hard work; the truck was heavy and old and had never seen oil in its life.

The weather worsened and ice formed on the guards' moustaches. The Germans were short-tempered and bored; they hated being outside in this icy blast. Peter had his head down when he was alerted by laughter and voices in German. Then a shot. Peter looked over his shoulder in the direction of the noise. The lantern-jawed guard they'd nicknamed Big Jaw was pointing his gun at Archie and making him undress.

'What's up?' hissed Peter.

'Dunno,' Neb said. 'Quick, get that last sleeper out and we can push the truck back up and see.'

They worked more quickly, but by the time they got up to the loading area Archie was already shivering in a floral print dress, his arms horrifyingly pale. His greatcoat and uniform straggled on the ground where intermittent sleet was soaking it.

'Work like a woman, dress like a woman!' called Big Jaw in English to the rest of the prisoners, grinning.

The three other Germans sniggered at the joke. Catcalls and whistles followed. Harry stood off to one side of the stack of sleepers, hands thrust deep in his pockets. Peter saw him conceal a smile.

Peter understood enough German to grasp that the dress belonged to one of the officer's wives and she'd been throwing it out.

'*Nun, arbeiten!*' came Big Jaw's command. Archie did not move. One of the soldiers fired a shot at his feet and Archie panicked and jumped into motion. Wearing the dress meant his legs could only take small steps. Harry was built like a wrestler; he hoisted his end from the top of the stack easily, and waited for Archie to lift his. Archie struggled, the veins standing out blue on his arms. The guards watched Harry and Archie manhandle the sleeper into the truck

'You. Get back to work.' Big Jaw had seen Peter and Neb staring.

They continued for another half-hour, and the next time he got back with the truck Archie was still in the thin dress. Despite his clenched jaw, Archie's teeth were chattering now. Harry ignored his working partner, but threw glances over towards where the guards were standing.

After ten minutes Peter couldn't stand to see the sight of Archie's skinny white arms. He left the wagon and went over to the gaggle of officers. 'Please, he'll freeze. Let him have his coat at least,' Peter said to the youngest, fresh-faced guard.

The guard shrugged, smiled, eyes shifting sideways to his companions. 'You think he needs a coat? Then give him yours.'

Peter saw Harry turn up his collar, pretend not to hear and walk away. He picked up the end of another sleeper, waited silently for Archie to join him.

It made Peter angry, and before he really understood what he was doing, he stood in front of the young German and deliberately unbuttoned his own coat. Once he felt the warm weight of it in his hands though, and the sudden chill on his back, he hesitated.

The German guard glanced knowingly at his companions.

Damn him. Peter would not back down; he walked over and handed Archie his coat. Archie shook his head, but Peter let the coat drop on to the concrete platform in front of him and returned to where Neb was waiting. When he turned to look back from the track, he was relieved to see Archie was wearing the coat over the dress.

They whistle blew for their half-hour break to use the ditch as a latrine and for a smoke. Peter did not dare sit in case he was too cold to get up again. The missing layer made his shoulders tight and his neck ache with cold. He hugged his arms around himself and banged his fists against his back to beat some warmth into it. His knees were numb.

'You're daft,' Neb said. 'Anyone can see he's not going to last. You've got to look after yourself.'

'I couldn't see him freeze.'

'You religious?'

'No, not particularly.' Peter paused to blow on his hands. 'Or at least not in a churchy way. But if we stop being kind, what's the point? Isn't that what England stands for? What will we be if we lose all that?'

'Alive.' Harry appeared beside him, buttoning up his flies. 'Look after number one. The first rule.'

Peter was too cold to argue any more. But as the whistle blew to start work again he was relieved to see Big Jaw, who had got bored with the game, kick Archie's clothes over to him, and gesture for him to take off the dress and put them on. Archie dressed slowly, painfully slowly. His fingers fumbled with the fastenings of his battledress and he almost fell trying to pick up his greatcoat.

Peter was in such a state of tension that he thought that any moment Big Jaw would get impatient, lose his temper and shoot. He and Neb had unloaded two more sleepers by the time Archie was dressed. When they took the next truck back Archie handed Peter his coat.

'Thanks,' he said dully. 'But you shouldn't have done it. It wasn't worth the risk.' Harry raised his eyebrows heavenwards and tried to exchange a meaningful look with Peter, but Peter ignored it.

'That's what friends are for,' Peter said.

When Peter put on his coat, it was still slightly warm inside from Archie's body heat; he felt its weight and comfort straight away, and just the feel of it improved his spirits. He marvelled that something as simple as a coat could make such a difference.

The next day Peter could see Harry talking to Archie and Archie shaking his head vigorously. It looked as though they were arguing. Peter felt the hairs rise on the back of his neck; he'd learned the scent of trouble. But the sleeting rain lashed down, making further talk impossible, and they were all wet through and low.

As the light began to wane they struggled to push the dripping truck back to the concrete platform next to the entrance to the mine workings. Here there was a set of buffers that the truck ran up to. Archie and Harry waited there, heads down against the sleet, with a pile of sleepers ready for stacking into the truck.

Peter and Neb rolled the truck up the line. Maybe now he'd find out what was going on between Archie and Harry. He gave the truck one last shove to get it up to the platform, and as he did he saw Archie move.

A quick movement, away from the stack of sleepers.

From then, everything happened very slowly. He didn't understand at first, what Archie was doing; he saw his hand fractionally too late. White fingers against the concrete wall. It was a reflex action, to leap in, pull Archie out of the way, but he wasn't quite quick enough. Peter dragged him backwards, but Archie's hand was right in front of the buffers.

A moment later a spurt of red on grey concrete, and Archie slumped.

Archie had crushed his hand between the truck and the buffer on purpose.

'*Was gibt's?*' The German shout came as Neb and Peter strained to pull the truck backwards, heaving with all their strength, the wheels creaking, as they tried to get a purchase on the wet wood.

Archie was on his knees. Two fingers were mangled, blood and rain dripping on the track. Someone blew a whistle, the sound of running boots. A moment later they were all lined up, Sten guns pointing at them.

They took Archie away to the hospital. Peter avoided walking over the trail of blood for the rest of the shift. The image haunted Peter; he imagined he heard the noise of Archie's bones cracking. Archie hadn't made a sound, almost as if the hand was not his. Peter felt guilty. He could have stopped the truck. But then, Archie might have found some other way. Fool. What did he think he was doing?

At roll call Peter was called out along with Neb. Apparently Big Jaw had been round to see Harry, and Harry had told them Archie did it on purpose. Harry was probably intimidated in case he got the blame. They thought Peter and Neb had planned it with him, so they were each sentenced to five days' solitary on reduced rations as a punishment. Injuring yourself was apparently 'sabotage'.

'What did I say?' Neb said. 'I told you, that friend of yours is a bloody liability. I'll do for him if I ever set eyes on him again.'

14

1955 Rhoda

A NEAT PILE of photographs and shoeboxes awaited me on Helen's lounge carpet, striped by shafts of sunlight streaming through the window.

'How's Peter?' Helen asked.

'He was busy this afternoon, with the cricket team. Some sort of meeting.' I sat myself down, leaned forward to look down at the photographs. 'That looks exciting.'

She narrowed her eyes. 'You didn't tell him, did you, that you were coming here?' She did not sit.

'I was going to. I did try,' I said. 'I asked him about the war. I saw in the paper there was a wartime film on at the pictures last Sunday afternoon, so I asked him if he'd like to go. It didn't help. He just clammed up.'

Helen sighed and pursed her lips and began to open boxes and sort photographs in a too-efficient way that showed me she was cross. Then she stomped upstairs, and I could hear bangs and thumps above my head as she pulled out more boxes in the spare bedroom.

I really had tried. On Sunday, rain had kept Peter and me indoors. Peter was marking more essays in the kitchen. 'There's quite a good film on,' I called. '*The Cockleshell Heroes.*

With Trevor Howard and José what's his name. About men trying to knock out German ships in the war.'

'I thought you'd grown out of Trevor Howard.'

'He's all right, I just don't like him in those romantic things. It sounds good.'

'I thought you liked weepies. Like *Brief Encounter*.' A pause, in which I felt myself stiffen. 'Isn't there anything else on?' He emerged from the kitchen and took the paper from my hand. 'What about this instead – "*Footsteps in the Fog,* a detective drama"?'

'I'd rather see the other one. I'm interested. There's so much I don't know about the war.'

Peter ignored me. 'Well, if we can't agree, let's not bother. If it clears up I could do some jobs in the garden. Would you like a cup of tea? I'm just making one.'

'Oh, all right then. Yes, please. We've never talked much about it, have we, darling? The war, I mean. I don't really know what you did.'

'Yes you do. I spent the whole bloody war in a work camp.'

'But what was it like? I've never really asked.'

Peter shot an impatient look at me from the kitchen door. 'Look, there's nothing to tell. I was a prisoner of war, okay? We had to do forced labour for the Germans. It wasn't exactly a picnic. I survived it and here I am. Thank God for peace, is all I can say. Do you want a biscuit with it?'

Then he'd clattered about, banging the tins on the worktop and slamming the cupboard doors. A few moments later he called out, 'It's on the table. I'm off to the paper shop. Want anything?'

'No, thanks.' I shook my head in frustration. So that was the end of my attempt to get Peter to open up to me.

'Here we are!' Helen's voice and her footsteps coming

downstairs caught my attention. I looked down at the piles of photographs and the boxes laid out on the carpet. 'Lamsdorf', said one. Archie must have been an organised man; they were all neatly labelled in tidy upright print.

We had a look at the things Helen had brought down – a big box of army records and faded misty photographs of men staring unsmiling at the camera from bunk beds. A lot of the things in Archie's boxes were baffling and we couldn't understand why he'd kept them – old scraps of label from food tins, a child's scribbled drawing of a house.

When we'd looked through the boxes downstairs, Helen finally took me up to the spare room where Archie had kept his collection. The rest of the house was eerily spotless, but the spare bedroom was piled high with ramshackle boxes.

'Blimey,' I said.

'I know. Sorry it's a bit chilly in here, but there's no room for a paraffin stove or anything.' Helen blew dust off a hanger draped in a sheet, and then flipped it back to reveal an old greatcoat. 'This is Archie's, but Peter would have worn one just like this,' she said.

It was stained with dirt, worn black around the pockets. She was going to take it off its hanger to pass it to me.

'No, it's okay,' I said, retreating to the door. 'Best leave it where it will stay protected.' I didn't want to touch it, it was filthy. And it was a shock – I hadn't expected anything like that. Peter had nothing with him at all when he came home, just his new civvies.

Helen grabbed a dusty cardboard box and we went back to the warm. We studied the pictures of the camp and maps of Poland where Peter and Archie had been interned. There were pamphlets too, with photographs. I'd never seen any pictures before. Probably they weren't in general circulation. It gave me a queasy feeling, imagining Peter there in those desolate muddy barracks. Helen kept up a non-stop commentary about it all; Archie said this, Archie said that.

'Nobody else lets me talk about him,' she confessed. 'They try to change the subject. They're embarrassed to mention him. Since he died, it's as if they want him never to have existed. But when you love someone, you want to talk about him, don't you?'

I nodded, but thought, *no. I never did.*

On the way home on the train I settled back to read some pamphlets Helen had lent me. One of the books listed atrocities that men from Peter's camp had suffered on the march across Czechoslovakia and Germany. Helen's stories showed me a different Peter, not the tidy headmaster in his white shirt and tie. It made me want to cut him open like a surgeon, look inside, extract the memories to see what else was hidden there. A longing for something lost flared in me.

In the train window my reflection was blurred, wistful. War had made a sad, long-faced woman of me, grey with worries, like a Pathé News version of myself. No wonder Peter hardly noticed me any more. Where was Rhoda, the jaunty young woman in the red lipstick, with such great plans to change the world?

Was it too late to go back to how we had been? I sighed. We'd got used to not hearing each other. And I didn't know how to make him see me, see another Rhoda.

The next morning I opened the paper to find it was full of the story of Ruth Ellis, who was to be executed in a few weeks for shooting her lover.

'Do you think they'll hang her?'

Peter looked up from his breakfast plate. 'Probably.'

I was taken aback. 'You can't seriously believe they'll go ahead. By all accounts her boyfriend beat her senseless.'

'It doesn't matter. She still took his life.' He lifted the paper from my hands, and scanned the headlines before thrusting it away in disgust. 'It makes me sick, all this sympathy for her. What about the victim? She fired six shots. Six. That means she had to pull back the trigger six times. But even if it was only once, she took a man's life. Don't you understand? They can't bring Blakely back, they can never bring him back.'

'But if they hang her, that will be just as bad! Surely in this day and age, they could just imprison her. She's not likely to do it again, and I can't bear the idea that in a civilised country like this, we're going to actually take a woman to the scaffold and kill her. It's barbaric.'

'So she gets away scot-free, does she? What about Blakely, and his family, for God's sake? Nobody spares a thought for them. But that's just typical of you.' He stood up, grabbed his jacket from the back of the chair. His face was beet-coloured with anger.

'What's the matter? What have I said?'

'You're as bad as all these people, getting hysterical over it, all sentimental, turning her into some kind of national heroine. She's a murderer, don't you understand? And as for barbaric, you don't know the meaning of the word.'

'Peter—'

'Don't "Peter" me. Don't try to get round me.' He swept up his briefcase from beside the stairs and a few moments later I heard the door bang.

On the sideboard lay the pile of exercise books he'd been marking the previous night. He'd forgotten them. I stood and gathered them up to run after him, but moments later he surged back in, snatched them out of my hands and stuffed them into his briefcase. For the second time I heard the door slam.

What was the matter with him? It must have touched a nerve somehow. Surely he couldn't really want to keep the death penalty? I picked up the paper. It gave all the details of how it would be done. The noose, the trapdoor. All the people who would be present to witness the obscenity of it. It made me nauseous. That poor woman would be waiting right now, knowing what was to happen to her. It was this that seemed the most cruel. People are usually spared the date of their death. Even if they are ill, they cannot know the exact moment. It comes suddenly, mysteriously. The way it did with Matthew.

I took the breakfast plates away and scrubbed them hard with the brush. I thought back to the day Peter put his fist through our door. The image of the shattered glass haunted me. There was something about that day, a darkening, even before I heard the glass break.

Perhaps Peter had seen a hanging in the war. Helen was beginning to help me understand about Archie and Peter, the things they went through. But he wouldn't talk to me about his feelings; in fact there was so little feeling between Peter and me now, it was hard to find it at all.

I dried the cups. My mother had given us this china as a wedding present, floral with a gilt trim. I dangled the cup from my hand. What did it feel like to smash something? When I let it drop, it broke in two on the hard tiled floor. The second one smashed into too many pieces to count.

We are both going mad, I thought, *and nobody knows.*

15

1940 Peter

THE SOLITARY BLOCK was a cellar storeroom in the German quarters of the mine. Big Jaw searched Peter at gunpoint and yelled at him to empty his pockets into a bag. Peter panicked, dropped his precious letters. He leapt to scrape them up from the snow and black grit on the ground. He didn't want to lose a single one. They were the ones Rhoda sent him before he embarked. Big Jaw squashed them unceremoniously into a bag. *Please, don't lose them*, he thought.

He was forced to take off his boots. With his hands above his head and a rifle butt between his shoulders he picked his way across the icy cinders in his shreds of socks. He could barely breathe. A nudge in the back propelled him down some steps to where a heavy iron door gaped open. Behind him, the door slammed. The clang reverberated like a shockwave up his back. No windows. A smell of coal and urine. He had the feeling his heart was shrinking inwards, solidifying like a lump of coal. Fear was with him all the time, the fear of a small child bullied by the bigger boys.

He felt his way around the walls. Powdery deposits — mould? A slatted sleeping bench with a thin blanket that smelt of damp. The floor sloped slightly towards the door, which didn't fit at the bottom and let in a draught of air; here his foot caught something and he heard the ring of metal. A bucket, he guessed, for the necessaries.

He buttoned his coat up tight, wrapped the blanket around his feet. To be alone was actually a relief. He'd have five days of it, if he could survive on half-rations and didn't go crazy. Even though the bench was hard and narrow, to just let his body rest was bliss. He dozed, his breath clouding hazy before him. When he woke, his bones ached with cold, and his knees would hardly bend. It was then he realised he'd have to exercise every day, or when he got out, the work would kill him.

Doggedly, he began some physical jerks. When they were done, he felt his way back to the bench and wiped his forehead with his sleeve. A distant church bell reminded him it could be Sunday. Back home the band would be playing in church without him, all in their peaked black hats with the patent brims and gold-chain chinstraps. Afterwards they always went to the village hall and he could almost taste the weak tea and biscuits, feel the smooth handle of the china cup, hear the clink of the teaspoon as he stirred. Rhoda's face, looking at him through the hatch. Her trim figure and glossy dark hair. He pictured her smiling to bossy Mrs Bickerdike as she turned the cups the right way up on the saucers.

By now Rhoda should know he was safe, a prisoner of war. They'd had to fill in forms and get them stamped. His mother would have told her. But he could be here years, he knew, whilst the war ground on.

Let there be no bombs in Carnforth. His chest constricted. *Please let Rhoda be safe.* And then a plea that went even deeper. *Let her remember me. Don't let her forget.* His eyes smarted. She said she'd wait, she promised. He groaned in frustration, punched out at the wall once, but it skinned his hand and he knew it to be a waste of effort, stupidity to hurt himself. It made him wonder about Archie; he hoped he would never be so desperate that he'd do what Archie had done. Poor Archie, he was only a boy really, didn't seem to be able to cope.

Five days was a long time to be alone with his thoughts. He picked over different scenarios in which he'd turned right instead of left. Men had died because of him. His thoughts ground on, in a never-ending loop, toiling over the same events until he groaned and had to clap his hands against his head to give himself some peace.

After twenty-four hours, Big Jaw threw in a hard crust of bread, and Peter crammed it in his mouth, though he could feel the grains of dirt from the floor on his tongue, and did not know how old the bread was, if it was even edible, but it eased the painful cramp of his stomach for an hour or so. Then he curled up again on his hard bench, head on his knees. He was like an animal, crouched there in the dark, an animal in a neglected zoo.

When they let him out of solitary, the world seared his eyes. The sky flared too bright, the grim conditions of their barracks exhibited themselves in intricate detail. In solitary he had had relative safety; now the scent of fear reached him in the wary looks of the men. He had expected life to be different when he emerged, like some sort of rebirth into the world, but no. Still the same shoddy wooden huts on their concrete bases, still the coils of barbed wire. Still dirty washing strung everywhere that would never be decently clean or dry because there was not enough water to wash it properly and besides, the water was impossible to heat. The energy drained from his limbs.

He looked about for Archie, but there was no sign of

him. It gave him an empty feeling, not to have him close by, as if something was missing.

He was put straight back to work. Thank God he had thought to keep fit.

'Hell, wasn't it. Work with me?' It was Harry.

Peter smiled, and nodded. It was good to see a face he knew. 'You seen Archie?'

Harry grimaced. 'Hospital. Not seen him since then. What a jerk. You okay?'

'*Schnell!*' The Unteroffizier motioned them to carry on working. They made a good team; Peter had renewed strength and Harry was much stronger than his short physique would suggest.

They worked on in silence, until the guards went off for their walkabout and smoke.

'Saw the Red Cross truck come in last night. Might not get a parcel each, but we'll get shares. Something to look forward to.'

'What about post?'

'No telling. Anyway, some men hate it. Say it's like picking a scab – the more you hear of home, the more you wish you were there. Best not to think about it. If it comes, it comes.'

When they got back to their billets that night Peter had only just sluiced himself at the tap when he heard someone behind him. Wary, he turned, still dripping. Archie stood there, his arm in a sling, his left hand a big paw of crêpe bandage poking out.

'I'm back,' Archie said.

'They fixed you up then.'

Yes.' Archie looked at the ground, shoulders hunched, as if he could shrink away beneath his clothes. Peter felt his presence as a sudden oppression, but he brushed it aside.

Archie watched him dry his face.

'Damn fool thing to do,' Peter said.

'I couldn't have stood it, not another day.'

Peter shoved his drying rag into his pocket. 'Still, it was stupid. What will you do now? They can't make you work, can they?'

'Stone loading. For the track bed. Carrying buckets of stones with my good hand, until the other one's fixed.'

'Will it be okay?'

He shrugged. 'Two fingers are smashed. I'll manage. They took one off, but the other's splinted.'

'Sounds painful.'

'It'll be all right if it doesn't get infected … it's not so bad, not when …' His mouth worked as though to say more, but nothing came out.

'Did you see Brodie in there?'

'He's gone.' Archie looked down at the ground again and trod a stone into the mud. 'They took him away. Dead, I think.'

'I thought they'd be able to do something.' Peter rubbed at his neck with the cloth to dry it.

'They didn't try. They take them away, the ones they think won't be good to work again. In a truck. It takes about ten minutes. I watched the truck turn off into the pines, then it came back empty with the two guards. There's no town there, nowhere for them to go. You hear shots, then you never see them again. A man came in from the mine, screaming blue murder; a rock had fallen on his chest. Same thing. Bundled on to a truck and taken away. They look us over and then decide if we're worth keeping. If we'll be able to work.'

Peter didn't know if he was hearing the truth or not. 'What about the rules? The Geneva Convention?'

Archie shook his head. He looked up at Peter with his big blue eyes. 'I wasn't to know, was I? It was an accident. When I dropped that rail on him, I wasn't to know.'

'You can't be certain what happened to Brodie. Maybe you're just imagining the worst.'

'I'm not imagining it. Oh, I know what you and the other fellows say, you think I've a screw loose or something. But I haven't, I tell you, they shoot us. The ones that can't make it.'

'All the more reason to make it then. You've got to brace up. Not play silly tricks like getting yourself injured. I can't look out for you all the time. We're here until the war's over whether we like it or not, and I just haven't got the energy to cope with more trouble than we've already got.'

Archie's face turned red. 'I thought you'd be glad to see me. I thought we were pals.'

Peter sighed, frustrated. He picked up his mug from the ground and stuffed his washcloth in it. He said, 'I am. But you should try and get on with the others more. It's no use making enemies, getting people's backs up.'

'It wasn't my fault about Brodie. It just slipped.'

Peter felt the conversation sliding round again on to the same track. He shook his head, turned and walked away back to the hut leaving Archie waiting there. He felt terrible, but just being near Archie made him feel tired. Perhaps Harry was right after all, and he was better off without him.

That night there were five food parcels for their hut, and Harry and some of the others lit the coal stove in celebration so they could boil up some Klim condensed milk and have milky tea. Just the heat of the stove made life more civilised. They'd had to sneak coal back in their pockets. You wouldn't think there'd be a shortage of coal since the prisoners spent the entire day digging it out, but they never got enough to make a good fire from what the Germans gave them. So everyone's greatcoat pockets were grimed and gritty from bringing back coal. Tonight the stove groaned and made mournful whooping noises as if it was struggling back to life.

Peter saw Archie stand hopefully at the back of the crowd huddled round the fire. Nobody called to him to join them, they just ignored him. After a few moments his face closed up and he walked away. A twist of compassion tightened Peter's chest, but the warmth of the fire was so enticing he could not bear to leave the cosy circle.

Morale was high that evening and the men sat around exchanging anecdotes, smoking their precious cigarettes and eating squares of Nestlé's chocolate. The sudden sugar in their diet made them light-headed and voluble. Games of poker and dice for stakes in the parcel sparked sudden roars and cheers.

But nobody looked for Archie or asked after him. Stupid bugger. Peter knew he was in the hut somewhere and his thoughts kept straying towards him. Eventually he wandered over to find him huddled on the top bunk facing the wall, nursing his bad hand. Peter spoke to his back. 'Hey, Archie, come and join us. It's warmer by the fire.'

'I'm all right here.'

'Come on, Harry's cooking up Spam fritters.'

Archie turned over then and shouted, 'I don't want his bloody fritters. Damn you all to hell.'

Peter retreated. When he got back to the fire one of the men said, 'He's crazy. Leave him alone. More for us anyway.'

But Peter felt as though there was a hard lump behind his breastbone. Some emotion wanting to move, but it was trapped, locked in behind barbed wire like himself.

That night he could hear the scratch of Archie's buttons as he shifted restlessly above him in his bunk. In the morning Archie was up and away first, and the following few weeks this pattern continued with Archie avoiding Peter and keeping sullenly on his own. If he saw Peter in the queue he'd bow his head and move away. He was always on his own though, never with a friend.

It still bothered Peter. He told himself it didn't matter, that things were different in war; that friendships were likely to be of short duration, and he'd soon forget. He told himself he didn't care. If Archie wanted to be so bloody awkward, then sod him.

One night over the snores of the men, Peter heard the sound of Archie groaning from the bunk above. It went on intermittently, calling for his attention. Eventually, frustrated, he got out of bed and hissed, 'What's the matter? I'm trying to sleep.'

'Nothing.'

'Is it your hand?'

'No.'

'Then go back to sleep.'

'I can't. I thought I'd just get a few days' rest in hospital. Now look at me. I'm a mess. I'll never be able to explain to my father.'

Peter sighed. 'Now's not the time. We can talk in the morning. Just get some sleep, can't you.'

'It hurts too much.'

Peter resigned himself to dealing with it. 'Have you heard from them, your parents?'

'Yes. From Mother. It came today. Oh God, Pete, she'd be ashamed. I had a letter from her at Lamsdorf, but Father wouldn't write. He thinks I'm a waste of space. That's why he sent me away to school. He always wanted me to be braver than I was, you know, to dive off cliffs, that sort of stuff.'

'Shh!' A disembodied voice from further down the hut.

'Keep your voice down,' Peter said.

'I couldn't be like him. That's why he sent me to boarding school. At first I thought it would be good to get away from him, but of course it was a school he'd chosen. The Blue Coat School. It was brutal. They picked on me because I was bad at sport. When I got out last holidays, I thought, even the army can't be worse than this, so when war came I faked my age and joined up.'

'How old are you?'

'Seventeen last week.'

Peter rubbed his hand through his hair. A kid. He was just a kid.

Archie paused, picked at a hole in the blanket with his good hand. 'He's spitting mad I went behind his back. He'd have wanted me to go for a commission after he spent a fortune on that school, but I signed up as a private without telling him. Even when I was signing the papers I knew I'd be a crap soldier. And can you imagine me as an officer? Ha. I thought I'd get myself killed and then he'd be sorry.'

'I hate to break it to you, pal, but you're still here.'

He didn't laugh. 'When I was leaving I stood in the hall with my kitbag and Mother wept; she was terrified I wouldn't come home. But Father? He was so angry he didn't even bother to shake my hand. Mother begged him to report me as underage, but he wouldn't. He just stood there and said he supposed at least the army might make a man of me.'

'Did he serve in the last war, your father?'

'Did he! He treats every day like a war. With me, with my mother. He was a captain, but he got invalided out doing something incredibly heroic. And here I am, stuck in a

Jerry labour camp with an injury I did to myself. He'd die of shame. I can just see my mother trying to explain this one away to him. I'll never be able to go home.' His face twisted and contorted. 'I miss her. I missed her at school too. I just want to go home.' He turned his face to the wall, his shoulders heaved again, but he suppressed his emotion. 'And I don't think I can do another day shifting sleepers,' he whispered.

Peter reached out an arm and patted him on the shoulder. Archie turned over, looked at him. 'My legs keep buckling. The men all laugh at me. Sometimes I just want to run and hear the noise of fire and for it all to be over.'

'Shut the heck up! Can't a man get some sleep?' Harry Tyson's voice. 'If you don't zip it, I'll come and put my fist in your mouth.'

Peter whispered, 'Don't ever talk like that, do you hear me? You're going to get through this. Whatever went on before, your mother will be worried to death. She'll just want you home safe. It'll all seem different in the morning, now get some sleep.'

Archie was up first as usual but the next night when Peter came back, Archie's pack and belongings had vanished. He asked everyone if they'd seen him, but nobody had.

He did not like the sight of that vacant bunk. Maybe Archie had done something stupid. Peter was uneasy. Perhaps he should have talked to him more last night, been more help. He folded Archie's blanket, put it neatly on the end of the bed.

What Archie had told him about men being taken away and shot preyed on his mind. What if Archie was lying in some ditch somewhere? All day he looked out for him, scanning the tired hungry faces, looking for Archie's blonde hair and red ears, but he was nowhere to be seen.

By curfew he was angry. If Archie was on a work party, why the hell hadn't he told him he was moving on? Hadn't he looked out for him all this time?

But at night the darker thoughts came. Peter could not sleep listening for some sign, some inner feeling, that Archie might be alive. But he heard no comforting noise from the bunk above, nothing but the wind and the hailstones rattling off the roof.

16

1941 Peter

WHEN HIS SECTION of the railway was finished, Peter, Harry and Neb spent six more months side by side loading coal into hoppers on the railway – filthy, heavy work. They never queried where the hoppers went until they had to spend another six months unloading them at the other end of the track through the heat of the summer and into the autumn. Peter's muscles bulged at the expense of the rest of his emaciated frame.

He worked as slowly as he dared, reluctant to fuel the German war machine, but left with no choice. Now the rail to the mine was finished and joined up to the other track, the one that led out to where trucks could take the coal by road. He and Harry began to talk about how they would be redeployed; Peter dreaded being sent down the mine where the air was foul and conditions much worse.

Peter missed Archie. Harry never told Peter much about himself; if he asked him about home, he got an evasive answer or he changed the subject, so that the real Harry remained an enigma. Harry liked to fraternise with the Germans, and one day Peter asked him, 'Can't you try to find out what happened to Archie Foster?'

'Not still pining after him, are you? Dead probably. He had it written all over him.'

'Just curious, I suppose.'

'Don't even ask. It'll only stir up trouble. Anyway, he was a waste of space if you ask me.'

But Peter still wondered.

Mail was getting through at last from Rhoda and his mother and it had lifted his spirits, just to know that the familiar little world of Carnforth still existed; the market and the library, the Roxy and the railway station. Rhoda's writing was like Rhoda, tall and elegant. Just the sight of her handwriting was enough to give him fresh determination to keep going.

That was until an announcement by the camp Kommandant informed them that they must pack their kit and wait by the main gate the next morning. There was no warning, no reason given. The news was met with unease.

'Do you know anything?' Peter asked.

'Not a thing,' Harry said.

Harry was standing from habit with his back to the unlit stove. He looked nervous for a change, smoking a hand-rolled tab end down until the end burned his lips. He couldn't keep still. For the first time Peter saw that despite his air of non-chalance, Harry too was scared.

'There's a padre coming this evening to lead us all in prayer,' Neb said.

'Bad sign, that,' Harry said.

'Thanks a bunch.' Peter said. 'Do you fancy going along?'

'What, to some toff spouting a load of claptrap?' Harry threw his tab end into the stove. 'God's not shown his presence much in this lot, has he? A man who's just come in says the SS have been building extermination camps. For the

Jews.' He laughed. 'God's chosen people. If that's true, he's mighty slow with the thunderbolt.'

'I heard that too. But it's probably only a rumour, to lower our morale. I can't think they could get away with that. Someone would blow the whistle,' Peter said.

Neb said, 'Oh thanks, Harry. Extermination camps. You've cheered us up no end. Very tactful. Specially as we've no idea where they're bleeding taking us.'

'Well, I'm going to hear the padre,' Peter said, 'see what he says. It'll be something to do, take my mind off tomorrow.'

'Missing school assembly, are you?' Harry smirked.

Peter was about to riposte, but Nebs said, 'Go on then, I suppose it can't hurt to have God on our side.'

The prayers must have worked because they had gone from railway builders to agricultural labourers in less than a week. Peter's heart sank when he saw the vast ploughed field that awaited them.

They were to plant up cabbages to feed the 'Fatherland'. It was demoralising, working to feed the German army. Still, at least they were safe, not considered dispensable just yet. And it looked like easier work than lugging sleepers.

This thought was short-lived. They worked in pairs, one digging and one planting. Whichever job you did was hard. The digger had to lift the sodden earth and blister his hands on spades that looked as though they'd come from the Iron Age, and the planter had to bend double most of the time. The rain made the top of the ground claggy so that their boots collected clods of earth as they went. In the furrows water slopped into the holes in their boots as they squelched through it.

'Ever thought of trying to escape?' Neb whispered.

'I've decided not to try,' Peter said. His father came to

mind. He could almost imagine his voice giving out advice about journey times and mileages. He added, 'Not enough intelligence about where we are, or what's happening. Can't do anything without intelligence.'

'I might give it a go,' Neb said. 'I had you down as a possible. Harry too. Orders are, to try if we can.'

'Not sure those who gave the orders knew we'd be stuck in the middle of nowhere with not even a map.'

'Suit yourself,' Neb said, but did not press him.

As the rain dripped down his neck, Peter worried over it. It was disturbing, confessing he wasn't going to make any attempt to escape. As if he'd given up. Was he making excuses to himself? Did it mean he was a coward, if he wanted to survive the war? He turned his attention back to the work. A small patch of England moving on the vast German continent.

Peter's hands were numb and white, his fingernails black, from pushing seedlings into the earth, following Neb's clumsily dug furrow. He worked mindlessly, like a zombie, too depressed to care.

Another group were working their way towards them from the other side of the field when Peter's attention was caught by one of the men planting. It looked like Archie. He watched the man covertly, trying to squint through the drizzle and make him out. But the man was never close enough for him to get a proper look.

The next day he saw him again. He planted faster so he could move down the row to get nearer. He cursed Neb who was slow with the spade, his breath coming in grunts as he heaved the clay to the side.

It was Archie, he was sure of it.

The man hadn't seen him; he was bent over, the bucket of seedlings slung over his right arm, planting with his left.

The man stood up for a breather, put his left hand to his back and stretched. It was him. Peter's face burst into a grin.

'Archie!' His voice came out as a croak.

Archie looked round puzzled, but did not see him. After a moment he bent his head back down to planting.

The rest of the day Peter watched him from the corner of his eye. A weight had melted from his shoulders. He noticed the calls of the birds, the ring of the spades against stones, the distant whine of an aircraft engine. It felt good to see Archie there, companionable, even though they were moving further away from each other again, to opposite sides of the field.

At the end of the day his back and legs had stiffened and he had to limp to roll call. This time, instead of only listening for his own name and number, he listened out for Archie's. He couldn't see him as there were two hundred or so men in the yard, but he heard him reply. Archie's voice was firmer, more robust.

Archie was staying in another accommodation block in an old barn adjoining the farmhouse. Of course the German officers had use of the rooms in the actual farmhouse itself. Tall posts and wire fences topped with the obligatory rolls of barbed wire dwarfed a series of agricultural buildings in the middle of open ground. Rusting corrugated-iron roofs, sentry boxes on stilts. To the left, about a hundred yards away, stood a sparsely wooded area of what looked like silver birch and ash, though most of the branches were bare, stripped to bone by the wind.

When he got to the other block it was open and several of the men were up on their bunks. 'I'm looking for Archie Foster. You know, with the bad hand?'

A man who was reading a battered book looked up from his bunk. 'Over there. Last bay but one.'

Peter thanked him, but before he got there Archie was already leaning on his bunk, waiting for him. 'I thought it was you.' His expression was wary.

Peter rushed in, ignoring Archie's aloofness. 'I saw you in the field. That was me shouting. God, was I glad to see you! I'd thought the worst when you just disappeared. How are you, man?' Peter couldn't resist clapping him on the back.

Archie thawed a little. 'Better. The hand's still not right, but it's getting there.' He held it out. One finger was still tightly wrapped in a filthy bandage, and there was a livid purplish stump where the other had been.

'We finished that track. Nearly finished us, too.'

'They caught me by the front gate.' Peter saw him let go of his grudge and crack a smile.

'I knew it was you, soon as I saw you.'

'I should've learned by now, never to stand near the front gate. I was scared as hell when they told me to fetch my gear and get in the truck. I didn't know where they were taking us. I thought I was going where Brodie went.' He paused to brush his flyaway hair out of his eyes. He looked shyly at Peter and away.

'You look well.'

'It's all right here, out in the fresh air. No cramped spaces, nothing dangerous. Just hard work and harder weather. Still lousy rations though. But the guards are older, less likely to take a potshot. They've sent the younger ones off to bigger camps or the front.' He paused. 'I thought I'd never see you again.'

'When you'd gone, I sort of missed having you about.'

Archie pressed his lips together in a pleased kind of way. 'I can't get over it, you turning up here. Mind you, we need someone like you to organise us all.'

Peter snorted, but he was flattered all the same.

They stood a moment, smiling at each other, before Peter said, 'You'll never guess what. Neb and Harry are here too.'

Archie did not look thrilled.

'Harry's on the bunk below me. You'd best say hello.'

'I don't think—'

'Come on, they'll be mightily surprised.'

Neb leaned over a rickety table hammering metal into the blades of a small fan. He was constructing a 'blower' – a small stove made out of Klim tins.

'Look who's here,' Peter said.

'Hello, Neb.' Archie hung back.

Neb looked up through narrowed eyes but dropped his head again towards his contraption. 'Hey, Pete, I need another can to hold the fuel. You don't know where I can get one, do you?'

Archie coloured and shifted from foot to foot. 'Maybe you'll have to wait for the next Red Cross parcel.'

'I need it tonight or it'll hold me up,' Neb said.

'How does it work?' Peter willed Neb to make a more friendly response on Archie's behalf. 'I've seen chaps using them, of course.'

'Same principle as a forge,' Neb said.

Peter squatted down for a better look.

'See, the fan forces air down the tube and over the fuel. Incredibly efficient. You can boil a mug of tea with just a few scraps of cardboard. And the best thing is – it weighs nearly nothing.'

'I can try our barracks,' Archie said.

'Good idea,' Peter said.

'If you like.' Neb went back to flattening the metal. Peter

saw Archie pause a moment, obviously wondering whether to go or not. Peter gave him a nod and he hurried off.

When Archie had gone Peter said, 'You don't like him, do you?'

'I never said that.'

'I couldn't believe it when I saw him coming towards me across that ploughed field. I thought he was dead.'

'So did I. He's trouble. It feels risky being around him. You never quite know what he'll do. He stuck his hand in between the buffers of a train, for God's sake. And he got us all into solitary.'

'That wasn't his fault. It was—' Peter looked over his shoulder. Harry was bearing down on them. 'Anyway, we're all under strain. It comes out in different ways.'

'Oh, please. Don't start with that Freudian stuff.'

'What's up?' Harry said.

'We're talking about Foster. Why he injured himself.'

'He's here,' Neb said. 'I had him down as a goner.'

'Sheesh. Well, I'll be. Too lazy to work in the mine, that's all. When I said they'd likely put us down there, I saw his eyes go – a crazy sort of look. Next minute he was lying on the ground with his hand in a pulp.'

'Oh Lord. He's claustrophobic. I thought you knew. He'd never survive being underground.'

Harry said, 'Soft, you mean.'

'He's just a kid. He's only seventeen. Anyway, he seems to be all right now, more cheerful.'

'We're still better off without him. Here, hold this.' Neb beckoned Harry to press down with his finger whilst he crimped the edge of the metal to hold it together. His long slim fingers seemed to know exactly what they were doing.

'Neat,' Peter said.

'A Canadian chap showed me. At Lamsdorf.'

'Is this for what I think?'

Neb looked up. His dark eyebrows furrowed in warning. 'Don't say a word.' He glared at Peter. 'And especially not to your cuckoo friend.'

Peter had no time to react because Archie appeared breathlessly, waving an empty Klim tin. 'Look! I got it for four cigarettes. I don't smoke, so I had spare.'

'Great, Archie. Isn't it, Neb?'

'Yep,' Neb said, holding out his hand for it.

'Will they let us take it out to the fields, do you think?' Archie said. 'A hot brew out there would really be something.'

'Yes,' Harry said, 'and they'll let us just sit down on a blanket too, for a picnic.' He raised an eyebrow at Neb who suppressed a smile.

Peter frowned and turned away from them. 'It was great you bartered for that other tin,' he said to Archie. 'Can you play draughts? One of the lads has made a board.'

'A bit. Mother taught me.'

'Come on then, we'll sit a while and have a game.'

He took Archie out of Harry's earshot. 'Don't mind them. They're just a bit tense.'

Archie's face showed he was not convinced.

They sat down on Peter's bunk, and put out the pieces, cut from old leather and cardboard. Peter rubbed his eyes, they were blurred. His head ached. He was suddenly tired; tired of himself, weary with how he always tried to smooth over troubled waters. It was no use trying to get Harry and Neb to be nice to Archie.

Archie was a child, ill-equipped to make decisions for himself, and Harry was the opposite – too knowing. Neb was surly, quick to take offence. He didn't share a single interest with any of them. In his previous life they might never have been his friends. But here – well, they were who he had got to know. And he needed friends, he realised. It was difficult to live together and be civil in these conditions. Here he was, hungry and cold and afraid, and still he was trying to play draughts. How bloody stupid.

But perhaps this was what civilisation was. To move pieces round on a board instead of shooting each other.

17

1941 Rhoda

I took Melvin from Patty and dandled him on my knee whilst she went off to the Ladies. He was a fine toddler, in his blue romper suit, with chubby cheeks and a cow-lick of blonde hair just like in the knitting adverts. Melvin chuckled at me as I gave him a bobbin to play with.

It was my morning off and we'd spent it in the WVS room at the station, making balaclavas and gloves, between doing tea for the troop trains. When Patty came back I asked her, 'Don't you mind knitting for the troops when you're conscientious objectors? It seems funny to me, that.'

'I don't mind a bit. I think of it as keeping people warm. Thank goodness we can't knit guns! Then I really would be in a dilemma.'

'Is Frank all right?'

She gestured for me to hand Melvin back, and I gave him a little squeeze and plopped a kiss on his forehead before I passed him over.

'Not really. It's a lot harder for him than it is for me. It's not the farm work, but other people's attitudes. Last week they made him eat his dinner out in the cowsheds instead of in the farm kitchen with the rest of the workers. Even though it's harvest time.' She paused to put Melvin down where she had tumbled out a set of wooden bricks.

'That's terrible.'

'Even the Italian prisoners of war are allowed to eat inside with the family. Frank feels it, when they treat him like that. He tries not to show it but I know it gets to him. And one day last week whilst he was eating, the door to the cowshed opened and someone threw a white chicken in with him. He said he just looked at it, pecking and scratching happily round the floor, and wished he was the chicken. It's hard when all his friends cut him dead.' She sighed, shook her head. 'Have you heard anything more from Peter?'

'His mother and I both had a letter from him last week. He doesn't say much about the camp, just not to worry. It's always such a relief just to know he's all right. He's been asking for us to send warm things before winter, but the letters take so long, I think it'll be spring by the time he gets them. Anyway, I thought I'd make a set to go with this balaclava — you know, gloves and a scarf.'

Patty laughed. 'I can't see Peter dressed in that lot. He always used to look so smart in his tweed jacket and tie, and his nice trilby. Balaclavas make me think of grubby little boys.'

'Like Melvin, you mean? Aw, I didn't mean it.' I reached out to ruffle Melvin's hair and was rewarded with a gummy grin. Melvin was the most delightful little boy, I could almost eat him.

'No, it's a good idea. As long as he's prepared to wait until next Christmas.'

I made to slap her, but she ducked away, giggling. 'Only joking.' She picked up her needles. 'I bet you miss him.'

'Every day,' I said.

She reached over, patted my arm. But as I knitted I

wondered if I did miss Peter in the same way. Nearly eighteen months had gone by since he'd left. It seemed longer. My life was so busy I barely had time to think – what with my job on the bookstall and all this voluntary work. When I did think, I was restless. Life was passing me by. I envied Patty, cooing over Melvyn and telling me all her plans for a nice new home when the war was over, whilst my life was on hold, like a telephone line waiting to be plugged in and connected.

Sun mottled the table in front of me. I looked out of the window. It was a warm October, yet I had barely set foot outside into the fresh air for weeks. I longed to get out of Carnforth, up to the Lake District, to see the leaves blowing golden off the trees, to breathe in the scent of the wind from the fells.

I wound the khaki wool round my needles, knit one, purl one. Uncertainty about the future knotted my stomach. The war might drag on, and as long as it did, Peter would be stuck in Poland. Germany had taken Yugoslavia and Greece and was now invading large swathes of the Soviet Union. The papers told us Smolensk had just fallen. Carnforth under German control was just unimaginable. Nobody ever said we would lose the war, but we all felt the fear of it, as each of the other nations capitulated and fell, as more troops were lost at sea and on the ground. And what would happen to Peter if we lost?

18

1941 Peter

PETER CHOPPED ONE of the turnips in two with the blade of his spade. It gave him a strange satisfaction so he lifted the spade and brought it down again and again until the turnip was mashed into a gritty pulp and sweat poured off his brow.

Archie appeared at his side. 'Stop it. They'll see you.'

'I can't help it. It just gets to me. The whole bloody thing. The boredom, the stupidity of it all. We're traitors, did you know that? If we were at home we'd be hanged for this – helping the enemy.' He prodded at the pulpy mess with his boot. 'For Christ's sake. Some German is probably shooting down our men, with his fat belly full of food that I've provided. Doesn't it get to you?'

'Course it does. But I'm just glad we're here, not in the mine, or some other worse camp. My mother was always telling me I needed fresh air and exercise.'

'Don't joke. I don't think I can take it today. I just woke up and wondered, what's it all for?'

'We just need something else to think about, we've had no news for ages. Quick, bury that mess, the guards are looking.'

Archie was right. No letters or parcels had arrived, no new prisoners with outside news. They probably did lack mental stimulation, a sense of direction and achievement. But after a long day digging or grafting in the fields there was no point in trying to organise sport or games, the men were too exhausted. But then he had an idea. Maybe they were too tired for football, but people could read, couldn't they?

The next day Peter put up a makeshift plank shelf, and persuaded some of the others to donate reading material. Even though the guards confiscated anything with news, it was a start, he told himself. Mentally, he called this 'the library', though it was hardly literary – two well-thumbed magazines, *Blighty* and *Razzle,* alongside a *Prisoner of War* magazine and a tattered Bible donated by one of the more religious *kriegies* as they called themselves, short for *kriegsgefangener,* the German word for war prisoners.

Peter was delighted when more books found their way to his 'library' and encouraged by the success of this idea, he stuck a notice up and asked for anyone interested to come along to discuss the idea of having some lectures.

'Keep still,' Archie said. He was giving Peter a haircut with a blunt pair of scissors he'd traded with a guard for fags, and Peter was trying to write himself a list for the talks on his lap.

'Watch you don't lose your ear,' Harry said, as he passed.

'Hey, Harry.' Archie paused in his snipping. 'Are you coming to our meeting tonight? Peter's organising it.'

'Dunno. What's it for?' Harry said.

'It's so we can share ideas.' Peter looked up from where he was writing on the back of a chocolate wrapper.

'Oy,' said Archie. 'Stop moving your head.'

'We can teach each other,' Peter said. 'If one person knows a bit about something – German, say, they can give a talk to the rest of us.'

'I'm not learning bloody German,' Harry said.

'It's so we can better ourselves, not waste our time when we're here,' Archie said.

Harry's eyebrows lowered. 'And I suppose it's people like me you think need bettering?'

Peter leapt to Archie's defence. 'No, I'm sure Archie didn't mean—'

'Yes, you did. The bloody rich throwing crumbs to the poor.'

'It's not like that,' Peter said, standing up and pointing to the paper. 'It's the idea of sharing, everyone's equal in this.'

'Except some are more equal than others. You and your teacher's pet. Always putting yourselves above everyone.'

'Come on, Harry, don't be like that,' Peter said. He waved the list encouragingly. 'You could offer a subject yourself.'

'Offer a subject? God, you can't even see it, can you?'

'What's the matter?' Archie said. 'Don't be so uppity. We're all English, aren't we?'

'That's just it.' Harry shoved his face close up to Archie. 'Which England do you live in?'

Archie took a step back.

'I bet it's church fetes, newspapers through the door in the morning, jam on the bloody table. Posh bloody haircuts.' Harry's words tumbled over each other. 'Well, it's not my England. My England is watching my mam take in other people's dirty washing for two shilling a week when she can't even afford to keep her own kids clean.' He turned to look at Peter with contempt. 'There's no green lawns in my England.'

Peter held out his hands in a gesture designed to restore calm. 'I know. That's just it. If she'd had an education—'

Harry lowered his voice. 'Oh yes, that's your answer to it all. You want to educate us.' His chest rose and fell, his eyes glittered. 'Well, what if we could teach you a thing or two? How my mother made that two shilling feed a family of six, for instance. Once you're poor you stay poor. My father was poor and his father before him. Why? Because you lot keep treading us down, that's why.'

When he'd gone Peter and Archie sat in uncomfortable silence for a while. Peter brushed the stray hairs from the table with his fingers.

'That was some blow-out,' Archie said, wrapping up his scissors.

'It gets to us all. Being stuck here. He'll calm down. He's talking rubbish. My grandfather was an iron-worker. Besides, we can't just let our minds go to waste,' Peter said, 'or when we come out we'll be fit for nothing. If I don't make the effort to do something I'll have lost years and years, with nothing to show for it.'

Archie said, 'He's just got a chip on his shoulder. Plenty of others will want to come to the talks, you'll see.'

In fact only two other people turned up, George Henderson, an older chap who used to be a canal worker, and Neb, both of whom were there more out of loyalty than any desire to study. But Peter wouldn't give in, and the following week Neb gave a talk on ornithology, complete with impersonations of bird calls. A few *kriegies* gathered and cheered him when he'd done. The next week, word had spread and the barracks was crowded when George stood up to talk about boat mechanics. Everyone crammed into one bunk bay to listen, and George did his best with pencil diagrams passed round from one hand to the next.

Peter grinned when the applause came. His idea had taken off. George's face had turned pink with pleasure. The only thing that spoilt it was that Harry never came to listen. He just hung round in the barracks deliberately making distracting noises with his card-playing cronies. Peter resisted the urge to tell him to keep quiet, knowing it would just sir up more animosity.

A week later he asked Archie if he'd give a talk. Archie made a face.

'It doesn't have to be long. You could teach a bit of German, that'd be useful.'

'I'm not much of a public speaker.' Archie paused. 'Anyway, it's only school German, and I don't exactly want to advertise the fact that I can speak their language.'

'Oh. I suppose so. There must be something. What did you do at home in your spare time?'

'The usual. Cycling. Collecting things. Stamps and stuff – I had quite a good stamp album, and when I was a kid I used to collect birds' eggs, feathers, fossils. That kind of thing. Isn't it nearly time for roll call?'

'Sounds interesting.'

Peter knew Archie was resisting and his bland useless face made him cross. Why was it always him, Peter, who had to do everything? More insistent than he meant to be, he said, 'Oh, go on. Be a pal. I need another person before me. I'll put you down for a talk on stamp collecting – philately, we'll give it its proper name, shall we?' Peter scribbled Archie's name on the list. 'You'll need to make a few notes. It'll only need to be about half an hour, and lots of that will be questions and answers.'

'All right. As long as it can be short.' Archie went back to darning his socks.

On the day of Archie's talk, as an even bigger group of men gathered expectantly, Archie's neck grew steadily more mottled and red. He clung on to the bunk, under the one bare electric bulb, embarrassed to be the centre of attention. In his hand was a dog-eared piece of paper covered in tiny notes.

Peter introduced him; Archie cleared his throat. Cleared his throat again. When he finally began, it was in an apologetic whisper.

'Can you speak up a bit?' someone shouted from the back.

Archie raised his voice, started his speech over.

Peter put his hand to his forehead and squinted under it. Oh Lord. He should have realised how hard it would be to give a talk on stamp collecting with no stamps or pictures. Archie had obviously prepared, but it was as though he was reading from a particularly dull manual.

Archie kept the notes up near his eyes, so his mouth was hidden from the audience and it made it all the more difficult to make out his words. Peter's heart sank. He willed Archie to make it more interesting, to tell a few jokes, a funny story, anything to liven it up, but Archie continued to doggedly read from his notes, his red face looking deliberately down from the men in front of him.

People began to shuffle and fidget. After about five minutes, a few at the back sneaked off. The door shut behind them with a bang.

Archie obviously heard the door and gabbled on in a monotone, as if he was desperate to finish. 'Edward VIII stamps are sought after because he was only on the throne—'

From the back of the room he heard a voice shout, 'Get off!' and a burst of laughter. Peter shot to his feet to see who it was. It sounded like Harry's voice, but he couldn't be sure.

Archie stopped, swallowed, looked around at the men as if really seeing them for the first time. His cheeks flared red as a plum. He shoved his notes in his pocket, clenched his hands together. Peter stepped in to get the thing moving again. 'So, have we any questions?'

'Yes, when will it be over?' A hissed whisper from the back of the room. Harry, Peter was certain. A ripple of amusement went round the remaining audience.

'Quiet at the back, can't you,' George Henderson called.

'Yes, we're trying to listen,' Peter said, glad that George had spoken up. 'Have you ever seen a Penny Black? I've heard that they change hands for a fortune. Have you ever found anything valuable like that?'

Archie looked venomously at Peter. 'No, I haven't. They're incredibly rare.'

'It was early, that one,' George said. 'Queen Victoria's time.'

'What's it worth?' shouted someone.

'I don't know. A fortune, I should think,' Archie said, bristling.

George said, 'Well then, the most valuable stamp you've got?'

Archie answered looking at his boots, his arms folded tightly across his chest. 'I haven't got any valuable ones,' he said. 'I just like the history, the look of them, seeing the different designs from other countries.' He closed his lips tight and looked down at the floor, his hands in his pockets. It was clear he wasn't going to speak again.

Peter and George exchanged glances.

'Put your hands together for Archie Foster then, lads.' Peter clapped rather too loudly, and the rest of the audience gave a perfunctory smatter of applause. Behind the main group a sudden volley of cheering and overenthusiastic clapping. Peter stood just in time to see Harry going out of the door laughing. Nobody came to congratulate Archie, or ask him questions afterwards as they usually did, not even George Henderson. They were soon standing in an empty barracks.

'That went well, didn't it,' Archie said.

'It was fine, honestly, really interesting.'

'No, it wasn't. Don't treat me like a school kid. You've made me look a fool in front of all the other men. It was a stupid idea. Harry was right. Stamp collecting. Jeez. They'll all be laughing at me now.'

'Well, you could have made it a bit more lively. It wasn't exactly scintillating material—'

'It was your bloody idea! I told you I didn't want to, but you – Mr High and Mighty – knew best. You make me sick. You set me up! You knew I'd be rubbish.'

'I can't help it if you can't string two words together, can I?'

A moment when Archie clamped his lips together. 'Piss off.' When the words came they were like a bullet. Archie pushed past, the door slammed and Peter saw him through the window, head down, shoulders hunched, shambling away.

Peter snatched up the lecture list and tore it in two. There was only one more name on it anyway, his own. He felt like grabbing Harry Tyson by the lapels and punching him in the teeth. It was all Harry's fault. If it hadn't been for him heckling they could have salvaged it somehow. The talks had been going so well, just building up nicely. Now the whole idea was ruined.

He felt bad about Archie. He couldn't stand to be in the empty barracks so he went to stare out past the wire fence, to where the bare branches of the trees were silhouetted in a purplish haze. All he'd tried to do was to make things more bearable, take their minds away from hunger and danger and the fact that they'd failed. But what was the point? Nobody ever thanked him.

He wished he'd never had the idea. A weariness came over him again; he watched the clouds scull by, indifferent to what was below them. Later they'd pass over green fields maybe, or little villages. Places where people slept peacefully at night and life was normal.

He shouldn't have press-ganged Archie when he wasn't keen. Now he'd humiliated him. It reminded him of school, when he asked the weaker pupils to get up and read out their essays in class, because it always made him squirm to listen when he had to make them do it. He'd never been able to decide whether it was cruel, or a necessary part of their learning, to push them to do better.

School. He'd recreated a school.

He supposed he was trying to impose some sort of control over his life by sticking to what he knew. When he left school he went straight to university and from there to teacher-training college and from there back to St Cuthbert's. It was the only world he understood.

But this wasn't a boarding school and these weren't his pupils. He squeezed his fists in his pockets. Did Archie do what he told him to do because of his teacher's manner? Or did he behave like a teacher because Archie was just a kid? Which came first, the chicken or the egg? How did he come across to the other men – did he seem pompous, or bossy? Probably. And he was only a driver, after all, he'd seen no action, done nothing whatsoever for his country. The others, like Harry, they were the soldiers, the real men. His face burned.

A rage boiled up inside him, but it had nowhere to go but to turn into a sour and bitter lump in his solar plexus. Sod them all. If they wanted to waste their time doing nothing, who was he to stop them? And as for Archie, from now on he could bloody well take care of himself.

19

1955 Rhoda

LEWIS'S CAFÉ WAS busy, but I saw Helen sitting at a table for two, and waved.

I took off my linen bolero and squeezed into the seat opposite, plonking my string bag on to the table. I pointed to it and said, 'Would you believe, I've read them all.'

'Any use?'

'It's fascinating. Do you think Barker's tales are true? About the camp, I mean. There's so much I didn't know. Lamsdorf, the conditions, the sheer numbers of men held there.'

'Yes. We went back there, two years ago I think it was. Not much left now, just a few lumps of concrete overgrown with grass. Archie was moved to see it again though. I couldn't really understand why, because I got the impression his time there was pretty grim.' Helen took the bag off the table and looked inside.

'It's all there,' I said.

A sulky-looking waitress appeared so we ordered our usual soup and sandwich.

'Peter came again last week, like he always does,' Helen said. I was aware of my face becoming suddenly watchful. 'It felt awkward. I didn't know what to say. We've been meeting ages, and I still couldn't mention you. He said you'd been out a lot with your friends and that these days he hardly ever sees you.' She paused as if to gauge my reaction, but I picked up the menu again, pretended to study it.

She was still waiting for a reply. 'It's not up to me,' I said. 'It's up to him to tell me. He's the one who kept you secret all this time.'

'But now you're keeping secrets from him. Two wrongs don't make a right. You should tell him because I'm worried that—'

'I can't. We don't talk any more, not like that. I keep trying to tell him, but I just can't. It would seem like I'm accusing him of something, and I'm not, not really. I'm only sad he won't confide in me.'

Helen looked embarrassed. 'Is everything all right between you?' she asked, 'I mean generally?'

'I suppose so. We're like any married couple, ups and downs, you know.'

Helen nodded, leaned in towards me to hear more. Something about the way Helen hung on my words made me uneasy. 'Anyway,' I said, 'he can't accuse me of being out too much, he's out at cricket or wretched school meetings all the time.'

'Is he?' Helen asked. She rolled her napkin into a tight ball and clung on to it even when the soup arrived.

When we'd finished eating I said, 'I still don't understand how he kept you secret. Why did you or Archie never call on us? Why didn't we get a Christmas card or a postcard?'

Helen was daydreaming, her eyes unfocused, staring into the middle distance. She dragged her attention back to my question. 'We did send the odd postcard. But I guess he kept them from you. And he always came to us because he said train travel cost too much, and he was better paid than Archie.'

I raised my eyebrows. I did not like the idea of our finances being discussed with other people. It was just not done.

'Of course we protested,' Helen said, 'but Peter was insistent. Now I realise it was because he hadn't told you, but we'd just got used to the routine of him coming. It seemed normal to us, we never thought to query it. And we never sent him a Christmas card because he always came to see us right before Christmas. Archie always gave him a big bar of Nestlé's chocolate, some sort of daft private joke between them. We gave him his card then – it was always addressed to the both of you. Even now, I can't believe he never told you, it seems so underhand – really out of character. To be honest we just thought you were a bit … I don't know, unsociable.'

Unsociable. So that was what they thought.

Helen seemed to want to make up for her earlier comment. 'Sorry. But you know I've enjoyed our get-togethers. It's nice to have someone I can talk to about Archie. And he would have been so thrilled someone's taking an interest, particularly you. I've brought you another batch of books, and some pamphlets, if you want them. There's a book about war production, that's an eye opener. Did you know more than four million of us were employed in munitions factories? We must have made an awful lot of bombs. When Archie read about the scale of it all, it seemed to upset him.'

'I didn't know you worked in munitions.'

'Yes, along with four million others!' She laughed, shaking her head.

I laughed along with her, but felt a niggle of jealousy. Helen must have looked like that when Archie was first courting her, all lit up. It would be nice to be courted again, feel the sheer champagne fizz of excitement. I looked down at my empty soup bowl.

'I was telling Peter about the factory last week,' Helen said. 'Oh, we had such a giggle. He's such good company. I was telling him how once, there we all were – searched and checked for metal buttons in case of a spark, whilst outside there was a flipping thunderstorm, lightning bolts setting fire to all the barrage balloons …' She tailed off. 'What's wrong?'

'Nothing. It's just it's getting late, and I have to be going.' I couldn't bear it, the idea of their cosy little chats.

'Have I said something?'

'No. I'm just tired.' I'd never seen Peter giggle in all the years we were married.

On the way home I saw the headlines. *Mrs Ellis is Dead.* They'd actually done it. I bought a paper and found out she had eaten a good breakfast before they killed her. It seemed obscene – giving her sustenance, whilst all the time knowing that they were to break her neck only a few hours later.

Even more sickening, the warders had gone to great lengths to ensure Mrs Ellis could not commit suicide, and thus deprive the public of seeing justice done. The ultimate power over someone, to decide for yourself when they live or die. I suppose like the Nazi captors had over Peter. I began to see how awful it must have been for him, not knowing if he'd ever come home. Helen's words came back to me, how she had laughed and chatted with him about the war. It stung. I had a sudden desire to hold him, to bring him home to me.

20

1944 Rhoda

I INHALED THE smell of steam and soap from the twin tub. 'Pa not back yet?'

Mother dragged another soiled shirt from the laundry basket. 'No. He's been out all day again. But the Home Guard's a waste of time, he'd be better off digging in our back yard. Hitler's not coming here. The leeks need lifting, and I can't do it all. Not with Andrew's school uniform to do, and the WI bottling and everything.'

'That's right, blame me,' Andrew said. 'I have to have a uniform, don't I? Unless you'd like me to do my exams in the altogether?' He scowled as he took the plates from the sideboard and set them out on the cloth.

'Don't be cheeky. Get that table laid, and properly, mind.'

When Mother turned her back to lift the dripping washing basket he pushed out his tongue at her. I gave him a warning look, but he ignored me.

Taking the cutlery from the drawer I said to Andrew, 'Go see to the rabbits, I'll do this.'

'What's the point? Rabbits are for kids. I'm nearly fifteen. Anyway, we're going to *eat* them in the end, aren't we? And I'm not going out while *she*'s out there.'

Mother's back was visible through the window as she pegged out the shirts with quick sharp movements, shaking them out as if they had fleas.

'Come on, Andrew. She doesn't mean to be so cross. She's just got a lot on, with the WVS and everything.'

'She says I don't do anything except make work. But I brought the coal in yesterday, and I mended that blackout blind in the bathroom.'

'It was you that tore it.'

'I didn't mean to. I was only trying to close it. See, you're on her side. Nobody's on my side.'

'There's no such thing as sides. Why don't you—'

But it was too late, he'd jumped up and I heard the clang and rattle as he dragged his pushbike away from the front door.

'Andrew!' Mother's frustrated voice. 'Andrew! Where are you going? Tea's nearly ready—' She blustered in through the back door with the empty basket. 'Where's he gone?'

'I don't know. He's upset. He thinks we're ganging up on him.'

'What did you say to him?'

'Nothing. I think he feels neglected. We're all so busy. All he needs is a bit of attention. And we could praise him a bit more, when he's helpful.'

'I have to ask and ask before he'll lift a finger. He didn't offer to put out the washing, did he? Or empty the swill bin? He'll get praise right enough, when he does something worth praising.' She sighed. 'If he expects me to chase round the streets of Carnforth looking for him, he's got another think coming.'

'I'll go. It would be a shame for that stew to spoil. You see to Pa and yourself and I'll go and fetch Andrew.'

I pulled my gabardine coat on again and jammed my

felt hat over my ears. Our kitchen was poky, and sometimes it felt as though I just couldn't breathe in there.

I found Andrew easily because I knew exactly where he'd be – where he always was, given half a chance, outside the bike shop looking at the latest shiny model in the window. After much cajoling he agreed to come home, but even at our gate I could hear Pa shouting from inside.

Andrew and I paused, looked at each other, not wanting to go in.

'It's not fit for pigs, that.' Pa's voice. I pushed open the front door and the smell of burning caught in my throat. 'And here's me, working all hours to put good food on the table, and all you can do is ruin it.'

Mother was tearful. 'It's only just caught. I'd only popped out to put the washing—'

'It's burned black. You can't even cook a decent meal. And look, it's raining. What's the point of putting washing out in the wet?'

We hovered in the hall, and I heard the noise of a spoon scraping on a pan before I plucked up courage to walk down the hall to the kitchen.

Pa swivelled in his chair. 'You're late.'

'Sorry, Pa.' Andrew slunk to his chair.

'Your mother's burned the stew.'

There was no point in replying so I just sat down.

'I break my back to put this food on the table, so you'll all eat it, every last scrap. We're not wasting it. If you don't like it you can blame your mother.'

The meal was taken in silence. I watched Mother scrape my serving of stew from the bottom of the pan and almost gagged when I tried a forkful. It was bitter. I held my breath whilst I tried to get it down.

Pa finished his without flinching, put his knife and fork together at the side of his plate. Mother had changed out of her apron, but she still looked grey and haggard as she struggled to finish the blackened carrots.

I forced myself to swallow. I had been hungry, but my appetite was gone. I wondered what had happened to us. It was as if we all sat at the table, but somehow none of us was really there.

Andrew picked at his food and pushed it round his plate. 'I can't eat any more, I'm full,' he said.

'Then it will be served again tomorrow until you do. Take it to the larder, Jean.'

Andrew's mouth twitched but he didn't say anything. Mother wordlessly picked up Andrew's plate and took it away.

Andrew picked at the embroidered flowers on the table-cloth with a fingernail. I knew he was reluctant to ask to leave the table, but nor did he want to sit there either.

'It's time for the news.' Mother came back from the scullery.

Pa nodded at her and she went over to tune in the wireless. The hiss and crackle was a relief in the strained silence of the room. Father frowned as she fiddled with the knob trying to get it tuned in, until at last we heard the plummy accents of the newsreader saying, 'The Battle of Monte Cassino finally ended today with an Allied victory. Polish troops hoisted their red-and-white flag on the ruins amid cheers. The Germans have ceded it to Allied troops and departed.'

'At last, we seem to be getting somewhere,' Mother said.

'Shh. Let's listen.' Pa glared at her and she disappeared into the scullery. We listened to how the Allies had taken an important air base in Burma, and how Japanese resistance in the Admiralty Islands had finally crumbled. It all seemed so far away from Carnforth. I wondered if this meant that Peter might be home soon.

'Reports suggest an increase in the Allied bombing of strategic targets in France,' the newsreader said.

'We must be planning something,' Pa said, using a royal 'we' as if he was in the know, and not just a member of the Home Guard. And somehow it was all right for him to talk over the news.

'Will it be over soon, do you think?' Andrew asked.

'I hope so. Everyone's worn out.' He stood up as the tones for the end of the news pinged out, and said, 'I'm on an overnight tonight. Up to Carlisle.'

Andrew prodded his fork into the tablecloth. 'But it's Sunday. You said we could go fishing tonight.'

'Not tonight. Can't do it. And not the rest of the week either. I'm on split shifts, and when I'm not driving I'm on Home Guard duty. See, there's so much more rolling stock on the lines, what with carrying troops and munitions and food about the place.' Pa opened the door to the stairs and went up.

'I wish I'd left school. I never wanted to be an engine driver like him anyway, too much like hard work.' Andrew was sulky.

I felt sorry for him. Mother had no time for him, nor Pa. 'Look,' I said, 'Let's have a game of Ludo or something.'

'Ludo?' His tone was scathing. 'No, I'm going down the canal. Take my bike.'

'What about your homework?'

'Done it.'

I hadn't seen him touch a book all weekend, but I didn't feel like arguing with him again. 'Well, for heaven's sake tell Mother if you're going out.'

I might as well have talked to the wall because he

clattered past Mother in moody silence. I sighed. Above me the hollow sound of Pa's footsteps clomping down the stairs. He was dressed in his overalls with his bag for his up-and-down box and his peaked cap in his hand.

'I'm off, love,' he said to me.

Mother appeared at the kitchen door. 'Hold on, I'll get you something for your box.'

'No time. I'm on the seven twenty-eight.'

She tried to take the box from his hand. 'But you can't last all night without a snack, let me get—'

'Stop fussing, woman. I'll get something from the refreshment room. Can't a man have a little peace?'

And with that he grabbed his uniform jacket from the hall hook and was gone.

'A little peace,' Mother said grimly. 'I guess we could all use a bit of that.'

21

1941 Peter

PETER WAS NERVOUS, his empty stomach cramped with tension, causing him to double over, clutching at the griping sensation. There was a mist hanging low over the fields; the sky was grey as ash. He wondered when Neb would make his move. His heart jumped in his chest every time there was a sudden movement or noise – a crow landing by the fence, or the tractor on the farm starting up.

It was coming on to winter again now and they had grown used to the life, physically, if not in other ways. Their arms were weather-beaten, muscled from hard work. Their stomachs had shrunk, but they never became used to the discomfort of hunger; they still felt the need to scavenge in the waste of the produce they harvested.

Peter marvelled that the guards could not sense something – the men's unease, their bodies ready to run or to dive for cover.

He loaded the beets into the barrow. If he could get away with it he pissed on them when they were in the lorry. Small acts of sabotage kept him going. Peter paused a moment, stretched his back. Harry's eyes were also trained on the edge of the field. It was nearly changeover time. He guessed this was what Neb had been waiting for.

Harry nodded at one of the guards, who in turn raised his arm to another man near the gate to the compound. That man began walking rapidly down the hill and out of sight. What was all that about, Peter wondered?

When it happened, it was so quick there was barely time to hit the ground. Men running, scattering in all directions. Peter dropped fast. It was what Neb had told him to do. It was a split second before the firing began, the ear-shattering rat-a-tat drilling him further into the ground. When it stopped and he heard an engine start, he raised his head a fraction to look. The field was strewn with bodies, but how many were escapees, and how many just terrified men like himself he couldn't tell.

'*Stehen Sie auf!*' The call roused people to stand.

'*Hände hoch.*' Hands up. It reminded him of Judgement Day, all these men rising out of the earth, arms to the sky. Peter staggered to his feet but several others did not stand. Peter thought they might be alive but in shock. At least he had known it was coming. He flicked his eyes over towards the woodland, saw figures dashing between the trees.

A battery of gunfire, flashes and smoke in the brake of trees. Some men fell, others ran in zigzags trying to dodge the line of fire. It was hopeless; they didn't stand a chance. Someone had tipped them off; they'd been waiting for them.

Guards came to round up the rest of the workers. 'Stand up!' A guard spoke in English. With a flood of relief Peter saw Archie at the other end of the field, but many prisoners still did not stand, perhaps too scared to do so. The guards let rip with machine guns to make sure they were dead. At least one was obviously alive because when he realised what was happening he began to rise, but too late. The bullets caught him in the neck and he jerked. Blood spurted; he clasped at his throat with a bewildered expression, then flopped back to the ground.

'It is a very bad thing you have done,' said Fuhrmann, one of the older, flabby-cheeked guards. The irony was not lost on Peter, who was too angry to trust himself to reply, even if a reply had been called for.

After they were force-marched back to the barracks, Fuhrmann took away their boots and locked the door on their billets. The staccato noise of distant machine guns and the barking of dogs sent ripples of apprehension up his spine. He hoped Neb would make it. He found he was holding his thumbs tight in his fists, willing him on.

Harry was white-faced, jumpy. When Peter touched him on the arm he spun round so quick it nearly knocked him over.

'Did you see Neb?' Peter asked.

'How the hell should I know? Just leave me alone.'

An hour later the message came to line up for roll call.

The temperature had dropped and the cold ate through Peter's clothes, turning his skin to gooseflesh. He wondered if they were going to keep them standing there all night. But no, after forty minutes or so a cart pulled by a bedraggled shire horse was ushered through the gates. Hauptmann Weinart appeared and ordered Fuhrmann and another guard to drag the English bodies off the cart. They yanked them off by the nearest limb, and let them slap anyhow into the mud. Peter could not see properly, past the men in front, who they were.

The bodies steamed, still warm. There was absolute silence in the yard. He counted twelve bodies. He was willing Neb to have got away, that he wasn't amongst them.

It was a lesson. To show them how many had failed. When he'd been marched back to his billet, Peter was shaking and could not stop. His teeth chattered with it so he could not sleep. He'd called himself a coward because he hadn't tried to escape with the rest. He'd been ashamed he and Archie had funked it. When Neb had asked him, he had been inches away from saying yes. But if he had, he would likely be one of those out there now, face down in the mud.

In the morning they had to march past them to the day's work. Carrion crows flapped on the corpses with their black wings. It was a shock to see some other creatures so close up. They had glimpsed mangy-looking cats and even rats before, streaking past them from the farm. Someone always wanted to trap them and eat them. Peter had the urge to stop, to study the crows' elegant flapping wings, watch their sharp beaks, their bold button eyes, but at the same time he wanted to scream at them and chase them off. In the end he just turned his face away, his fingernails digging into his palms.

Archie was already in the field, unloading spades and buckets from the truck. 'He didn't make it,' Archie said, dumping another spade on to the pile, his gaze flicking to the two guards who were about twenty yards away.

'Are you sure?'

'Yes. I passed quite close. I recognised his hands. Neb had such big hands.' Peter glanced to Archie's mangled hand. Archie thrust it out of sight into his pocket.

'Poor bugger.' Peter dragged a hoe off the truck.

'Two from our hut went too.'

'Brave lads. I didn't try, because I didn't know if I could.'

'You'd be all right. You're sort of invisible. I mean, you don't stand out. You just look, kind of ordinary.'

'At least it's not an ugly mug like yours.'

'You wouldn't really have a go, would you?'

'Don't be daft.' Peter slapped him on the shoulder.

'What will happen to them? They can't just leave them in the yard, they've got to let us bury them. It's law, isn't it?'

'Don't know,' Archie said, handing him another hoe. 'But I know I couldn't afford to try anything. They're already watching me to make sure I work – because of this hand. And I want to have that drink with you at the King's Head. And a huge plate of steak-and-kidney pie and chips with gravy like we promised.'

'Don't. My stomach feels like it's squeezed dry.'

Another morning of back-breaking work followed by orders to dig graves in the copse for his comrades. Archie wasn't picked because of his bad hand. The ground was heavy with clay and riddled with tree roots. A deliberate choice. In the end they had to send for picks to do the job. After an hour or so of digging in the increasing rain, Peter cursed Neb and all the other foolish buggers who had tried to escape. Escapees just made conditions harder for those left behind.

'Someone must have known they were going. Or how come they'd got men in the trees?' one of the men asked as they walked back to the compound.

'I saw Foster talking to the guard when he was unloading from the truck yesterday morning,' Harry said. 'Best ask him what he was saying.'

Peter leapt in: 'I was with Archie then and I never saw that. And anyway, Archie wouldn't give anyone away.'

'He's unpredictable though, isn't he. That hand injury, he did that to himself.'

A rustle of interest went round the rest of the men. Peter said, 'That's unfair.'

'You saw him though. You were there. He did, didn't he?'

'That was a long time ago, not long after he'd been taken, and he was still suffering from trauma.'

'Suffering from trauma.' Harry imitated Peter's voice. 'Well, I've news for you. So are we all.' He looked round the gathered men for their sympathy. 'So are we all, but we wouldn't give our mates away.'

'How do we know it's not you?' Peter flashed back. 'I saw you nod at one of the guards. You're the one who's in with the Jerries. You shouldn't make accusations without having firm evidence.'

Harry laughed, as if the whole idea was ludicrous. 'I didn't accuse him of anything. Don't start flinging mud at me just because I ask questions. I'm just saying its worth asking him, that's all.'

Peter could not trust himself to speak. He set off ahead of the others, marching up near the guard, until he realised that even that might be the subject of speculation. Reluctantly he slowed. Archie knew nothing about it, he'd swear. And he wasn't going to let poor Archie be a scapegoat for this.

By the time he got back to camp four of the corpses were in flimsy wooden coffins. Someone had found a flag from somewhere to drape over one of them. Only ten men were allowed at a time to take each man for burial, as the Germans could only spare two guards with dogs.

Peter and Archie were allowed to march Neb to his resting place. Peter was at the head end, but there was no coffin for Neb, just a stretcher. Neb had machine-gun holes in his chest and his uniform was caked with blood and mud, but otherwise his face was expressionless. It was this that was the hardest to bear. Peter wished he could summon Neb back, ask him what he was thinking, where he'd gone.

The wind had risen, and the few trees on the knoll of the hill creaked and rattled. When they got to the site they upended the stretcher to tip his corpse into the hole. Archie and Peter got in with him to straighten him before Peter climbed out to throw the first spadeful of earth over him. It seemed sacrilege to cover his face like that, as if he wouldn't be able to breathe. But of course he'd never breathe again anyway.

'Shall I say a few words?' Peter asked. 'I'm not a vicar or anything, but we should say something for him.'

'Not just for him,' Archie said, 'for all of them.'

'For all of us, you mean,' said George Henderson.

'Maybe the Lord's Prayer?' Peter suggested.

'Oh no, not that again,' George said.

'Does it matter?' Peter said. 'He's dead. Someone just say something.'

Archie took a breath:

> *'Half a league, half a league,*
> *Half a league onward,*
> *All in the valley of Death*
> *Rode the six hundred.'*

Archie recited the poem with the noise of the wind blustering behind him. His voice was quiet and they had to strain to catch it, but they were all entranced by the familiar words:

> *'Forward, the Light Brigade!'*
> *Was there a man dismay'd?*
> *Not tho' the soldiers knew*
> *Someone had blunder'd:*
> *Theirs not to make reply,*
> *Theirs not to reason why,*

Theirs but to do and die:

Into the valley of Death

Rode the six hundred.'

He paused. 'Sorry. That's all I can remember.'

The wind dropped eerily into silence. Peter was choked. The words of the poem had taken him back to school, to boys reciting in the fuggy classroom, to the sound of the school bell, the scrape of chairs.

'Neb would have enjoyed that,' George said. 'Bloody stupid. Just like him.'

They laughed then, and the wind rose up to whip the branches overhead, and those with tears in their eyes were able to dry them.

Later that evening Archie appeared next to Peter's bunk as he was trying to write a letter home. 'Some men from Neb's barracks came by and asked me what I knew about the escape attempt.' His tone was accusatory.

Peter put down his pen and said, 'So?'

'I told them I knew nothing, but they didn't want to believe me. They said you'd told them I was talking to the guard.'

Peter swung his legs out. 'I said no such thing.'

Archie studied his face as if searching for the truth. 'I can't believe you'd think I had anything to do with it. I didn't know anything, didn't even know they were going. Why the hell didn't you tell me? Why am I always the last to hear of anything round here?'

'Calm down. I didn't want to risk anyone who wasn't involved. I helped Neb with his German papers, that's all, because I speak a bit of German.'

'You could have told me. My German's better than yours.'

'I wanted to tell you, but I promised Neb I wouldn't.'

'It was awful. I didn't know what they were talking about. It made me seem stupid, suspicious. They think I tipped off the guard. They all stood there like some sort of official delegation. They didn't exactly say it, but from their questions I knew that was what they were thinking. How could they think I'd do that?'

'It's not your fault. Harry Tyson set the idea in their heads.'

'Why?'

'Who knows? Maybe Harry wanted to move the blame further away from himself. No, I take that back. That was uncharitable. You didn't talk to a German guard yesterday morning, did you?'

'You saw. You were right next to me. What is this?'

'I know, I know. I just needed to be sure.'

'You mean you don't trust me.'

Peter shook his head, sighed. 'Look, I do. I'm sorry. I'm just on edge, upset. It's been a hell of a day. We all want someone to blame. Harry too. It doesn't mean anything. Everyone's on short fuses, that's all.'

Archie sat down on the side of the bunk, looked at his boots. 'You don't understand. It's bad enough with the work. But the toughest part is not being liked.'

'Don't be so hard on yourself.'

'No, listen. It's true. So don't insult me by pretending it's not. I know I'm not Mr Popular.'

'I think we all feel that way sometimes.' Peter reached out to touch him on the arm. 'Don't let it get to you.'

Archie shrugged his hand away. 'It's all right for you. The men respect you.'

'You're just having a bad day, that's all. Tomorrow it will—'

'Why, Pete? Why don't they like me?'

Peter looked at his earnest face and couldn't answer. Perhaps it was just that Archie looked as though he needed a friend too much, perhaps it was that they sensed some weakness in him. And despite Archie's pleading eyes, Peter could feel himself recoil, as if even Archie's question was pushing him further away.

22
1955 Rhoda

'HOW'S PETER?' HELEN asked, as she handed me cheese on toast.

We were eating at Helen's kitchen table, a modern red laminate with matching chairs. Helen always had a vase of flowers standing on it and the kitchen was immaculately tidy, with the coffee and tea in little square canisters, and Italian spaghetti in a tall jar.

'He's all right,' I replied. 'Same as always. Spends too much time at school meetings. He had one on Friday and was back really late. And now he's got an allotment too.'

Helen turned her back to me and moved over to the stove to light the gas under the kettle. When she turned back to me her face was pink.

'What does he grow?' Helen asked.

'Oh, I don't know. Veg and stuff. You know, he used to say allotments were for people who hadn't got a garden. But he met someone at school who has one as well as a garden, so then Peter had to do the same, and I'm telling you, he's never out of there.'

Helen had sat down and was leaning forward, listening. 'Don't you ever go down with him?'

'Me? Oh no. I'm useless with plants. And anyway, I don't think he wants me getting in the way.'

'I should think it would be nice, being out in all that fresh air. I wouldn't mind. It would be a chance to chat, catch up on things.'

Something about this remark irritated me. Perhaps it was just that Helen had obviously had a better relationship with Archie than I did with Peter.

We ate our cheese on toast while talking about the slides that Helen was going to show me of their trips abroad, the sites of the PoW camp and other places Archie and Peter had been held in the war. 'That's if I can remember how the damn thing works!' she laughed.

Whilst Helen set up the projector, I went upstairs to the bathroom. As I washed and dried my hands I noticed that the bathroom too was immaculate. Curious, I looked inside the wall cabinet. It was almost empty. A wrapped bar of Lux soap, some Avon face cream in a jar, and a toothmug with a single toothbrush and a tube of Pepsodent. It was nothing like our own overflowing cabinet, with its dusty jars of tablets, athlete's foot cream, eyebrow tweezers, old bottles of shampoo and fading forgotten bath salts.

Fascinated, I pulled open the airing cupboard door to see the towels neatly stacked in a pile of rose pink and white. I stared at them, at their appealing plump softness. What sort of person has time to fold and stack towels like that? The answer came to me all at once. A lonely person. A person who hasn't got a husband constantly asking what's for dinner and asking them to wash cricket kit. Someone who has lost someone, and the gap shows, even in the airing cupboard. I felt a rush of sympathy for Helen.

I went downstairs to see her kneeling behind the slide projector. The curtains were drawn and the room was in gloomy semi-darkness. 'Good job it's a dull day,' she said. 'They're all lined up, but I hope you don't mind if I skip some, the ones that are too boring.'

'No, I'm looking forward to seeing them. I haven't seen any recent photos of Archie, and it would be nice to see what he looked like.'

'He never changed much, at least not to me. And he used to say Peter never changed either. I guess people don't when you know them well. You take them for granted.'

The square of light blinked and stuttered against the screen until it was replaced by a picture of a younger Helen and presumably Archie standing by a ferry, in mackintoshes, the wind blowing their hair around their faces.

'Dover,' she said. 'I'll skip through these until we get to France.'

Helen and Archie's faces snapped past, looming large and small, all with the fixed smiles of people who knew they were posing. I'd hoped it would give me a sense of who Archie was, but his bright smile, his wispy fair hair, betrayed nothing of the real person.

The hour passed as I was given a tour through views over French beaches, fortifications, obscure German villages, sites of work camps and abandoned railway stations, long roads with ruined farms. Archie had taken slides of nearly everything.

Helen's commentary was peppered with exclamations, bursts of laughter. 'Oh, look at Archie's terrible tie!' The slide carousel clicked round like a clock, wiping each image with the next. Through them all and the hum of the projector Helen and Archie smiled and smiled.

Their happy faces filled me with an ache, a nostalgia not for the past, but for a future that never came. We hadn't had many holidays, and Peter didn't even own a camera, let alone a slide projector, so there would be no photos of Peter and me smiling like that. There was nothing to tell anyone where we'd been or what we'd done. Sad – as if we didn't really exist.

Besides, Peter didn't like to be away from his garden. And now there was the allotment too. His dahlias and chrysanthemums got more attention than I did, half the time. Strange, because before the war he was all for travelling, said he couldn't bear to be stuck in boring Carnforth all his life. But now he never liked going away. He insisted we could have just as good a time at home. So I'd settled for days out or trips to the Lakes, and he'd never contemplate us moving from Carnforth.

'Are you all right?' Helen said. 'You've gone quiet.'

'Just thinking about Peter and me. About our holidays.'

'Are you going somewhere nice?'

'Nowhere. I mean, we mostly holiday at home. He's a bit of a home bird.'

'That must be relaxing. Archie was always wanting to go off abroad. To tell you the truth, it got a bit wearing sometimes. But then, we had some good times – I wouldn't have changed it.'

'I suppose we always want what we haven't got. It's human nature.'

'Yes, human nature.' She took out another box of slides and popped open the lid. 'The grass is always greener.'

We were silent a moment; the projector was stuck on a slide of a road somewhere in Germany.

'Peter would know all these places, but he won't let me show him.' She let the words drop into the stillness. 'I don't know why I'm showing them to you. I'll switch it off now.'

'No, don't.' Something about the darkness, the fact that I couldn't see her face, made me say, 'I can't talk to him. I don't talk about those years.' In my head a picture of Matthew rose up.

Helen began to speak but I spoke over her: 'Whilst he was a prisoner of war, I fell in love with someone else.'

Silence.

She turned to look at me. Her head was silhouetted against the screen so I couldn't see her face.

When she didn't speak, I asked, 'Are you shocked?'

'No. Of course not.' Her voice was brisk. 'People do it all the time nowadays. Times have changed, and these things happen. People grow apart, change, want what they didn't want before.'

'And it's so long ago now, it seems crazy that I've never told him. I knew he'd be hurt and it seemed like he'd been through enough. It's why I tried to put the past behind us.'

But even as I said this, the thought came that you can never put the past behind you, because the past is a part of you.

'Well, I suppose it was a long wait for those left behind.' Helen picked out some slides and fiddled with them. After a moment or two she tidied them into the box. 'And you've kept it a secret from him all this time?'

'Yes. I never told him ... no point. You see, Matthew ...' I took a gulp of air; just hearing his name on my lips again after all this time was like an explosion in my mind. Oh Lord, I was going to cry. I bit my lip, took a deep breath, but it was no use, tears were seeping from my eyes. I put my finger under my eyelashes to avoid smudging my mascara.

Helen stopped packing slides into boxes and knelt beside me on the carpet. 'He was the love of my life,' I said, tears now pouring embarrassingly down my face. The words sounded stupid now I'd said them out loud. I'd carried this thought in my head all these years but hearing it made me realise it was a young girl's thought, not the thought of a thirty-five-year-old woman.

'Here.' Helen went to the bookcase and fetched a box of tissues. 'Cry it out, it's always better.' Somehow, as soon as she said that, I lost the desire to cry. I wiped my eyes.

'What was he like, this chap?' Helen asked. 'Was he in the forces?

23

1945 Rhoda

ORDINARILY I WOULDN'T have remembered the two men at all, not at a busy lunchtime with tables filling and emptying every few minutes. People flooded in and out of the station buffet all the time, on their way to work, or like now, off to Lancaster or Morecambe for shopping in the January sales. I'd got used to the droves of hurrying men in uniform, shouting over the guard's announcements; the drab khaki and air-force blue designed to blend with land or sea.

Patty and I were on our lunch break when the two men came in. We could not help but watch them. The younger one wore a paisley-patterned scarf with a lemon silk lining knotted loosely around his neck. Both men were expensively dressed, in warm-looking pale fawn coats that were certainly not the utility overcoats we were used to seeing. Their sharp trilby hats, unlike the flat caps most railwaymen wore, turned them into silhouettes clipped from the moving background.

The men ordered at the counter. In their voices I heard the sound of a world I'd never seen, an affluent world of wine, jazz and cosmopolitan London. It sang in my memory, so that later I would recall it – the first time I ever set eyes on Matthew Baxter – and marvel at how a single moment can cling for so many years.

They were obviously discussing the place, staring round at the walls with frank appraisement as if looking for signs of decay or dilapidation.

'They're saying now that it will be over next month,' Patty said, stirring her weak cup of tea. 'Have you had any news?'

I dragged my attention back to her. 'No. Not since the camp at Oeringen. Not a dicky bird. Sometimes I think I imagined Peter, imagined all my life before the war.'

'I know what you mean.'

'Sometimes I have terrible thoughts, Patty. Like, he could be already dead, and we just don't know.'

She frowned and shook her head. 'You would hear if that happened. It's regulations. The United Nations is very clear on that. They have to inform you.'

'I keep thinking he might have forgotten me.'

'Don't be a silly, he won't have forgotten you, it's just that the mail is so uncertain.' She leaned over to squeeze my arm. 'Sometimes I marvel that any letters get through at all, what with bombed trains and ships and everything. People often wait for months for news.'

'Sometimes when I'm busy, I forget him, though. Then I get awful guilt. It's hard to keep on writing. Do you know, it's nearly two years since I heard? It feels like I'm sending letters into outer space.'

'Is it really? That long?' I saw the shadow of worry cross her face before she could replace it with composure.

Over Patty's shoulder the two men continued to examine the walls and ceiling and point at them as if they were the most interesting thing they'd ever seen. The younger one had a briefcase with him and he slapped it down on to one of the tables and opened it.

'Are you listening?'

Patty had been talking and I'd missed what she said. I leaned in and whispered, 'Those two men behind you are behaving a bit strangely. I think they're from the ministry. They look like they might be requisition officers.'

Patty swivelled round to look. By this time the younger one had his notebook out and was pencilling notes. The older man paced the floor deliberately, counting his strides. The one with the notebook looked up to see us both staring and smiled.

Patty turned back quickly. 'Nice-looking chap,' she hissed, raising her eyebrows with a grin.

'They're not from round here, anyway.'

It wasn't just their clothes, but more than that, it was their confidence. As if they could hold their shoulders back and know the world would always be good to them.

'Is that the time?' Patty glanced at the clock above the counter, and grabbed her string bag from the back of the bentwood chair. 'I must be going. I only got Mam to mind Melvin and Margaret for an hour, and Margaret will be ready for her feed. Now where's my hat?'

'Under the seat.'

She fished it out and put it on, fluffing out her blonde hair at the sides. 'Now you take care. I'll see you later.' She gave me a perfunctory hug.

I watched her go, and she had to brush past the two men who by now were standing right in front of the door. The good-looking one in the paisley scarf was sketching into his notebook. He startled as she said 'Excuse me' but then apologised and stood aside to let her pass.

He glanced back to my table but the way they were scrutinising everything made me nervous, so I dropped my gaze to my plate.

Evelyn, the frazzle-haired waitress, brought the tray

round to the two men and eased it on to their table. 'Don't let it go cold now.' Her manner suggested that if they did it would be a personal insult.

'We won't,' the man in the scarf said and winked at me.

I smiled and watched them covertly for a few more minutes. The older one made a face at his friend as if to say the tea wasn't very good. But then they looked down again to scribble in their notebooks.

There was much laughter. They were enthusiastic, lively, in the grip of some great idea. Every now and then, the young man with the curly copper-coloured hair would glance my way, as if to see if I was listening. I tried to pretend I wasn't.

I could not help staring. It was as if they were from a different England altogether, one where young men didn't die, where clothes were always new and well pressed. It was like two parakeets arriving in a world of sparrows.

And I recognised the pang, the lure of it, even as I nodded to Evelyn on the way out. As I left, I let my eyes drift back to see the young man still watching me, and I shivered, shaking off some feeling I couldn't quite name, an excitement, as though he'd seen right through to my core.

I heard the clank as Andrew propped his bike against the drainpipe in the yard. 'Hey, Mother, they're going to make a film here in Carnforth,' he said as he slammed the back door. 'Stanley Holloway's in it.'

Mother raised her eyebrows at me. 'Don't talk rubbish. They wouldn't make a film round here.'

'They are. They're using the station.'

'Our station? No. Your father would have said.' Mother dismissed it.

'And nobody mentioned it when I did the tea run this morning,' I said. 'Are you sure?'

'Mr Emmett at the newsagent told me, so there, Miss Clever Clogs. I passed him on my bike and he waved me down to tell me. They're bringing a film crew and everything.'

'What's it about?' I asked, curious.

'Don't know. But he said they're going to build a film set on the platform and advertise for people to be in it. Do you fancy it, Rhoda?'

Mother aimed a mock slap at Andrew, but he dodged and she missed. 'Get the plates out and lay the table. There's a war on. There's no time for play-acting and carrying on. Your father will have a fit. On his station? What do they want to make a film there for? There's nothing there except the munitions dump and the goods yard. They'd be daft – the station's so busy with troop trains coming and going, they'd never be able to film a thing for the noise.'

I barely heard her. Those men on the station, they must be something to do with the film. At last, something new was happening in Carnforth, right on my doorstep.

24

1941—1945

Dear Rhoda,

Just in case my last letter went astray, I am safe and well. Please let my parents know too as I'm still waiting for a letter from them. I've been moved again to a different POW camp where we are farm labourers. Feeling homesick more than ever. Not much I'm allowed to tell you about life here except I am surviving. Still pulling up cabbage and loading it into trucks. I never want to see another cabbage again in my life.

The fellows here are okay and at least here the whole business of the British Army is less rigid. At [censored] the S.C.O.'s expected us to parade to keep up morale and show how British we were, and as you know I never really wanted to be a soldier. I dislike the whole life and spirit of the Army intensely, though I concede their attitude may be very efficient as far as us winning the war. But I've always hated all that business of someone else telling me exactly how to fold my trousers or how to wear my hair. And all that pointless marching. I hated being marched to my meals, marched to my football game and even to the church service for prayers.

At least here I'm being told what to do by [censored] and not by my own countrymen, and do you know what, it's easier. I feel justified in my resistance to them. Though they [several sentences censored].

We have little entertainment here except what we can make ourselves, so when you get this letter, please send me a good book. Something not too highbrow and not too depressing. It would be wonderful if you could because it would go a long way, I'd pass it along to the other chaps so we'd all get the benefit. Shaving materials wouldn't go amiss either, I look like a bit of a tramp right now, patchy bristles all over. We haven't had a Red Cross parcel for a while.

Here's hoping for good news from you, I kiss your picture every night.

Your Peter x

16th December 1941

Dear Peter,

Just got your card telling us where you are. I tried to look it up on the map but it's [censored].

We are all well. I am recovering from a cold, it has been such a hard winter. Pa is busier than ever, on nights a lot, and he says there's so much freight on the lines, mostly [censored] which worries me to death. You would laugh – I have been conscripted to signal work on the line and the bookstall is being staffed by WVS volunteers. Can't tell you much, 'loose lips sink ships' and all that. But by golly the training was hard. So much to remember, but fingers crossed there've been no trains going the wrong way or accidents yet.

Andrew is the same as usual, though he's growing up quickly, I saw the beginnings of a few hairs sprouting on his upper lip, but he is so embarrassed about it he won't let Pa show him what to do. He's mad about the war, wanting to join in with the fight, but I'm glad he's not old enough. I hope it's soon over – the thought of him having to fight would finish Mother.

With it being almost Christmas I've hurried to send a parcel to you with some books and some things I've knitted for you. I won't say what, surprise! I'm afraid I sent an earlier parcel to your other camp. I didn't know you were moving. I hope they forward things on to you.

There's not much time for anything else but the signal box and the WVS – I still meet with Patty when I'm off signal shift to take tea to the troops. Every time I do I think of you. I sent a letter to Father Christmas wishing you could be home for Christmas.

With love

Rhoda x

12th September 1943

Dear Rhoda,

*I have run out of rationed letters so am using postcards.
We had photographs taken so hope I shall be able to send
you one shortly just to show you how I am. Still miss you
like mad. Tolerable here except still no word from you.
Would love to hear news from Carnforth. How are the
band faring without me? Please check Mother has asked
my bank to put my money into War Saving Certificates.
Cheerio for now. Please write soon, and keep safe my love,*

Peter x

3rd January 1944

Dear Rhoda,

*Happy New Year! Hoping 1944 will mean an end to
all this. I think there must be a conspiracy against me
because I haven't heard anything at all from Mother or
from you even though it's been Christmas. Our Christmas
Day was just like all the others though a padre came to
take prayers. He looked ridiculous in his dog collar and
battledress. A living oxymoron if ever there was one. On
bad days I think we've been forgotten in this corner of
Germany, miles away from anywhere. Sometimes I wonder
why I'm bothering to write any more. Does anybody get my
letters? They won't tell [censored].*

*Pretty depressing here, winter very cold, ice makes the
work more difficult. Trying to keep cheerful, hoping for
good news soon.*

Dearest Rhoda, if you get this, please, please write.

Peter x

4th August 1944

Dear Rhoda,

I don't know why I am writing to you as I haven't had a reply for 1 year 2 months and 4 days. I just have to hope that your letters to me are stuck somewhere in a German post office, and that you haven't given up on me. Don't give up on me, will you, darling? I haven't lost hope that we'll be together when all this is over. I am too tired to write much, it is busy at this time of the year on the land. But I can't forget about my girl.

Please if you get this write soon.

Your loving Peter x

Unteroffizier Hans Drescher collected the mail from the wooden postbox by the farm canteen once a fortnight. From there he drove it thirty miles by jeep to a pick-up point in a barn on the road to Lamsdorf railway station, where the mail was supposed to be collected by another jeep doing the rounds of the work camps. Mail destined for the return journey to the E22B prisoners was supposed to be dropped at the barn too, so he could pick it up at the same time.

For two years, everything went smoothly; the system was efficient and Hans enjoyed being the bearer of post for the English prisoners. But one week when he went to deliver, the last bag was still sitting where he had left it, and no new bags had arrived for collection. The next time it was the same so he complained to his senior officer that nobody had been to collect or deliver the post.

'Not our business,' Offizier Fuhrmann had said. 'Just do your duty. They've probably more important uses for the jeep than ferrying English letters. They'll collect when they're ready.'

As the time went by it offended Hans seeing the mail sacks sitting there, when he had clearly done his own job in delivering them. The prisoners were complaining, demanding to know what was happening.

He asked again, and Fuhrmann said he'd look into it.

Months went by. Hans got used to just pushing open the barn door and shoving the mail inside. Nobody ever came and soon he gave up looking to see if there was any post for delivery. He avoided the looks of the English prisoners, kept his distance. It worried him though, the burden of all those letters. He often remembered them at night, couldn't sleep for wondering how many thoughts were tied up in those bags, how many anxious children were waiting for letters from their fathers.

Again he asked his commanding officer what to do.

'Nothing,' Fuhrmann said. 'Don't worry about it. It's only a few letters. The younger men have been redeployed, sent to the Soviet lines. Maybe there's nobody to collect. Just follow your orders.'

Hans continued to drop off the mail even though it never moved, until one day in the autumn of 1944, he arrived to find the mail had gone. The barn was empty. It looked strange after all this time to leave his lone bag in the vast empty space. He wondered if the sacks had been stolen, but then breathed a sigh of relief. Wherever they were, they were no longer his responsibility.

25

1945 Peter

'Is it true? We're moving again?' Archie said breathlessly, leaning over Peter's bunk.

'Guess so.' Peter had already sensed something amiss because the Germans were scattered, their attention here and there. But they were still armed and even less predictable, so nobody took chances.

'But it's minus something out there,' Archie said.

'Aw, poor baby. Then take your vest,' Harry said. 'Hey, George, can I team up with you?'

George Henderson, who was on the next bay, leaned round the corner and said, 'Sure. We're best to stick together.'

Peter exchanged a rueful look with Archie. They'd already arranged to team up with George too. He knew neither of them particularly wanted Harry's company, but could hardly protest.

George was talking, 'One of the men in number four has a radio. I've just heard. They're saying some of our men got away in Berlin, even in this weather. They went in with the Romanians and they spoke good Czech, so they managed to get out to the Allied lines. Once we're out of this compound, you never know, we might see an opportunity.'

Archie called to him, 'Maybe.' He turned back to Peter.

'We're not for trying anything though, are we? Not until we know what will happen or where they're taking us. It would be stupid to try anything dangerous now.'

'Oh yes, we mustn't try anything *dangerous*,' Harry said, overhearing. 'That's why we joined the bleeding army, isn't it?'

'Oh, lay off, Harry,' Archie snapped.

Peter ignored them. The constant bickering was getting to him.

George called out, 'I'm getting ready. If the rumour's right and we have to move, it will be in a hurry.'

'Why are they moving us?' Harry asked.

'Man in hut seven says the Soviets are making headway on the Eastern Front – they've got Jerry on the run.'

All just rumours, thought Peter. He said, 'We don't know anything. It's just hearsay. Three and a bit years we've been stuck in this camp. What's going to change now?'

Archie sat down on Peter's bunk. 'That's not like you. It's usually you geeing me up.'

'Guess I'm brassed off. Every time we move we just seem to get further away from home, and no nearer the end of the war. I feel numb, like there's no man left inside me. That I'm just an empty body walking around going wherever Jerry tells me to go.'

'I know,' Archie said. 'Numb sounds good. I'm scared, Pete. I worry about what will happen if the Soviets get here first, before the Yanks. I'm not sure whether they're part of the Geneva Convention or not. And I wouldn't put it past them to finish us off rather than hand us over. Less trouble.'

Peter turned to look out of the mud-spattered window to the icy landscape outside. Maybe he had become institutionalised. Here was a world they knew. Not a comfortable world, granted – one of hunger, fear and humiliation – but at least they knew the rules, and they had survived so far. They had followed the turning of the year, the sowing, the planting, the harvesting. The earth here seemed as if it was their earth, even though they had dug it for the Germans. There was something reliable about nature, about things growing, about the weather.

Out there was an unknown quantity.

He looked at Archie's worried face. A surge of affection rose up from nowhere and threatened to overwhelm him. 'Come on, everyone,' he said, rising with a great effort, 'thinking just makes it worse. I guess if you lot are going, teacher had better come and keep an eye on you.' He took his pack from where it hung on the end of the bunk.

George, the practical one, said, 'I'm buggered if I'm carrying a pack.'

An hour later George brought back a bit of old corrugated-iron roof that had blown off in the last storm, and with much sawing and bending it back and forth, they managed to make rough-edged runners for a makeshift sledge.

Except for the machine gunner's turrets, the goons were nowhere to be seen, busy making their own preparations.

'You're not taking those?' Archie pulled out a pair of trousers from the box on runners, and held them up.

They were the last piece of Peter's original uniform, though they were far too big for him and the bottoms were rotted with mud. The men had all shrunk since arriving at the camp, but nobody said so. It was one of the things they just did not talk about. The trousers Peter wore now were second-hand. Nobody had uniforms with insignia or stripes, they were all the same rank – English, unwashed, defeated. After this long, they were all wearing dead men's clothes.

'Someone might need an extra layer,' Peter said.

'He's right.' George whipped them from Archie's hand and stuffed them back in the trunk. 'The weather could worsen, and we don't know where we're going.'

Peter folded a ragged grey blanket and pushed it down to the bottom. Most of the room in the box was taken by clothing, a spare greatcoat, blankets, food from Red Cross parcels and cigarettes.

Thank heaven for the Red Cross. A parcel had arrived a few days earlier and as soon as they knew they were leaving there was a great rush to cram as much food in their shrunken bellies as they could. From his window he could see discarded tins littered everywhere. Nothing could be wasted; what couldn't be carried had to be eaten.

The parcels had also contained some knitted hats, new, made cleverly to fold out into scarves, all in the regulation colour. Peter pounced on one amid the scuffle, and managed to pocket it.

Archie was subdued when Peter brought it out of his pocket to show him. 'They're new,' he said, awed. 'Fancy them knitting these. Englishwomen sitting by their fires at home thinking of us. My mother might have knitted one of these, or your Rhoda. Or someone else's sweetheart. That's who we're fighting for.'

'Fighting? You're one to talk. You haven't done any fighting for years,' Harry said. 'If you ever did.'

'You know what I mean.'

Peter did. He pictured his mother's hands moving quietly with the needles. 'I got it for you,' Peter said with sudden generosity, passing it to Archie. 'I've still got my balaclava.'

'Really?' Archie's face broke into a delighted smile. 'I don't know what to say. Thanks.' He put it on and pulled it down over his ears. 'Snug as a bug.'

Peter smiled, but then caught sight of Harry's sour face watching him.

George had just got the lid on their box when the voice of Hauptmann Weinart on the tannoy made them all tense their shoulders to listen. His voice was followed by that of an English officer translating. Prisoners were to line up, take only essentials, and those who refused would be shot. 'No chances, eh, lads?' crackled the disembodied English voice.

Peter kept the small bundle of letters from Rhoda in his pocket. Perhaps it was stupid and sentimental, as he hadn't heard from her for so long. She might have forgotten he existed by now. But he hadn't even thrown away the envelopes. They were a sign that normality existed somewhere – that people would lick the envelope, go to the post office for a stamp, and perhaps seal it with a kiss before slipping it into the box.

He took them out now for a last look. When he saw Rhoda's writing his mind immediately conjured her soft dark curls, her trim waist, her smile. But it was so painful to remember that he screwed up his eyes against the memory. She did not belong here amongst the stench of mud and sweat. It was the least he could do – keep her from this. He put the letters away again.

This time he hoped he was going home. Even if he had to walk there.

26

1945 Peter

Two hundred and fifty men emerged shuffling and coughing into the cold, men whose chests were full of phlegm and had no medicine to get better. The only thing they knew was that the weather was bloody awful and they were going to be marching.

The landscape was bare and mist-shrouded; the hard-packed snow burnished pewter from the tread of men's boots. Even the labels of the cans discarded only a few hours earlier outside the barracks were unreadable, grey with frost.

The four of them stood together, Archie and Peter at the back of the sledge, George and Harry in front. It was oddly quiet, no lorries or trucks, no vehicles at all. The silence was too much for some who feared they were to be marched to their deaths and began to weep and moan, until the crack of a pistol rang out a warning and the group subsided to shivering silence again.

They heard the staccato noise of an engine starting up, before a truck drove past bearing Hauptmann Weinart, Fuhrmann and two others. It veered by in a grinding of gears and exhaust fumes. Another vehicle took up the rear. In between, the camp guards patrolled. 'No chance of a lift then,' whispered George.

Harry glared at him, not wanting any trouble. They took the hint; Archie and Peter closed their ears and mouths and, when the order came, they followed the rest, boots slithering on the ice. They were about halfway down the line, Peter guessed.

At noon the pale sun melted the surface of the ice into grit and water and it became warmer. With the warmth came the ever-present itching from lice, and the chafe of the stiff fabric of the uniform. Designed to be hard-wearing, the trousers were harder wearing than Peter's soft skin, and after a morning's marching the creases at the backs of his knees began to rub. He walked in a strange stiff-legged way to try to minimise the sting of his sore legs. As they walked into the afternoon, they were joined by more POW's from other Allied work camps.

'Do you know where we're going?' Archie asked. The same question again and again, to which there was never an answer.

The four of them guarded their box jealously. They walked for what must have been eight hours, gauged by the fact that the snow was beginning to grow long shadows, and ahead of them the men had become one dense black moving shape. The rhythm of footfalls had deteriorated into a general rumble. To keep going, Peter counted his paces; eighteen thousand, nineteen thousand, twenty thousand, reciting the numbers like times tables. As dusk thickened Peter looked to the sides for the first time. All those hours he had been walking, just staring down at the rough wooden lid of that box, or ahead at the bobbing backpacks and balaclavas of the men in front.

Now he saw he was moving through a forest. Dark stripes of trees towered to the left and right. The trees gradually greyed and glistened, and he began to see his breath. The temperature was visibly dropping. White frost crept along the branches of the pines. The beauty of those trees after the sameness of the compound made him want to fall to his knees in prayer, but he dare not stop. The crack of ice grew in the puddles as he walked. His nose began to tingle. He wrapped a scarf over it, pulled his hat down to his eyebrows.

He passed over a crossroads and then suddenly: '*Halt!*'

The order to stop rattled down the line as the men literally fell where they stood like dominoes. For a moment Peter couldn't speak. None of them could. They were unused to walking, their backs bent like bows from planting. They were weak before they set off with malnutrition and now exhausted from the sheer willpower of putting one frozen boot in front of the other. There was no sign of any dwelling or camp. No light anywhere, no birdsong or other sound.

George rubbed at his legs, with hands encased in old mismatched socks. 'I think that's Czechoslovakia. Over those mountains.'

'What's there?' asked Archie.

George answered, 'My guess is, we're going to the camps in Bavaria. That is, if we can avoid the Soviets.'

'Hell, I'm ready for them,' Harry said, shifting his bottom a little to avoid the ruts in the road.

'How far?' Archie asked.

'Don't know. Far enough,' George said.

'Stop gassing and get out the grub.' Harry struggled to his feet, pulled off one glove and blew on his hand before levering open the box which had seized shut with frost. His wrists were bony and the veins stood out on the backs of his hands. They were all drooling by the time he prised open the can of Spam. In doing so he cut his hand and George had to bandage it up. It was a surprise to see the blood – this evidence that they were still alive, that blood still flowed through their veins, hot and red.

The Red Cross Spam had a slimy salty texture that felt strange on the tongue after their diet of watery potato swill, and it was almost a relief to tear off some of the old stale bread they'd been hoarding in their box. Peter was still eating when the order came to set off again. To stand was a torture. *Please let it not be frostbite.* He hoped his feet were only blistered in his boots.

They set off again, buoyed only by the fact that there were so many in front and behind. If they had wanted to stop they couldn't have.

'Are you all right?' he asked. Archie had stopped pushing and was lagging behind.

'Sorry, Pete. I can't push it. I can hardly walk. I can't feel my toes.'

'You can't stop. You know you can't. Put your hands on the box and count with me. Each count is a second nearer, you hear? Each count one second nearer, right?' Of course he didn't know nearer to what, but the sense of arrival somewhere was what Archie needed to hear. Some end, some place to stop.

He nodded. Peter began, 'One, two, three …'

Long after he'd fallen silent himself, he could hear Archie doggedly counting into the thousands. That's how he knew it was about another four hours before they stopped at a deserted farm. The walls had been shelled on one side and the farmhouse itself was empty. The officers went inside the house. The prisoners had to crowd into two dilapidated barns with rubble for walls, and smell the pungent woodsmoke and cooking from outside.

Nobody complained. It was dry at least and warmer than being in the open. Most lay down in the first space that came to them. Three of them dragged out the blanket from the box and huddled together, but George curled up on top of their possessions with the old greatcoat over him. Nobody was going to get near that box except over his dead body.

Peter slept. They all loved the sweet oblivion of sleep and had learned to savour the hours when the nightmares that came were not real. Sometimes in his sleep Peter would remember Rhoda, the soft swell of her breasts under a pink lambswool cardigan, the curve of her ankles in a film of silk stocking. Inconceivable textures now – the softness of lamb-swool, the smoothness of silk.

'Hey!' A voice made him sit up stiffly, his teeth already chattering with cold.

Harry was shaking him. 'Someone's taken our blanket. Whipped it right off our backs.'

'What?' Peter looked about, still croaking with sleep, but all around there were men packing knapsacks and bags with blankets. The helmeted guards prodded people to their feet with the butts of their guns. Impossible to tell who had taken it. Nobody could tell who looked guilty amongst these defeated-looking men who could barely pick themselves up.

'Never mind,' Archie said, still dozy, 'Don't waste your energy.'

'We'll freeze to death without it. I'm going to get it back.' And Harry began to push his way through the men who were half-standing or sitting up. Peter saw him remonstrating with one man who sent him packing. By now the guards were mobilising the men and lines were already forming. Peter's eyes were still bleary and he squinted at Harry through the morning light.

'What's up?' George sprang to his feet as if he'd never been asleep.

'Someone took our blanket. Harry's gone after it.'

He turned to look to where Harry tugged at a blanket that another man was holding.

'Damn fool,' George said. 'I'll go and get him.' He set off towards the two men, but by now another man had stood and was clinging to the blanket, and Harry was shouting, pulling harder to get it from their grip. Two guards pointed, exchanged words.

'Hey, Harry!' George's movements were more urgent as he picked his way over legs and packs.

One of the men shoved Harry hard in the chest but he clung on, keeping his balance, and aimed a fist back at his face. It was a neat jab, a boxer's left hook. Another man began to shout. One of the German guards raised his gun.

'Harry!' Peter yelled a frantic warning but it was drowned by a shot. The man who was about to hit Harry buckled and dropped to the ground.

Archie covered the backs of his ears and his head with his hands and flung himself to the ground where he stood. Like an infection, all the other men followed suit.

'*Auf! Heraus!*'

Around him men staggered slowly to their feet again all except one. Harry tugged at the blanket he was lying on.

Archie stared a moment before turning back to Peter. 'When we get home, we'll tell them, like we always do. Tell his folks he died fighting. Fighting the Germans. We leave Harry out of it. That's all.' He brushed wet from the front of his coat, his shaky hand pulled up his collar. They manhandled their sledge out into the open and pushed it into the road. Peter pushed, the other two pulled.

A few moments later Harry came up beside him. He put the blanket on the chest. He and the blanket were spattered with blood.

'Leave it,' Peter said, trying to push it off. Just the sight of it made him angry.

'No, we'll need it.' Harry fumbled to hold the blanket down.

George turned. His expression was cold. 'You heard what Peter said. Leave it. A man died because of you and that bloody blanket. A man who would be here now if you hadn't been such a damn fool.'

'It was his own fault, he shouldn't have taken it. It was ours.'

George lost his temper. 'It's no use to any of us now, you stupid bugger. None of us will sleep well under it now, will we? Covered in that man's blood.'

'Come on, it wasn't my fault the Jerries took a potshot.'

'Just go away. Your face makes me sick.' Peter shoved the box viciously forward, and it began to slide on its runners. Archie and George took up the slack.

Harry was left standing in the road, holding the blanket.

'Nazi bastards,' George said.

Peter did not reply, imagining the dead man's family. A bit further on he asked, 'What shall we do about Harry? His things are still in here.'

'I don't know. I wish we hadn't said he could come with us,' Archie said. All Peter could see of Archie was his nose poking out from beneath his new knitted hat.

'It's harder work with only three,' George said. 'And he's strong. We should dump his stuff really if he's not pushing.'

The ground had got rougher; there was less snow covering it and they had to march uphill. Peter watched his friends' backs as they pulled. Archie was wearing a greatcoat but it drowned him, his shoulders shrunk to be too narrow for it. George's shoulders were wide but stooped from working in the labour camp underground followed by more than three years of digging cabbages.

Peter took the chance to pull his hands away a moment to blow on them, for they were almost numb with cold. Then he pushed again. The top of the box had a deep score in it from his knife. He'd decided to keep track of the days. He'd be able to tell his father how far he'd marched when he got home. If he got home.

A flurry of snow hit them sideways, and he struggled to keep his balance. It was much harder work without Harry. He had to wipe the surface of the box to stop snow collecting there, and he had just done this for the umpteenth time when another pair of hands appeared next to his. They were clad in worn woollen gloves and the sleeves of a ragged jersey were pulled down over the wrists.

Harry was back pushing with him, his stubby nose red with cold. The offending blanket was wrapped around his shoulders. Archie and George looked back at the sudden decrease in weight, but said nothing. Peter ignored Harry, it was just too much effort to stop and get him to remove all his things.

'Bit of an accident, that,' Harry said, the faint note of an apology in his voice.

'Don't give me that.' Peter was not ready to forgive him. 'It was your fault. You can't bring a dead man back. And I keep thinking of his mother, whether anyone will ever know he's there, stuck in that barn to rot.'

'Let it go, Pete. Come on, Harry, push if you're going to,' George called over his shoulder. Peter concentrated on keeping time with the men in front. He saw Archie lift his hands, wipe his eyes with his coat sleeves, forming frozen crusts over his cheeks.

'They'll march us to death,' Harry said. 'Like the Japs did to the Yanks. A man just told me.'

Archie turned to look their way, his eyes shadowed with fear. Peter had an urge to strangle Harry. He'd broken the first rule of the silent code that existed amongst them all. Never mention the worst. He tried to speak calmly, 'George says we're just going to another camp out of the way of the Red Army, that's all. That's why we have the Geneva Convention.'

'What if George is wrong? Chap back there says it's not just us, that there's—'

'Shut the fuck up and push,' Peter snapped, tired of it, cutting him off.

The snow was falling thicker now. He could not look at Harry. He was sick of him, his bullish face, the way he made everything and everyone his personal enemy. He tried to reason with himself. Nobody likes having their fears exposed for everyone to see, and Harry was only telling them what they already half-suspected.

27

1945 Rhoda

PATTY BARELY LET my customer pick up her magazine before she leaned over the counter and said, 'Guess what! Those two men who were looking at the refreshment room – they're location scouts for a film. They're not army requisition officers at all.'

'I know, Andrew told me.'

'Oh. Anyway, I was on shift last night after you left and they were right there on the platform again. I asked them whether they were going to use the station, and guess what? They're going to film at night. Oh, and I'll take a copy of *Woman's Weekly* whilst I'm at it.'

I handed Patty the magazine and counted the coins, still warm from her hand, into the till, and pushed the drawer shut with a ping. 'Why at night? What about the daytime scenes?'

'Can't be any. That's why they're doing it here, because they'll need lights and they can't risk them blazing away in London. So you might not see much of it even though you work here. But you'll never believe it, they're holding auditions. For extras. It's true, I asked the stationmaster – Stanley Holloway's coming and a young star called Trevor Howard.'

She paused expectantly, waiting for my reaction.

'I don't like Stanley Holloway much,' I said. 'I can't

bear his monologues. People think he's northern, but it's just insulting.'

'Did you not see *This Happy Breed*? That was a great film.'

'I've never even heard of this Mr Howard. What's he been in? Now Dirk Bogarde, I wouldn't mind serving him the tea.'

'Yes, if he comes, bagsy first look-in. And don't tell Frank! But look, the auditions are Saturday in the Station Hotel. I kept the clipping from the *Visitor* for you. She unfolded a cutting from her pocket.

'I don't know –' I said, when I'd read it.

'Oh, go on. I'm going. We need a bit of extra money with two kids and another on the way. Come down with me. It will be fun. I'll even let you have first go at Trevor Howard.' She raised her arched eyebrows and patted her hair where it was tied up under a scarf.

I made a face and laughed. 'Oh, very generous. Assuming he'd look at either of us! Go on then. But I don't want to be in the film. I'd be awful.'

'Why? You've got time now they've laid you off signalling. And you've got that nice speaking voice they all want. Not like me – I can't get rid of my Barrow accent. I've tried, but I just end up sounding as if I've swallowed a barn door.'

'No. You know I'd not be able to do it because I've got my shifts back at the bookstall, and the WVS tea run. My hands are full already. But I'll come with you for the outing.'

'That's more like it. I'll meet you in the refreshment room on platform two then at half one. There's bound to be a massive queue.'

'Okay, but don't tell my father. He'd have a fit if he thought I was doing that instead of something useful.'

'Right-o. Hey, that's the bell for the next train! I'll have to get a shift on. Mam's minding the kids and she'll think I've got lost!'

When the day came for the audition Patty was all dolled up with her hair curled into stiff waves and a red-and-black scarf kirby-gripped to keep it on. Over the last few years we'd lost weight with the rationing and all the extra exercise. Patty used to be plump and buxom, now she was just buxom. It suited her. She was wearing a second-hand winter coat that was too big and obviously designed for when she was further along with the baby, but she'd belted it in tight. She'd have three children soon. Where did the time go?

At the hotel, a big Victorian edifice of blackened sandstone, there was a queue running right round the corner. Luckily, as we joined, it began to move, and we all squashed in through the glass-windowed door. A smart Brylcreemed young man behind a table took Patty's name and gave her a brown tie-on label. Next to him was the copper-haired young man I'd seen before, in his paisley scarf.

'No one under eighteen. If you're under eighteen we can't take you,' he called. His voice was cultured – all precise consonants and rounded vowels.

Quite a few younger lads and girls shoved past us, muttering, 'Swizz,' and 'Not fair.' There must have been a hundred or so there, come from all over, so I stuck with Patty whilst she waited. She was very excitable and kept waving at people she knew, until we got near the front when the Brylcreemed man said, 'You need to fill in these forms.' Patty took one, but I said, 'No, thanks.'

'You're not auditioning?'

'I can't act. I just came down with my friend.'

'Me neither,' the man in the paisley scarf grinned. 'Just a backstage boy, me.'

Patty handed in her form and tied her name label on to her button, and they were all told to go through to the back bar. In the foyer a black-uniformed waitress was serving tea, so I ordered a pot and sat down with the paper to wait.

The middle pages of the *Visitor* showed long-distance and close-up views of battleships in the churning grey sea off Morecambe. The beach was empty, swathed in barbed wire to prevent the enemy from landing. The picture made me sad. I mourned the loss of the jolly Morecambe in my memory; the Morecambe with shows and the pier, the striped deckchairs next to the Lido with their seats flapping in the wind. Patty always joked that if Jerry landed in Morecambe now, they'd think it so dull they'd turn round and go back.

Within about fifteen minutes a whole batch of disgruntled people emerged from the double doors to the back bar.

'They only want young folk.' One of the men shook his head. 'Why they couldn't have said that in the first place, well, it beats me.'

I turned and smiled sympathetically at him as he jammed his cap on to his head. Patty was still in there. I hoped she'd stand a chance. After Peter had gone it was only Patty who really cheered me up. And since she'd met Frank she'd calmed down a bit, was a bit less brash, and she was devoted to him and the children. Heaven knows, if anyone needed the money, they did, with all those mouths to feed.

Peter and I would probably have had children by now if it hadn't been for the war. The idea was unbelievable, though. I'd almost forgotten who Peter was. Waiting for him was like having permanent grit in my shoe – I'd stopped noticing how much it rubbed.

I glanced down at the engagement ring on my left hand. I didn't know what to do about it. Peter had given it to me right under the station clock just before the train came that was to take him out of England and to France. He hadn't even had time to ask, just thrust the box into my hand.

When I'd got it home I'd opened the box and stared down at the velvet pad. At the little ring of pale gold with the chip of diamond. Did it mean I was engaged? I'd slipped its flimsy band on my finger, but it felt empty somehow. Not just because the ring was a little big, but because he hadn't asked and I hadn't said yes. But I'd put it on all the same and Mother was thrilled to bits. Of course I didn't know then that I wouldn't see him again for all this time.

I was a different person now at twenty-four years old than I had been at nineteen. Working on the signals had given me confidence. I stopped twirling the ring. It made me depressed. I turned to look at the door. Patty was taking a long time. The copper-haired young man saw me looking and came over.

'They'll be ages,' he said. 'I was at the London auditions and they were a whole afternoon. Your friend's still in there, so that's a good sign.' His face was open, eager.

I nodded and smiled politely. It wasn't an invitation but he sat down in the chair opposite me anyway. He took off his hat and put it on the seat next to him, and pushed a long forelock out of his eyes. 'Nippy, isn't it? That's the North for you!' Then he rubbed his hands together before he offered me one to shake. 'Matthew Baxter. I'm the assistant location manager.'

'Oh. Rhoda King.' I shook his hand which was warm and dry. He was looking at me as if expecting a question. I obliged. 'I'm afraid I don't exactly know what a location manager does.'

'I'm just the assistant. Finding the places where we'll film. They've got to look right, have the right atmosphere. Little details make a difference. Like the station here having ramps instead of steps, and a nice curve in the platform. But I do all the organising, the running about. Timetabling with the locals wherever we're on location. Are you local?'

I nodded. 'Just up the road.'

'Yesterday I had to look at all the train timetables and work out when we could get a train and driver for a few hours in Carnforth. It's hard to get one without disrupting the rolling freight or the munitions trains. And boy, it was even harder to get a driver that didn't mind being on film.'

'Did you get someone in the end?' I thought, *Well, it wouldn't be my father, that's for sure.* Pa would never agree to be on film.

'Yes – an old chap called George Farrer, and he recommended a fireman called Alf. George wouldn't do it unless Alf would. Do you know them?'

'Everyone knows George and Alf. They're friends of my father.' I relaxed a little. 'They've worked the trains on the Barrow line for as long as I can remember. They're like Laurel and Hardy.'

He laughed. His laugh was like a cough, wheezy and breathless. There was a silence while I tried to pour tea and discovered the pot was empty.

'Hey, you can't be running out of tea – England's fuel, that! Let me get you some more.' He lifted the pot out of my hand and set off to fetch a refill. I noticed the way he strode confidently up to the counter, a bounce in his step. When he set the pot down again he said, 'I expect you're wondering why I'm not fighting.'

I wasn't, but I could see he was going to tell me anyway.

'They wouldn't let me. It's asthma. I was glum to begin with. Everyone else I knew was signing up. Back home they were all talking about gunboats and fighter planes. My sisters' husbands, people at Denham. Ridiculous really, the way they were talking, as if it was a great big adventure. All of them ballooned up with optimism. He sighed and looked out of the window. 'Half of them are dead now. Sad.' His face was earnest. 'Sorry, I didn't mean to go on. Still, I'm doing my bit. The government assigned me to this. And this is war work too in its way, to keep people entertained. Keep some culture.' He was leaning forward, trying to convince me. 'Not that I don't love it. All this, I mean.'

'I expect it's really interest—'

'Do you like photography?'

A momentary flash of the pictures on the mantelpiece in Peter's mother's house.

'I've always loved photography,' he said, without waiting for a reply, 'ever since seeing my first Box Brownie. It's marvellous, just to fix the image there so that it never fades. I think that's what memory's made of. Photographs. Sometimes I can't remember my childhood holidays, but I can picture my father's photographs. All of them. And film – well, that's even better. To preserve a whole way of life through moving pictures. One day I want to be a cinematographer, or work for television. Do you know, I read in the paper that the whole country will have television after the war's over? They're setting it up through the local radio networks. Rediffusion, it's called.'

'Really?'

'I'd love to make film for television. I've got so many ideas – but hey, I'm boring you.' He laughed, knowing he wasn't.

'No, I love films. And I bet you get to meet all sorts of people.'

'Well, you have to start somewhere. And yes, you do. I meet all sorts. Like you – it's been nice to chat to you.' He smiled at me with twinkling eyes. 'You never know who you might meet.'

'Are you from London?' I stirred my tea, suddenly self-conscious.

'Yes, we all are. We're up here because we need a lot of outdoor shots, and it's just too much of a risk in London. Jerry would see our lights and there wouldn't be enough time to get everyone clear.'

'Is it very bad down there? We hear a lot about the V-bombs, the doodlebugs.'

He shook his head, blew out through his mouth. 'Awful. But you can't keep Londoners down. I tell you, it's wonderful to get away. I'm sick to death of dust and rubble and sad faces. It's so grey somehow.'

I glanced out of the window at the drizzle misting the windows. 'It's pretty grey here, too.'

'Not from where I'm looking.'

I blushed and gripped the red silky scarf that lay in my lap.

When I looked up he was still staring at me through narrowed amber eyes. 'It's night filming, so I'm free in the daytime if you'd like to take tea again.'

Gosh, he was bold. It took my breath away. There was a moment before I crashed back to reality. 'I'm engaged to be married,' I said bluntly. I drew my hand out so that the ring was in view.

His face lost its animated smile. 'Oh. Lucky man. Sorry to be so forward. I just thought it might be nice to have company. No offence meant.' His face had become distant, polite.

'None taken. Thank you very much for the tea.'

He did not seem to know how to continue, and I was too embarrassed, so after a few minutes while we both watched the rain trickling down the glass, he picked up his hat and stood, shifting his weight from foot to foot. 'Guess I'd better go and see how they're getting on. Maybe your friend's landed a part by now.'

I lifted my hand as if to wave, but then let it fall. I watched him as he strode over to the double doors. Matthew Baxter. I repeated his name to myself. Matthew Baxter with asthma. He probably asked girls out everywhere he went. And he did not look as if there was anything the matter with him, he looked as young and fit as them all. But he had brought Peter back to me like a thump in the chest.

A wave of guilt made me pull my coat round me, and look round to see if I could see anyone coming out of the other bar. Where was Patty? I wished they'd hurry up.

The double doors flew open and a crush of people crowded into the foyer, all talking at once.

'I'm in!' Patty grabbed me by the shoulders and gave me a smacking kiss on each cheek so I had to rub the lipstick away. 'I've got a card and everything!' She thrust a brown card in front of me with 'PASS' stamped across it in red ink.

'Oh, Patty, that's wonderful! Have you got a speaking part?'

'Course not. They only wanted extras, to walk up and down the platform and get out of trains and that. But won't it be exciting? I'll be able to get you Celia Johnson's autograph.'

We began to follow the others all trying to funnel out through the double doors. I turned once to see Matthew Baxter chatting animatedly with another young woman in a checked swing coat and fashionable turban. It gave me a stab of envy to see their smiles, and all at once I felt angry. He'd moved on quickly, hadn't he? But I mourned the glimpse I'd had of some possibility; the freshness of something new beginning. I wished I hadn't let the chance slip by, that I could call it back.

28

1955 Rhoda

HELEN LOOKED DIFFERENT. She'd had her hair cut and styled shorter so that it framed her face and made her look ridiculously young. She was wearing what looked like a new summer jacket in a soft green cotton. It suited her.

I pushed through the queue to get to her. Lewis's was busy as usual, with shoppers out for a summer bargain.

'I've ordered our usual,' Helen said. 'Is that all right?'

When we'd got our soup in front of us and had exhausted the small talk, I said, 'I was thinking, you've told me loads, and I've got really interested in all this stuff about the war, but it still doesn't tell me much about Peter during the five years he was away. I've spent hours in the library, but there's not much about it there. I was hoping I'd find out more, somehow.'

Helen stirred her spoon round in the bowl. 'Yes, I used to wonder why Archie liked doing all this collecting. Now he's gone, the souvenirs seem a bit empty without him to tell you the story. Sometimes I look at it all and it just looks like a pile of junk. But it all meant something to him. Evidence I suppose, that he was there.'

'I thought you might be able to fill in the gaps. Peter won't tell me a thing. He's got even worse lately, snappish with me whenever I ask him anything. Like he's given up on me.'

'Hmm,' Helen said. A moment later her face looked hot and shiny, and she stood to take off her jacket. 'It's gone suddenly warm,' she said.

'It's wonderful to have this good weather at last, isn't it?' I paused as she dabbed her face with a napkin and stuffed it in her handbag. 'You wouldn't tell him, would you, about what I told you last time – you know, about me having an affair?'

'Course not. What do you take me for?'

'Because I think he would still be hurt, even though it was so long ago. I don't think you get over that sort of thing. I'm lucky, Peter's always been faithful to me. His only vice is the cricket. He's out again on Saturday, some big match at a club in Manchester.'

Helen stirred her soup round again, staring into it instead of looking at me. 'You're not eating much,' I said. 'Is it all right?'

'Oh yes, it's fine. It's just, I'm not very hungry.' She was shifting in her seat, looking uncomfortable.

'It's the heat. Maybe we should have gone for a sandwich instead of soup. How are things with you? How is it at work?'

Helen cut me off before I'd finished speaking. 'Fine. Look, I'm not feeling very well. I think I need to go home.'

'Oh.' I put down my spoon. Was it something I'd said? 'You poor thing. What is it? Do you want to go to the Ladies?'

'No, no –' She was already up out of her seat.

'Can I get you a taxi or something? Or I'll walk you to the—'

'Please don't fuss. I'll be fine. It's a migraine, that's all. I get them sometimes. I can feel when one's coming on. Sorry about this.' She looked flustered, searched her handbag. 'Sorry. Look, here's some money for the bill.' She pressed some coins into my hand.

'I'll pay, don't worry.' But she was already gathering her bags. I stood up.

'Call me,' she said, and kissed me without making contact on the cheek.

'You take care,' I called after her retreating back.

I contemplated her untouched soup. Had I offended her in some way? I thought back over our conversation. Could she be upset that I thought she'd tell Peter about Matthew? She'd seemed rattled, not in pain. I had a niggling sensation something wasn't quite right, but try as I might, I couldn't put my finger on it.

29

1945 Peter

THEY HADN'T KILLED them yet and there had been plenty of opportunity. So the column must be going somewhere after all. They had got themselves near the front of the line, probably because their packs were on the sledge. For most, their packs banged against their backs, and the extra weight was intolerable to such weak men. Now the walk was uphill, some men were falling behind with exhaustion.

That morning Peter saw a couple of men jettison the cans of meat from their Red Cross packs, to make their burdens lighter. Harry leapt after them, and they all dug in their boots, trying to hold the sledge from sliding back. For they were skirting the edge of a mountain, winding slowly up. After they passed a crossroads the snow became muddy and flattened.

'Someone's been here ahead of us,' George said.

'Probably more war prisoners.' Peter scanned the road for evidence. There was a tin can with a ragged edge by the side of the track. A scrap of bloodied rag trodden into the slush here, a twist of tinfoil from a cigarette packet there. He didn't look too closely round the ditches at the boot prints and brown stains where men had stopped to relieve themselves.

'Do you think they're far ahead?' Archie asked.

'Can't tell. Not whilst we're still moving.'

Peter hauled on the rope with renewed enthusiasm, peering into the whiteness ahead for a sign of more men. In front of them, the truck slowed and its wheels skidded in the snow as it went off the road to avoid some obstacle. The wheels spun round and slush flew up in slashes of wet. The engine whined, then it seemed to find traction and slewed its way forward.

Lumps of grey baggage lay in the road. It was a moment before Peter realised the shapes were men. The snow had covered them with a fine film, but there was no mistaking the colour of their uniforms. Three men sprawled on the road, two face up, one face down. They were dead. They must be.

The two men marching ahead of them glanced down and one swivelled to look at them, made the *kaputt* gesture – finger across his throat – then pulled his coat tighter around himself and walked on. The other sped up his step to keep pace Peter was alongside the bodies when he heard a moan. The man who was face down twitched.

Peter let go of the sledge and made to hurry over. 'Better not.' Harry said. He grabbed hold of Peter's arm in a tight grip. 'Leave them! You'll get us killed.'

He wrenched his arm away and took no notice, bending down to the man and then rolling him over. The man groaned and pulled up his knees to his stomach. 'Here, fella,' Peter said, 'we're going to get you up.'

Archie hurried over. 'Let me. I owe it to Brodie.'

'Who's Brodie?' Peter asked.

'From the mine. The accident.' Peter remembered. But it seemed so long ago, he'd almost forgotten.

The man on the ground opened his eyes and focused blearily on Archie. Once he had made eye contact Peter saw

Archie's face soften. 'You're going to make it, mate,' Archie said. 'We're going home.'

A stupid promise, but Peter couldn't help liking Archie for it. Neither of them could bear to leave the man there, not if he was still alive. Peter felt the heat of the man's forehead with the tips of his fingers. His face was rosy despite lying in the snow. Peter's heart fell. A fever. He didn't reckon much to his chances.

'George! Over here. Help us,' he called.

Harry stared as George and Archie heaved the man to his feet. 'He's a Yank,' he said, 'look at that uniform.'

'So what?' Archie said.

'He's not one of ours. Leave him.'

'They're our allies, aren't they? We're expecting them to save us, for God's sake. Aren't we?'

At that moment Hauptmann Weinart and his aide appeared alongside in their truck. Peter stood out in their way so they had to stop.

'Please, we need transport for this man,' Peter said in German, standing up tall, though he felt dwarfed by the German's well-fed bulk, his smart green overcoat and fur-trimmed collar. He gestured to George and Archie, to the prisoner propped between them. 'He's ill. He needs a hospital.'

Harry, who was still by the sled, said, 'Don't, Pete.'

Hauptmann Weinart looked Peter up and down from the comfort of his seat. He barely glanced at the man hanging between the other two men. Then he shrugged. They all spoke enough German to understand the answer. 'We have no transport. If you want to bring him, carry him yourselves.'

'Right.' Archie's eyes took on a determined glint. Wordlessly he and George half-dragged the man to the makeshift sled. 'We'll lay him over this.'

Harry put his arms over the sledge. 'No. It's suicide. We can't take an ill man. What if we catch it?' Harry tried to drag the sledge away, but the runners meant it could not travel sideways.

Archie pushed his chin out threateningly at Harry, who backed off. 'He's coming with us. If you don't want to be part of it, then get your bloody pack out of our box and carry it yourself.'

Harry stood back, unable to find words. Archie squared his shoulders, his face was belligerent. It was the first time any of them had ever seen a spark like that in him. Around them the men parted to trudge past. The ill soldier hung over the box like a rag doll.

Archie turned to Harry. 'If it was you, wouldn't you want someone to stop? Or should we just leave you there, like those other poor buggers?' Harry dropped his eyes. 'Do something useful and get him some water.'

'I don't have to take orders from you.' Harry was mutinous.

Despite the fact that the man was skin and bone, they struggled to pull the extra load. He stank too. Dysentery probably; Peter had seen enough of it in camp to recognise its stench. Harry brought back water, but his expression was sour. Peter took the container from him and gave the ill man a drink but it just dribbled from his mouth. They did not ask him his name, and he did not tell them.

Every few hundred yards Peter had to stop to heave the ill man back on to the sledge because his inert body kept sliding off, and his legs and boots trailed in their way.

'Told you we should have left him,' Harry said.

They'd dropped much further to the back, just ahead of the twenty or thirty stragglers.

When Peter looked behind, one man was staggering

from side to side. The rear Wehrmacht truck ignored the followers and was keeping up with them, the main body of men. Peter had become so used to the drone of the engine that when it sputtered to a halt he stopped in his tracks to look round.

Two officers got out and tried to get the truck going again with much cursing. After banging about in the bonnet and boot, and a few more futile attempts to restart it, they unloaded their guns and gear from the back.

'I'm going to walk to the back, see if I can help the Jerries get it going,' Harry said.

'You mad bugger,' George said. 'Why? They won't give you a lift, you know. You'll only have to walk back up this hill again.'

'Doing them a favour might be useful.'

'Whose side are you on?' Peter said, more sharply than he meant to.

Harry gave him a cursory V sign, hitched his coat forward and tightened it round his neck. The snow was falling quicker now. Peter watched his hunched shoulders as he walked away, a dark silhouette against the white. Peter found even his walk irritating, the way his arms hung stiffly away from his body, the set of his neck in his shoulders. Harry hadn't gone more than ten yards when one of the guards spotted him and waving his rifle, yelled at him to get back in line. The guard was angry about the truck. Harry blundered back to them, tail between his legs.

'Told you,' Peter said.

Harry glared at him. Whilst they watched the Germans, Archie sucked nervously on a cigarette and coughed, as if he could feel the prickle of tension in the air.

The big guy cursed the truck again then picked up

his gun and fired at the ground. The stragglers fell flat, whimpering.

'*Auf! Auf!* Run!'

They were making the stragglers catch up. More shots were fired, the weary men fell into a ragged line. The smaller guard prodded the prisoners in the legs with his bayonet till they jumped and staggered forwards, grunting, desperate, arms flailing with the effort.

'We should do something,' Archie said.

'You going to pile them all on here then?' Harry said.

'Harry's right,' George sighed. 'We can't save them all.'

'If we don't try, what the hell's it all been for? Have they spent five years in a labour camp just to die out here?' Archie said.

'Some of them look pretty bad,' George said. 'As bad as this chap. And we could be marching for days more.'

Archie kicked at the snow. 'I can't bear to see any more like that, just left there to die. When we stop I'm going to try to help them. Someone has to.'

'That's the last thing we bloody need,' Harry said. 'Some do-gooder trying to save the world.'

Peter closed his ears. The constant bickering was driving him crazy He just wanted to end it. To get some peace. As if it wasn't enough to contend with, just the sheer effort of walking. The numb feet, the driving snow. The fear of becoming one of those grey lumps left to rot on the road.

30

1945 Rhoda

'HAVE YOU SEEN those new carriages over on the siding?' Patty said.

Patty and I were doing our usual – knitting in the refreshment room whilst we waited for the next train. 'Stationmaster says they'll be the refreshment cars. They're cleaning them. Where the stars will eat and that, when they're filming.'

'Won't they eat in here?'

'No, they have their own cooks. There's too many people for in here, he says.'

'Too many people?' I paused and knotted on another ball of khaki wool. 'How many are they bringing?'

'He reckons near on eighty.'

'You're kidding! Are there that many in the film? I thought it was only a shortie, a B feature.'

'They'll have all the technicians and sound men to feed. And us extras. And they'll want meals at all hours if it's night filming. Maybe we'll get London food. Heck, I bet they can get potatoes. I couldn't believe it last week when they started rationing potatoes.'

But I was no longer listening. I was wondering if I'd see Matthew Baxter again. Something about him had stuck in my mind. The way he held himself, the free and easy way he'd talked to me. I told myself it was just because nobody had complimented me for a long time. I was flattered, that was all.

The next day, Sunday, when I went up the ramp to get to the WVS room, there was already a building on the station where there hadn't been one before. Worse, it was right in front of my bookstall. It was a strange-looking wooden contraption, like half a wall, stuck out on to the platform. Trailing cables dangled out from two arc lamps overhead. The walls were made of painted canvas and wood. It looked flimsy and unconvincing. Two men in brown bibs and braces were up stepladders hammering it together. On a Sunday!

I'd no option but to walk past them. I paused and looked up at the window where they were attaching fake coping stones. 'Hello, miss,' one of them called cheerfully as I passed. 'WVS, is it?'

'Yes,' I called. 'Is this part of the set?' Which was a stupid question, but he didn't seem to mind.

'The outside of the refreshment room.' He pushed back his flat cap to look up at it. 'It doesn't look like much now, but you wait till it's lit.'

'What about the bookstall?'

'Don't worry, pet. It's only flattage. It'll come down in the day, be stored in that big wagon outside.'

I nodded, and looked over to the real refreshment room which was nothing like the wooden edifice he was constructing. Seeing my dubious face, he said, 'The inside will be filmed in the studio at Denham.'

'Not here then?'

'Can't get the right camera angles here. We need to have a missing wall at the front, so we can dolly in and out. But they're recreating it at Denham exactly the same as it is inside.

The set builders are brilliant. You won't be able to tell. Right down to the counter and the Whitbread plaque on the wall.'

'I'd no idea they went to such trouble.'

'Mr Lean always wants it right. I've been on all his films. He's a nice gent, but very keen on details. Someone's in there taking notes for him right now.'

The refreshment room was usually closed on a Sunday, but today it was open for all the carpenters and crew. When I pushed open the door the first thing I saw was a blaze of bright light, and Patty's back – her blonde hair and the wide padded shoulders of her coat. But it was the person opposite her who stopped me in my tracks. Matthew Baxter. He looked up as the draught from the door made the fire waver and smoke. I struggled my way past a tripod in the middle of the floor, and stepped over another black rubber cable. He stood up to greet me as Patty glanced over her shoulder, shielding her eyes from the glare of the lamp.

'This is my friend Rhoda,' Patty said. My shadow hovered over the table.

'We've been introduced already,' I said, 'at the audition.'

Matthew smiled at me, and I gave a half-smile back before I sat down and shrugged off my coat. The room wasn't very warm but I needed something to do. I took my time hanging the coat over the chair. Damn, the light would be showing up my face and I had no powder on. I got out my bag with the half-finished knitting and placed it in front of me, all the time acutely conscious of his eyes on me. I didn't dare look at Patty. She was sharp as a tack.

'Gosh, it's bright,' I said. 'I'll see all my dropped stitches.'

'They need to get every detail,' Patty said. 'Mr Baxter's been taking photographs and measuring up for the set they're making in London. That's why there's all these lights.'

'No point taking a picture if the light's wrong,' Matthew

said. His camera was on the table in its leather case right in front of me, a big expensive camera by the look of it. His conversation at the Station Hotel came back to me. I hid my hands under the table, slid my engagement ring round and round on my finger.

'Have you ordered anything?' I asked Patty.

'Evelyn's bringing tea. She's in the back.'

'I've just had a good idea,' Matthew said. 'I need to get an idea of scale. Will you two stand behind the counter there and I'll take a picture?'

'Oh, I don't think –' I shook my head, protesting, but Patty hauled me back to my feet, and Matthew was already attaching his camera on to its tripod.

'What a lovely idea. Come on, Rho, it'll be like we're in the film. Where do you want us?' Patty bustled me behind the counter and leaned forward on to it with her elbows, smiling broadly with her 'pose for the camera' look. I hung back, embarrassed.

'I think standing up – now hold on, I'll just move that out of the way.' He moved the empty glass cake-stand to the side. Can you put your arms around each other's shoulders – Patty? Now smile when I say "Ready".'

'Hey, what's all this?' Evelyn appeared grumpily from the kitchen.

'Come on, Eve, get in the picture,' Patty said.

I moved over and smiled tightly, knowing that I would look bleached out next to Evelyn's red lips and sooty mascara.

'Ready.'

A moment's silence, then a pop and a flash that made me jerk my head back. And another and another.

'Okay. I think I've got it. Thanks a million. They'll be really useful. When I've developed them I'll do you some copies. There's a printer in Morecambe who said I can use his studio. What luck, hey, finding a chap who'll let me use his darkroom! I might manage it tomorrow if I can get on the blower and Mr Havelock-Ellis lets me have a few hours off.'

'I'd like a copy,' Evelyn said. She gave him a toothy smile before going back to the kitchen.

'But don't go to any trouble for us,' Patty said.

'I need the shots for the designer at Denham, so it's no trouble at all. I'll get the lamp out of your way now. Can't have the station blazing away and attracting enemy bombers, can we?'

'Oh, I don't know. It might liven it up a bit!' Patty said.

I laughed with her, but sat back down, feeling awkward as Matthew carefully packed his camera into its case, making sure all the components were slotted into their correct places. He was absorbed in it for a moment before he disconnected the plug and cabling from the lamp.

'I'll go and put these in the holding truck –' he held out the cabling and tripod, '– and I'll come back for the lamp. Don't touch it, ladies, it will be hot.'

The door banged behind him.

'Well!' Patty's look was triumphant.

'Have you got your gloves finished?' I said. 'I've more wool here if you haven't. What time's the next train due?' I fumbled for my needles.

'He's a bit of all right, isn't he? Your type, I should think.' She was watching me closely through calculating eyes.

'Give over. I don't know what my type is. Peter, I suppose.'

'You know, a bit intellectual. Thoughtful. And there aren't many men about. I haven't seen a handsome man in ages. I hope a few more like him will be coming up for the film. He's got nice eyes.'

'Don't be silly, we've only known him a few minutes. He might be a complete bounder.'

Then I felt guilty. He'd behaved perfectly. Funny about Patty remarking on his eyes though. Hazel, brown flecked with gold. When had I noticed their colour? I squeezed my own eyes shut, as though that might erase him from my mind, along with the tingly feeling in my stomach.

Patty was watching me, winding wool from her ball. 'You're blushing,' she said.

'It's just warm in here. It must be that lamp. I'm glad he turned it off.'

'It's all right. I won't tell anyone. He is good-looking. But don't get any ideas, remember, your Peter will be home soon. I was reading the *Daily Mail* this morning and the Red Army are in Germany. There was a headline as well about our tanks smashing the Roer line. It will only be weeks now, they say.'

'I know Churchill's called for surrender, but nothing seems to be happening. And I've still not heard, I don't even know where Peter is any more, they—'

A noise of a horn, and the door banged open. Matthew hurried in with his trilby pushed back on his head.

'That horn means the cars have come for us,' he said, breathless. 'We've got to go back to the Low Wood Hotel now for a meeting with Mr Lean.' He licked his finger and touched the lamp with the tip of it to test its heat before picking it up. 'And when we're filming the station will be closed to people who haven't got a pass. So I might not see you again. If not, it's been nice meeting—'

'Oh, I've got a pass,' Patty said. 'They took me on as an extra, remember? And Rhoda works on the bookstall.'

I felt myself clam up, as if she'd said something embarrassing. But Matthew looked directly at me and smiled. 'Oh, that's good. I hoped I'd see you again. I'll stop by and buy a book. And if you change your mind about afternoon tea, you can leave a message for me with anyone on the crew.'

Patty glanced at me sharply, before saying lightly, 'What a shame. You work in the afternoons, don't you, Rhoda? And anyway, Mr Baxter, her fiancé will be back soon. He'll be first on that plane when the troops come home.'

His eyes dropped and there was a moment's pause, during which I clenched my hands in my lap. He took a breath and it looked as though he would reply, but in the end he just tipped his hat with his spare hand and walked out of the door.

'Patty, that was uncalled for.' I rounded on her.

'What?' She patted her curls into place as if it was of no account.

'Telling him about Peter. It was embarrassing. He was only being friendly, not asking me out or anything.'

'It looked more than "just friendly" to me.' Patty raised her eyebrows.

'You've changed your tune. A minute ago you were all for it. Who was it who said they hoped there'd be more handsome young men from London?'

'That was just a joke, you know it was. I didn't really think you'd actually do anything.'

'I'm not "doing" anything. Pass me that wool. Let's forget about him. I've already told him I'm busy. I'm not interested in Mr Baxter.'

But as we sat knitting together, I wondered if he would develop our pictures. I imagined him in the darkroom, tilting the developing fluid back and forth under the red light, watching my face appear out of the white paper, grainy and dark.

31

1945 Rhoda

IT WAS A hell of a day at work. A batch of troop trains were delayed and then they all arrived at once and the soldiers had to hang about the platforms. The bookstall was besieged by impatient men wanting their papers or something to read, and giving me sharp words when I couldn't serve them quick enough.

By the time I got home in the evening I was tired and not in a mood for any nonsense, so I was even more annoyed to find Mother in a state. Andrew had gone missing again.

'Can't you go and look for him, Rhoda?' she asked me. 'We had another spat. I told him off for being lazy and he shot past me again.'

I sighed. 'Do you know where's he gone?'

'I've no idea. He's beyond me. I can't seem to cope with him these days. He's so tall and awkward, and he just won't listen.'

'It's just a phase, Mother. He's ready for work, and hates being treated like a kid. He'll get over it.'

'And your pa doesn't help.' She indicated with a jerk of her head the shed at the bottom of the garden. 'He thinks everything's my fault. His idea of discipline is to ignore him until he needs the belt, and now he's just too old for that. Don't tell him Andrew's gone again, promise?'

'Come on, Mother, sit down. I'll make you a cup of tea. We've both had a hard day by the sounds of it. Let Andrew take care of himself. We'll have a quiet few minutes before they come in demanding their supper.'

'Would you?'

'Sit there now, and I'll bring the tea.' I spooned the precious tea into the pot, adding a bit extra that I knew I shouldn't, and poured on the water until it steamed from the spout. When we had our cups in front of us I said, 'You shouldn't let Pa shout at you that way, you know.'

She pursed her lips as if to reject the idea, but then sighed. 'I don't know. I don't know how to stop him. He's in the habit of it now. You'd never believe it, but he used to be such a quiet young man, before he went to war in France. I don't think he thought we'd see another war in our lifetime.'

'I don't know how you stand it, how he treats you.'

'I have to. Sometimes I see something soft underneath, the old Billy, but then it gets squashed out by his temper.'

'Do you think you could manage without him?' The words were out before I had time to think.

She shook her head wordlessly, emphatically, before answering. 'Don't be ridiculous. He's my husband. Whatever he is. I can't do that, think of the scandal of it. And I couldn't do that to him.' A moment whilst she looked down at her cup and saucer. 'I've no complaints. He's been a good provider.'

I stirred my tea, watched her mouth set into a stubborn line. I paused a moment, aware of some chasm opening before I said, 'You might be able to live with it, but I don't know if I can stand it any more. I can't bear his rages. They make every day like treading on eggshells.'

For a moment her voice wavered. 'You're not thinking of moving out? Not yet, where would you go?'

'Mother, I'm twenty-four. I'll have to some time. The war will be over, Peter will be home and I shan't be living here for ever. And I worry about you, about what will happen when Andrew and I have both gone. You know – how you'll cope, with him.'

She stood. 'This tea's not hot enough. I'll put some more water in it.' She went to the stove and put the kettle back on the hotplate. She did not turn again to face me, but I saw her back, her shoulders rise as she folded her arms, the straps on her apron tighten. I saw how her hair was escaping from its grips at the back, and how suddenly forlorn it made her look. After a few moments of standing there, she pulled open the oven door and bent to look inside. A smell of sausage drifted out. 'Nearly done,' she said. Her voice was brisk.

I watched her tip more water into the teapot in a deliberate stream and replace the patchwork cosy. When she came back she smiled brightly. 'Let's cross that bridge when we come to it, eh, love? And let's have a bit more respect for your father too.'

After that I drank my tea silently. One thing I was sure of, I wanted more out of life than my mother had. I had to get out of there, I was suffocated. It was not just my father, it was the sense of life passing by without me. Five long years I'd waited for Peter. A rush of restlessness rose up in the pit of my stomach. Life was running through my fingers like water. As for Peter, I sometimes thought he was more my imagination and memory than a real man at all.

'Brr, it's parky tonight!' Patty bustled her way into our hallway in a flurry. Mother looked up and down at her worn-out teddy-bear fur coat and woolly hat as if assessing how much longer they might last, but Patty did not seem to notice as she was in full flow. 'Edna's poorly and they need another helper to serve in the canteen so I told them Rhoda'd come down. It's good money. And you get to see all those film stars.' Mother opened her mouth to interrupt but there was no stopping Patty. 'They need people to serve up, Mrs King,' Patty said. 'It's just the one night.'

'What about your pa?' Mother was doubtful, worried. 'How will you get in? What time will you—'

'I'll take a key, don't wait up.' I grabbed my gabardine and my felt cap from the hooks by the door and slipped the key from the sideboard in to my pocket. We hurried out of the door all giggles.

'Wait! You'll need an overall,' Patty said.

'Oh, flip!' I rushed back for it. 'See you later, Mother,' I called, cramming my pinafore into my cloth bag, and we hurried away. As we went I saw Pa just coming back from work.

'Quick, in here!' We dodged into the back alley whilst he passed. I knew there'd be trouble once Mother told him where I'd gone, and I didn't want to hang around long enough for him to stop me.

Patty's heels clacked on the pavement as I clung to her arm to avoid tripping over anything in the dark. There was a lovely moon which silvered the rooftops and I could almost smell the frost beginning to bite. I breathed in a huge gulp of cold air, felt my lungs expand.

The station yard was full of big generating wagons, and knots of people waiting in their outdoor coats. Light poured upwards in a big square shaft from the railway platform into the sky. A train must be in too as there was a thick plume of smoke billowing upwards. As we got nearer a sleek Rolls-Royce with its headlights shadowed slid past us and pulled up in front of the main entrance.

Patty grabbed me tight. 'That's Celia Johnson and her dresser. Come on, run! If we hurry we'll see her.'

We pelted down the road, coats flapping, in time to see the driver hand Celia Johnson out of the car. She was a tiny slim figure in a pale pink coat and a rather ridiculous hat, but we couldn't get close enough for a good look because an attendant was hooking a rope back across the entrance gates to stop us going in.

'Does she get dressed here?'

'No, she always comes ready to film, in the costume and everything, but there's a fire lit in the Ladies Waiting Room too in case they need her to change.'

The attendant grinned when he saw Patty, and I realised it was Mr Naylor, our council street sweeper, in a new uniform, but still with his old woollen scarf wound twice around his neck, and his habitual pipe on his lip. He sucked at it, and then greeted us: 'All right, Patty, Rhoda.' He seemed taller and straighter now he was a doorman, instead of just the man I used to watch from the window scraping up old Player's packets from the gutters.

By the time we got into the station proper, Celia Johnson and her dresser had vanished. Patty seemed to know her way around, and hauled me past the obstacles of lights and cameras on trolleys, bogeys full of plugs and cabling and round to the refreshment-room kitchen. They'd already filmed Patty's part on the first day and then told her she wasn't needed any more. But typical of Patty, she'd managed to blarney her way in on the action. Even if it was just peeling potatoes.

I was nervous, unsure whether I'd be any earthly use in the kitchen, but already the burners were going and several girls I didn't know were peeling turnips in a very business-like way.

'Here, take these.' A tall, dark girl with a London accent

and her hair tied up in a headscarf pushed a bowl towards me, and handed me a knife.

Patty winked and started on a pile of potatoes with gusto. Kidneys and bacon were coming up on the trains, but there were still onions to chop, potatoes and turnips to peel, then the ovens to get going. When Patty had collared me into saying yes, I hadn't really expected to be peeling turnips with not a film star in sight. But I hadn't seen so much food in years. Mother would have fainted dead away at the sight of it.

If I could bring in a bit of extra money Mother would be able to pay the doctor for her bad back. I'd do one night anyway, see how I went. I smiled at the dark girl opposite who was obviously in charge, and she nodded at me. 'Hilary,' she said, before scalping the heads of the turnips with enthusiasm.

We got everything done and the sautéed onions smelt divine. I'd almost forgotten that there was a film being made on the platform outside, except I glanced at the clock above the door and saw it was one o'clock in the morning. How on earth would I be fit for selling papers tomorrow?

'You okay with waiting on tables?' Hilary asked. We were to be waitresses in these makeshift 'canteens' which were really railway carriages joined together. One First Class and one Third Class. 'You'll do Edna's shift in First Class, then,' Hilary said.

'I'll take that one if you like –' Patty jumped in – 'as I've already done a few nights.'

'No,' Hilary said, 'you stay where you always are. It'll make it more awkward when Edna comes back otherwise.'

'You jammy animal,' Patty whispered. 'First is where the stars eat.'

'Oh.' I brushed down my overall and hoped I looked tidy. Then thought, so what if they're film stars, they still have to eat like the rest of us. I glanced at the clock guiltily. Mother would probably still be awake, waiting up for me.

The food had to be carried on the station luggage trolleys in steaming metal pots down the subway and up the ramps to the dining cars. After being in the hot kitchen the cold air made me shiver. We hitched the trolley over a lot more cabling and wheeled it past cameras that looked like leggy black insects.

There was nobody about except a man in a homburg hat taking a cartridge out of one of the cameras. Thank goodness Carnforth Station has no steps, I thought as three of us girls dragged the soup up the slope. Even the trolleys themselves with their iron wheels weighed a ton.

I glanced up at the clock on the platform and saw that it had stopped. 'Look, the clock's wrong,' I said. 'They'll need to get it fixed.'

'It's not our clock. It's one they've put up specially. It's got hands they can move round,' Hilary said.

'People will miss their trains,' I giggled.

'No, you dumb cluck, they take the false front off in the morning,' Hilary said, but she was laughing.

'I hope they forget.' Patty tugged at the handle as the trolley was stuck in a rut. 'That'd be a lark.'

The dining-car door swung open and two smartly dressed railway porters got down to help Hilary and me lift the food containers up through the narrow door.

'Toodle-oo.' Patty dragged the trolley with the other vat of soup away down the platform.

I clambered into the carriage, which was the last word in luxury with velvet curtains festooned with a bobble fringe, candle lamps on all the tables, and pristine white cloths. It was noisy and convivial with much laughter, and hazy with smoke from cigarettes and pipes. Unfortunately it was also so cold you could see your breath, and with the steam from the soup the windows soon fogged up. I saw one chap wipe at the glass with his sleeve, despite the fact that the only view he'd ever get was of more trains stuck in a siding.

I didn't recognise a soul; all the so-called stars were muffled up to the ears in coats and scarves.

The porters and Hilary and I served the soup. Nobody took any notice of me – it was as if I was invisible. They just carried on talking and laughing in their bright London voices. As I put the bowl down in front of one of the men, a slightly stooped chap with a mournful expression, someone else nudged past and I slopped the mushroom soup on to the tablecloth.

'Careful!' the mournful man said.

'Sorry, sir,' I said, and rushed to fetch a cloth to wipe it up.

'That's Trevor Howard,' whispered Hilary.

He flapped his napkin at the stain with a lot of sighing and tutting. When I tried to wipe underneath his plate he frowned impatiently. After we'd served the main course and then the dessert of bananas and custard, and not a single one of them had even smiled or said thank you, I marched back down the ramps, bristling with annoyance.

I threw off my overall. 'How do you stand it?' I raged to Patty. 'They treat us like dirt!'

Everyone stared at me. There was a moment's silence. I caught a glimpse of Hilary's wide eyes.

'Do you know, they were complaining about the sweet? Bananas! We haven't even smelt a banana for years, and there they are complaining about it, pushing it round their plates. There's people up here would kill for a banana. They don't know they're born.'

'Well, we get to take home the leftovers, so I don't know why you're complaining,' Patty said.

'I don't want their leftovers.'

'But a minute ago you said you'd kill for a banana,' Hilary said.

'I didn't say that – I said I don't want their leftovers.'

'Do you want bananas like them, or not?' Patty shrugged impatiently, 'I don't understand. What do you want?'

I was at a loss to explain. I didn't know. I looked at Patty hopelessly. I couldn't really understand myself. I wanted a different life, maybe their life. But at the same time there was something not right about them expecting to be waited on like this, not when men like Peter were fighting for their liberty, and for the first time I understood why the word 'sir' had made Peter go to war.

'Sometimes I just don't get it with you,' Patty said. 'You don't know you're born. Other girls would give their eye teeth to wait on Trevor Howard.'

The atmosphere between Patty and me remained strained but I was determined to finish the shift and be paid. Once the pots had been scrubbed I was free to leave. Hilary packed me four portions of leftovers in a biscuit tin.

'Waste not, want not,' she said cheerfully, handing me the weighty tin, which made me feel even worse about my earlier outburst.

On top of the tin was a small brown envelope. I had to go out the back way because they were filming. Once out of the door I paused, set the biscuit tin on the window ledge and took out a cigarette. I had a churned-up feeling in the pit of my stomach. I needed something to calm me. One match couldn't hurt, I thought to myself, not when the whole sky was ablaze with arc lights.

But I struggled to get the damn thing to light; the matchbox must have got damp. Giving up, I tore open the brown envelope instead and was astonished to count out twenty-six shillings. More than I earned for a whole week at the bookstall. And that just for scrubbing turnips! It was silly money. I thrust the coins into my pocket.

I was just about to pick up the tin of leftovers and cross the road when I heard voices. Matthew Baxter and two older men in trilby hats were walking across the car park to one of the big Ford vans. The other men were loaded up with lights and cabling and tripods, and one was pushing a bogey full of wicker baskets and suitcases. Matthew was going to pick up one end of a basket, but the man with the moustache wrestled it from his hands and said, 'No lifting, remember.'

I should get on home. The van doors clanged shut and I heard the engine growl into life. Matthew and his friend turned to go back to the station. Afraid they'd see me, I shot back behind the corner of the building but my elbow knocked the tin off the ledge and the whole thing clanged down.

'Oh!' I let out a cry. The lid had burst open so kidneys and bacon and mash had slopped all over the pavement. Of course there was no hiding then. I was scraping the mess off the flags with the lid when two pairs of neat brown brogues came into view.

'You all right?' Matthew said, bending over, hands on his knees.

In the background the van revved up. Lights grazed across the building, making me blink.

'I'll survive. My own stupid fault. I dropped this tin. What a mess.' I stood up, the tin lid covered in gravy in my hand. Matthew straightened and I caught a glimpse of his amused expression.

'Heavens,' said the man with the moustache. 'What on earth is it?'

'Kidneys and mash, leftovers. I was taking them home.'

'Oh, those – jolly tasty I thought. Good not to waste them.' He smoothed his moustache with a finger. 'I have to say, I hope they're not going home now they've been on the pavement!'

It was a relief that someone had enjoyed the meal. I relaxed a little. 'Actually, yes. I will take them. My father keeps a pig, so he'll think he's in clover. The pig, I mean, not Pa.' We all laughed.

Matthew said, 'This is my friend Ed Owen. Ed, this is Rhoda. She works on the bookstall, isn't that right?'

'How do you do.' I went to hold out my hand but realised I was still holding the dripping lid. Ed grinned and mimed shaking my hand.

Matthew stooped and gingerly picked up the tin and held it out whilst I manoeuvred the lid on to it. 'Here.' He brought a handkerchief out of his pocket with his free hand and passed it to me.

'Thanks.' I wiped my hands and then realised I couldn't really give it back to him, all covered in gravy like that, but he held out his hand for it, rubbed it over the tin, then stuffed it back in his jacket pocket.

'Have you got far to go?'

So far I had avoided looking directly into his eyes, but now I looked up. There was a sudden tension between us, like a wire. 'No, just around the corner.'

'Let me see you home then,' he said. I felt myself grow hot with embarrassment, but hoped neither of them had noticed in the dark.

'There's no need, it's only a step.'

'Oh, go on,' Ed said, 'he'll be hell to live with if you don't let him. Anyway, he's harmless, our Matthew.'

'All right then, if it's no trouble.'

'A pleasure,' Matthew said, but I couldn't help seeing the sly wink that Ed gave Matthew as we went.

The town was deserted; out of range of the railway station there were no lights anywhere. The stars glimmered above the grey silhouettes of the rooftops. We walked up past the post office, crossed the road and turned right into the terraces with their taped-up windows. In the dark I could hear Matthew's breath, a regular rhythm as he walked. Neither of us spoke; I didn't know what to say to him, and he didn't say a word.

'This is it,' I said. It had come so soon. I paused near the corner of our street and got out my key. I didn't want to risk any of the neighbours seeing me.

'Can we go round the block again?' he said. 'I've been thinking how to put it. Come on, just a few more minutes. It won't matter, it's late enough already.'

So we walked past the end of the street and up round on to High Street. After a moment I heard him take a deep breath. 'I'm sorry,' he said. 'I know you're engaged, and to a good chap too. But I just wanted to say, I wish you weren't.'

My heart began to hammer in my chest. I stopped and he stopped too. A cat ran across the street, a blur of ears and tail. In my pocket, the evening's coins slid warm over my fingers.

He turned to look at me. 'I mean, there's something about you. I had the pictures developed, and they're lovely. You're very photogenic, did you know that? I'll have to show you. I watched them develop and then I just spent a long time looking at your face. It's the sort of face that I ...' He stopped speaking then, and I realised I was hanging on his words, longing for him to continue.

'The sort of face that sank a thousand ships, you mean.' I was flippant, but it was because I was flustered. I needed to try and get back some sort of equilibrium.

'No, 'he said softly, 'the sort of face I'd like in my life, that's all. He's a lucky man.'

'Not so lucky. He's in a prisoner of war camp. In Silesia.' I saw Matthew register the information and his eyes close tight to shut out his embarrassment.

'Oh Lord. Look, I'm sorry. I've gone straight in with both feet again. I seem to be always apologising. How long has he been—?'

'Five years. Almost since the beginning.'

He shook his head and let out a whistle through his teeth. 'Sheesh, that's rough.'

Tears sprang into my eyes, and I put my hand up to my nose. He didn't try to comfort me, just stood and watched. 'I can't give you my handkerchief. Not unless you want a face full of gravy.' His eyes crinkled and I burst out laughing.

How quickly the heart can change. One minute I was sad, the next helpless with laughter. Suddenly everything seemed incredibly funny. I laughed until I was doubled over, and so did he.

'Oh, don't!' he said, as if it was all my fault. He propped himself up against the wall of the hotel, wheezing with laughter until he had recovered enough to speak. 'Look, I'd better be getting back or Ed'll think the worst of me.'

We walked back, still giggling, the way we had come, until it subsided and the silence rang loud in our ears.

At the end of my street I stopped and he turned to face me. 'Are you working tomorrow? On the bookstall?'

I hesitated. A small war of my own went on in a split second. 'Yes,' I said.

'Then I'll come and buy a book. We can be friends. Shake?' He held out his hand.

Without thinking I took it. His fingers were warm; they squeezed mine and I made no attempt to free them.

'Goodnight, Rhoda,' he whispered, and let my fingers hang a moment before they dropped. My name sounded different, sophisticated, from his lips. As he walked away he turned to give a salute, his coat swinging as he went. I let out a long shuddering breath. My legs were shaking. I almost ran down the street, fumbled to get my key in the lock and crept inside.

The house was cold, the fire out, but Mother was asleep in the chair, her slippered feet resting on the hearthrug. I glanced at the wooden clock on the mantel – ten to four. Next to it was a picture of Peter in uniform. His mother had brought it round for me; they'd had it taken the day before he left. Peter's eyes seemed to be following me as I crossed the room, his face a silent reproach. I turned it face down.

32

1955 Helen

THE TELEPHONE RANG and Helen leapt towards it, but stopped with her hand over the receiver. She let it ring three more times before picking up. She waited with her heart thumping for the operator to connect her.

'Hello, Helen?' The voice was crackly, nasal. A wave of disappointment. It wasn't him.

Helen tucked her hair behind her ear so she could hear better, and put on her bright voice, 'Hello, Rhoda, how are you?'

'Listen, I'm coming down to Lancaster to do some shopping on Friday and I wondered if I could call in, for a coffee, and to see some more of Archie's things. In the afternoon some time?'

Helen paused. Conflicting thoughts were running through her head. 'Both of you, or just you?'

'No, it'll be just me.'

Helen exhaled, relieved. 'Yes, that'll be fine. How about half-past two?'

After Rhoda rang off Helen went and sat on the sofa in the lounge and picked up one of the photograph albums she'd got out last night; not Archie's wartime albums but the personal ones of holidays and the family. She thumbed over the pages until she came to photographs of Peter and Archie that she'd taken about four years ago in the back yard.

It had been a lovely day and she'd put the dining chairs out there so the men could chat in the sun. She'd taken the picture from the kitchen window, the Box Brownie pressed to her stomach. When she called out 'Cheese!' both men turned, surprised. Archie was blurred – he'd turned too fast – but the photo had caught Peter well. She could almost feel the startle in his eyes.

She examined him, the man she talked to almost every day, his slightly Roman nose, his dark hair parted to the side. A handsome face, distinguished-looking. His calls had got more frequent. He phoned from his office at school as he always had, sometimes before she went to work, sometimes in the late afternoon when her house calls to patients were done. She knew she shouldn't encourage him, but she looked forward to it, and she told herself there was nothing wrong. They'd known each other for years, hadn't they?

Lately, he'd taken to telling her what he was going to listen to on the radio, and then in the evenings she'd sit and know he was listening too. She never pictured Rhoda sitting next to him. She had put them in separate compartments in her mind. Part of her knew it couldn't go on, but she was unable to help herself. She snapped the photograph album shut, put it down on the settee and rubbed both hands over her face.

The telephone was mutinously silent. She willed it to ring. These days she hurried home from work, in case he called. What if she was out? She'd miss him and then she'd have to wait ages before she could hear his voice again. When it rang though, she always let it ring a few times, so he wouldn't know she'd been sitting waiting.

She stared at the geometric pattern on the carpet without

really seeing it. The thought of Peter made her insides churn with anticipation. Until recently he had simply been Archie's old pal from the war. Of course she was aware that he was an attractive man too, but since she had been on her own, friendships with men had taken on a new significance. She knew it, and so did they. Was it her imagination or were men different with her now?

Maybe she was being silly. Perhaps Peter only meant to be a friend and there was no more to it than that. It was treading a dangerous line, she knew, coming between a man and his wife. She liked both of them. She knew she should tell Peter she was meeting Rhoda. It was dishonest not to, and he'd be hurt if he found out they'd deceived him. But wasn't it up to Rhoda? Surely it was Rhoda who should tell him.

33

1945 Peter

THE MEN WERE in a bad way. More had been left behind, the rest clung to each other for support. The blizzard caused them to look only at their boots, at the tracks of the man in front. Talking was impossible in these conditions, the spittle froze on their lips. There was no longer any sense of being guarded because the weather was so appalling the guards could not see to shoot straight even if they'd wanted to.

Towards the end of the column Peter and Archie pushed the sledge, half-leaning on it to prop them up. The man on top had ceased to groan. Dead, probably, Peter thought. He felt for a pulse in the man's neck. Nothing. He was cold as a fish and stiffening fast. Peter gestured to the others to help and they carried the corpse off to the side of the track.

Behind them a bottleneck of men formed, waiting until they could move again, too tired to care. The wind blew snow in swirls around them. Archie fumbled through the man's pockets looking for something. His fingers could not open the buttons of the man's coat. 'His papers,' came Archie's muffled voice from under his scarf, 'so we can let his family know.'

But it was too much for Archie to do, too much effort. Understanding, George beckoned him away.

'Wait,' Harry said. He pulled hard at the man's boots.

'What are you doing?' Peter shouted over the wind.

'Mine leak.'

Bloody Harry. There was something not right about taking a dead man's boots. Peter pulled him away. Harry protested, but George came to help Peter drag him off.

They left the snow to cover the soldier, struggled on. Such a feeling of relief once the extra weight was gone. The lightness of the sledge, the easy slide of the runners. For a while this sensation was all that bore Peter forward; he couldn't think straight, not with the whistle of the wind, the invisible sky whirling a blur of white.

He didn't like to admit it, but Harry had been right, it had all been a waste of their effort. But carrying the sick man had bonded them together, reminded them they were a team, given them a common purpose. It had been Archie's idea. Peter looked sideways at Archie, doggedly plodding on. He could not help but feel a glimmer of admiration for him.

Some hours later they hit a main road, a track churned by tanks and armoured vehicles. Maybe this meant they were approaching a town or a village, somewhere to rest, get in front of a fire. Their coats were wet and needed to dry if they weren't to freeze hard at nightfall. He kept a lookout for a signpost to tell him where they were, but there was none.

The road was wide and clogged with people fleeing in the opposite direction. The carts, which teetered on the rutted compacted snow, were piled high with trunks, cooking pots, even sticks of furniture. The refugees were as miserable-looking as the English prisoners. Bundled up in rugs and cloths to keep out the cold, they were mostly women and children – a people which could have been any nationality,

Czechs, Poles or Germans. Weary and haggard, hollow-eyed with fatigue and fear, they did not even look their way.

One thing was certain, it must be worse where these people had come from to make them want to take to the roads in this weather.

'I heard shelling earlier,' Harry said.

'I didn't hear anything,' George said.

Peter listened, straining to hear distant fire, but there was no noise except the creaking of frozen leather boots and the stamping of feet, the jingle of metal against metal on backpacks.

Some time later they were assigned new guards. These were older than the previous guards and the rumour quickly went round that all fit Germans were being sent to the front to fight the Russians. The new guards were sour-faced and surly and anxious to be moving. They did not want to stand about in the cold, despite their fur-collared coats and sturdy gauntlets.

Peter looked to Archie, 'You okay?'

Archie gave him a ghost of a smile.

Peter counted the notches on the lid of the box. Seventeen. It seemed far longer than that. It was important to remember what day it was. He thought of his father, his meticulous record-keeping. He had kept note of the days for him. And of course for Rhoda. She had become like a guiding star, not even a thought any more, but just a feeling, a sense of direction. He wanted to lie back in that womanliness, breathe in softness and scent, to get away from uniforms and armies, and unwashed men.

But from now on it would be harder. They'd been ordered to leave the box behind.

Thank God he and Archie had spent their previous years labouring in the fields. Their muscles were used to working, they had built up endurance through hard work in the outdoors. Many officers who'd had a softer regime had given up, been left by the side of the road to fend for themselves or die.

Stomachs groaning with hunger, the four men devoured what was left of the Red Cross parcels rather than carry it.

'Better in than out,' Peter said.

They saved one tin of meat for another day, but shared the milk powder out, pouring it into tin mugs between cupped hands to stop it blowing away. Mixed with snow it gave them a few sweet fizzy mouthfuls. Archie found a small bar of chocolate that had fallen through to the bottom of the box. He cracked it solemnly into four pieces. 'Emergency rations, lads,' he said.

'Hey! That's not fair. What if we get separated?' Harry said as George made to stow the last remaining tin of meat in his pack.

'I can't cut the bloody thing in half, can I?' George said. 'And I can cope with the extra weight.'

'*Schnell!*' The old guard shouted and gestured to them to hurry.

Peter stuffed his ration of cigarettes into his stiff damp pack, along with spare socks and underwear. Odd how these garments represented in some strange way the civilised world, though actually they were only any use if you were a crazy man and prepared to undress in below-freezing temperatures.

'Bye, old chap,' George said, patting the box on the lid.

Without it, they felt as though they'd lost their last defences.

That evening they were issued with a rare portion of stale black bread brought by truck from one of the villages.

'No! Save some of it,' George said, as they fell to tearing it with their teeth.

It was too late for Harry, who had already devoured his. But Peter saw Archie stuff some in his pocket, and forced himself to do the same.

Another night by the side of the road, this time in a tumbledown barn surrounded by fallen masonry part-buried in the snow. Sleep was fitful, and Peter dreamt again of market stalls full of fruit. He wanted to stay in the dream, but there was a smudge of light coming. Dawn.

He kept his eyes shut, hoping for a few more minutes. A boot in his ribs, as Archie almost tripped over him in his haste to get up.

'Give it back,' yelled Archie.

Peter opened one eye. 'Bloody hell, Archie! Can't a man get some sleep?'

He was just in time to see Harry dodge away, with Archie running after him, reaching out to seize hold of him by the coat. Harry roughly pushed Archie away, but one hand was still trying to cram a hunk of bread into his mouth.

'Bastard!' Archie grabbed Harry's wrist and pulled it down, tried to pry the fingers open.

Peter jumped up, but his legs were numb and he almost fell. 'What the—'

'He took the bread from my pocket,' Archie said.

Peter leapt in to help. He got hold of an arm to restrain Harry but Harry was writhing, pulling to get away.

'Let go!' Harry swung the fist with the bread at Archie, a practised left hook, and it connected with the side of his face. Archie staggered backwards, clutching his jaw. His eyes widened in shock and pain. Peter heard a whooshing noise in his ears, his stomach seemed to come upwards into his chest. The view turned grainy, and he could no longer see anything except Harry's satisfied face.

From somewhere a rush of fury came.

He grasped Harry by the lapels. Harry raised a hand to strike out, but he was too late. Peter let go of his sleeve. The whites of Harry's eyes glinted, looking feverishly left and right for escape even as Peter's arm swung back.

When Peter's balled fist came forward it was backed by a tide of five years' frustration.

Harry's chin jerked back and he lifted up off his feet into the air.

A crunch as his head hit the ground; his woollen cap landed like an upturned cup in the snow. The air exhaled gradually from him, deflating like an empty sack.

Peter stood panting, holding his hand where the knuckles had smashed into Harry's chin. Where had his strength come from? Harry was splayed on the road. Peter was ready for him to jump up and come for him. He held his fists up, his knees bent to spring forward.

But Harry did not move. His hand was open, the black bread resting next to the open fingers.

Archie did not go to pick it up. 'Jesus, Pete. What have you done?'

Peter could not talk. His mouth felt stopped. He wiped his brow.

From under Harry's ear a slow trickle of red.

George appeared, knelt down. Felt Harry's chest, listened at his nose. Lifted his head. Underneath was the edge of a boulder embedded in the snow. It was slick with blood.

Peter backed away as Archie hurried in.

Archie squatted next to George, shouting in Harry's ear, 'Harry, come on. Harry.' Archie looked to George for reassurance. 'He's not dead. He can't be. He took my bread from my pocket. He hit me.' He turned to look at Peter. 'He hit me, didn't he?'

Peter nodded, trying to bring some sense back to the world.

George looked up. 'Christ. I think his neck's broken. '

Peter felt his legs go from under him, then nothing. He covered his head with his hands, rolled himself into a ball, hugging his knees. He knew nothing else until Archie came and hauled him to his feet. 'Don't think. Just get your feet moving. We've got to march on.'

'I can't. What about Harry?'

'He's dead. You know he's dead. We've got to keep going or be left behind.'

A guard shouted at them to get moving. Nothing made sense any more; something had happened and he could not think. His brain was like cotton wool.

'Where are we going?'

'Who the hell knows. Come on, take hold of my arm and walk.' Archie towed him forward. 'Walk, for Christ's sake.' Peter felt his legs strain to get a grip against the icy ground. Ahead, George's bent figure ploughed on, his boots skidding to get purchase, the pack bulging on his back.

Next to him was an empty space where Harry used to be. Peter shrank into himself.

They were leaving Harry behind.

His thoughts struggled to make a purchase, just as his feet did. He could never go home. The picture of Harry's open fingers against the snow hung transparently over all his thoughts. In England his mother would be ironing the table-coth as usual in the kitchen, unaware. Rhoda would be smiling at ordinary people over the counter in the bookstall.

He could never go back there, never look into their faces knowing what he had done.

34
1945 Rhoda

ANDREW SAT AT the table, his homework books out in front of him, but he was gazing into space, chewing the end of the pencil. As I passed I saw his previous mark of four out of ten and a lot of red writing. At this rate he'd never get his School Certificate. Andrew saw me looking, frowned, and covered the page with his hand.

I scraped the cinders from the fire and saved the biggest black ones, discarding the chalky residue. Mother was baking in the scullery, her usual Friday task ready for the weekend.

'Who was that you were outside with last night?' Andrew asked.

'Nobody.'

'It was a man. I saw him out of the window.'

'It was just Frank, Patty's husband. He walked me home.'

'It didn't look like Frank.'

'Well, it was. Now shut up and get on with your work.'

I stood up from laying the fire and saw Peter's eyes looking straight out at me from the photograph. Mother must have stood it back up. I picked up the frame and stared at it, hoping to feel something, but there was nothing. I couldn't see past the image no matter how I tried; couldn't conjure him up in my mind any more. The last letter from him was years ago, and I'd stopped sending any to him since I'd had no reply.

Was it my imagination, or did he look sad already, even in that photograph? I put out my finger to touch the slight lines around his eyes. *Are you alive?* I asked him silently. *Speak to me. Tell me.*

No answer. I could hear the scrape of Andrew's pencil, the drumming of his heels on the chair legs. 'Aw, you soppy thing,' Andrew said.

I put the photograph down hurriedly. 'Oh, be quiet.'

Cross, I twisted paper into knots and laid the fire. When I lit it, blue smoke leaked out in my face, making me cough. I held a newspaper over the fireplace to encourage it, squatting on my haunches. Should I go back to the canteen tonight?

A flutter of excitement. I remembered the sound of Matthew's laughter, full-bodied as if it shook his whole chest. I said his name in my head. He'd said he wished I wasn't engaged. Then again, he probably said that to every girl he met. What made me think I was so special? But there was something. I knew there was something between us – a tingling recognition I had never felt with Peter.

I was so deep in thought the paper whooshed into flame and I had to thrust the whole thing into the fireplace where it blazed into flakes of black soot.

'Is it lit?' Mother called from the scullery.

'She's only burning the blooming house down,' Andrew called.

Whilst the fire took, I carried the photograph of Peter upstairs and put it in my drawer. I felt bad sliding the drawer shut, but I didn't want him looking at me all the time like that. When she came in, Mother noticed its absence straight away.

'Where's that picture of Peter?'

'I took it up to my room.'

'Never mind, love.' She came over and put her arms round my shoulders. 'I know you miss him, but it will soon be over. Everyone says so. I bet he'll be back walking through that door the minute they let him out.'

I shrugged her off. She meant to be kind, but she just did not understand. 'I'll be out tonight again,' I said.

'You were very late last night. I must have dozed off.'

'Pa was in, wasn't he?' I said, to divert her.

'No. He got called off, on another night shift.'

'Where is he now?'

'God knows. Carlisle? Manchester? He doesn't tell me anything any more.' She sighed. 'You look peaky. Are you sure it's a good idea, working nights?'

'It's good money.' I went to my pocket and counted out a whole pound on to the table.

'Oh my Lord! Where did that come from?'

'From last night. For you, so you can pay the doctor for your bad back.'

'I can't take that.' She stared at it, wiping her hands down her apron.

'Yes, you can. There'll be more. I'll work tonight and over the weekend. It's only peeling potatoes, any fool could do it.'

'But what about the WVS, and the bookstall? The Illingworths rely on you.'

'It won't affect them. We all have to do a bit extra these days, and I'll just do it for the weekend. I don't know if I can keep it up during the week, I was nearly dead on my feet today. They don't finish until dawn – they're making the most of the night filming time.'

'Oh, love, it's good of you.' She came over to hug me,

pressed me to her apron. 'You're the only one who cares a fig about me. You're my rock. Heaven knows, I'll miss you that much when you're wed, stuck here with only Andrew and your pa.'

The chair behind me scraped and I turned just in time to see the door slam.

'Andrew!' Mother shouted, but it was too late. We saw him drag his bicycle past the window. She looked to me and shrugged her shoulders helplessly.

When I got to the kitchens Patty was there already. 'Sorry about yesterday, Patty. Do you still need me?'

'We need you all right,' Hilary called. 'Look at this lot.' She pointed to a huge pile of filthy carrots on the draining board.

Patty was tying a leopard-print scarf around her head and tucking in her hair. She smiled and it lifted my spirits.

'Am I forgiven?' I asked.

'Suppose so. Course. But if you want to make it up to me you can swap jobs.' Patty said.

'You want to peel all my carrots?'

'No, cheeky. I mean, you can have Third Class and I'll have First.'

'Go on then,' I said. 'I know you're dying to get your hands on Trevor Howard.'

She flicked her overall at me before tying it on, winding the tapes around twice and pulling them tight to her waist.

'Is Frank minding the children?'

'Yes. He doesn't mind. The pay'll go towards our new house. We're wanting to move out of lodgings next year, when it's all over.'

'That's good.' But I was barely paying attention. I would be in Third Class, serving him. Matthew Baxter. My stomach was already tying itself in knots. I scrubbed at the dirty carrots with the bristle brush, and topped and tailed and sliced, breathing in and out through my mouth, telling myself to be calm.

Mother thought I was doing this to earn a bit extra to help her out. Patty thought I was doing her a favour. But I knew the real reason I was here, though I would not have admitted it to myself, not then.

'Will you go and tell the stationmaster it's ready?' Hilary said.

I dragged my coat on over my overall and popped my head out of the door. Lights on the platform buzzed a faint noise and around them moths flitted and danced despite the cold. On the other platform a group of extras had gathered around a camera, their breath making standing clouds before them, and a cameraman was shooting a pile of luggage on a trolley. I ignored them and knocked gently on the stationmaster's door.

'Come in,' came a faint voice from inside.

A warm fug of heat blasted from a cheery coal fire. The room was chock-a-block with people leaning up against the walls or sitting on bentwood chairs. I must have looked taken aback.

'Quick, shut that door,' the stationmaster said, standing with his bottom warming, and his bowler hat still on his head.

'Hilary sent me to say that dinner's just about ready.'

'Two down – "Supposed force in Eastern Front covered by flashy stuff causing cricket problem..."' Celia Johnson looked up from the newspaper, pen in hand.

'How many letters?' Stanley Holloway asked her.

'Eight, seven. I'm completely stumped.' She looked up at me. 'Are you any good at crosswords?'

'She works on the bookstall, so she should be,' said a voice I recognised. It was George Farrer the engine driver.

'Oh, hello, Mr Farrer. I looked back at Miss Johnson. 'Sorry, I'm not much use at crosswords, not the cryptic ones anyway.' I was fascinated by her face; it was flawless, her skin luminous and smooth. Her big doe eyes were even more striking in reality.

'Can't we finish this first? It's so cosy in here, and the dining cars are draughty as blazes,' Miss Johnson said.

'Draughty as blazes – that makes no sense. A blaze can't be draughty,' Mr Holloway said, flicking at her paper with his finger.

'You know what I mean. Anyway, I'll have to brave the arctic carriage eventually because I'm starving. That last take was sheer torture. I thought he was going to keep me out there until I froze to the platform. I won't look so lovelorn with an icicle hanging off my nose, will I? Oh gosh, I hope it was all right.'

'It will be fine. You'll be great, just as you always are.'

She looked down at her paper and I realised with fascination that her eyelashes must be false. Nobody could really have such long lashes.

'Come on, everyone,' said the stationmaster, 'if Rhoda says it's ready you'd best get on over there. I'll damp the fire before I go off duty so it will still be in afterwards.'

The stars stood up and began to wrap their mufflers round their necks and replace their hats. I took the chance to slip away back to the kitchen.

'You've been ages,' Patty said.

'I talked to Celia Johnson.' I was breathless with excitement. 'She's doing the crossword in the stationmaster's office.'

'Jeepers. Did you get an autograph?'

'Flip. I didn't think to ask.'

Patty raised her eyes to the ceiling as if I was a complete idiot.

Five minutes later we were pushing the food trolley over to the platform. When I got to the third-class carriage it was nothing like the other one had been. The tables were cheap dealwood with no cloths, and grey blinds masked the windows.

I let Hilary serve Matthew, but as I passed he put a hand out to stop me. 'Hey, Rhoda, want to watch a scene? They'll be doing a few cutaways, about two-forty-five.'

'I'd love to, but we might still be clearing away.'

'If you wait in the stationmaster's office at about half-past I'll come and find you.'

I could hardly keep the grin from my face. 'Will it be all right? I mean, I won't be in the way?'

'Not if you're with me.'

'I don't know if they'll let me, but I'll try.' But I knew I'd be there. I was almost breathless. I tried to behave normally, but my heart was galloping.

The kitchen girls sat down at the table with Yorkshire puddings like the ones we'd made for the crew. It was real eggs too, not the dried stuff we'd been eating at home for months. Beef had come up on the train. It was delicious, but I was too nervous about meeting Matthew to eat much. I watched Patty chattering away, cramming her mouth with forkfuls of pudding, and felt sick. Washing the pots seemed interminable. The water wouldn't boil and we had to wait ages before there was enough for washing the greasy skillets we'd cooked the puddings in.

I kept glancing at the clock above the door as it inched its way round to half-past two.

'I'm just going out for a spot of air before we start the breakfast prep,' I said, grabbing my coat.

'Don't you want tea?'

'I'll have some when I get back.'

'Don't let it go cold,' called Patty, but my hand was already turning the brass handle on the door.

In the stationmaster's office a game of poker was going on, at a small green-topped table. There was much hilarity as people played for matchsticks.

I watched the game a minute or two on tenterhooks. When the door opened and a rush of cold air hit my legs I shivered. It was him. My stomach seemed to turn inside out. 'Come on, I'll take you over,' he said and guided me out with a hand on the small of my back. I could feel the warmth of his palm even through my coat.

He was talking, leaning over as we walked. 'I'm afraid there won't be much to see — not a lot of action. It's not that kind of film. It's mostly close-up shots of Laura Jesson and the doctor. That's Miss Johnson and Mr Howard. But I think she's going to be very good. She can turn it on really well, and she's sort of mesmerising.'

I could understand why someone would be mesmerised by her. She was beautiful. I wished I was able to mesmerise someone the way she could. I wanted to be her, to be somebody, not just the too-tall girl on the bookstall.

Matthew walked me slowly up the ramp, explaining about long shots and close-ups and how there were three kinds of lighting — front light, back light and fillers. The names of the lamps were strange — foufous, broads, bashes. His enthusiasm for lighting was like a drug, it had me bewildered but fascinated.

He kept cocking his head to one side to check I had

heard him. Every time our eyes caught, I felt my heart give a little jump. It was freezing on the platform and normally I would have hunched my shoulders and stuffed my hands in my pockets, but I wanted to make a good impression so I kept my shoulders down and walked tall, hoping to look elegant, despite my chattering teeth and thin winter coat.

Filming stopped whilst everyone waited for a munitions train to rumble through. The locomotive chuffed by with no warning hoot or signal, pulling its deadly chain of rust-coloured carriages. I shuddered. They were all full of explosives – truck after truck, all destined for the poor people of Germany.

'Good job there's no V1's up here,' Matthew said. 'That train would make such a blast if it went up. We're official evacuees, did you know that? The film crew. Stupid, isn't it. We had to fill in a form and everything before they'd let us come up here. Mind you, I'm glad we came.' He looked at me and smiled, a lopsided smile that crinkled the corners of his eyes.

'Me too,' I said, as we strode down the ramp and up to the other platform. The camera was rehearsing the scene when we arrived, with one of the surly set-builders standing in for Miss Johnson.

'There's Ed,' I whispered.

Matthew moved close to me so he could speak in my ear. 'Yes, he's the focus puller. Watch how smoothly he pulls the lens as the cameraman moves in. It's the hardest job of all, that. Ed's a master – you need acute vision and a sensitivity of touch. The audience often don't notice it, but their attention is shifted by where the sharp parts of the image are. We'd soon notice if Miss Johnson went all fuzzy and the wall behind her got sharp.'

His hand rested lightly on my arm. It sent a thrill through me. I moved a little closer.

The men seemed satisfied with the tracking forward, and Ed removed the lens from the camera and scrutinised it carefully under an arc lamp. 'He's checking the gate,' Matthew said, 'making sure there's no dirt on the lens.' A faint odour of soap, tobacco and warm wool as Matthew tightened his hand on my sleeve and leaned in to point ahead. A train was waiting and a man sprayed more smoke from a machine around its wheels. 'Look,' Matthew said, 'they must be nearly ready.'

Miss Johnson took her position on the white tape where the workman had been standing. A quiet, like a spell, came over her and over everyone else. How she managed the scene without her teeth chattering I don't know. She was watching a train depart. Such a simple thing, you'd think. But it was amazing to watch the nuances of expression shift over her face: her hope, her guilt, her regret. She could make her thoughts visible. I hoped mine were not as transparent as hers.

I was just thinking this, when someone in Carnforth slammed a front door and they had to do the whole take again. 'Quiet, please!' yelled Mr Lean. Once filming began I was completely drawn again into Celia Johnson's face — despite the cold of the platform eating through the soles of my shoes, despite the silhouette of the camera in front of me.

'Cold?' Matthew whispered. He pulled me back by the waist to lean into him. The feeling made me light-headed.

Once the shot was done and the clapper boy chalked up the scene, we had to stand aside to let everyone pass. Matthew explained the film was supposed to be set in a small provincial town, and the station would be called Milford Junction.

'No wonder they chose Carnforth then,' I said. 'We've

always been a bit behind the times. The war might actually reach us in another five years or so.'

He laughed and squeezed my waist. I glanced over his shoulder to where Trevor Howard was waiting. He was immaculately suited, his newspaper in hand, leaning on the rails by the ramps, keeping his cigarette smoke out of shot. I looked back to Matthew. His hat shadowed his face, showing his sharp features. He looked just as much a film star as Trevor Howard. At night, under these lights, the whole station was transformed into a place of glamour and romance so that even the towering coal hopper became architectural, significant.

I looked up at the clock. It was stopped at eight-forty-five. Damn, it was the false time. I turned, pointed to my wrist and raised my eyebrows. Matthew looked at his watch. 'Three-thirty,' he mouthed.

That time already. 'Sorry, got to go.'

'Come on then!' He grabbed me by the arm as we hurried under the subway.

A rumble in the distance.

'The *Royal Scot*,' he said. 'Quick! We'll just be in time.'

He took hold of me and held me steady, away from the edge of the platform, his arms tight around my shoulders. His lips found mine just as it whooshed through the station in a rattle of wheels and a cloud of steam.

I kissed him back.

'Gosh!' he said, delighted.

'I must go and help in the kitchen – they'll be wondering where I am,' I blurted.

'Look, I'd like to meet you for tea. After work one day next week? Is there a place round here that's decent?'

'I don't know. My mother always expects me to—'

'Go on,' he said. 'Be a devil. You only live once and

every now and then you have to grab life with both hands. It's only tea. Not a weekend in Paris.'

I laughed, despite myself. 'A weekend in Paris might tempt me more.' Too late I realised what I'd said. Me and my big mouth. He'd think me fast, and I only meant it as a joke. I took out a handkerchief and blew my nose, even though it didn't need blowing.

'Tea first,' he said seriously. 'Paris later.' I looked at him, trying to read his face. 'When the Germans have gone.' His face cracked into a wicked grin.

'You!' I pushed him on the shoulder and we laughed.

Back in the kitchen Patty said, 'There you are. We thought you'd got lost. The tea's stone cold. There's all the bread to do. And the marge's making holes in the bread. We've tried warming it, but soon as we get it away from the stove it goes hard as a rock. The butter knife's over there.'

I set to spreading bread, all the time thinking of Matthew Baxter and the feeling of his warm mouth against mine.

'How many have you done?' Hilary's voice interrupted my thoughts.

'She's been dreaming,' Patty said. 'She's gone star-struck.'

I put the margarine on quicker after that. But Patty was right; her words described exactly the feeling that tightened in my chest.

35

1945 Peter

THE DAY'S WALKING passed in a blur. Archie and George chivvied him to walk, but did he imagine it, or were they more wary of him now? More convoys of fleeing civilians passed close by. The road was narrow so they had to stand away to one side to let them pass.

Somewhere behind them Harry lay still on the side of the road and would never get up again.

Peter stretched his hand where he had hit him, feeling the pain of the knuckles which were bruised and swollen. Snow fell clean and white, melted into beads of water on his palm. His hand. This hand had caused another man's death. It did not seem possible that hands could be so deadly. He thought of all the naked touches Harry must have had in his life, the mother's tender stroking, the lover's caress, the brush of a friend as he passed you a cigarette, even the push of a German guard as he put you into a wagon. All those touches, unnoticed, hardly ever remembered. And yet Peter's was the last touch, the last sensation Harry would ever have felt. The fact of it was momentous, so large he struggled with the scope of it.

He stuffed his hand back in his glove. 'I'm sorry,' he said, over and over under his breath as he walked. But it didn't ease the feeling of utter emptiness that hung over him like a fog.

The rhythm of his footfalls was the only thing that kept him connected to the earth. He watched the goings-on around him as if from a vast distance away, the other men's voices drowned by his bleak thoughts. Archie pushed him forward every now and then from behind when he got too slow. Archie's touch had taken on a new significance to him, a proof that he was still here, however briefly, in the land of the living.

His attention was caught by a scrawny chicken in a cage on the back of one of the carts creaking by. Several other men had obviously seen it because there was a sudden hustle of silent activity, then scuffling as the victorious man plunged back into the line out of sight of the German guards, the struggling chicken clamped under his arm. The man with the chicken shoved past, and Peter stepped sideways. His elbow connected with Peter's ribs, and Peter hung on to the sensation.

At the same time, Peter felt his boot turn over on a rut in the ice. A sharp pain, and an audible crack in his ankle. He gasped and fell heavily on to his side where another man tripped over and fell on top of him. The weight knocked the breath out of Peter's chest. Both winded men were dragged back up to their feet by the men around them.

As soon as he stood he knew that something was not right. He was nauseous and a shooting pain went right up his leg to his hip. He started to walk but found he could not put any weight on his foot. He hobbled as best he could but the ankle was throbbing and he found himself dropping further and further back. Archie and George were out of sight now amidst the shamble of men.

After about a quarter of a mile, his ankle had already

DAVINA BLAKE

started to swell despite the cold, and now the top of his boot cut into his leg, but he dared not stop and sit to look at it. If he did, he might not get up again. He began to count, as he had earlier with Archie when Archie had been close to giving up. One, two, three. Each step was torture. Finally he was weeping with the pain and this froze his lashes so that all he could make out was a blur. When the order came to halt, he just let himself collapse where he was.

His cheek burned where it lay on the ice. He wasn't going to make it. It was what he deserved, retribution for Harry. Maybe there was a God after all, and he was keeping a tally. Boots pounded past his ears. The thought came to him that, just like Harry, he had survived all these years of the war and now it would end here. Nobody would know where he was. He thought of his mother at home in her neat little kitchen, his father filling in the crossword in the newspaper in his meticulous capitals. And he thought of Rhoda, when he pressed the little leather box into her hand, and her anxious face as she waved him off at the station.

A lethargy set in. He could not walk another mile, let alone twenty to the next filthy barn or frozen field. He had seen other men left behind with his own eyes; those too ill to walk just died, or were shot by the German guards. The membrane of time was so weak, people so fragile. A single second could separate a man from his life.

His ankle throbbed with heat so he curled up and put his hands on it to warm them. He felt his mind drift. It was a relief to let go. He imagined the band playing in the sunny Memorial Hall, thought he'd sleep. A voice in his head told him he would not wake.

Someone was shaking him and shouting. He curled further into himself, ignored it. If they shoot, they shoot, he thought.

'Come on, get up.' The voice was irritating, he wanted to brush it away like a fly.

'Can't,' he mumbled. 'Leave me alone.'

'Help me.' He heard the voices but it was as if they were in a distant room. For a moment he thought he was still in the Memorial Hall at home, but then he was dragged to his feet. The sudden pain in his ankle brought him round.

Archie and another man hauled him up and Archie propped Peter's shoulder under his own. 'What the hell's the matter?' Archie said. 'George is waiting up the road. Come on, we're not going without you.'

'I can't walk.' The world teetered on its side and then slowly came back into focus. He gritted his teeth against the pain.

'Come on, I'll help. Is it the runs?'

'I can't. My ankle. It's broken.'

Peter saw Archie hesitate whilst he weighed this up. Then he saw him come to a decision. 'It's not broken, just sprained. Here, lean on me.'

They made their way back into the column then, Archie bearing the weight on Peter's bad side. It was slow progress. The pain seared so he could not speak, only clamp his jaw shut. He could barely hop or shuffle, dragging his injured ankle through the snow. George was way ahead and Archie was not strong enough to carry Peter's weight as well as his own for long.

Nobody else offered to help. It was each man for himself. They were out of reserves, everyone was close to starvation and running on empty. Gradually they found themselves further down the line. 'We're going to make it to the next billet, then we'll find a medic, get it looked at. Right?' Archie said.

Peter could only groan in agreement. He did not know

if he could make it that far, and even if he did, they hadn't seen any sign of a doctor in the ranks, either English or German. They struggled onwards, Peter's dragging foot collecting snow as it went. Archie changed sides every now and then to relieve his shoulder, even though one side was much less efficient. Breathless and frustrated, Archie even tried to piggyback him, but it was too hard to keep upright on the slippery ground, and Peter feared it would draw the guards' attention.

By the end of the afternoon a few hundred men had passed them and they were near the end of the line. Behind them they saw the stragglers and the four German guards and their dogs, helmets down into the wind, rifles over their shoulders.

'Leave me. You've got to,' Peter begged.

'No. We can make it,' Archie said, but as he slipped again, 'Bloody snow.' Peter saw he was almost weeping with the effort and awkwardness of propping him up.

They stopped, both filled with the hopelessness of what they were attempting.

Another convoy of fleeing civilians was passing and they needed to shunt off the road. In desperation, when one of the horse-drawn carts was approaching, Archie put himself out in front of the horse. The cart lumbered to a stop. A muffled female voice told him in guttural German to get out of the way.

Archie took cigarettes and the remains of his Nestlé's chocolate from his pocket and held them out on his hand. There was a small girl on the cart watching them with soulful serious eyes. Peter could not hear what Archie was saying but realised he must be trying to strike a bargain with the woman driver. Peter swayed on his feet.

Sometimes an action happens in a blink of an eye. One of those lightning reversals that twists fate back on itself. A decision is made as if it has been made for you, as if you've become caught in the net of the decision and it snaps you to its will.

The woman clambered down. Peter saw the chocolate was in the little girl's hand. A piercing in his ankle as Archie and the woman manhandled him on to the back of the cart and covered him over with something that smelt of woodsmoke. The next he knew he was jolting down the track back the way they had come, away from the column of men, away from his countrymen. Back towards Germany. In disbelief, from the corner of his eye he saw the blurred white ditches and hardened drifts pass by.

He was jerked awake by the cart going over a rut. He could barely feel his body, it was so cold, but he leaned up on one stiff elbow. He saw that he had been covered by an old chenille curtain; the brass hooks were still left in at the top, but it was dusted with a powdering of frost. He squinted into the dawn light. There was not a German guard in sight. Instead the landscape was dotted with moving blobs of people, small pockets and larger groups all struggling down the road. Around them stretched fields of snow bordered by the dark haze of trees in the distance.

Archie sat next to the woman. He was wrapped in a dirty yellow knitted blanket which looked to be stained with dried blood, and he had his hat pulled down over his face and his scarf wrapped about his chin. The little girl was sitting on his lap. With his weeks-old beard he did not look like a soldier and nobody stopped them. Peter knew they were heading further back into enemy territory instead of away from it and they would certainly be shot if anyone asked them for papers or became suspicious. But he would have died left by the side of the road anyway, so what was the difference?

The little girl turned to look behind and gave a tentative smile. It split him open. True, he did not know where he was or where he was going, but the picture on the front of the cart represented some sort of sanity. A man, a woman, a child. There had to be kindness where children were. If a child smiled at you it was impossible not to smile back, no matter what the circumstances. He wondered if they knew they were taking a murderer with them.

Life had delivered him, when so many others were dead. Why? He could think of no reason. Death was a fact, but the mystery of it was like weed beneath the water: grasp for it and it would sway out of reach. Peter stopped striving, stopped resisting, distanced himself until he was mere bone and blood and muscle, a carcass. He lay back and just let his body be carried. The trundle of the cart was rough on his back.

The woman stopped the cart beside a clump of trees so that Archie could relieve himself. Peter had a sudden panic that she might drive off without Archie, but she waited. Peter took the opportunity to thank her. '*Vielen Dank*,' he said. 'My leg,' he pointed, '*kaputt*.' The little girl jumped as if she had forgotten he was there and turned to stare.

The woman looked back over her shoulder. 'I speak English,' she said. 'I studied it at school. My name is Annegret.' Her eyebrows were very straight; straight nose, square chin. She was angular, almost sexless, somewhere in middle age. The comparison with Rhoda came almost straight away. It was odd to be so near to a woman after all this time. She too was appraising him.

'I'm Peter,' he said, though his name sounded as though it no longer fitted him.

'Yes.' She indicated Archie with a wag of her head. 'Your friend told me. My daughter is called Klara. Her father is dead. At the Soviet front line. We can take you to Dresden. There will be many refugees there, much confusion, so perhaps you may find your way home.'

Home. Just the word made him swallow. She seemed to see his pain but said nothing, waited impassively for him to recover himself.

'Dresden,' he said finally. 'I've only heard of it from books. It is supposed to be a very beautiful city. I've seen pictures of the cathedral. How far?'

'Three days, maybe four. I don't know. My mother and her sister are there, in an apartment. But it is better to have a man with us on the road. Even an Englishman.' She leaned towards him. 'The Soviets, they came to the village next to ours. They do not treat German women well.' Her voice dropped to a whisper. 'They rape us, even old women. They do not care who. Then they kill us. My daughter is only eight, and I heard that ...' She stopped, looked away, suppressing her words. When she turned back she was angry. 'Keep your face hidden, look old. Young men are suspicious, they should be fighting for the Reich.'

She climbed down, emptied a sparse handful of oats from a sack and fed it to the listless rough-haired horse. In a tin bucket she scraped snow to get water. She seemed to know exactly what she was doing. Her feet were encased in a pair of man's shoes several sizes too large and stuffed with paper, and the soles slipped on the hard-packed snow.

She grasped the edge of the cart for stability and addressed him with a stubborn gaze. 'You will help us. Or I will throw you off.'

'I'm not sure we can be any use. I've a bad leg. And we're not armed.'

She pulled open her collar with a gloved hand and drew out a knife, which she held out to him before jamming it back under her coat.

'There are other knives under that bundle. See.' She came around to the back of the cart and lifted the bundle. Three kitchen knives lay there. None looked sharp enough to even cut a cabbage. 'Take one, put it in your coat.'

Peter shook his head. Suddenly the idea of having a weapon, even this knife, was frightening. After what had happened with Harry, he did not trust himself.

'Please,' Annegret said. 'If the Soviets try anything and I am dead, you must use it. Don't let them take her their way, better a quick and painless way.'

Peter said nothing. What could he say? He did not think he could kill a child. Even though the child's mother might ask him to. And with that old kitchen knife?

Annegret grabbed the knife and held it towards him. The movement was half-threat, half-offering. 'Three to protect her is better than one,' she said. 'I could leave you behind.'

A beat. Reluctantly he pocketed it. His ankle was so painful it was too much effort to resist.

She sighed, relieved, and nodded at him.

When Archie returned he set to cooking a meal under Annegret's supervision, with a few sticks that she had brought in a bundle to make a fire. Archie found oats and used milk he had from the rest of the Red Cross parcel. He melted snow for their drinking water and for the horse, and then cooked with one eye on the horizon, for he too had been given a knife and instructions to use it should the Soviets appear.

Archie brought a bowl up for Peter to eat before eating his own. Peter smiled his thanks. Annegret and Klara shared the other bowl. The little girl sat on the front of the wagon, watching all the proceedings silently with serious eyes, spooning in the food with concentration. She was wearing a too-big coat and her head was wrapped in a knitted scarf from which her hair straggled, the ends stiff with frost. After all those weary men her face looked so fresh and clear, pink with the cold. She watched them speaking though she could not have understood a word.

Peter let the warmth of the hot food spread through him until he felt drowsy. He heard Archie ask, 'Have you heard any news? Will Germany fall to the Soviets?'

'No. We are waiting for the Americans. Hitler is finished. It is over. This is why I pick you up. If we meet Americans you will speak up for us.' She wiped out the plates with deliberate movements. It wasn't a request. 'The Poles are taking back their lands, they shout at us, "Get out of here, you Hitler folk." They point guns at us and tell us to get out. We have had to leave everything, just these few things we could bring. The Red Army also come at us on our tails and there is nowhere safe for us to go, except west, where our relations are. We are a people without choice now. To be slaves to the Soviets or the Americans.'

'We've been prisoners of war for five years,' Archie said. 'We'd be finished now, dead by the side of the road, if you hadn't stopped. Peter's leg's broken, I think.'

'I'll look now. See what can be done.'

Peter heard her clamber up beside him but really did not want anyone to touch his ankle. So Archie had known it was broken all along. He flinched and moved away.

'Lie still and let me see,' Annegret said. 'I was the pharmacist in my village. I know a little.'

She untied his bootlace with determination. Her breath steamed above him. She seemed to have more energy than both the men. Even to do that would have defeated Peter.

But then, she had not spent years on half-rations, had not already marched miles in the snow. She was purposeful and strong. 'Pass me those sticks,' she said to Klara in German.

Klara fetched the bundle of kindling over and Annegret picked out two long straight sticks. 'I need something long to tie it on.'

'A splint,' Archie said, realising what she was doing. 'Hang on.' He reached under his yellow blanket and pulled out a battered first-aid pack from his greatcoat pocket.

'The real thing,' he said, pointing to the white circle with the cross on the pack. 'Army issue.'

'What's in it?' Annegret was curious. He showed her: the field dressing, the lint, the round pencil.

'What's that for?' she asked, pointing to the pencil.

'Dunno. It's what they give us. The scissors were taken off us when we got to the camp, but they let me keep this.'

'Pah. Nothing for the pain? No drugs?'

The army issue of Elastoplast, pencil and bandages seemed suddenly hilarious in these conditions. Archie started to laugh.

'They send you to war with these! Ha!' Annegret began to laugh too. 'Not even us Germans are so stupid!'

Whilst they were laughing Annegret made a sudden twist on Peter's ankle and he yelled with pain.

'The only way,' she said. Then she splinted it and bound it tight. 'You're right. It is broken, but it will mend if you rest it. Six weeks' rest should do it, doctor says. Shame you must walk from Dresden.'

They laughed again. Through it all, the daughter Klara did not make a sound, but the more noise they made, the more she cowered away.

'Come, Klara,' said Annegret in soft German, pulling

her towards her in a bear hug. 'It is all right to laugh.' Then quietly, 'Dieter won't mind.'

'Who is Dieter?' asked Archie.

'Her brother. The Poles shot at us to make us leave our house in Stary Zamość. A stream of bullets hit him in the back. We wrapped him up in that blanket, the one you're wearing. We brought him with us, and I tried to save him, but there were too many wounds. He bled to death. After two days we could not bear to carry his body any further, and had to leave him behind in the snow.' Peter, who had propped himself upright, looked to Archie who loosened the blanket around him and shook his head. 'It is all right,' Annegret said. 'The dead do not feel. It is the living who feel.'

Abruptly Annegret stood and wiped the bowls with a cloth over and over, long after they were clean. Then she climbed into the driving seat. Her lips were pressed tightly together. She made no attempt to move off, just put her arms around her daughter. Klara's small hands in their mismatched gloves crept around her neck.

A few moments later she passed Klara back to Archie's knee and clucked the horse onwards. From his viewpoint in the back of the cart Peter sat up and stared backwards at the road behind them and the sky. Today it was a blank nothingness, mist receding into mist. Snow came in intermittent eddying flakes. His thoughts swirled with the snow, for he still could not leave Harry behind. He carried his face with him as the miles melted into miles.

For a time they were the only people on the road. As the landscape rolled by Annegret just stared fixedly ahead, her shoulders squared, as if that in itself was keeping her going. Peter marvelled at her stoicism. She must be dog tired. He hadn't seen her sleep, though he'd seen the heads of Archie and the girl loll and jerk from time to time. The sight of her courage moved him, for she'd lost a son, shot in front of her, yet she seemed to have a backbone of iron. She had enough to contend with, without him being a burden too. He must pull himself together, do something useful.

'Have you a map?' he asked.

Archie turned, surprised.

'Yes. In the green holdall.' Annegret did not turn.

'May I take it out and look?'

'Yes. But I know the way,' Annegret said. 'As long as we can stay on these roads. You can look if you like, but don't get it wet.'

Peter eased his way over to the bag and took out the map. As he did so he saw the holdall was full of photographs, a hairbrush, a child's doll, all jammed together as if hastily thrust inside. He extracted the map and tried to work out where they were. 'What was that last village we passed?' he asked.

'Jänschwalde.'

She spelt it for him, and it was reassuring to find the name on the map, although it was hard to read because it was written so small. He felt as if he was in control again, to have this small piece of information. 'But it's about a hundred miles from here to Dresden,' he said.

'I know that,' Annegret said with contempt.

36

1955 Helen

'I'VE BEEN READING the latest Graham Greene. *The Quiet American*. You'd like it,' Peter said.

'I've not read that one. What's it about? Apart from being about a quiet American, I mean.' Helen heard herself giggle, and stuck her finger in her hair and twirled it the way she used to do when she was much younger.

Peter leaned forward to put down his coffee. 'It's one of his best, I think. About a journalist in the Indochina War. Typical Graham Greene stuff. But it's good. It goes into all the reasons why someone might want to fight for his country and do everything right to be the perfect military man, but lose himself in the process.'

'It sounds like just my sort of thing. I'll see if our bookshop's got it.'

'I'll lend you it, if you like, next time I come over.'

'No, no. If you've recommended it,' she said, 'I'll just go down to Smith's and get it.'

'I'd love to know what you think. When you've read it, maybe we could meet up for lunch one day in town, make a change.'

Helen felt heat rise to her face. 'That would be lovely.'

She knew this was the edge of something, the prickling feeling of discomfort mingled with excitement.

'Do you know, it's so nice to talk to someone who likes the same sort of things as I do.'

The clock pinged the hour. 'Is that the time? I'd better be getting back.' He did not mention Rhoda, but she might as well have been there in the room with them. 'I'll call by again next week as usual, see how you're doing.' It was the excuse he used just after Archie died, and had kept on using though they both knew it was long redundant.

'Lovely, I'll look forward to it.'

He kissed her on the cheek, and then surprised her with a peck on the lips.

After he'd hurried off to catch his train, Helen exhaled. Her face broke into a smile, and she hummed a tuneless little riff as she went to take the rubbish out to the bin outside. By the time she came back in she was more sober. She had begun to think of what Archie might think if he could see her now.

The book was in her bag, and Helen held it tight under her arm. She was early. She'd been so terrified of being late that she'd more than forty-five minutes to kill. So she walked up the road by the museum and then back to the canal, looking in the chemist's, the shoe shop and the hairdresser's window. In the hairdresser's window she'd caught sight of herself – a short woman with slightly wild hair – and it did nothing to boost her confidence, though when she set off she'd thought she looked nice. She glanced at her watch again.

Helen hurried back down the street, aiming to be there just one or two minutes late. The weather was perfect – bright sunshine with a little breeze – and outside the canal pub knots of office workers were gathered round the tables in little groups, spilling out on to the towpath.

Peter waved at her from an empty table and she wove through the crowd to join him. He stood as if he was going to hug her, but then must have thought better of it and sat down.

'You look lovely,' he said, smiling. 'That's a nice dress.'

She was about to sit when he stood up again. 'Let me get you a drink. What will you have?'

'A dry Martini, please,' she said, finally taking a seat.

She watched his back as he strode up the steps into the pub with his distinctive limping walk. He looked nice – tight trousers and a button-down shirt, with a dark jacket. No tie. She was used to seeing him in his suit, but the sight of his casual clothes made her more relaxed; she'd been worried she wasn't dressy enough.

He came back with Martinis for both of them and they chinked glasses and said 'Cheers'. The tart taste of the Martini reminded Helen of holidays with Archie; it was a long time since she'd had a drink. She asked after Peter's garden and allotment and took a big gulp of her drink to ease her nerves. Even a few mouthfuls made her light-headed.

Peter drew pictures with his hands a lot as he explained about staking tomato plants and dahlias. He had nice hands, solid and practical. She did not really hear a word he said. He leaned in close to her to talk so that she could see the sprinkling of hairs where his shirt collar met his neck.

He was looking at her intently. She lowered her eyes. His hand lifted as though he might rest it on top of hers.

'Peter!' The voice was jovial. Peter dragged his hand away hastily. An older man in a navy blue blazer, and a strawberry blonde with a pencil skirt, bore down on them. 'I thought it was you.'

'Oh. Hello, Malcolm, hello, Sylvia.' He stood up to greet the other couple.

'Good to see you. We're just having a spot of lunch.' Malcolm shouted with the voice of one who is slightly deaf. He turned to stare at Helen.

Peter introduced them. 'This is a Helen, wife of an old friend of mine. Archie Foster. He was my best friend. Fifteen years we knew each other ...' Helen stood to shake hands, aware that Peter had introduced her in a way that made much of the fact that she was married to someone else.

'Have you had lunch?' asked Sylvia. Her voice had a trace of an accent, Liverpool perhaps.

'No, not yet,' Helen said.

'Then why don't you join us? Give Malcolm and Peter chance to catch up?'

Peter looked sideways at Helen to gauge her reaction. She looked at the floor, awaiting the inevitable.

'All right then,' he said. 'You go on in, we'll finish our drinks and join you in a minute.'

'See you inside then.' Malcolm took Sylvia's arm and steered her towards the inside of the pub.

'Sorry,' Peter said as soon as they were gone. 'I had in mind a quiet lunch with just the two of us, but it will look odd if we ignore them. They've been friends of ours for years.'

'Friends of you and Rhoda?'

'Yes, from the Parents' Association.' His shoulders gave an apologetic shrug. Tension showed in the furrow between his brows.

'I see.' The disappointment was almost unbearable. The novel still lay there between them on the table. She'd go. This had been a stupid idea. 'I think perhaps I might leave you to it. You go and catch up with your friends, I'll just finish my drink and—'

'I won't hear of it. I promised you lunch, and you're having lunch.' He must have heard the crack in her voice; his expression was stricken. 'Look, I'll go and tell them that as it's such a lovely day we've decided to eat outside. They won't mind. It was thoughtless of me. I'll bring some menus.'

Whilst he was gone Helen scratched miserably at the wooden tabletop with her fingernail. She saw that the whole idea was impossible; penetrating someone else's marriage was like breaking into a fortress that was fenced in on all sides. A flurry of activity near the door made her look up. Peter was there, a false smile on his face, followed by Malcolm and Sylvia.

'What a good idea, eating outside,' Malcolm said. 'It's so stuffy in there. Here, have a menu.'

'Thank you,' Helen said, taking it, her stomach sinking. Peter did not look at her, but she could feel his discomfort by the way he pulled at his collar as if it was too tight.

For the next hour she endured Sylvia telling her about her new twin-tub washing machine, their planned holiday in France, and how Rhoda was splendidly good at manning the bric-a-brac stall on school Sports Day. It was a world Helen knew nothing of and it only served to make her feel more uncomfortable, but Sylvia did not notice Helen's silence. She kept up a stream of chat, interspersed with the rattle of her gold charm bracelet and much laughter at her own jokes.

They ordered the three-course lunch, but Helen could only pick at her pâté and her stroganoff. When the dessert menu came, she said, 'No, thank you, I'll pass.'

'Oh, but you must!' Sylvia said. 'I can't eat dessert on my own. Rhoda always has the trifle. It's very good, and I won't feel so naughty then.'

'I'm already—'

'It's very light. Strawberries and cream. Go on.'

Helen capitulated, and dutifully praised the trifle when it came, though eating it made her feel too full. She felt as if she was suffocating. They divided the bill and then at last Malcolm and Sylvia got up to leave. Helen exhaled.

'Thank you for lunch,' she said after they had both stood to shake hands with Malcolm and Sylvia again. She looked at her watch. 'Oh, is that the time? I should be going.' It was all wrong. She'd had such romantic notions about the afternoon, but an hour with Sylvia and Malcolm had spoilt it all.

'Really? Do you have to?' Peter said. 'I thought we might have a walk – it's a nice stroll down the towpath, and we could walk off our lunch.'

He was cajoling her, and it made her want to resist.

'No, I have to go. I promised a neighbour I'd sit for her children later.' It was a lie, but she felt out of her depth. She wasn't ready for this deception. She just needed to get away, somewhere where she could breathe. When she stood she was unsteady on her feet from the alcohol. She picked up the book from the table.

'Helen.' He stood and reached for her shoulders. 'I'm sorry.' Then he pulled her to him.

She let him hold her, and they stood like that for a long moment, she with her cheek pressed to the buttons of his shirt, hearing his heart beating under her ear. How stupid, her eyes were full of tears, tears of frustration, tears for something long lost. She pulled away, sniffed. 'It was a lovely lunch, but I don't think I'm ready for this,' she said.

'Can I drive you home?'

'No, no. I'll walk. It's a lovely day. I'll get the bus.' She was retreating as she spoke, waving the book, to keep a distance between them.

He took a step towards her, but stopped. His face was

hurt, puzzled. She turned and bit her lip, walked as quickly as she could, back up the road past the hairdresser's. After about five minutes' walking she slowed. She longed to go back, back to his arms. She savoured the feeling of it, the smell of the warm cotton of his shirt, the firm circle of his arms pressing into her shoulder blades. She hesitated. Pride was the only thing that stopped her running back, calling out, 'Yes, yes, let's take that walk!'

But it was too late now, he'd have gone. Driven away in his Ford Zephyr. And now he'd be offended, and their friendship would be awkward. Archie would be looking down on her and shaking his head. She pictured his disappointed face. *You're an idiot, Helen,* she told herself, *you've ruined it all.*

37

1945 Rhoda

TUESDAY WAS A day off, at least a day off from the bookstall. I was so tired that it was nine o'clock before I could drag myself up and out of bed. I had heard the noise of Pa shouting below and put my pillow over my head.

A moment later my door banged open and he was standing there, in his shirtsleeves with no collar. 'Your mother tells me you were out all hours last night.'

I sat up, clutching the sheets and blankets up to my chin. 'I was working on the filming, Pa. In the kitchens. It's good money.'

'You kept her awake, coming in so late. They're a right nuisance, all those people cluttering up our station.'

'She wasn't awake, she was—'

'You're not going back.' His face was white and taut. 'What are you doing it for? You've got a good job already. And the war's not over yet. The WVS still needs volunteers if you've got so much spare time.'

'Mother was worried about the doctor's bill. I only wanted to help out.'

He looked at me as though I'd slapped him. 'That's nothing to do with you. I provide the money in this house, and if you need anything you come to me. Understood?'

'Yes, Pa.'

'Get up then, and make yourself useful. The rabbits need feeding out the back.'

He whipped the blankets off the bed and tossed them on to the ground. I heard his tread go downstairs. It was silent down there as if the house held its breath. A few minutes later the door slammed.

I pulled my nightdress tight around me and listened. The crackling music of the Andrews Sisters' 'Rum and Coca-Cola' drifted up from below. I exhaled. He had gone out, and Mother was able to pull herself back together and listen to her programme in peace.

When I got downstairs she was pushing a small piece of scrag end through the tabletop mincer. She said, 'He told you then.'

'I know there's a war on, but for heaven's sake, we all need a bit of entertainment.'

'But you'll heed what he said?' Mother stopped winding and fixed me with a warning look.

I looked away from the sight of the meat coming out of the mincer. 'I don't know. I don't like being shouted at like that. He's a big bully. He seems to forget I'm not six years old any more.'

Mother blasted the tap over her hands and said over her shoulder, 'Don't start, Rhoda. I won't hear anything against him, not today'

I scraped the worms of mince into a bowl and covered it with a tea towel. 'Well, he's gone out, so let's just forget about him, hey?'

The market was bristling with people bartering home-made preserves, vegetables and eggs, and there were a few stalls with second-hand woollens and books. I got a few things on

Mother's list, then I stopped at the second-hand stall looking for something to read, and saw a box of sheet music.
Beethoven. It reminded me of Peter. I picked it up. And then
put it down again. Left it where it was, moved my finger
along the spines of the books.

My conscience prickled me, but I reassured myself. I had
done nothing wrong, only agreed to have tea with Matthew
Baxter. Just tea with a friend, that was all. And Peter could
be dead, for all I knew. I tried to conjure him up in my mind,
but he was vague and indistinct – saying goodbye to him
seemed aeons ago.

Later, on the way back from market, I passed the station. It looked just like any other morning. People were hurrying for a train that stood belching steam at the platform,
ready to take passengers to Morecambe. I'd been there only
a few hours ago, in the incandescent glow of the film lighting. The whole memory of the night before had turned into
a film; the haze of diffuse light and smoke, the emotion on
Celia Johnson's face, the dark shadowed features of Matthew
Baxter under the brim of his hat.

The sun emerged momentarily from the clouds to dazzle me and I shielded my eyes. I looked about and saw how
good life was, that the business of living, the bustle, the sheer
activity was right there in front of me – somehow all these
last months I had managed to shut it all out. *Sorry, Peter,* I
thought, in words that were clear as cut glass in my mind, *but
I've waited long enough.*

I left the market with a spring in my step. All the way
home I looked about me with fresh enthusiasm. At the first
yellow daffodils peeping up from the neighbour's garden, at
the sparrows haggling over a discarded peeling in the gut-
ter. Life was here and Peter was not. Time to make my life
amongst the living. I could not wait to see Matthew.

When I got home there was a car parked outside our gate. A new black Humber with a long deep scratch all the way down one side. Raised voices were coming from inside, but this time it seemed to be Mother shouting.

The front door was open and the black-suited figure of Mr Jones the undertaker was taking up most of the space in the hallway. His hat was still on his head and he had backed Mother and Andrew up to the kitchen door.

Mother was wearing an exasperated expression. 'It wasn't me,' Andrew shouted, red in the face.

'I'm telling you, I saw him hanging round before I went in the shop,' Mr Jones said. 'He looked suspicious, so I went upstairs and looked out of the window and saw him get something out of his pocket.'

'I didn't! I—'

'You did,' he said. 'Mrs King, I saw him duck down behind the car and I just knew he was up to something. So I came back out, and saw that. A bloody great scratch, right down one side.'

'I didn't do it,' Andrew said, looking at me for support. 'I saw it was scratched and went over to have a look, that's all. I was just looking at it. It's a nice car. I've done nothing. Nothing!'

'Did you touch that car, Andrew?' Mother scrutinised his face.

'No.' He scowled.

I interrupted. 'Look, let's be calm about this. If Andrew says he hasn't done this, then he hasn't. I'm sorry, Mr Jones, but you can't just accuse him because he happened to be in the street. Anyone could have done it.'

Mother shot me a grateful look.

'It was him, I'd bet my life on it. I'm not satisfied. I'll

come back later and have a word with his father. Someone's got to pay for this and it isn't going to be me. If I get no satisfaction, then I'm sorry, Mrs King, but I'm going to have to go to the police.'

Mr Jones did not remove his hat but just strode away, calling, 'I'll be back later to talk to your husband.'

Mother turned to Andrew. 'Get out of my sight. Go on. Up to your room. We'll see what your father has to say when he comes home.'

Andrew slouched away. Mother shut the door to the stairs after him.

I was halfway into the kitchen when a rhythmic banging from upstairs made me stop in my tracks. Furious, I yanked open the stairway door and shouted up, 'Stop that!'

But the thumping continued just the same. I glanced at Mother. She was slumped over the table, head in hands. I raced up the stairs two at a time and threw open the door. The room was dark because of the blackout blinds, with only a shaft of light from an open window. Andrew was lying on the candlewick counterpane, kicking his heels into the bedhead over and over.

I shouted over the din, 'I said stop it! Haven't you caused us enough trouble already without making it worse?'

'I knew you wouldn't believe me. Nobody ever does.'

'I didn't say that, and you know it.'

I heard the creak of springs as he rolled over. 'But you don't believe me, do you?' His voice was miserable.

I sighed, and sat down on the bed next to him. 'Look, Andrew, I don't know what to believe. What were you doing hanging round the undertaker's anyway? Why weren't you at school?'

'It was PT. I hate PT. People always blame me for things when it's not my fault.'

'We don't. You're imagining it. But you're in a right blinking mess now because Mr Jones will come back again to talk to Pa. You'd better have a good excuse ready as to what you were doing out of school, because you know as well as I do, he won't stand for any nonsense.'

'What do you think he'll do?'

'How should I know? Like all of us he just wants the truth. Tell him the truth – that's always the best thing to do.'

I reached out a hand to comfort him, pat him on the shoulder, but he flinched. 'Go away! Just go away,' he yelled.

I had no option but to leave. He was so prickly, the least thing set him off. I went slowly downstairs, and thought back to when I was his age. Was I as moody as him? It was hard to remember. I suddenly had an image of doing my homework at the kitchen table, and my parents shouting at each other in the scullery.

When I got downstairs Mother was still sitting with her arms on the table, her forehead on her sleeve. Her eyes were puffy as if she'd been crying.

'What are we going to do?' she said. 'Your father'll kill him.'

We waited on tenterhooks for the noise of Pa's key but it was after curfew when a sudden rapping made me almost jump out of my skin.

'I bet that's Jones again, and your father's still not back.' Mother hesitated near the door. But then the hammering again, really hard and insistent.

She wiped her hands on her apron. 'You go – tell him he's not home.'

I undid the chain and turned the key. I pulled open the door a crack but it was not Mr Jones. Two strangers stood there; one was a policeman and one the ARP man in his helmet. 'Can we come in?' said the ARP man.

'Is it about Andrew?' I asked.

'It's your father. He's had an accident. We need to speak to your mother. Is she in? This is PC Tomlinson.'

Mother was already at my shoulder at the sound of the unfamiliar voices, and with the sixth sense she always seemed to have.

'What? What is it?' Her voice held rising panic.

'It's all right, he's at the hospital. They've taken him to Lancaster, to the Royal Infirmary,' PC Tomlinson said.

She was already reaching to the peg for her coat.

'An accident with the firebox. The blackout curtain caught light. The conductor, a Mr McCarthy, went for help, and they've taken Mr King there by ambulance. He was conscious, but he was in quite a bad way – he tried to put it out.'

'We've come to offer you a ride down,' the ARP man said. 'There's enough petrol in my car.'

'Oh, that's kind,' Mother said, looking pale and distracted. 'Rhoda, can you stay here and sort out Andrew's school things?'

I squeezed her shoulder. 'You go, and take care now.' I passed over her coat. 'Send word, won't you, when you know more.'

'Don't wait up. I'll stay until he can come home. Make sure Andrew takes his P.T. kit, his clean shirt is in—'

'Never mind all that, Mother. Just go with the gentlemen now.'

I watched her wind her scarf methodically round her throat and put on her felt hat as if she was going to church. Then she grabbed me by the shoulders and kissed me hard on the cheek. My eyes welled up.

'Thank you,' I said to the ARP man. 'It's kind of you

to take her.' The constable opened the door and helped her into the car.

'You look after your brother,' said the ARP man. Then in a low voice, 'I don't think she'll be back for a few days anyway, he was in pretty bad shape. Let us know if there's anything we can do.'

'Yes, yes, I will.'

I shut the door and turned to see Andrew standing there in his pyjama bottoms, his eyes scared. 'I don't need looking after,' he said. And then, 'He's not dead, is he?'

'No,' I laughed. 'Course he's not dead.'

I held out my arms, but he looked away, embarrassed. He was too old to be comforted. Instead, he took a step back up the stairs. 'What will happen about Mr Jones?'

'Bother Mr Jones. He can go whistle. We've got other things to worry about, now Pa's in hospital – like how we'll manage without Mother. And without Pa's wage.'

'Can I go and see him?'

My heart went out to him. A few minutes ago he'd been terrified of his father. 'Best wait here for news. Mother will get a message to us soon as she can. Now get along up. You've got that test tomorrow, and you're going to school, whether you like it or not.' I saw his mouth begin to protest. 'But tell you what, I'll bring you some cocoa like you used to have when you were a kid. Special treat.'

Thus bribed, he went upstairs. When he'd gone I poked the fire and made myself a piece of toast and dripping. I pictured Mother, her wiry figure all alone in the big hospital. Like Andrew, I still had soft feelings for Pa, I realised. Even if he scared us all. I didn't like the idea of my big strong father lying in a hospital bed. I hoped he wouldn't need to be there too long. Otherwise how would we pay the rent, let alone the hospital bills?

When I woke I managed to press-gang Andrew off to school and get most of the chores done before work. No news had come by lunchtime so I was about to close the bookstall and go to the hospital, but then the fish delivery man from Lancaster came into the station with a hastily scrawled hand-written message:

> *He's very bad. Hands all burned. He's shouting blue murder. Hold the fort for me a few days, will you. Keep an eye on Andrew. Sorry my ration book's here in my bag, so you'll have to use your own coupons or manage somehow.*
>
> *Mother x*

Oh Lord. Poor Pa. He always said that those blackout curtains were an accident waiting to happen. How were you supposed to stoke the fire with a curtain in the way? Mind you, I suppose it was better than the train being bombed.

I pocketed the note and went into the busy refreshment room to order some lunch. I could barely think amidst the clang and clatter of the plates and cutlery. What on earth would Mother do if Pa couldn't work? They'd need my wages more than ever, and Pa might need nursing too. With sicken-ing clarity I saw my precious free time slipping away. When it came, the dried-egg sandwich turned out to be tasteless, and the tea weak, eked out with water to make it go fur-ther. I sighed and pushed them away. Even if the war ended tomorrow I would still be stuck in Carnforth with Mother, nursing Pa and fetching Andrew out of trouble. It was just too depressing.

We were thronged with customers all afternoon, so I didn't have much time to dwell on it, but when the rush abated, I glanced up to see a flurry of small flakes coming down over the edge of the platform. Snow. That was all I needed. And coming up the ramp, Andrew. He shouldn't be out of school yet, so what was he doing here?

I had to serve a customer before I could speak to him. 'What happened?' I asked. 'You're out early.'

He looked down at his feet. 'Des let us out early, because of the snow.'

I was suspicious. 'But it's only a few flakes. And don't call him Des, it's disrespectful.'

'He said that the buses would be off because of the snow. Have you heard anything from Mother? Is Pa all right?'

'What did Mr Measures say?'

'Just that school's closing early. He lives somewhere Morecambe way. Maybe he was worried about getting home. What about Pa?'

I really didn't think Mr Measures would have shut the school for a scattering of snow, but I couldn't face a confrontation. 'I had a note saying he's burned his hands. Mother's staying there a bit longer so it'll be just the two of us. Come on, get your bike.'

'How bad?'

I skirted his questions. 'Don't know yet. Mother says bad, but we'll see when he gets home.'

We mounted up and cycled home through the snow which had now turned into sleet. It stung my face and made it hard to see, but the light covering of white meant it was easier to navigate our way in the dim-out.

Once indoors I lit up a fire and set some potatoes to boil.

'I'm starving,' Andrew said. 'When'll it be ready?'

'About twenty minutes. Get a slice of bread if you can't wait.'

He rummaged in the pantry. 'There's only a crust left, and the butter ration's finished,' he called.

'Get some dripping then.'

'Where is it?'

I put the peeler down in frustration. 'For heaven's sake, just look.'

It was quiet a while and then, 'Rhoda!'

'What?'

'I think the fire's gone out.'

'Well, why weren't you watching it? I can't cook dinner and watch the fire. You have to do your share. See if you can get it going again.'

At least the potatoes should be nearly done. I glanced up to the clock on the mantelpiece. Four-thirty.

Four-thirty! Wednesday at four-thirty. I stood stock-still and stared at the clock. How could I have forgotten? I was supposed to meet Matthew Baxter at the Belmont Tea Rooms. It was as if I'd been suddenly drenched with cold water.

'Andrew!' I was already putting on my coat. I switched off the heat under the pan and hurried to put on my galoshes. 'I've got to go out for half an hour, I won't be long—'

'Why? Where are you going? What about tea?'

'I said, I won't be long, but I have to go now. Right now. I'm late for something at work. I'd forgotten about it.'

'Can I come with you?'

'No, you can't. Look, the potatoes are ready and there's tinned ham in the pantry. I'll be back in fifteen minutes—'

'You said half an hour.'

'I'll see you soon,' I said desperately. 'Just get on with your homework whilst I'm gone.'

Oh gosh, would Matthew still be there? I jumped on my cycle and pedalled away. It was hard going. I had to get off and push the bike up the hill. Snow was coming down thickly now and the front of my coat was plastered white.

I was out of breath by the time I pushed open the door into the café. The clock over the top of the counter said five past five. My heart sank. There were just two elderly ladies sitting there, frowning at me for not closing the door quickly enough and letting the light out and the blizzard in.

Embarrassment did not stop me from asking, 'Was there a young man in here earlier?'

The girl behind the counter said, 'A man in a nice overcoat, Southern accent?'

I nodded.

'Yes. He waited ages. He kept looking at the door every time it opened. He had a cup of tea and a toasted teacake. You've just missed him.'

'Thanks,' I said. 'I got held up.' I didn't want the women to think badly of me and they were staring. I realised it was because I was dripping water on to the nice clean linoleum.

'What will you have?' asked the girl, holding out her pad and pen.

'Oh, nothing. I don't want anything, thanks.' I turned and went out through the door. As I shut it I saw one of the old ladies shake her head at the girl behind the counter.

He'd think I'd stood him up on purpose. I wheeled my bike quickly away, full of nervous agitation. I forced myself to slow and breathe deeply. Perhaps it was a good thing. He was only going to be here a few weeks, and with Pa's accident and everything, it would be hopeless.

What could I have been thinking? I must have been mad. I'd just leave it. Probably best that way. My reasoning mind kept on talking, persuading me that it was for the best, when all the time I was really angry at myself for forgetting, and ashamed to have let Matthew down, for it went against all my feelings of what was right and proper, to do that to someone.

When I got home Andrew had eaten all the potatoes and made a mess of turning the key on the tinned ham so that the tin wouldn't open properly any more, and he'd tried to dig it out with a fork. The fire was out and the room was cold and cheerless.

He was sitting at the table with his empty plate next to him, crumbs of pork jelly blobbed on the table, scratching at some homework. 'Is there any pudding?'

'No.' I was close to tears.

'He'll be all right,' Andrew said, jumping up and putting an arm over my shoulder. 'Mother'll look after him.'

'Yes, I know.' I sniffed and took a deep breath. I couldn't tell him what was really the matter – that Matthew Baxter would think I didn't like him.

38

1945 Peter

'SOMEONE MUST STAND guard,' Annegret said. 'Peter, you will be first.'

He accepted her orders as though she was his commanding officer. They had found a derelict school to give them shelter as the temperature plummeted outside. The school was already home to about twenty other dazed and ragged refugees.

Archie said, 'I'll wait with him. You and Klara go and sleep.'

'No. Peter will wait alone.' Her voice was uncompromising.

Peter knew what she was thinking – that they might take the cart and all her belongings and leave her and Klara there.

Annegret refused to get off the cart until Archie went with her. As she went, she called back over her shoulder, 'If anyone tries anything, shout loud.'

Peter watched the three of them go, struggling with the thin straw mattress and blankets. Klara looked like a bundle of clothes on legs, she was so wrapped up. Peter put the cart round the side of the school out of the wind. He had never driven a horse before, but using the cracked leather reins he managed to steer it the few yards he had to go. This raised his spirits, to be actually deciding things for himself, to be alone for the first time in years.

Above, the weather had cleared to reveal pinprick stars behind ghostly clouds. The sky had a stern beauty. Such clarity was not a good sign as it meant a severe frost, and his extremities were already numb. It would be risking frostbite, to be out here in the open. The cold had kept the swelling down on his ankle though, so he took a handful of oats from the small sack and hobbled round to feed the horse. He did not dare uncouple it, and it stood bedraggled and bony, head hung low.

Afterwards, he huddled inside his greatcoat with his back to the grain sacks and Annegret's bags. He was so tired. It came from allowing himself to come back a little, to a place where he was an individual, not just a number. The slow thawing of a man coming back to life. He must have dozed a little because a slight movement of the cart alerted him – someone else was there in the dark. 'Archie? Is that you?' But there was no answer, and hearing nothing more, he went back to sleep.

When he woke the cart was on a slant. He sat up, disorientated. It was only then that he realised the horse had gone.

Annegret took in the situation but said nothing. What could she say? She stared, unmoved, at the empty traces and Peter's face. He began to apologise, but she waved it away. 'Save your talk,' was all she said. Peter hung his head, could not look up. When she finally walked away, he watched her bend to prepare food for Klara by digging out snow to make meltwater and mixing it with barley for a mash. She looked old, suddenly, tired and old. The remaining straggle of refugees began their trudge away from the shelter in the opposite direction to the Soviet lines.

'We're really stuck now,' Archie whispered.

'It's my fault. You must go on without me,' Peter said. 'I'll be safe enough here. I'll just wait. Nobody will take any notice of me as long as I keep quiet and don't act like a soldier. I'll just have to stick it out until the Soviets or Americans come.'

'You said that before, and you know I'm not doing it.'

'But you can walk with the others. Go with Annegret and her daughter. Help them carry their things. Oh God, I feel terrible. I never heard a thing.'

'Don't, it won't do any good,' Archie said. 'The horse was on its last legs anyway.'

It did not make him feel any better. Peter leaned against the back of the cart, to keep his bad ankle off the ground. 'Is there another route to Dresden? A shorter one?'

'You'll have to look at the map. But I wouldn't fancy it myself. You'd be much more obvious away from all these refugees. We've been lucky so far, but you'd be a sitting duck in open country. And it's so frustrating not to know what's happening or where the Soviets or the Yanks are.'

Annegret handed Peter a bowl with the remains of the food, and came to lean up beside him against the cart, with Klara holding her mother's coat as if she might suddenly run away. Peter dare not look at them. He took a spoonful of the mash with a feeling of disgust for himself. He had done nothing but cause Annegret trouble, yet she fed him just the same. The gruel was bland and cold and his shame made it stick in his throat. He passed it on to Archie.

Annegret said, 'We will unload the cart so we can pull it. We will take turns. Peter can ride sometimes if his ankle is bad.'

'No. You must go on without me.'

'I will splint it again, make a better splint. And I need Archie to pull. He won't come without you. So you will come.'

'But—'

'An end to it. We have to take the wagon. Klara needs sometimes to ride because she is so small and it is so far.' Her lips pressed together in a stubborn line.

Archie said, 'There is a station at Spremberg. I've looked at it on the map. We could go there, see if we can get a train to Dresden.'

'You are crazy,' Annegret said. 'The stations are run by the SS and German army. If you want to stay alive, keep away from them.'

'But Peter won't be able to walk all the way, and maybe the British will have taken the station by the time we get there.'

'And maybe Hitler might be St Nicholas.'

Peter and Archie pulled or pushed the shafts of the cart whilst Annegret and Klara rested a while. It was not as painful as Peter had thought it might be. The cart had large wheels and the landscape was relatively flat. Annegret had strapped his leg firm and bandaged it around his boot. His feet were both numb with cold so it was hard to feel anything anyway. She'd tied a flat slat of wood to his boot too so it slid along the ground and he didn't have to bend his ankle. So now it was only his hip joint that ached, and his arms.

All over Germany people were on the move. Everyone was fleeing from something, and the whole population was in flux, filtering in long lines through the snow-covered landscape. Many had been thrust from their homes with only one bag, while many more had lost parents or children to an enemy that kept changing its face.

Peter sent up a prayer of thanks for Archie and Annegret, that they didn't leave him behind. Annegret had dumped her possessions by the side of the road without complaint. He winced as they helped her haul off the cooking pots, the carved three-legged stool and the framed portrait of a young man in black Victorian clothes that was obviously a family heirloom. What they couldn't wear or eat, they left behind. Other refugees hurried to see what they had discarded, making off with anything useful, picking it over with skinny dirty fingers.

Annegret had given Archie and Peter blankets which they belted over their coats, and woollen hats and scarves to wrap over their faces. Few other men were on the road except for the elderly or the very young. The sun fizzled through the cloud briefly at noon to melt the surface of the road. Annegret's shoes splashed in the water making the hem of her skirt sag with wet.

It was heavy going because despite the thaw, the road was rutted with ice. They stopped every ten minutes or so to rest or change places, but as the day wore on they pushed on harder, hoping to make a village or shelter before nightfall and the bone-creaking cold. Peter ached all over from effort. Just when he thought he could go no further he felt Archie stop pushing the cart. Up in front was the tail of a long line of drab prisoners. Even from here the yellow stars on their backs were clearly visible.

'There'll be German guards with them,' Archie said.

Annegret sensed something the matter and jumped down. For the first time Peter saw how gaunt she had become and that her eyes were shadowed with fear.

'Jews,' she said. 'From one of the camps. We will have to pass them. Cover yourselves well. Here.' She tucked Archie's scarf in round his neck and pulled his hat further down over his eyes. 'Keep your heads down and act old. If they get suspicious I will have to say you held me ransom, and hand you over.'

'What about Klara?'

'You tell her nothing, you hear me? Leave her sleeping. And whatever you do, go slow.' Annegret took the side of the cart closest to the patrol guard and Archie moved over to the right side. He pulled his belted blanket tightly over his greatcoat to hide its origins, and hunched his back. Peter shuffled his way to alongside the cart on the side furthest away from the line of prisoners.

Barely breathing, Peter leaned on the wooden edge of the cart, felt it bump along the track. The noise of the Jewish men's clogs on the wet ice was more like a scraping and scratching than a definite footfall. Peering over from the other side Peter could not see Archie's face beneath his scarf, but Annegret's was grim with tension.

The Jewish prisoners, about fifty of them, were clad only in their striped suits, no coats, gloves or proper footwear. Their progress was slow. They looked to neither left nor right. To Peter they already appeared to be fading away. It wasn't just their skeletally thin wrists poking from their sleeves, their roughly shaven skulls. No, something about them was already ethereal in comparison with the shiny-helmeted guards in their bulky green coats. Peter averted his eyes as they drew nearer, catching them up with each turn of the wheel.

Though Peter's nerves were screaming to get past them, Archie turned his gait to a shuffle. The cart slowed to a snail's pace. Peter was aware of his breath, of every step. He hunched his head into his shoulders, looked down at the muddy ruts of the ground.

Closer. From the sides of his eyes he saw the last few

Jewish men were so weak they could barely walk. One slid silently to his knees, but was dragged to his feet by the others. Under the chassis of the cart Peter watched their shadows extend like black fingers. Without warning a volley of shots sliced through the air and the shadows crumpled. Nobody screamed, nobody cried out.

Don't look, he told himself. *Just keep walking.* But the cart had stopped dead, and he had to stop with it.

'Mutti! Mutti!' In the cart Klara shouted for her mother. He glanced at Archie who was stock-still, cowering against the side of the cart.

'Was liesen Sie?' shouted the guard to Annegret. What are you looking at?

'Nichts,' she replied.

'Gehen Sie auf.' Then get moving.

'Ja. Heil Hitler.'

The cart stuck a moment and Peter saw Archie and Annegret pushing hard, feet trying to get a grip on the slippery surface. Another shot rang out, this time spattering the snow close to Annegret's feet. Klara whimpered and shouted to get down. Annegret panicked, strained against the shaft, just as Peter clamped his teeth together and pushed with all his strength. To his relief the cart lurched off. In the cart Klara lost her balance and toppled over from where she'd been clinging to the side. She began to cry.

'Be quiet,' Annegret said sharply, and miraculously Klara stopped howling.

They moved quicker now, but not too quickly, along the line of grey men. Every step seemed to take an age. Peter could feel his heart thump behind his ribs. One of the guards with a German shepherd dog on a leash came to his side of the cart, to see what the disturbance was. Peter dragged his foot more and cast his eyes to the ground. The dog put its brindled head down and sniffed at his leg but Peter willed himself to ignore it, and to his relief, the guard jerked on the lead and dragged the dog away.

After he had passed, Peter snapped a furtive glance behind. Four grey heaps lay spreadeagled in the wet. Like waste paper, they could almost blow away. Four more who would not make it home.

A sudden yearning engulfed him. To turn back time, to go back to before the war, back to sanity, back to warmth and comfort and a safe place to sleep at night. He had to press his trembling lips together and push the thoughts away as he concentrated on putting one painful foot before the other.

The guards ignored them, let them go by. The Germans themselves looked miserable enough, their faces sullen and pale. They were intent on their charges, the last vestiges of some concentration camp too close to the border.

The cart passed the front of the column without incident, on past a brake of dark trees, the only feature in the landscape. Peter looked back; the Germans were leading their charges into the trees. When they had got about a quarter of a mile away from the Jewish column, another burst of machine-gun fire split the silence. This time longer, the noise ricocheting over and over.

Annegret hoisted Klara off the cart and into her arms. Klara put her mittened hands over her ears, screwed up her eyes. Archie appeared too, to stand next to Peter and look backwards up the road.

A moment's peace. Black rags of crows erupted suddenly into the air, wheeling above the trees, and then, rising, the faint grey of smoke.

'I hope she will be able to forget.' Annegret's voice shook. 'Not all of us are like this.'

'She will,' Archie said. 'She will grow up to be a peace-keeper, and a beautiful kind woman like her mother.'

Annegret moved over to Archie and he put his arms around them both in comfort. It moved Peter, this meeting. Annegret was not beautiful, not in the old sense. But her strength made her something. And Archie – with his scrubby beard, the lank greasy hair, his complexion red with wind and weather, looked like a tramp. But the outside didn't matter. The boy from Lamsdorf who needed someone to like him had gone.

39

1945 Rhoda

I SLEPT FITFULLY, worrying about Matthew Baxter and what he would think of me not turning up. A knock at the door woke me early. When I opened it, still in my dressing gown there was Patty.

'I heard about your pa,' she said. 'I'm sorry. Sounds like he'll be off work a while. I told Hilary and she says there's still work for you at the station canteen – you'll be needing a bit extra for the doctor. And my mother says she's happy to have Andrew overnight, while you're working. She'll feed him, and he can help her babysit Melvin and Margaret.'

'Oh, Patty, that's so nice of her. I don't know though, Andrew can be …' I paused, not knowing how to tell her that Andrew wasn't exactly helpful at home.

'It's only for a few weeks and the money's too good to turn down, you know it is. By then your mother and father will be home and things'll be back to normal. What do you say?'

'I don't know—'

'It'll be all right. You can knock off at four and get a few hours' shut-eye before you have to be at the bookstall, and then get a proper kip after work. You can start at eleven, Hilary says.'

'Go on then. Tell Hilary I'll be there. And thank your mother. I'll tell Andrew to go round after school.'

At eleven prompt I arrived at the station kitchen again, stamping to rid my boots of the melting slush. The air was damp and it made me shiver, so I was glad to be in the warm. I was set to mixing a big vat of dried milk for the pudding, all the time dreading what might happen when Matthew Baxter saw me again.

Patty was glad to see me, a scarf tied round her head to keep the kitchen smell out of her hair. She was chopping turnip to make mash.

'I've seen the papers,' Patty said. 'Looks like the news from the Crimea is good.'

'Everyone's sick of fighting,' I said.

'They were reporting from the Yalta Conference on the BBC – some are saying there might even be an official peace declaration tomorrow.' Patty scooped the turnip into a big metal bowl. 'I can't wait now, I just want it to be over. What will be the first thing you'll buy once rationing ends?'

'Stockings,' Hilary said. 'Mine are more darn than stocking.'

'A great big cream cake made with six eggs and loads of butter and double helpings of strawberry jam. Mmm.' Patty licked her lips.

'Oh, we're not on food again,' Hilary said. 'Shut up dreaming, everyone, and get on with mixing that pudding.'

When the food was ready I nipped round to the stationmaster's office to tell them. Mr Neame, the producer, and Mr Howard had their shoes off and were toasting their socks on the fender before the fire. Mr Howard's sock had a hole in it, and it made him seem more approachable and less of a film star.

'Food in about five minutes,' I said.

'Here,' he said, thrusting a *Daily Express* at me. 'Looks like it's nearly over.'

'Yes, my friend Patty just told me.' I glanced at it and took in the main gist of the headlines – the Germans had sent in tanks at Cleves, but we'd fought past them. Some of the Germans had surrendered. Koniev was getting nearer and nearer to Dresden, and the Soviets were mustering massive forces. Some Germans said they'd rather surrender to us than the Soviets because the Soviets were ruthless and they were afraid of them. I thought of Peter then. I'd not really thought of it before, but of course these German troops would feel fear too. What a whole bloody mess.

'Did you see that bit about the cost of the war?' Mr Neame said.

'Where?' I said, scanning the sheet.

'Bottom-right column. Fifty-nine thousand five hundred million pounds – that's America's war bill to us. We could have made a few feature films with that. How on earth did they work it out, though? Beats me.'

'There's probably someone adding up all the bullets and putting it in a little notebook. Or more likely they just made it up,' Mr Howard said.

I handed him back his paper, thinking of Peter's father and his notebook obsession. 'Thanks.'

'You got anyone out there fighting?' Mr Howard's eyebrows raised in question, and I suddenly got a glimpse of his handsome film face.

'No. I mean …' I hesitated, shoved my left hand with my engagement ring into my pocket. 'My brother's not old enough. But my father's in the Home Guard.' I didn't mention that he was in hospital. And I said nothing about Peter either, and my conscience fluttered briefly before I turned to go.

When we set off with the trolley we were in time to see one of the engines just arriving in a stink of oil and steam, ready for the next take.

The cold air revived me. On the other side of the station Matthew was deep in conversation with Mr Neame and Mr Holding, the production manager. They were pointing at the platform and seemed to be indicating that the train had come in too far. Before long it was reversing slowly out again. I watched Matthew surreptitiously as Hilary and Patty chattered.

'Hello, girls.' It was Ed Owen. 'What's cooking?'

'If you mean what's for dinner, it's steak-and-mushroom pie come up from London, and turnip mash by yours truly,' Patty said. 'Mind, Hilary says you get prizes if you can find any steak in there.'

Hilary laughed.

'I bet it's very good,' said Maggie, the continuity girl, joining us. 'I always enjoy the food.' Patty smiled and they were soon deep in conversation about the rationing.

'I say, you haven't a spare smoke, have you?' Ed said.

'I thought you Londoners were the flash ones,' I said.

'Here, have one of these.' Maggie handed him a green pack of Craven Plain before turning back to Patty.

He thanked her, and offered me one but I shook my head.

'Where do you come from in London?' I asked.

'Oh, I'm not from London, I'm from Dorset originally,' Ed said, striking a light. 'But I live there now. I share a flat with old Matthew. Keep an eye on him.' I raised my eyebrows and he took a puff before adding, 'Watch he doesn't

get involved with the wrong type.' He winked at me knowingly, and I felt myself redden.

'Come on. Food's getting cold,' Hilary said.

When we served the meals Matthew didn't say a thing, and I
couldn't speak either. It would be too embarrassing in front
of all those people. I didn't meet his eyes, just left him to
Hilary. But he was waiting for me when I finished, shoulders
hunched against the cold.

'I've only got a few minutes,' he said. 'They've ordered
the car to take us back to the Low Wood. Did you forget
about yesterday, or did you not turn up on purpose?'

'I'm really sorry, I tried to come, but we'd had a bit of a
crisis at home, and I got there too late.'

'Look, it's too cold to talk, stood out here. Let's go in
the stationmaster's office. The others won't mind.' He ushered me through the underpass and on to the platform.

We passed people packing up cabling and lights into
skips, and hauling trucks of equipment into the left-luggage
store. I saw Ed look up at us and glance away as if he knew
we did not want to be seen. The room was warm but empty.
I wasn't expecting that and it made me suddenly wary, like an
animal on unfamiliar territory.

I paused a moment until Matthew had taken a seat and
then I joined him at one of the card tables.

'Shoot,' he said.

I told him about Pa. He looked into my face all the time
I was speaking with an unnerving attention. I was conscious
of my hands fiddling in my lap, the ring on my finger. But
then he stopped me by reaching out for my hands and stilling
them between his own.

I looked up and swallowed. 'I don't think I can do this.'

'Shh,' he said, stroking my hand. 'We'll just sit a moment, shall we? Quietly, whilst there's nobody here.'

I nodded and his hand continued to stroke mine. My neck was hot, my scarf felt tight. It was as if the world had shrunk suddenly to the size of my palm, the subtle sensation of our twining fingers, of his hands exploring mine. I thought I might faint with the feeling of it.

'Matt?' A voice calling on the platform. He jumped, and his hand jerked away in reflex, leaving mine empty. I looked down at my knees, filled with a sense of loss.

'The car's here,' he said. 'Look, we'll see each other again, won't we? The café, Saturday at four-thirty?'

'Matt?' The voice was frustrated now, and suddenly the door flew open.

Matthew stood up to go.

'Come on, we're all waiting.' Ed frowned at us both.

'You'll be there this time, won't you?'

My 'yes' came out as a whisper.

In a few seconds he was gone and I was left in the empty room. The cold draught from the door had blown ash over the floor. I scuffed it back towards the hearth with my shoe, my senses fizzing. The room looked too mundane for what had just occurred. I realised with horror that I was in love.

40

1955 Helen

'I KNOW IT wasn't ideal. I'm sorry, they rather ruined our lunch, didn't they?' Peter said.

'It's all right. It couldn't be helped,' Helen said, doodling frantic spirals on the telephone pad.

'You're not upset about it?'

'No. Why should I be?' She changed ears to relieve the pressure.

'Nothing. You dashed off, without ...' Peter's voice died away.

'It's just I felt awkward. Your friends kept talking about Rhoda, and it made me feel terrible. Cheap, somehow.'

'Oh, Helen, that's nonsense. I'm sure they didn't notice anything, didn't see any harm in it.'

'But that's just it, there is something, isn't there. I mean ... I got the impression you'd like us to be more than good friends.'

There was a silence. Helen thought, *oh no, I've gone too far, scared him off.*

'Yes.' He cleared his throat. 'I suppose you're right. I hadn't quite got that far in my thinking – no, that's not true. I had hoped, well, I didn't know how you felt. I just wanted to spend more time with you, that's all.'

'Sorry if I'm a bit blunt, but you know me, I like to know where I am. And when Malcolm and Sylvia came, well – it became impossible to pretend that Rhoda doesn't exist.'

'Yes, yes. I realise, I put you in an awkward situation. But Rhoda probably wouldn't care anyway – she doesn't take much notice of me when I am there. She's always out at one thing or another. Of course you've never met her, she always had some excuse or another.'

Helen knew this was an economical version of the truth and felt a twinge of outrage and sympathy for Rhoda, but she didn't pick him up on it. Inside she wanted to keep Peter up on his pedestal. Men, she thought, why did they have to manoeuvre everything to suit themselves?

'Anyway,' he carried on, 'I'd like to see you again, that is if you'd like to. I promise we won't be interrupted this time.'

Helen said, 'But what about Rhoda?'

She heard him sigh. 'I don't know. Let's just see how it goes, shall we? All I know is that I like your company and I'd like to take you out to dinner.'

Helen found herself wavering. 'I don't know.' The doodling had turned into jagged zigzags.

'What about next Saturday night? I'll pick you up at seven o'clock.'

'You're twisting my arm.'

'I know I am, and I promise not to rush you into anything, but … oh, I don't know, let's not squash it before it's begun, eh? It will be a chance to talk. Go on, say yes. Someone told me about a nice French restaurant over Slyne way.'

'All right, but—'

'Wonderful. I'll pick you up Saturday, seven o'clock.'

She hung on until he'd rung off, then caught sight of herself in the hall mirror, her face red and glowing, eyes shining. So she was right, it was 'something' after all, he did see her as more than a friend. Just see how it goes, he'd said. But she knew she liked him. She always had, ever since they'd first met all those years ago. Archie had always said Peter was a hero, that he'd saved Archie from going crazy in the first few months in the camp, and she supposed the idea had stuck; her Peter had always had a golden glow around him. She'd been impressed by him too; being a headmaster of a school.

She used to get dressed up when she knew he was coming, even in the old days when Archie was alive. Her memory began to replay a dozen little scenes she thought she'd forgotten. She remembered baking cakes and scones, making the house smell sweet and homely; Peter's legs sprawled out in front of him in the lounge, taking up too much room so she had to step over them on the way to the kitchen.

She sighed. A heady mixture of nostalgia and excitement. She went through to the kitchen and absent-mindedly rearranged the canisters on the worktop. She cared for him too much already, she knew, and it might only end in tears. The calendar on the wall caught her eye. Next Tuesday's date had 'Rhoda 2 p.m.' scrawled there. She paused, pen poised over Friday's date. She couldn't put his name. Instead she filled in the square with a big asterisk like an exploding star.

41

1945 Peter

BETWEEN THEM THEY worked out a route to the railway station. From there, Peter hoped to get to Dresden and find concrete news of where the English or Americans were. Annegret had talked to another German woman, who had told her the German army was in retreat and the Soviets and Americans were shrinking Germany, squeezing their grip from both sides. But these were just rumours.

He had to make it to England somehow. He had come too far, lost too much to think otherwise. His mind skated around the thought of Rhoda. He had been away nearly five years. Would she even know him when he returned? He did not want her to know the prisoner of war Peter. He was too ashamed. He'd have to clean himself up, become the trustworthy teacher again, the man who could look a class of twelve-year-olds in the eye without flinching. But that would be just the outside. What about what was inside? It wouldn't be so easy to clean that away.

It was thanks to Annegret they'd survived so far. He admired her. She had shared her food and her fire with him, even though he was her enemy. The pain in his leg was bearable now and it might even heal itself. He had given Annegret precious little in return. The Red Army had not come, he had not had to use the knife that still pressed cold against his chest. He was in an enemy country heading for an enemy town where, if he was found, he would certainly be shot. He was a liability, he knew. Without him, Archie would be able to move much more freely, yet Archie showed no signs of leaving him, had stuck by him all the way. He wondered why. Perhaps it was just that to die with a friend was better than to die alone.

He was filled with a sudden rush of affection and grate-fulness. With Archie he didn't have to explain.

Just outside Spremberg they decided to leave the cart and go on without it. It would make them less obvious, and now the distance was shorter they might be able to manage the last mile or so free of it. Annegret carried a small leather suitcase and a tied bundle over her back. Archie carried her larger case for her, as well as his own pack. When anyone spoke to them, which was rarely, it was always Annegret who answered, not Peter or Archie, even though their German was passable.

Klara walked, holding hands between Archie and Annegret.

'We're going on a train, Klara,' Archie said. '*Der Zug.* Chuff, chuff.'

'Chuff chuff,' Klara said. She had begun to talk more now. She smiled up at Archie. Her worn-out scarf and thread-bare coat only emphasised the pallor and youth of her skin.

Peter limped behind, a pack strapped to his back, each step a struggle with his bad ankle. Now that there was no cart to prop him up, a stick, hastily made from a fallen branch wrapped with cloth, did its job well enough, though after half a mile the pressure on his hand gave him blisters. The weather was warmer though, and the snow had melted into patches of dirt road and paving.

Just outside the town they passed a man hanging from the lamppost by his neck, his feet dangling only a few feet from the ground.

Annegret hurried past, trying to distract Klara from the sight. Klara did not even flinch. It made Peter sad to see her, that a child should not find this sight shocking. But further down the road there was another, and another. All the lampposts had dead men hanging there. One of them, a young lad by the look of him, in a Sunday suit and no shoes, had a scrawled placard tied around his neck. Peter limped over for a closer look. It was easy to translate.

'I have been hanged here because I am too cowardly to defend the Reich.'

Peter shivered. If anyone mistook him or Archie for a deserter or a man who wouldn't fight, then the same fate would await them. Annegret turned to him. 'The SS. They have been here. Are you sure you want to carry on? They will control also the station.'

Archie said, 'We haven't got a plan B. It's dangerous wherever we go. We'll just have to trust to Lady Luck.'

Peter stopped. 'We're a risk to you, Annegret. We'll go a separate route if you'd rather.'

She seemed to consider this a moment. 'No. I've got used to you. Klara likes you. We have seen too many uncivilised men. Would you hang your own countrymen? No. With you stupid English we feel safe.' She smiled a rueful smile.

He laughed. Annegret put her arm out to him so he leaned on her as they walked on down the road towards the station. It felt companionable, this brush of human contact. The thought that it might be his last touch made his eyes well up. He glanced sideways at Annegret's determined face under her blue-patterned headscarf, as she bore his weight on the shoulder of her faded woollen coat. A surge of love hit him so painfully it made him falter.

Many more folk had had the same idea of trying to get a train, and worse, the station looked to be a depot for the German Armoured Division. From above, the long red-brick station must have looked like home to a seething mass of brown ants. All of humanity was there. Refugees and the dispossessed trying to go one way, and German militia trying to go the other. Cattle trucks screeched to a standstill to be loaded with crates of shells. Ragged queues stretched in all directions, some people unsure where they were going, most desperate to be on the move in any direction as long as it was not on their own two feet.

They joined a line of refugees. Across from them, fresh-faced, clean-shaven young German boys in uniform joked and laughed, though the air about them bristled with tension. They knew they were going to the front, and the way they sucked quick drags on their cigarettes showed their fear. None of them paid the refugees any attention. It was as if by joining this horde of women and children and the elderly, Peter and Archie had become invisible. They kept their heads down and did not speak, did nothing to draw attention to themselves.

Klara was fascinated by the Hitler army and stared, her finger in her mouth. One of the young men saw her staring and winked, smiled back at her. It made Peter wonder if he had sisters at home. To keep her occupied Archie tore out a piece of paper from his precious notebook and gave her the army-issue pencil to draw with.

'*Was kann ich zeichnen?*' Klara asked.

'Draw Grandma's house. *Deine Grossmutter.* Where we're going,' Archie said.

She shook her head. '*Mein Haus. Ich zeichne gern meinem Haus.*'

She became completely engrossed until the clang of the station bell announced the arrival of a train and the people behind them surged forward, pushing them from behind until they were jammed together. But it was going up the line, and the queue of German boys in their neat black boots and carefully arranged caps pressed forward and on to the platform. Peter breathed a sigh of relief when they went; he felt safer with civilians.

The crowd spread out again to give more standing room.

'Will you be all right?' he asked Archie, knowing what he was like in crowded places.

'I'll have to be,' Archie said.

'Try not to be sick on my boots this time,' Peter joked, but Archie ignored it, glanced tersely ahead to the milling crowd.

Annegret asked Klara, 'Give me your pencil.'

She turned over Klara's picture and squatted down, leaning on the notebook to write. When she had done she handed Peter the paper. 'In case we get separated,' she said. 'The address of my mother in Dresden.'

'Thanks,' he said, smiling at her. 'Thanks for—'

But the bell clanged again and he had no time to say more; the press of people carried them forwards towards the barrier at the platform. As Peter got nearer he saw what he had not seen before – that the barrier was staffed by SS who were checking everyone's papers.

He grabbed Archie's arm to pull him back. 'No!' he said. 'The SS!'

In that moment the train trundled into the station. There were only four carriages on the train, not enough for all these people.

'I've got this far, I'm going to risk it,' Archie said over his shoulder.

'No, please,' Peter said, 'it's madness'. He clung on to Archie's arm.

People pushed and shoved to get past them, cursing. Ahead of them Annegret was carried forward by the crowd. She looked over her shoulder, but could not come back against the tide. A tumult of voices, different languages, the noise of a baby crying. Someone pushed Peter violently in the back and he staggered forwards, but still he would not let Archie go. Annegret hoisted Klara on to her hip. Klara turned back to look for Archie, her hand stretching out to him, but had to grab tight to her mother's shoulder as she was jerked forwards by the surge of the crowd.

'Let me go! I'm going with them.' Archie twisted sharply and swam towards the barrier.

Annegret paused, searched for her papers in her pockets, but finally held them up to the guard who nodded her through. She cast one look back at them before the rest of the mass of people closed in around her. Archie fought to get nearer the barrier, but Annegret's suitcase caught on people's legs. Peter could do nothing; he was helpless in the movement of the crowd.

Too late, the SS guards closed the metal gate, raised their guns in front.

The people sighed and fell back. On the platform Annegret's blue-patterned headscarf moved forwards amongst the other hats and caps and up into a carriage. He couldn't see Klara – she was too small – until a large woman hoisted her up and crammed her into the train. Annegret's arms came out to meet her, before they were both pressed out of sight.

The train left and soldiers cleared the platform of those who could not climb on board, pushing people back behind the barriers at gunpoint. Archie left his place in the queue and came to lean against the wall next to Peter. His knees shook, his face was white. He leaned back and closed his eyes a moment before dropping to the ground. There, he hoisted Annegret's suitcase on to his knee, and buried his head and arms on top as if clinging to a raft.

So now they were on their own; two men together who stood out from the families fleeing from the east. The dark shadowy arches of the station suddenly appeared more hostile. Peter whispered, 'Let's get away from here – we stick out too much.'

Archie raised his head, tearful. 'They're on their own now. I don't like them being on their own.'

'But you saw – they were looking at everyone's papers. You'd never have got through. We'll have to try some other way. I've got the map in my pack – we should try to go to where we might meet some Allied troops.'

'And where the hell's that?' he snapped. 'I've no idea.' His face was pinched with pain. 'We're out of touch, all we've heard is Nazi propaganda. We've no solid evidence to say the Americans are anywhere near here. They could be miles away. Annegret said—' He paused.

Peter looked up. There was an older woman in a black pinafore staring at them. Their conversation might arouse suspicion. So he smiled and nodded at her and kept quiet. She did not smile back.

Archie stood and went a little further away from the woman. Peter watched him light a cigarette. At that moment he hated him – he was hurt that Archie had nearly left him behind.

Archie took a drag, then said, 'You should have let me go with them. Our only chance is to try and bluff our way through on to the next train.'

'There's got to be another way.'

'What way? You can't bloody walk.'

'I'll manage.'

'Well, I'm going to try it. You can either come with me or go your own way. It's up to you.'

'I'm not prepared to risk it.'

'Then give me Annegret's address.'

Peter felt in his pocket for the paper. He passed it over without a word.

Archie took it and stuffed it into his pocket. He held out the unfinished cigarette.

Peter was about to thank him, until Archie dropped it in front of him, crushed it under his boot and walked off to join the queue which was already snaking around the side of the long brick building.

From habit Peter bent to try to salvage the dog-end from the wet. Archie couldn't really mean to go by himself, could he? He'd be shot if they caught him without papers. A flood of panic. Without Archie, then the chances of him getting home by himself were slim. Worse than slim. Peter could not stay still. He paced the platform, limping, cursing his bad foot, wondering what to do, unable to go nearer the gate. Never in his life had he felt so alone.

42

1945 Rhoda

IT WAS AFTER lunch when the ambulance came bringing Pa home. There was a slit of light in the upstairs window when I got home from work. I would have to make an excuse – this time I was determined to get away again in time to meet Matthew.

I took my key out of the door and pushed it open. Mother called, 'Is that you, Andrew?'

'No, it's me,' I called, already heading up the stairs.

'Where's Andrew? Is he with you?'

'It's all right, Mother, he's with Mrs Goodhalgh – you know, Patty's mother.'

'It was only then that she let the door to their bedroom swing open and I could see Pa lying flat on his back in bed. Mother and Pa had always had twin beds, and he was in Mother's nearest the door, which was all wrong. He didn't sit up.

'It's Rhoda,' she said to him.

'I know,' he said irritably, but still he didn't move.

'You'll have to lean over him – he can't move much because of the pain.'

I went around the side of the bed, noticing that it was

piled up with crocheted blankets and a slippery feather quilt usually put away for best.

'How are you feeling?' I asked.

He didn't answer me. I reached over to pat him on the shoulder and saw his head flinch away. He'd lost his eyebrows and his nose was blistered, his lips peeling and raw. 'Go and get our Andrew,' he said with difficulty. 'He should be home. What's he doing with that woman, anyway?'

'He stayed there last night so I could work. We'll be needing extra now you're off shift.'

'He's not staying there with them, do you hear? Not with Jack Howarth who won't lift a finger to fight. And you've no—' Here he broke off into a fit of coughing. His face and neck suffused red, he could hardly catch his breath. I tried to help him sit up but he yelped as I touched his arms. He was a dead weight and I could not shift him.

'It's the smoke, love,' Mother said. She fussed me out of the way and helped him take a drink from a cup with a straw in. His hands were big wedges of bandage. He couldn't even clasp the cup.

It was the cup that did it, his helplessness. He was suddenly an old man, his head small on the pillow of the bed, his strength buried under the heap of blankets. I made a pretence of straightening the quilt. It was clear he was unable to use his hands, and the slow realisation of what that would mean was only now dawning on me. A weariness came over me, not for me but for Mother. I saw what it would mean for her, knew she would shoulder this burden just the way she had dealt with every other disaster life had thrown at her.

'I'll send Andrew over later, Pa,' I said. 'You just rest now.' I exchanged a look with Mother. Her face was unreadable, but the lines around her mouth seemed to be etched deeper. 'We'll manage,' I whispered, and squeezed her arm.

The slogans said that a nice cup of tea could cure anything but it couldn't cure this. He would be an invalid until his hands were recovered and we would just have to get used to it. A nurse was going to come the next day to tell us how to do the dressings. His hands would be badly scarred, Mother said, and he'd be lucky to get his grip back. The nurse would tell us exercises we could make him do.

We tiptoed around the subject of caring for him, neither of us wanting to truly take responsibility for it. All the while I could see the clock ticking around to four o'clock, four fifteen.

I knew I couldn't leave Mother. She was overwhelmed with just the thought of it, and drained with four nights on a chair at the hospital.

'What happened?' I asked her.

'They still have to have the firebox covered. In case the lights are seen by enemy aircraft. It was windy and the cover went up. Bertie Hammell's new, he couldn't cope. He just panicked. The thing was blazing away, and shreds of flaming cloth blowing back towards the carriages. By all accounts your pa put it out with his bare hands. Typical. Both hands straight in without thinking.'

'Poor Pa. Is Bertie all right?'

'Not as bad as your pa, but burns to his chest and arms. It'll kill your pa, not being able to go to work. I don't know how I'll cope.'

'Look, Mother, you must rest. You can have my room. Get a good sleep. I'll go in and see to him while you get some kip, then when Patty calls for me I'll wake you. It'll be all right.' I saw that the clock on the mantelpiece had reached four-thirty. Matthew would be waiting. But I couldn't go, couldn't leave Mother. He'd probably give up, now.

Mother interrupted my thoughts. 'What about Andrew?'

I rubbed my face, let out a long breath. 'He's all right staying where he is for now. Tomorrow we'll sort it all out.'

'But there's dinner to cook, and what if your pa needs ...' but she tailed off. The realisation of the care he might need made her tearful and she brought out a crushed handkerchief.

'It'll be fine. I'll make us something. You go and put your nightie on.' I hugged her tight and she leaned on my chest. 'It's only one night. Then the nurse will be here to tell us what to do.'

She went up, and I grabbed the teacups and went to the scullery. What could I have been thinking, to even consider some sort of relationship with Matthew Baxter? I imagined him sitting waiting again in the café, in his good-quality overcoat and paisley scarf with the yellow lining. I pictured his slim hands turning the pages of the *Daily Express*, a cup of coffee half-drunk in front of him. The whole thing was impossible. I sighed, took a limp pinafore from the back of the door and slipped it over my head.

Mother was at last resting in bed, and the house was quiet. I got a taper and lit the gas, then half-heartedly put some dried apples to soak to make an apple charlotte with the leftover bread.

A knock at the door. Who now? I wiped my hands on my pinny and opened the door.

Matthew Baxter stood there, his hat in his hands.

Panicked, I pulled off the pinafore with a quick movement and hurried out on to the step.

'When you didn't come, I thought something must be the matter, and I couldn't sit and wait not knowing,' he said.

'Who is it?' Mother's voice from upstairs. Trust Mother. She wasn't sleeping after all.

I called back up, 'Rest up, it's only the papers.' I threw

the pinafore over the top of the mangle and tried to shut the door on our kitchen. I didn't want him to see how we lived.

'He's late today,' Mother said.

'Don't fuss, Mother,' I shouted. 'I'll deal with it.'

I propped up the snick and pushed the door closed behind me. 'I'm sorry,' I said, whispering. 'My father's just home from the hospital and my mother needs a bit of help.' I hurried out on to the pavement and gestured for us to go around the corner. 'Sorry. I meant to come but I couldn't get away. Pa can't do a thing. His hands are in a terrible state.' Matthew began to make sympathetic noises but I took a shaky breath and hurried on over him, 'And I'm sorry if I led you on, but I can't do this, Matthew. It's getting too deep, and it's just too complicated.'

He watched me talking, but I got the sense my words were like rain, just running off him.

'You do like me ... don't you?' he said. It was a statement of fact more than a question.

'I can't see how we'll get the time. Besides, you'll be going back to London soon, to your other life, and then it will be hopeless. And I'll be needed at home more than ever.'

'There's a week or so before that, and there are such things as trains, you know.'

I turned to look over my shoulder at the house, which was pulling at me as if I was held there by a length of string.

'Is it him? Your fiancé? I haven't forgotten he exists, but I know my own feelings too and in wartime you have to seize the moment when it comes because it might never come again. Rhoda?' He took me by the shoulders. 'I look at your picture every night.'

It was like being caught in the glare of headlights; it was so bright I could barely see.

'Do you love him?'

'No. I mean, I don't know. It's Pa, he's really bad. And as for Peter, I've had no word. I don't know if he's dead or alive. And it would be terrible to do this to him if he's waiting for me in some German camp somewhere, and … oh Lord, even worse to do this to him if he's dead. Disrespectful somehow.'

'So what should we do? I can't turn off my feelings for you.' His voice was very calm, his gaze fixed on mine.

I backed off. 'I need to think of my family and put them first. You'll soon forget about me.'

'I doubt it.'

I swallowed, shivered in the cold. 'Sorry, but I just can't.'

He reached to pull me towards him but I was conscious of the neighbours and the windows behind me.

'No,' I said, jerking away. 'I have to go. Look, I'll see you later. We can be … friends, that's all. I have to go.' And I turned and ran. I heard my heels tapping against the pavement. As I rounded the corner I saw him from the corner of my eye, still standing there, his slim silhouette sharp against the grey road.

It was only when I got inside that I allowed myself to be angry. It was all right for him. He was free to do what he chose. He didn't have such a complicated home life. My chest felt as though it had been run over.

'Rhoda. Rhoda!' Pa wanted me.

I hurried up into the bedroom. 'Shh! Mother's sleeping and don't you dare wake her.'

'I don't mean to be a trouble.' His voice had taken on a whingeing tone. 'I need a drink. And when's tea going to be ready? Your mother couldn't get me anything worth eating in that hospital.'

'You'll have to wait, Pa. It'll be ready in about twenty minutes. Can you sit up for it?'

'No. It's too damned difficult, and it hurts like hell. You'll have to help me.'

I sighed, fought the urge to just leave the whole damn mess and run after Matthew. In the kitchen I slammed the cupboard door so hard that all the crockery rattled.

43

1945 Peter

PETER USED THE wall to claw his way to standing. Nobody
wanted to lose their place so everyone slept in the road, heads
on their baggage. He was anxious. Archie had barely spoken
a word since Annegret and Klara had left, and he must have
been up early because he was much further down the queue
than Peter. He swallowed. Did Archie really mean to risk
it? It would be suicide. Nobody could get past those Nazi
guards.

Refugees were still pouring into the town. It reminded
him of something biblical, this mass exodus, a whole population on the move. Several trains rattled into the station and
out again. The military had commandeered all the trains at
Spremberg to send troops to and from the front. The queue
compressed towards the platforms.

Archie's head moved further and further away from
him down the line as the hours passed. Peter's ankle hurt
again, a deep throbbing pain. Several times he almost joined
the queue, but he was afraid. It was the same feeling he used
to have as a child when he couldn't swim and stood terrified
and shivering on the edge of the freezing pool, his bare toes
a few inches above the water.

At one point a fleet of army ambulances arrived. There

was a clamour from the crowd who hoped the trucks had come to deliver food or fresh water, but no, they were medical orderlies there to meet one of the trains. The train was a freight train of cattle trucks. The German conditions for their own wounded were as bad as for prisoners of war. Troops waiting for the train out were ordered to lug the covered stretchers bearing the bodies of men who'd died on the journey.

It seemed inhumane, this. That the young German soldiers were seeing the spectre of what they, in only a few days, would become. Sympathy stabbed like a needle in his chest. The German youths were white-faced and trembled under their caps. Their new uniforms were soiled with blood as they loaded the screaming men into waiting trucks.

When they'd gone, the crowd moved further down. Terror for Archie made Peter light-headed. He looked up the road. Another wave of refugees. If he didn't move now he would lose sight of Archie and be on his own. Archie wouldn't – he wouldn't leave him behind, would he? Peter craned to catch sight of Archie's head. A ripple of panic overtook him and he limped to the end of the line, just behind an elderly woman with a wrinkled blue-faced baby in her arms.

The clanging bell resounded in his ribs.

A train. In the right direction this time, but only four carriages again.

The crowd surged forward, everyone elbowing and jostling so that he cannoned into the woman in front. A bag on the old lady's back smacked him in the face as she turned to curse him. Peter couldn't see Archie any more – there were just too many people. The queue stopped abruptly, Peter almost tripped and fell.

Ahead of him there was a disturbance, the noise of shouting and a woman's cries. A rat-a-tat of gunfire. The people behind pushed him like a solid wall. Peter caught hold of the old woman's shoulders and tried to move her aside, but she couldn't move, she too was wedged fast.

'*Entschuldige mich*,' he said, trying to squeeze past a man on his left, but he was not quick enough.

After what seemed like only seconds he heard the rhythmic noise of the train accelerating and an audible collective sigh of disappointment.

He stood on tiptoe. He was about fifteen yards from the barrier; there was still a knot of people there, but he couldn't see Archie anywhere.

There was something lying on the track, surrounded by soldiers, but he couldn't see what it was. He stopped a woman coming back from the barrier with a hand on her arm. '*Was ist los?*'

She shrank away from his urgent manner. '*Tot. Keine Papiere.*' She pulled her arm away from him, called protectively to her young son to follow her.

Someone was dead.

Peter fought his way towards the barrier through the hostile crowd. He used all his strength, not caring who he was elbowing aside. One angry old man yelled at him in guttural German. When he ignored it he spat at him, gestured him to go back to the end of the line. Peter knew it was risky to draw attention to himself, but he had to know if Archie had made it on to the train.

He felt someone take hold of him by the waist. Peter turned in anger, to push the person away.

A pair of familiar pale blue eyes anxiously searching his.

Archie. My God. 'You stupid bugger. I thought you were a goner. Don't you ever do that to me again, you hear?' He shoved him hard in the chest. Archie doubled over. Shocked, he stood upright, flinched away.

'Don't. People will notice.' Archie beckoned him away from the barrier. 'You were right,' he said. 'They shot the man in front of me who could not produce his papers quick enough. It was horrible. His wife and kids were stood there screaming. He was shouting for mercy – Czech, I think. Anyway, a language I couldn't understand.' Archie leaned over, put his hands to his knees.

Peter rested a hand on his shoulder, felt him shivering through his clothes like a dog just out of cold water.

Archie inhaled a convulsive breath and stood. 'I'll be all right in a minute.'

Peter waited, rubbing his back.

'Sorry,' Archie said. 'It just got to me. As if he wasn't worth a farthing.'

'Not worth the risk then. We'll have to try to cut across country. Let's get somewhere we can talk, look at the map.'

'I hope Annegret and Klara are all right. I've still got her case, look.' Archie held up Annegret's suitcase. It was a battered old thing, tied together with what looked like the belt of a dressing gown, the leather corners warped and scuffed with use.

'If we're not going to meet them in Dresden there's no point in taking it with us,' Peter said.

'There might be something useful in it.'

'Okay. But let's look first, see if it's worth carrying. She won't mind.'

They walked away around the corner of the building, past the long straggling queue, and sat down, backs to the wall. Archie's hands were shaking so Peter untied the belt and opened the case.

'I don't like it, Pete. It feels like spying, to go through

her things,' Archie said, as Peter passed a white blouse and a hand-knitted jersey into his hands.

'I know, but they're no use to her. Not now we've got them anyway.'

There was a wedding photograph in a frame in which a smiling Annegret was seated with a bouquet on her lap. Behind her a handsome man in German military uniform stood with his hand resting on her shoulder. Peter gave it to Archie and saw him stare at it a moment too long before he said, 'He must be short, to have the photo taken with her sitting down. Old photographer's trick.' He thrust it at Peter. 'Put it back.'

Peter slid it to the bottom of the case. His hand felt some papers underneath what looked like a pile of school exercise books, a batch of documents all together. Peter picked one out.

'*Deutsches Reich Kennkarte*,' he read. He opened it to see the serious face of a boy staring out at him. Dieter Schönhorst. Annegret's dead son. The same straight nose, same square jaw. Here he was. It was sad to think he'd been so recently alive, a boy still so young his identification card was being looked after by his mother.

Another small square tan-coloured book caught his attention. '*Soldbuch*', it said, with a logo of an eagle clutching a wreath and a swastika in its talons.

'Look at this,' he said with mounting amazement. 'It's her husband's papers. Karl Schönhorst.'

'But he's dead, isn't he?' Archie scowled.

'Yes, but I think this is his paybook and ID. She's kept it as a memento.' Peter held it out towards Archie. 'How awful. Husband and son both gone, and so close together. But what do you think?' He raised his eyebrows. 'It's got to be worth a try.'

'No. Too risky. You didn't see them gun that Czech down.'

'Let's think it through, weigh it up.'

Archie was quiet for a few minutes, his forehead furrowed. 'Well, I've saved a photo of me and my mother. It might just be big enough for me to do something with. I could take the boy's permit and try and put my picture there instead of his. Pass me the boy's permit.' Peter watched him touch the face with his forefinger. 'He looks like her, doesn't he?' He sighed, braced his shoulders, 'It's possible. I'd have to cut carefully round those rivet holes, though.'

'What about the stamp?'

'Don't know. Suppose I could try to copy it. It's quite grey and faded. It might work. Have you still got your pencil?'

Peter patted his pocket. 'That will leave me with the soldier's pass then.' He looked through the booklet, trying to decipher the German as best he could. 'Oh Lord, I'm pretty sure this word says "deceased" here. What can we do about that? And I look nothing like him. Not to mention my uniform under this lot.'

They ruminated a moment.

'Here.' Archie whipped the book out of his hand and taking it to the edge of the road, smeared mud liberally over the pages and particularly over the word '*verstorben*'. When he had finished it looked as though the pass had been in battle somewhere.

'Hey, that's not bad.'

Archie grinned, pleased. It was the first time he'd ever praised him, Peter realised.

He tried not to show how cheered he was at Archie's reaction. With his pal by his side, life was suddenly brighter. Perhaps even getting home was possible.

He said, 'Shame I can't do much about the photograph. I'd need to be in uniform, so we can't change that.'

'Tell you what, though. I'll bandage you more, over your face.'

'Oh, fine,' Peter said. 'Why don't you just cover me completely like Boris Karloff in *The Mummy*.'

'I haven't got a better suggestion. You're an injured soldier back from the front, right? We'll have to hope they don't look too close.'

'I'm not sure. I've never been much of an actor.' Now he was wary of the idea just as Archie was warming to it.

'It's worth a try. We've had a few lives already. If we can only get to Dresden, Annegret might persuade her mother to take us in whilst we find out what's what. And there's no military bases at Dresden – it's supposed to be full of refugees. Come on, we'll just be two more. And won't Annegret be surprised when she gets her suitcase back.'

They were as ready as they were ever going to be. They'd familiarised themselves with the currency in Annegret's bag, and the likely train route to Dresden. Archie's *Kennkarte* was reasonably convincing at a cursory glance. Peter was to go a little ahead as his leg made him the slower of the two. Archie was to try and look as if he was with a family, so the pair of them would not be so obvious.

It was twilight by the time the train came. Peter limped towards the barrier, a dirty bandage over one eye and all across one ear. The closing dark was in their favour, but he was convinced the smell of his fear must be apparent to the waiting women around him. He positioned himself to the right so that his right ear and eye were unimpeded, and had to turn his head and squint to glimpse over to the left where Archie had placed himself next to an old woman who seemed to be alone, except for a baby strapped to her chest with a cloth. She had her *Kennkarte* in her hand. Thank God. It looked the same as Archie's. Archie caught Peter's eye briefly, then looked away.

When the train arrived it was the usual stampede. Peter thought his heart might burst out of his chest. He kept his head bowed, and held up his pass. *Please God,* he prayed wordlessly, his attention on the shuffling clogs of the woman in front, and her ragged hem.

A furtive glance sideways. The smooth-cheeked men at the barrier wore armbands and the caps with the eagle insignia. Appropriate enough, for their intent expressions reminded him of hawks scanning their prey.

Now. He pushed his way forward.

Nobody stopped him.

On the other side his head swam. He realised he hadn't been breathing. He sucked in great gasps of air. The train doors swayed open but the train was already inching forward. He turned desperately to look over his shoulder. Archie was behind him. He nearly yelled with euphoria. They'd done it.

He could not put all his weight on to his bad foot to lift himself up the carriage step, but was finally pushed up by the crush of people behind him, whilst those in front kept him upright.

There were not enough seats so they were standing. A German child in grubby lederhosen moved over to let Archie sit next to his mother. It brought a lump to his throat. So there was still politeness somewhere in this world. The train rattled off to the audible relief of those on board. Their progress would likely be slow. Peter recalled the awful train journey to Lamsdorf, and how they had to wait hours in sidings whilst other trains, presumably carrying German troops or supplies, passed them.

After a few hours nobody had been to collect their tickets so Peter relaxed a little. He made eye contact briefly with Archie and managed to find a squatting place near the door. At last he was able to get the weight off his leg which he stuck out in front of him, wedged in the doorway. The train jug-a-jugged into the darkness.

He must have slept because when he woke a station guard was standing over him asking him for a ticket. 'Dresden,' he said, holding out a *Reichsmark* note from Annegret's bag. The man wound the handle on his machine and the ticket issued. Peter nodded and took the ticket and change, went to put it in his pocket.

'*Frontsoldat?*' the guard asked.

Peter did not at first hear him, so he didn't reply. 'Shell shock,' said another passenger in German. 'I've seen it before.'

The guard moved off down the train shouting for everyone to put the blinds down now it was dark. Only then did Peter look to Archie. He was resting, his mouth hanging open, head back against the seat. And Peter slept once more. He was awoken by the sound of shelling. A deep rumble and boom of explosions. It suddenly occurred to him that the train could be strafed by Allied aircraft.

The lights in the train went out. Peter pulled up the blind to look out. He heard the drone of aircraft. Ahead of him he could see the distant wispy glow of target flares landing: Christmas trees, they called them. Children began to whimper. Unease manifested itself in the shifting of baggage. Others near the windows lifted the blinds hesitantly to peer out. The train creaked slowly, stop-starting. The faint thud of explosions. *Our boys,* Peter thought, *giving them what for.*

All seemed to be peaceful again. Peter looked out to see a distant orange glow on the horizon. For a moment the train picked up speed and then a deep boom shuddered up through the tracks and under their feet. The woman next to Archie gasped, and her little boy clambered squealing on to her knee.

More shelling followed, the echo first seeming close, then far away. He wondered what targets were being hit by these bombers. He could see no searchlights or other defences lighting up the sky, except for that weird orange glow on the horizon. The train picked up speed, though the sharp crack of explosions was louder. By now people were crowding to the windows to look under the blinds, eyes fixed on the horizon before them.

'Is that Dresden?' a young woman asked.

'No. Böhlen, maybe. Can't be Dresden. Must be the oil factory.'

But as they drew nearer, the glow in the distance became a roaring tower of flame. Now the noise of bombs had stopped. Grey smoke blanketed the sky. The train trundled nearer and nearer. Peter sought Archie's eyes. They met and held his before another small explosion caused Archie to lean over and stare, like everyone else, out of the window.

It seemed interminable, the long slow journey towards that orange glow. Now dark silhouettes were hurrying past them through the fields, and every road was clogged with the slow-moving shapes of cars and carts. In the distance, a lone siren wailed, but ahead, the whole horizon was ablaze and the black hulks of buildings were dwarfed by flames. The acrid smell of smoke seeped into the carriage. Several people coughed.

'*Gott in Himmel.*' The young woman next to Archie crossed herself.

The drone of more aircraft could be heard faintly over the noise of the train. People crowded to the windows to look out. Above them a cohort of planes flew in formation, so many they could be seen on both sides of the train, their dark fuselages visible against the grey smoke above. The compartment erupted into chaos. People screamed to get off. Peter stood up, swaying to find his balance, afraid he would be pushed out of the moving train.

The first hit was a crack followed by a deep roar. It rocked the train so it rattled on the rails. The ground shook. It was followed by more, wave after wave. In the compartment some women threw themselves to the ground. The carriage grew hot, the air dense. Surely the driver was not going to keep going? As they reached the suburbs a huge blast caused a clatter of debris to hit the train roof, and fiery fragments rained down either side of them. The train slowed, crawled onwards another four or five hundred yards. To their left another bomb fell. The train stuttered to a halt.

There was silence. Nobody wanted to get off now.

The train wheezed and creaked. Then slowly it inched backwards away from the station.

The woman next to Archie was weeping now, wringing a rosary in her hands.

The train shunted about a quarter of a mile back up the track and stopped. Outside a voice shouted, '*Auf! Auf!*'

The doors clanged open and smoke hit them like a wall.

They were to get off. Here. In the middle of nowhere.

There was a scramble to get baggage from the racks and to get out. Some were relieved, others terrified. Peter fell and rolled from the train; it was a long drop from the step. When he stood, he saw the old woman he'd followed onto the train; she was hesitating in the doorway, too frightened to jump, the baby clutched to her chest. Peter reached up his arms. She dithered a moment before handing the child over, then she too had to be helped down. Even in the darkness he was aware that the air was full of smuts, floating in front of his eyes. When he passed the baby back, its face was peppered with black ash.

He looked down the line and saw the doors disgorging their passengers. From inside the train, more shouting: '*Alles, los!*' Everyone off. Some people were already walking towards the blazing city. Others were arguing, some refusing to go.

Archie appeared by his side. 'Did you see those Lancasters?'

'Bloody frightening.'

'Do you think that's the end of it?'

'Don't know,' Peter said. 'But I hope Annegret and Klara are in a shelter somewhere.'

'They will be. She's tough. Dear God, it would be ironic if we got killed by our own bombers,' Archie whispered.

Peter pulled Archie to sit on the embankment. In the distance there was a roaring like the noise of wind through a tunnel. Another explosion briefly flared and a flurry of sparks showered upwards.

'You're not still thinking we should go there, are you?'

'Not until the morning. Give the fire crews some time to get to it. I want to see if Annegret and Klara are all right. And she'll want the photographs, I kept Dieter's picture, in my pocket. We can take her suitcase back to her.'

Peter didn't answer. They both knew that would be the last thing on Annegret's mind. But Archie was pretending they were in a world where a suitcase mattered. Peter said, 'Do you think that's what it looks like in London?'

Archie drew his breath in, shook his head. 'I don't know. Don't talk about it.'

Peter slept a while, huddled with Archie for warmth, arms

round each other. It was a comfort to hear Archie's heart beating. In the morning he woke to find his throat hoarse, his eyes prickling with the effects of smoke.

Around him there were many more people, some from the train, some escapees from Dresden. The smell of burned cloth was everywhere. In daylight they saw that the fire was still raging. The sky was dense with soot. Not a single train had come out of Dresden the whole night.

'It looks pretty bad,' Archie said in a low voice. 'They haven't got the fire under control yet.'

'They'll be all right,' Peter replied.

Around midday the vibration of distant engines forced the refugees to look to the skies, hastily scramble their possessions together and take cover in ditches. They could not see the planes, but the whine of their engines went right over their heads.

'Not again,' Peter said, as another explosion made the horizon shake.

'Christ,' Archie cried, grabbing Peter and dragging him back down the embankment.

It was one of the longest forty-five minutes in his life. The explosions shuddered his heart in his chest; though he had his hands over his ears the noise was almost unbearable. He felt the blows might knock the earth off its axis. More hot, molten debris rained down on the train track. Archie clung to him as if he could keep him from falling apart.

When it was over, they lay still a very long time, just grateful to be alive.

Peter looked into Archie's eyes. They mirrored his own. Shock, disbelief. He turned away from him, staggered to his feet. Nobody could survive under such a blizzard of bombing. That this sort of thing happened, he knew, but he could not grasp that his own countrymen were responsible.

They watched the city burn for another day before they picked their way towards it through the charred country-side. They did not look to the sides; they dared not. Peter was aware only of Archie. As they neared the city they came across bodies of people who must have been running, their clothes and hair burned away.

Peter and Archie were the only people walking to Dresden; everyone else was limping away. Peter struggled with his stick, their progress slow. It did not seem to matter. He had lost track of which side he was supposed to be on, what the war was supposed to be for, what his orders were. After all these years, what he'd been fighting for seemed remote; he couldn't remember. He was simply following Archie. As they grew closer, what met their eyes was not a city. Not a single building had four walls; rubble smoked everywhere, as high as a man.

Somewhere underneath there lay the population of Dresden.

A charred bicycle lay on its side in the road with the remains of a man consumed by flames. Trams were half-buried under blackened masonry. A burned-out car lay before them surrounded by a tangled charred heap of bodies.

Archie baulked at walking past it. 'I don't think I can do this,' he said.

Peter stopped too in the road. He didn't want to look, but his eyes were drawn there anyway. 'We don't have to. We can go back.'

'I have to know if they're dead.' It was the first time Archie had admitted the possibility.

'It will be worse in the centre.'

Worse. The word had lost its meaning. They walked further. Each step a new horror. More bodies. The buildings still smouldering. The place was pleasantly warm, from the stones that had retained the heat. Peter began to sweat for the first time in years. It was eerily quiet. The bombed-out windows stared blankly as he and Archie manoeuvred their way over the pitted landscape.

Peter wiped his eyes. He was weeping, the sort of tears that just flowed mysteriously from somewhere, even though his mind was so numb with what he was seeing he could not even think. Or perhaps it was just the smoke.

A few people passed them, their red-rimmed eyes the only part of their face exposed, their clothes blackened. Everyone had their face covered with a scarf or cloth, and Archie and Peter soon did the same. They walked over molten solidified tar with debris that had been glued to the road. Peter saw shoes embedded in it, a pair of blackened high-heels. There was no sign of the woman who would have worn them. When they came to a crossroads a work party crossed right in front of them, grey-faced British prisoners of war armed with picks and shovels. Two dazed-looking armed guards followed behind.

A man dragging a small wheeled wooden cart full of unrecognisable charred items passed them, his head down. Peter couldn't be sure, but he thought it was a child's body.

Peter took hold of Archie's arm; he could bear it no longer. 'Let's go.' He was ashamed. They shouldn't be there; it was disrespectful. There had been rumours that the Germans had committed atrocities, but nothing could match this. 'Come on,' he said again, more urgently.

Another old woman was limping towards them. Archie shook Peter off and called after the woman. '*Bitte, wo ist Engelstrasse?*'

She turned. '*Da. Verbraucht. Alles, mein Leben, meine Kinder. Alles verbraucht.*' She pointed up the road. It was the voice of a young woman, made old in one night. Peter understood her words: Gone. The whole city has gone. My whole life. My children. All gone.

Archie went a few steps forward before he stopped, his hands coming up to his head. He squatted down in the road as if to make himself as small as possible, like a foetus curled in on himself.

Ahead of him the centre of the city was a blackened hollow crater surrounded by the silhouettes of broken masonry.

Peter took Archie gently under the arm and guided him away from Dresden following the railway tracks, the way they had come. He was exhausted from limping so far with his stick and because the hope that had given them strength was gone.

'We should be dead,' Archie said, suddenly stopping. 'Why aren't we dead, Pete?'

'I don't know. Guess God has other plans.'

'God. You don't believe in him, do you?'

'No. Not now, no.' It was true. He didn't see that there could be any logic for a God. If he existed, why did he keep one person alive and not another? Why let Annegret and Klara escape death at the hands of the Red Army, make them walk all that way, then kill them in Dresden? *It isn't God, it's us*, he thought. *It's always been us.*

Archie sat on the embankment and took out of his pocket the pencil drawing that Klara had done on their way to Spremberg. He unfolded it on his knee. On it the house was still upright, all its windows and doors still there. The sun was shining its spiky little beams, and chickens still pecked lopsidedly by the wonky picket fence.

Without a word he folded it again and put it back in his pocket. A small tic moved at the corner of his mouth. Peter reached his hand out to put it on Archie's shoulder. As his hand made contact, Archie crumpled.

'What's the point?' he asked. 'What's the damn bloody point?'

There was no answer because Peter didn't really even know what he was asking him. Archie himself probably did not know what he was asking. The big questions are always the ones you can't even ask.

44

1955 Helen

HELEN ROLLED OVER in bed to reach for the Beecham's powders and another handkerchief. Her head throbbed, her eyes were dry and prickly. She'd known yesterday she was going down with something and had got the dusty bottle of whisky out from the bottom of the cupboard to make a hot toddy. She never drank spirits, but she had to do something. She had a sinking feeling of inevitability.

Not now, please. She couldn't be ill now.

Her evening meal was still uneaten on the plate in the kitchen because her back ached so much she'd had to lie down. But even then she'd been unable to sleep, her temperature rocketing one moment and plummeting the next, so she was either kicking off the covers or dragging them more closely around her. When she sat up in the morning, bleary-eyed, she was shivery and her nose red raw from blowing it.

Tonight was the night she was going to meet Peter at a romantic French restaurant, and she had flu. She should have guessed this would happen. It was probably some sort of punishment for having a relationship with a married man.

She dragged on her dressing gown and tottered feebly downstairs to make another hot drink, but immediately wished she was back in bed. Last night's dirty pans were congealed in a sinkful of greasy water, the cupboard door was still open where she'd searched for some honey to ease her throat. She lit the gas on the kettle and propped herself on the worktop with her elbows, leaned her face into her hands. Her forehead felt hot and damp.

She'd need to get word to Peter that she was not coming, or he'd be sitting waiting, wondering where she was. But it was not so easy. She couldn't just call him. It was Saturday, and he'd be at home. If she called Rhoda she might tell him she was ill, but she probably wouldn't as she hadn't told Peter anything about their meetings.

All the different possibilities rattled round her head. It made it hurt just to think of it. Everything was too awkward. She'd got herself so tangled up she couldn't unravel it all. What had she been thinking of? The idea of a love affair just seemed a far-fetched fantasy. She had no energy for this any more; she just wanted a quiet life.

She took the hot lemon upstairs and gratefully fell back into bed. He'd just have to wait. She couldn't be bothered to even think about how to let him know. If he was ill, she thought, then he'd have Rhoda fetching and carrying for him. There was nobody to even make her a drink. Being ill when you lived on your own was something else entirely. She closed her eyes, let herself wallow in self-pity.

Mid-afternoon the phone rang. She was asleep but groped her way downstairs, grabbed the receiver and croaked, 'Hello.'

The operator asked her if she'd accept his call. His voice – just the same. 'Helen? I'm in a phone box. I was just ringing to say I'm really looking forward to tonight—'

'I'm sorry but I can't come.' She cut him off. 'I've got flu. I'm in bed.'

There was a moment's pause while he registered the

information. 'Oh no. You poor thing. Are you sure you're not well enough to come?'

He wasn't ready to let go of the idea yet.

'Peter, I'm in bed,' she insisted.

A silence at the other end, before, 'Is there anything I can do?'

'No, nothing. I expect I'll just have to sit it out, let it run its course.'

'I can come over if you like, see how you—'

'No, don't do that.' The panic that he might made her hot. He mustn't see her like this, in her old dressing gown with her hair all damp with sweat.

'I could bring you some painkillers, whatever you need—'

'No, I'm best to get some sleep. I feel lousy and I just need rest. And anyway, you don't want to catch it.'

'I'll ring you up later then, just to check you're all right.'

'I'll be fine. You don't need to call, I'll probably be asleep. It's only flu.'

He finally gave up after she'd told him she'd be fine a few more times. She didn't feel fine at all, she felt terrible, and guilty too that she'd let him down, even though there was not a thing she could do about it.

Late that afternoon there was a ding at the doorbell. Helen struggled out of bed and opened the curtain to blink out at the bright daylight. There was a florist's van parked outside. She went down and opened the glass-panelled door an inch. It was a young man with a huge bunch of flowers wrapped in cellophane. 'Helen Foster?'

He held out the bouquet. Flowers for her? She couldn't be bothered to argue. She opened up at bit more and reached out her hand to take them. 'Thank you,' she said, trying to hide behind the door. 'I can't come out, I've got flu.'

She shut it, put the chain on, took the flowers to the kitchen. It was the biggest bunch anyone had ever sent her. Plump red roses, ferns, some other white fluffy-looking flowers, bright pink daisies. She looked at them hopelessly, wondering what to do with them. She hadn't a vase big enough for flowers like these.

The red roses looked unreal. She bent forward to smell them, but of course could smell nothing. Archie never bought flowers. With him it was usually chocolates so he could have a share of them. The thought of Archie made her tearful. He would have brought her lunch on a tray, and made her comfortable with the *Radio Times* on the sofa and the wireless within reach.

There was a card in a tiny white envelope. She took a handkerchief from her pocket and wiped her nose, opened the card.

Get well soon.

Peter x

He'd added a kiss. He wouldn't want to kiss her if he could see her now. She put it in her dressing-gown pocket. She couldn't think what to do about the flowers; a band of iron was tightening around her head. She couldn't face emptying the sink, so she filled a saucepan with water and stood the bouquet in it.

The next day Helen was still in bed, surrounded by the detritus of wet hankies, half-drunk cups of hot lemon, and bottles of aspirin when Rhoda rang. Rhoda had been planning to visit, she said. Helen told her she was ill and it would have to be another time.

At about two o'clock the doorbell rang again. Groaning, Helen heaved herself out of bed, went to the window and lifted the curtain, but she couldn't see anyone. She was cursing and about to retreat when Rhoda stepped back from the porch and looked directly up at her.

'It's only me!' Rhoda called cheerily, signalling for Helen to come down and open the door.

Oh no. Disgruntled, Helen shoved her arms into her dressing gown. Still wobbly, she went downstairs hanging on to the banister, and unhooked the chain.

As soon as she undid the Yale, Rhoda was pushing on the other side. 'Now you go straight back to bed, and I'll bring you a hot drink.' Rhoda was in the hallway, seeming even taller, even more commanding than usual.

It was easier to just do as Rhoda said. Helen had no energy to protest. It was only when she heard Rhoda running the taps in the sink that she remembered the flowers still sitting on the worktop. A hollow feeling grew in the pit of her stomach. She heard Rhoda wash the pots with a growing feeling of shame.

'When did you last eat?' Rhoda called up.

'I can't remember. Yesterday?' Helen's voice hardly worked. It was an effort to be polite and she hated the idea of Rhoda seeing all the dried-up remains of her last meal, the potatoes still in the pan, all the unwashed cups.

'You rest. I'll see what I can find,' came Rhoda's voice.

This was even worse, that Rhoda should be waiting on her like this. Helen curled under the covers, grasped hold of the sheets. Why did everyone have to make such a fuss? Why couldn't they just go away, leave her in peace?

'It's tomato.' Rhoda arrived with a tray of soup and

bread. The soup was in a bowl that Helen never used except for best.

Helen sat up. She was hungry, she realised. 'Don't come too near me,' she said. 'You'll catch it.'

'I've had it already. A couple of months ago. So I know how miserable it is. Anyway, it can't be that infectious because Peter never caught it, thank goodness. You know what men are like when they're ill. Always ten times worse than us.' She watched Helen as she struggled to put a pillow at her back and then passed her the tray. 'Those are lovely flowers in the kitchen. Do you want me to find a vase for them?'

'No, it's all right.'

Rhoda's eyebrows were raised in polite enquiry.

'They're from my sister. She heard I was ill,' Helen said quickly.

'Ooh, expensive tastes. I'll just trim the stems, shall I? It would be a shame for them to wilt.'

'No need, I'll do it later when I'm feeling better.' Helen hoped her face did not betray her embarrassment.

'It's no trouble. I'll just pop down and do it now.'

Helen heard Rhoda opening and closing cupboard doors. She ate the soup. It was strange how good Heinz tomato soup could taste. It had all gone by the time Rhoda returned with a jug of the flowers in her hands.

'I thought you might as well enjoy them,' she said brightly. 'I found this blue jug under the sink. It's all right, isn't it—'

'Yes, yes. It's fine,' Helen snapped. She didn't even want to look at the flowers.

Rhoda gave her a sympathetic look and put the vase on the dressing table, before sitting on the end of the bed. 'It's miserable, isn't it? When I had flu, I was really knocked out. Couldn't get up for a week. Peter had to bring me my meals and everything. He'd never let me do that for him, though.' Helen willed her to stop talking, but she didn't, just smoothed the bedcover absent-mindedly. 'Illness makes him impatient. He just goes on regardless. Nowadays, he'd be up and out in that garden even if he's at death's door.' She paused, knitting her brows. 'Do you know, he's changed. When he came back from Germany it was months before he could do anything at all. Was Archie like that?'

Helen shook her head, but it made her feel worse. She flopped back on the pillows.

'I used to despair – he sat at home every day, wouldn't go out. I couldn't persuade him to go back to work, to teaching. He said he hadn't the heart for it. But jobs were hard to come by and the school were keen, so eventually he did go back. On his first day he came home and shut himself upstairs in the bedroom. When I asked him what was wrong he said the sight of all the boys' faces had made him cry.'

Helen did not want to hear this. She did not want to hear that Peter wasn't the hero she imagined. She said, 'Archie had got over it all by the time I met him. He was angry more than anything. At the lack of jobs, at the way people treated him.'

'I never saw Peter get angry. He was just depressed, I think. Wouldn't talk, but didn't know how to put it behind him. And I was hopeless, didn't know how to help him. You see, I didn't know then about the camp, or the march. Any of it. I was so obsessed with my own grief. I just wanted him to go back to how he was. I couldn't prop myself up, and him too.'

Helen coughed, moved herself back down the bed. She wanted to put her head under the covers. *Please,* she thought, *just go.*

But Rhoda's eyes were distant, unfocused. 'When I think back to those first few years we were married, it was like we were living under a thick dark haze, an atmosphere. In fact, it wasn't until—'

'I think I'd like to sleep now.' Helen did not want to hear any more. She didn't know if the ache was in her body or in her heart, or both.

Rhoda jumped to her feet. 'Of course, sorry. It was thoughtless. You don't want me chatting on. I only meant to drop in for a few minutes, just to see if you were all right.'

'I'm fine.' Helen said. If she kept saying those words, maybe she would be.

'I'll be going then.'

'Thanks for the soup.'

'You go back to sleep. I'll wash the things for you on my way out.'

'Please don't. You don't need—'

'It's no trouble.'

As soon as Rhoda was out of the room, Helen groaned, stuffed the pillow under her head and pulled the covers up to her ears. She didn't want to listen. Downstairs, Rhoda was in her kitchen washing her pots. It felt too intimate, Rhoda knowing the insides of her cupboards, almost as if she could see inside Helen's mind.

45

1945 Rhoda

A DOOR BANGED downstairs and footsteps hurried up. It was Andrew. He breezed in, raindrops shooting from his mackintosh, dumped his wet schoolbag and plonked himself down on the end of the bed so it bounced. Pa groaned.

'Sorry, Pa, I forgot,' Andrew said, jumping back up.

'Just calm down, get a chair and sit by me,' Pa said. 'Tell me what you've been doing at school.'

'Well, they're telling us we're going to get normal holidays this year again, not long ones like last year. It's a swizz.'

'It's a good sign — it means things are getting back to normal,' I said.

'For some folks, anyway,' Pa said bitterly.

'Look, I'll leave you to it,' I said. 'I'll go and wring the washing. Mother went out to queue for brisket and she's not back yet. Shout for me if you need more aspro.'

As I wound the worn-smooth handle I could hear Andrew's voice upstairs loud and clear. On and on it went. Normally he never strung two words together, he was so surly. It was good; him and his father talking like this. Maybe Pa would encourage him, get him to go for a proper apprenticeship.

The door knocker went and I smoothed my hair and

brushed down my blouse and skirt and applied a dab of lipstick at the mirror in the hall. I could see a tall silhouette through the frosted glass. A momentary flutter in my stomach. It could be Matthew.

I opened the door to see our postman standing there with the second post; he was about to knock again. He held a thick bunch of letters, all tied up with string. 'Oh. Hello.' I hid my disappointment.

To my astonishment he handed the whole bundle over to me, and my first thought was that there were too many, far more than usual, and that they looked pretty tattered. 'Is this right?' I asked.

'I think so. I haven't untied it – it came from the depot like that, for Miss Rhoda King.'

'I'm Rhoda.'

'Looks like good news then,' he said and waved at me as he went. I took the letters indoors and saw that the top one was covered in different postmarks. The ink was smudged but I'd have recognised that slanted handwriting anywhere. Peter.

I sat down, the breath knocked out of me. I cut the string and spread the whole batch out on the oilcloth on the kitchen table. All of them were franked with the same date, of about six months ago. He must still be alive. The evidence was right there in front of me. On the mantelpiece the clock ticked.

I sat with my chin on my hands for a moment, just looking. One or two of the letters were just formatted cards with no envelopes. I turned one over. The last few lines were so cramped it took me a moment to decipher it.

9th October 1943

Dear Rhoda,

*I have run out of rationed letters so am using postcards.
We had photographs taken so hope I shall be able to send
you one shortly just to show you how I am. Still miss you
like mad. Tolerable here except still no word from you. I
only hope it is the post not getting through. Would love to
hear news from Carnforth. How are the band faring without me? Please check Mother has asked my bank to put
my money into War Saving Certificates. Cheerio for now.
Please write soon, and keep safe my love, Peter x*

21st September 1942

Dear Rhoda,

*We are being treated well. We are working growing veg-
etables and are outdoors most of the day. It is tiring work
so there is not much energy left for writing. Please write
soon, home seems a long way away. I hope your father's
allotment is keeping him busy. I asked Mother for warm
clothes in my uniform parcel but nothing came so just in
case if you get this please send gloves or warm clothes for
winter. If possible please send off as early as you can to
arrive in time. Please send my good wishes to your family
and my best love to you.*

Peter x

I could hardly believe it. I sorted them into chronologi-
cal order and realised the letters got shorter and shorter. He
couldn't have got any of mine either, because in all of them

he begged me to write. Bloody war. I couldn't sort out my feelings, couldn't take it in. Part of me wanted to send them all back, didn't want him to be alive. But then, horrified at even being able to think such a thing, I got a grip on myself. There was only one thing that was clear: the poor man had been waiting all this time for a reply.

Full of contrition, I hunted in the drawer for my fountain pen and ink and wrote a shaky note.

> *Dear Peter,*
>
> *All your letters arrived today. All at once. We thought you were dead. I can't tell you how relieved I am after waiting so long for any news. I'll send a parcel in the next post. Hoping to see you soon. More news in the next letter. In haste,*
>
> *Rhoda*

Should I put with love? I hesitated.

I added a tentative 'x' before sealing the envelope. I copied the address of the camp in capital letters to make sure it was legible, then stuck on as many stamps as I could find, fetched my coat and ran down the hill to the post office. I'd just missed it of course, but I put the letter in the box, and vowed to write a longer one the next day.

When I got home I collected my bicycle and put the bundle of letters into the saddlebag. No matter what my feelings about him, I knew I had to go straight to Peter's parents and show them the letters. They might not have heard from him and I couldn't in all conscience leave them waiting.

I followed the beam of my cycle as it wobbled through the dark, the words of Peter's letters swirling in my head. I opened the Middletons' gate and pushed my bike up the drive. A chink of light disappeared from the window of the front room as the curtain shut, and I knew they must have heard the gate scrape. There was Mr Middleton's car parked there, though it probably hadn't been anywhere for a year or more. There just wasn't the petrol.

By the time I got round the side to the back door Mrs Middleton was waiting, arms folded, on the step. She looked neat and trim as usual, straight from a Littlewoods catalogue.

'Have you heard?' I said breathlessly. 'I've got letters! The last one's dated only six months ago!'

'I know,' she said. 'You'd better come in.'

How could she know? I was trying to fathom this out when his father appeared.

'Oh, Rhoda. We've been expecting you.'

'Have you heard from him too?'

'Yes, last week.'

'Last week? But I only heard today. Why didn't you come and tell me?'

'Well, we thought ... I mean, we weren't sure from his letters if he was wanting to carry on, I mean, with the engagement. He didn't mention you much so we wondered if ... We talked about it, see, and we thought it best to wait, see if you got letters like we did.'

I was incredulous. 'You mean you went a whole week without telling me?'

Mrs Middleton fiddled nervously with the set of coral beads around her neck and looked to her husband.

Mr Middleton pushed his spectacles further back on his nose and cleared his throat. 'We thought it for the best. It's been a long time. His feelings might have changed. And we still don't know where he is now.'

How dare they? Fury made me struggle to get out the words. 'His feelings haven't changed. Look.' I brought out the bundle of letters and thrust them in front of them. 'He's been writing to me all this time. I can't believe you could be so unkind. It was the first thing I did when I got mine, to come over.'

'Well, we—'

Mrs Middleton shot her husband a look which clearly told him to hold his tongue. 'Won't you sit down, dear, and I'll get some tea?'

I couldn't bear the thought of it. Not tea in that stiff parlour. At that moment I hated them both. 'No, thank you. I've got things to do.' It sounded curt and cold. 'I just wanted you to know he was alive, that's all.' I aimed it like a barb in Mr Middleton's direction.

He stepped back, looking uncomfortable as I marched past him in the hallway. I thrust the letters into the back saddlebag and cycled away. I wasn't going to let them even look at the letters. I'd go and talk to Patty, at least she'd understand.

As I pedalled with my head bent into the wind I thought, how on earth could I bear to be married into a family like that? How would I stand it – the colourlessness of his mother, her timid repressed smile? His cold, evasive father? I rang my bell furiously, and a woman with a toddler, who was just crossing the road, jumped backwards out of my way.

The next afternoon Matthew came to the station bookstall, blowing his hands in the cold, as if he was waiting to buy a book. Oh no. I tried not to look at him as I served the queue of people waiting for the 4.14 to Barrow, but when he'd queued I had no option.

'I'll take a paper,' he said.

'You're early,' I said, aiming for normal conversation. 'Are you filming a day scene?'

'I got the bus from Kendal. I just wanted to speak to

you. When I got here, Patty told me about your fiancé. I'm glad he's safe and well. It's good news, so I wanted to check there's no hard feelings.' He looked impossibly handsome.

I rearranged the papers on the counter and tried not to show how glad I was to see him. 'No, no hard feelings. I got all his letters at once. I don't know what happened to them. It was so odd to see his handwriting again. Can you credit it, his parents knew more than a week ago, but they didn't even come and let me know.'

'Really? How awful.' Matthew listened as I told him about my visit. I was still angry at Peter's parents. Even now, something in me wanted to get back at them.

'Look, he's alive. That deserves some sort of celebration. Let me buy you a coffee later, no strings. I'll be good, I promise.' But his eyes said he wouldn't, and although I nodded, and said, 'I'll hold you to that,' my heart beat fast all afternoon in anticipation. Was I wicked, now I knew Peter was alive? I was all confused, my heart and mind at silent war with each other.

The refreshment room had a coal fire glowing in the corner and Matthew went to order whilst I positioned myself close to it, extending my flat-heeled brogues towards the fender.

'Here's to his safe return,' Matthew said. 'Lucky man.'

I smiled and he caught my eye. A piercing moment like a shaft of sunlight passed between us. A moment that made me feel as if I was drowning so I had to look away.

'It's no good,' he said. 'I can't really pretend I'm happy about it. There's something between us, isn't there?' He leaned towards me. 'There has been ever since I first saw you sitting in here with Patty, the first day we came up to look at the station. I thought, what a Northern beauty.'

'Don't be silly,' I said. 'Those were the words a film star

might use, not an ordinary person. But still, a feeling in my chest opened out, blossomed.

'I'm serious. You looked so self-contained. London girls always seem to need something, they're after what they can get. They size you up and make calculations. There was none of that with you, and I saw how you listened to your friend. I thought, that looks like a really nice girl. And I was right. You're the first person to listen to me when I talk about photography as if it really interests you.'

'It does interest me. But I get embarrassed when you compliment me.'

'Why?'

'I'm not used to it. It's not the way people behave round here. Nobody does much complimenting, we just get on with it.'

'That can't be true. I'm sure Peter must have told you how lovely you are.'

It felt strange hearing his name on Matthew's lips – all wrong.

Seeing my frowning reaction Matthew held up his hands. 'Okay, okay. Look, I'll change the subject. How's your father doing?'

I rushed in with relief, 'He's a bit better. He was talking for a long time last night with my brother. Andrew'd gone off the rails a bit. I'm glad in a way Pa's at home to guide him a bit. What about you? Are your parents in London?'

'Good Lord, no. Ruislip. Father's in the civil service, a pen pusher. And Mother's a volunteer nursing auxiliary. And I've got four sisters a lot older than me, married off with children and husbands in the forces. Stationed all over the place – I find it hard to keep track of them all.'

'So you were the only boy?' I stirred a lump of sugar into my coffee.

''Fraid so. Think it scarred me for life – all those dresses and dolls! It was hard when I was a child, being the only boy and so much younger. I'm very close to my parents, too close sometimes – they mollycoddle me too much.' He smiled ruefully. 'Actually, I think I was a bit of a mistake, though my parents would never admit it. But they're busy with the war effort, evacuees and so forth, so they don't get up to London often. But Mother fusses – sends me new underwear, as if I'm not old enough yet to fend for myself. And the most terrible knitted jumpers. Great big patterns in clashing colours. Lately I persuaded her to knit for my sisters' husbands instead, and I've got this image in my head now of soldiers crashing about at the front like targets in these ridiculous great pullovers!'

I giggled. 'They sound nice, your parents.'

'They're not bad.' I watched him butter his scone, spread jam liberally and then sandwich the two halves together. After he took a bite, he rushed to swallow it and wiped his mouth rather self-consciously on his cuff. 'Father likes to read and he sent me away with a great pile of books,' he said. 'I've just finished *The Citadel*. Have you read it? It will make you really think differently about doctors and how the poor have no chance at all really, poor devils.'

I was astonished. I never thought he'd have a social conscience. 'Yes,' I said, delighted, 'ages ago. It's a wonderful book. Though I could have cheerfully throttled Andrew Manson. When he starts to get above himself and forget how he got to where he was—'

'And that poor wife. What she had to put up with. But it made me realise how lucky I was, that my parents were able to pay for medical treatment when I needed it, and it made me wonder about your father's predicament. I mean I don't want to pry but if you need a little help –'

It pricked my pride. I shrugged it off. 'We'll manage somehow. Do you think we're all poor "up North"?'

He hastened to fix his blunder. 'Course not. It's just – I'm pretty well paid and happy to offer a loan ...' He saw my horrified face and said, 'Sorry, I've put my foot right in it. I didn't mean to – it's just I care about you.'

I took a moment to settle myself and had another mouthful of coffee before asking, to change the subject, 'What was the matter with you?'

There was a pause. He scraped the remains of the jam deliberately from his knife. 'Nothing. I mean, just the usual silly childhood things, like my asthma.'

I looked at my plate; neither of us had made much head-way with the scones.

To break the tension I asked, 'What else did he send you?'

'Who?'

'Your father. Which books?'

'Oh, he sent me some more Graham Greene. *Brighton Rock*. I loved *England Made Me*. Do you like him?'

I'd only ever heard of him, never read any. 'Absolutely.'

He looked up at me, delighted, and when his eyes met mine I almost stopped breathing. He reached out to press my hand where it lay on my lap. I did not move it, but I was aware of Evelyn behind the counter who had stopped drying a glass and was staring, tea towel in hand.

'Come on, we can catch the express!' he said, standing and almost dragging me away from the table. He paid hur-riedly by throwing his coins on to the counter.

He hauled me, breathless, on to the platform just in time to see the train hurtle past. He grabbed me by the shoulders and kissed me hard on the lips as the train whooshed past, the wind of it causing us to sway, the screech of its passing loud in my ears. I kissed him hard back. When he let me go I felt dislocated, dizzy, had to hold on to his arms to keep from falling.

'Gosh! That was worth waiting for,' he said. 'When's the next train?'

I laughed, my lips tingling all over.

'Mrs Goodhalgh brought us a casserole,' Mother said that night. 'Isn't that lovely of her? I never expected the neighbours to rally round like they have.'

'How's the patient?' I asked.

'A bit better. Still in a lot of pain. Nurse came again this morning with more morphine. But he's cheerful now he's got Andrew up there with him.'

'It's good – he needs Father's company.'

'Maybe they need each other's company. Andrew's got the card table up there to do his homework. Your father's helping him – if you can call it that. Mind, it's warmer up there now I've got the paraffin stove lit. Andrew actually brought up some paraffin from the shed. I'd no idea we had any left since rationing. And he filled the coal scuttle. Wonders will never cease.'

'Pa must be lonely, missing work.'

'His old pal Sol came round. He spent quite a long time up there this morning with him. Talking about fishing, most likely. I could hear them chattering away.' Fishing. It was a long time since Pa had had his rod out. 'Will you take him up this tea?' she said.

I took the tea with its straw sticking out and mounted the stairs, preparing myself – armouring myself, I suppose, for his reaction to Peter's letters. Mother would have told him I'd heard from him, but my lips could still feel the press of Matthew's kiss.

The room was fuggy with paraffin fumes, and an oil lamp stood on a pile of textbooks. Andrew looked up from his exercise book and said, 'Here, have my chair. I'm going down now to feed the rabbits. Glad Peter's okay, sis.'

Father adjusted his position in bed, wincing. Mother had put a bed tray over his knees, and now his face was peeling but his lips looked less sore. He had his dressing gown on over his shoulders to keep him warm.

'Tell me your news,' he said.

'Peter's in Poland,' I said. 'They must have moved him. To another camp. He has to work planting cabbages, for the German sauerkraut, I suppose. Anyway, he's okay, he says.'

Pa gave me a penetrating look. 'You don't seem very glad.'

'I don't think it's sunk in yet. All this time of preparing for the worst. And now he's all right – well, I don't know how I should feel.' I sat and glanced miserably at Andrew's homework – Francis Drake and the Armada. It seemed ridiculous now that we had U-boats and Spitfires. I looked back to Pa. 'I suppose I'd half resigned myself to Peter not coming home. It's a lot to take in.'

'It'll take time. Like my hands. They'll heal in time. There's no point me getting frustrated, I can't hurry it up. Nurse says a few more weeks before I can take the dressings off and get them moving. The morphine helps – it stops the pain and then I can think. I've done a lot of thinking, lying here. But I'll be back at work by the time your Peter gets home. He's not had a bad war, has he, not like poor Johnnie.'

I turned the oil lamp down to save fuel. 'Bad enough, I should think, being kept locked up like that. Oh, Pa, I should have written more often.' I shook my head. 'When no letters came back I just got disheartened.'

Pa pushed himself further upright on his pillows with

his elbows. He was unshaven and his arms looked thinner. 'Strange things happen in war, it's nobody's fault. Trains get bombed, ships get sunk, some letters probably never reach their destination. He'll understand.' He looked out of the window a moment before looking back at me. 'Terrible though. Just the thought of those lost letters pains me. Letters mean so much to a soldier. They remind you of what you're fighting for.'

'Did Mother write to you?' I could not imagine either of them being young and in love. Not now.

'She did. And without her letters I might have gone mad. I can't even speak of it. They were voices from another world. Somewhere clean and sane and good.'

From below there came the sound of a brush going back and forth, back and forth.

We listened to it a moment before I saw his eyes were filling with tears.

'What's up, Pa?'

'She's cleaning my boots.'

I went to the drawer for a handkerchief.

'I can't use one of those. My face is too sore.' I balled the handkerchief in my fist. Pa was still listening to the sound of the brush. 'I've heard that sound near every night for twenty-odd years and never heeded it. How much she does, I mean. But this last week I've sat here and heard the sound of her; the sound of her chopping up food, the posher banging in the wash tub, the oven door opening and closing. She never stops. I hear it now. The sound of her loving.'

'Aw, Pa.'

He spoke quickly now, with a catch in his voice. 'I'd forgotten. But you two, it's not too late for you. Peter's been lucky.' He looked straight at me. 'You've both been lucky.' He fixed me with a look. 'Andrew tells me you've been seeing someone else.'

Bloody Andrew. 'He doesn't know what he's talking about.'

'You'll stop that nonsense now, won't you? Peter's been writing to you all this time. He'll need to know you're here at home waiting for him.' He groaned and shifted in the bed.

'Does it hurt?' I asked, grateful for the distraction.

'Course it bloody hurts.' But he shook his head in frustration. 'Your mother waited for me. I said I'd never forget your mother waiting for me all that time, but I have.' I was struggling to keep up with the conversation, the odd fact of Pa's emotion. It must be the morphine. He was still talking; 'I've been terrible to her. But when I came round in the hospital she treated me like I was a hero for putting out that fire. A hero. Me.'

'You are a hero, Pa—'

'No, listen. I'm telling you, Rhoda, time dulls the pain, but it dulls the romance too, makes it ordinary. Death awakens all that. Death and the close call. When I woke up in that hospital bed and saw her sitting there waiting, it was all I could do not to cry. Don't tell her, will you?'

'Why? She'd be glad to know you care.'

'It seems weak, and that was one of the things about the trenches, not to show anything. Laughter, well, that was all right. It was fine to laugh when someone had their brains blown out, but not to cry. You got in the habit of hiding it all. I get mad when I don't mean to. When I try to be nice, I just can't manage it, somehow. Somewhere underneath all my bad behaviour I do care, but I don't know how to tell her, how to make it right.'

'You don't have to tell her,' I said. 'You could just show her by listening a bit more.'

The brush's steady rhythm continued below.

'Will you help her, love?' Pa's face was full of pain. 'She never stops.'

'I'll try.'

He nodded. 'When Peter comes home, well – he might have seen things. Things a man shouldn't have to see. We don't know how he ended up there. So go easy on him.'

'I know, you don't have to tell me.' I was snappish suddenly, caught between conflicting emotions. It was all right when Pa talked about his war, but I didn't want to think of Peter. It was as if I was suddenly reminded of a duty I did not want to do. My body still remembered the speed of the train as it rushed by, the feel of Matthew crushing me to his chest.

I went next door into my own room and sifted through Peter's letters until I found his photograph. A group of uniformed men, hair brushed neatly to the side, smiling at the camera. The front row had their arms folded. They looked tidy, if a little thin, but one funny thing – their boots were all different styles. One had what appeared to be light-coloured laces, one appeared to have odd boots. Peter was on the back row, so I couldn't see his feet. He had his arms clasped behind his back and was smiling fiercely in a way I had never seen before. I turned it over. '*E22B working party*' he'd written. Somehow this made it more of an enigma than if he'd written nothing at all.

46

1945 Rhoda

WHEN I GOT to the Third Class carriage to serve the dinner, Matthew gave me a huge grin.

'We've got to go up to a bridge in the Lake District for a recce tomorrow,' he said. 'Can you get an afternoon off? We need to scout it out before filming next week and it would be tops if you could come.'

I remembered my conversation with Pa about Peter, and immediately felt guilty, as if I was betraying them both.

'Come on, Rhoda, put the man out of his misery,' Ed said. 'He's talked of nothing else but you for the last week.'

'I'd love to, but only if you're sure I won't be in the way.'

Ed and Harry and the whole table whooped and banged their cutlery up and down on the table. Matthew looked sheepishly pleased, his face flushed red. 'Stop it, lads,' he said. I hurried away, aware that the whole compartment was staring at us with undisguised amusement.

The next day after lunch Matthew was waiting for me at the bookstall. His big camera bag was slung over his shoulder and a newspaper tucked under his arm. He tapped his foot, full of restless energy, 'Everything fixed?' he asked.

I felt like a naughty schoolgirl truanting. 'Yes, but I'll have to be back at the usual time. I didn't tell them at home, they'd only have made a fuss.' I looked down at my shoes, embarrassed, knew he wasn't taken in. He would guess I did not want to tell my parents about him.

'Ed will pick us up at about half-past. Let's go inside while we wait for the car. We can read the paper, see what's going on.'

The refreshment room was bustling with railwaymen on their break, but our table was free so we slid into our usual spaces, except this time, after ordering, Matthew came to sit beside me. He cleared the salt and pepper pots so we could spread out the paper.

I was so conscious of his presence that it was hard to concentrate on anything. I edged nearer to him so our thighs were touching. Matthew pointed to the headline. It read, *The Blasting of Dresden. Night Attack – 1,400 Planes from RAF Bomber Command.*

Matthew read it out. *'Fires seen by Koniev's men, crews of the bombers said they could see the glow two hundred miles away –* that's like seeing them from London to here; that must be an exaggeration. But even if it's propaganda it still must have been some sight.'

Evelyn arrived with the coffee. She gave me a knowing smile, and Matthew shut the paper.

'Enough of that,' he said. 'I don't really want to know the details, do you? It's too much to bear. Just whether or not we're winning.'

He reached for my hand, and gripped it too tight. The pain of it seemed to express something we could not say. I looked at his face, at the way his reddish hair was shaped around his ears, at the slight suggestion of freckles across the bridge of his nose.

He reached out to touch my cheek. 'You'll write, won't you? I can't bear it that this will soon be over. And I was hoping you'd visit. I'd like to show you round the studios. You could stay in the little hotel they use when we're filming. It's nice.'

'Won't it be expensive?' I was putting every obstacle I could think of in the way, yet all the time I knew that this thing was unstoppable, hurtling forwards like the *Royal Scot*.

He looked at me with tacit understanding. 'Please say yes.'

'But I'm engaged to Peter, and I worry you'll think I'm easy. And later, if it did work out, you'd always be wondering whether I'd be faithful to you, or whether I'd treat you the way I treated Peter.'

'I'd never think that.' He lifted my hand and squeezed it, his eyes full of tenderness, 'I'm not worried what people might think, let them say what they like. It's a rare thing, I think, what I feel for you, sort of … inspired. I mean, it makes me want to be a better photographer, to be a better person. To look forward into the future instead of back.'

I was moved by this outpouring. I reached over and threw my arms around his neck. He whispered, 'Does that sound stupid? Am I crazy?'

'Only as crazy as I am.'

'Then it's settled.' He kissed me a long tender kiss. I could have shortened that moment but I didn't, I didn't care. I just closed my eyes and kissed him back. When I opened my eyes I saw Evelyn glance away, pick up a dishcloth and look busy.

I had only ever been into the Lake District by train, so it was glorious to drive. Since petrol rationing nobody drove. What a view! Matthew sat with his arm along my shoulder, and as we passed Alan pointed out the Low Wood Hotel where they were staying; a huge place with gas lamps blazing away below its swanky sign, even in the day.

The sleek green Riley swerved off the road and into a gateway where we could park. It was a ten-minute walk from the parking spot to the location, and we giggled over the fact that I was wearing my best print frock and shoes. It was blowing a gale and the path was six inches deep in mud. Mother, who was brought up on a farm, would have laughed to see me picking my way around the puddles like a townie.

The bridge was rather quaint – a half-moon-shaped old packhorse bridge over a gurgling stream. A lace of ice fringed the edges of the water. Alan and Ed measured up distances with a cloth tape, examined the bridge for camera angles.

'Give me your camera, Matt.' Ed wound the tape back into its leather case. 'I'll take a picture of you both. You can stand in for Miss Johnson and Mr Howard so we can show Mr Neame.' He winked.

Matt turned to me, a little embarrassed. 'There's going to be a love scene on this bridge. Have to say, it's a wonderful location, isn't it?'

'You can't beat the Lake District. You should see it in summer – it's even more gorgeous.' I wanted him to see it then, I realised, bring him here again with his camera, just the two of us. A picnic, under bright blue sky and warm sun.

Matthew handed his camera over, with a barrage of instructions to Ed as to what to push and press. I was shy and a bit reluctant but hoped it didn't show. I couldn't help thinking, what a thrill, to be photographed by a real film man, in the very spot where Celia Johnson and Trevor Howard would stand in the film.

At last we got ourselves on to the bridge, and waved madly at Ed with the camera below. The wind whipped around us and I had to hold back my hair with one hand to keep it from my face. Matthew put his arm around me and Ed clicked the shutter. Only just in time because Matthew's hat flew off and Alan had to chase after it as it bowled towards the water.

Twenty minutes later we hurried back to the car, full of jokes and laughter. Matthew and I piled into the back seat and Ed turned the key. A choking cough, then nothing. He tried again. And again.

'Engine's flooded,' Alan said. As men do, they were soon out of the car and poking about under the bonnet, but it was no use, the blasted thing had died on us. I was uneasy. Mother would start to worry if I didn't come home as usual. What if she went to the station and asked after me?

The engine grunted and died again. 'Nothing for it. We'll have to walk to a telephone, get someone out from the Low Wood,' Ed said.

'Come on then, it's not far to the road. Maybe we can flag someone down.' Alan pulled an umbrella from the boot.

Oh no. My shoes were completely unsuitable for walking any distance, but I didn't want to wait alone in the car. Alan was tall and he and Ed set a fast pace and Matthew took my arm, but before long I was struggling to keep up, my fancy shoe straps cutting into the top of my foot.

Matthew too was slowing, as Alan and Ed got further ahead. After about ten minutes Matthew let go of my arm and staggered over to a wall, where he sat, his head in his hands. 'I've got to stop a minute,' he panted.

'Is it your asthma?' Even in the growing darkness I could see his face was pale and sweating and he was wheezing as though he could not catch his breath. 'Tell me what I can do.'

He could not answer, but the others had seen us and Ed

came running back. 'Oh Lord. I should have thought.' He sat down on the wall. 'Do you need your puffer?'

Matthew waved him away with his arm. 'No,' he snapped, coughing to try to catch his breath. 'Don't fuss. I'll be all right. Rest a minute or two.' He slumped with his head between his knees, sucking up air with rasping breaths.

'We'll go on ahead, come back for you,' Alan said.

'I'm staying here,' I said, knowing even as I said it that it would mean trouble at home.

'No, go,' Matthew said. 'I'll be fine … just rest.'

'I'm staying.'

'Best go before we lose the light,' Alan called, already striding out down the road. 'Follow the yellow-brick road!'

'We'll be quick as we can,' Ed said.

I sat down on the wall and took hold of Matthew's hand, rubbed his back with circular strokes of my palm as Ed and Alan disappeared round the corner. He took out a rubber bulb and a phial and puffed something up a tube into his nose. He was breathing easier now, though he was pressing hard on his chest with both hands as if to move the pain away.

I rubbed a while more, until his breathing calmed from a wheeze to a steadier breath. The lapping of the water in the lake was soothing. After a while Matthew smiled up at me and squeezed my hand tight. 'Thanks for staying. I'm glad you're here,' he said. 'We can walk a bit now, if you like, it's passed.'

'Is that medicine for asthma?'

'Yes. But it's okay, it's gone off now.'

'Let's sit a little longer. No need to rush. I'm sure they'll find someone soon and come back for us. Besides, I don't want to walk, my shoes are killing me.'

'What a cliché, hey?' he said. 'I promise I didn't arrange

for the car to break down. We'd all be groaning if this was a script for a film.'

'I like this cliché,' I said, and he laughed, and we sat in the quiet then as dusk came and night dropped around us. Matthew's breath settled to an even rhythm; I listened for it and tuned my own to his. I sat between his legs now, leaning back against his chest. He closed his arms around me, began to creep his fingers over my belly towards my breast. In the distance I heard the hoot of a steamer on the lake, and the first evening star appeared in the sky above. It gave me a feeling of longing, of loneliness; a pang in the heart. He turned his face towards mine in the dark, and brushed me with his lips. I heard myself moan softly, an animal sound that could have been pleasure or pain.

'You might have another asthma attack,' I whispered.

'What a way to go,' he laughed, coughed a little.

By the time they came back for us it was full dark. Headlights passed us several times but did not stop. Now that there was not a full blackout any longer the dazzle of them startled us. It sent a frisson of fear and excitement through me, to be caught suddenly, the light shining on what we were doing, the sudden illumination of bare skin. I'd turned now to sit facing Matthew. I was astride his lap, his hand had undone the buttons of my dress and snaked inside. My arms were clinging to his back, my legs were spread either side of his as he drew me towards him.

When we saw slow headlights approaching I hurried to fasten my dress, the parting an agony of desire and longing.

The car pulled up next to us and Matthew opened the door. I almost fell inside, disorientated. Inside the car I stole a glance at his profile, but he saw me looking and squeezed my fingers. On the return journey he lay back against the

headrest; he looked exhausted. I worried that what we had
been doing would make his asthma worse. I knew nothing
about asthma; I'd have to look it up in the library.

Back in Carnforth they dropped me at the end of the
street. Matthew kissed me again on lips already bruised from
kissing. When I opened the door Mother was there in the
hall, her face disapproving. 'Where've you been? We've been
worried to death. I went up to the station but they told me
you'd had the afternoon off.' Her voice dropped to a whisper.
'Why didn't you tell us?'

'I went out with some friends, up near Ambleside. The
car broke down.'

'Andrew says a man walked you home last week.'

Blasted Andrew. Couldn't he keep his big mouth shut?

Mother followed me as I went into the front room.
'Does he know you're engaged, this boy?' She was still whispering, to stop Pa hearing.

'He's not a boy, he's a man, and he's just a friend.' But I
knew she would guess.

'What's he called?'

'I've told you, it was a group of us. Ed and Alan and
Matthew.' I heard the slight delay in my voice before I said
his name. It felt strange to even say it, as if the name was too
small for this passion that was overtaking me.

Mother gave me a tight-lipped look then, the one that
meant she could see straight through me. She moved the
clothes horse away from the fire and began to fold up tea towels. 'According to the Home Service it will be over in a few
weeks. They're preparing for Victory in Europe Day. It might
take a while to demob everyone, but Peter will be home soon.
We thought, a summer wedding. June, we thought. We've
been saving our coupons, and when I heard war was coming

I put aside some extra. I could try and get some white silk, or at least a satin. How does that suit?'

'If you like.' I hung up my coat, turned my back so she couldn't see my face. 'We'll have to see what Peter thinks.'

There was a pause whilst she waited for me to turn to face her. As she talked she watched me. 'We saved you a bit of dinner. But it'll need reheating. You're not going out on the late shift tonight, are you?'

'I promised Hilary. It's only a few more days.'

Mother gave a sharp sigh, untied her apron and slipped it off. 'Rhoda, listen to me. I don't know what's going on with you, but I don't like it. You'll be getting a reputation. It's not nice to cheat on someone, especially when they've had the sort of bad luck Peter's had, stuck as a prisoner of war all this time. What would I tell his parents? Be sensible now.'

'His parents?' I gave a short laugh. 'They didn't even bother to tell me he was alive.'

'They were probably just waiting for the right time.'

'Well, they've never shown any interest in us, have they? She's never been here to ask after me, or invited us to tea, has she?'

'Well, I don't think a woman in her position … I don't think she—'

'You mean she wouldn't lower herself, don't you? They think they're too good for us, don't they?'

'But Peter's never been like that, you know he hasn't. He'll talk to anyone, Peter—'

'Mother, just leave it, for God's sake. I'm not a child. I'm twenty-four. I know I have to live here, but I'm old enough to make up my own mind and live my own life.'

'If it wasn't for the war, you and Peter would be married by now, with children and a nice house.'

'If it wasn't for the war, I wouldn't be here listening to all this,' I said, frustrated, and I ran upstairs to my room.

'Rhoda?' I heard her voice calling me but I ignored it. Through the thin bedroom walls I could hear Andrew enthusing to Pa about the serial numbers of engines and wagons. I stared at the wallpaper in my room – old-fashioned, a faded yellow with sprigs of flowers on a trellis. The bedsprings creaked under my weight. The room was everything I felt I didn't want. Stale, old-fashioned, cramped.

I looked through my bookshelves until I found a copy of a book by Graham Greene. It wasn't either of the ones that Matthew had mentioned, in fact it was one I'd got from the church jumble sale and started but found so dull I'd never finished it. Now I picked it up and looked at it with new eyes. I opened the first page, with determination, already sure I would like it.

Now the book held my attention. Suddenly it seemed so grown-up, so radical. So 'London'. It reeked of a bigger world. Before I went out I put my head round Pa's door. Mother had taken the blackout down and Pa was standing leaning one arm on the windowsill, staring out of the window into the garden. It was good to see him up. 'Bye, Pa. Just off to work at the canteen.'

He turned awkwardly to look at me. 'You work too hard. Still, it won't be for long. Your mother put the wireless in the hall where I could hear it. Our boys will all be home soon. She says you want a June wedding.'

I gritted my teeth. So Mother had lost no time in getting Pa on her side too.

'Bye, Pa,' I said again, masking my anger. I marched past Mother and slammed the door on the way out.

47

1955 Rhoda

'So how did they get home?' I asked Helen.

'Archie says they walked away from Dresden another forty miles towards Berlin where they met up with a bunch of Americans travelling by jeep. He says Peter just stood out in the road and yelled and waved something white. A blouse that belonged to Annegret.' Helen coughed, got out her handkerchief. 'Hold on.' She was still recovering from the flu. 'Wait a minute, I've got the suitcase somewhere. Archie said they were so ecstatic to see the Americans, they actually cried. He said he'd never forget it. It was such a great moment that he brought the blouse home as a souvenir. Of course I washed it for him and we put it back in the case with the other things.'

We were sitting in Helen's cosy front room. All around us lay biscuit tins of photographs, carefully documented albums and boxes of memorabilia. I picked up a 1944 copy of the *Illustrated London News*, one of a large pile. Of course I remembered these times, but I had forgotten all the little details. And now they were softened by nostalgia; I could no longer remember the peculiar taste of Spam fritters or dried-egg sandwiches. I glanced at the picture in front of me. The caption said, *'The stables where King George III kept 120 horses are now used for storing wheat.'* So much of the paper seemed to be about food – its shortage, its production, its distribution.

Helen returned with a stiff-looking leather suitcase and brought out a woman's blouse. 'This was Annegret's. The woman with the little girl I told you about. Look, all hand-stitched. She must have been quite a seamstress.'

'Archie brought this case back with him?'

'Wouldn't be parted from it. He said that without Annegret, Peter would be dead, him too probably. She was kind, even though she was German. Of course after the war nobody talked about things like that. It was called fraternis-ing with the enemy. You had to be careful – someone was bound to have lost someone they loved because of them.'

'This is what they waved when they saw the jeep?' I took the thin cotton of the blouse, ran my thumb over the pearl buttons, the picot edging on the collar. This belonged to a woman who had saved my husband's life. An unexpected surge of gratefulness passed through me. She must have been brave, too, to risk helping two British soldiers.

'Why do you think she helped them?' I asked.

'I don't know,' Helen said. 'Perhaps she felt bad about what her countrymen were doing, perhaps she had motives of her own. In war things don't always make sense, that's what Archie always used to say.'

Holding the blouse was like holding a mystery, some-thing living that had been in my husband's hands at the moment of his own personal VE Day. It almost felt as though it might contain some of that emotion, trapped in the spaces of the weave. I held it up to my face and smelt the unmistak-able aroma of Omo washing powder.

'It's lovely that Archie brought it home.' Helen looked up at me. There was an odd look in her eyes, one almost of pity. She said, 'Peter's always known that Archie had this collection tucked away in the spare room yet he's never once asked to see it. I wonder why.' She shook her head, as if to free it of its thoughts. 'They seemed content just to go down to the pub and have their steak-and-ale pie and chips. Always the same – steak pie and a pint or two of Whitbread.'

I laughed.

'I didn't realise that telling each other things is so important,' she said. 'There are so many things I wish I'd said to Archie, and now …' I saw her eyes turn thoughtful before she said, 'But I think it's probably better if you don't tell Peter about our meetings.'

I was surprised – a few months ago she'd been badgering me to tell him. I put down the blouse and gave her my full attention.

'It would seem a bit late, now we've been doing it so long. And you're probably right, bringing back the past won't do anyone any good.'

'And I was just thinking I might screw up the courage and tell him, isn't that strange? It seems so ridiculous now that we're such good friends that you can't call me up for a chat.'

'Guess I've come round to your way of thinking.' A bout of coughing seized her, and she went to fetch a glass of water. 'Sorry, it's a lot better than it was, this cough. I was saying, if Peter doesn't want you to know, then there must be some deep and dreadful secret he's keeping from you. I wouldn't rock the boat.'

'Yes, aren't men funny? It's probably something stupid, as you say, like him fraternising with the enemy.'

Helen began to pack the things away. She'd been restless ever since I arrived, glancing at the clock, full of a nervous excitement I couldn't understand.

'Are you all right?' I asked.

'Me? Oh yes, I'm fine.'

She hadn't finished speaking when the telephone rang. She leapt up, but then stopped in the doorway to the hall.

'Go ahead and answer it,' I said. 'Don't mind me.'

I heard her pick it up and answer with her number, and then a whispered reply, 'Sorry but I can't talk now … Ring me later … this evening, yes. Bye.'

I waited for her to come back through. When she did her face was pink.

So that would explain the bunch of red roses from before. I couldn't resist teasing her. 'Helen! You've got an admirer. Don't tell me you haven't, it's written all over your face.'

'No,' she said. 'I don't know what you mean. That was just the neighbour, thanking me for babysitting.'

She did not meet my eyes. This was so patently untrue that I didn't know what to say, but it took me aback, that she wouldn't confide in me. A niggle of discomfort made me anxious to leave. I suppose if I was her I would want to keep my love life private and yet…I was just being suspicious, wasn't I? I tried to quell my misgivings with the voice of reason. *Look, Rhoda, we've been through all that, there's nothing between Peter and Helen, they're just good friends.* Yet how well did I know Helen, and could I really trust her?

48

1945 Rhoda

FOR THE NEXT few days Matthew and I were together as many hours as we could muster. We could not get enough of each other. When I finished my day in the bookstall he was always waiting, hopping impatiently from foot to foot in his leather brogues. He was attentive in small ways, opening doors for me, holding my coat so I could slip my arms into the sleeves, taking hold of my hand at any opportunity.

One night when they did not need him for documenting the filming, we sneaked off to the Marine Ballroom on the Central Pier in Morecambe where they held a nightly dance. The Rhythm Club, they called it. I'd never seen so many people dancing at any one time. There were plenty of sailors and soldiers in uniform, such a crush of people revolving around the floor under two enormous glinting chandeliers.

I worried that dancing the foxtrot might set off his asthma. Actually it was hard to dance because the floor was so crowded, but we were able to hold each other tightly, which was all we wanted anyway. We danced only with each other and when I kissed his neck I tasted the salt of his sweat, and the feeling of being so close to him made me almost swoon.

At the end of the evening we caught the last train back to Carnforth and arrived just in time for his shift on set. As we alighted they were putting up the flattage for the exterior of the refreshment room again and the electricians were setting up the lights.

'Back to the kitchen for me,' I said.

'Like Cinderella,' he said, 'except that this time you have been to the ball.'

'Even better, I've come home with the handsome prince.'

'Not very handsome, I'm afraid, but I do love you,' he said, almost casually. 'You know that, don't you?' He plonked a kiss on my forehead. 'Make me something decent, not that tapioca again.' And off he sauntered before I could even reply.

At home things became more and more strained. Mother barely spoke now, just showed her disapproval in a frenzy of scrubbing and polishing. Fortunately Pa was still taking up most of her time with his need for nursing. He had become less demanding, more at peace and accepting. I noticed the change in him. He seemed content just to sit in his patched-up pyjamas and stare out of the window, opening and closing his fingers under the bandages with dogged determination.

When Mother suggested he should come downstairs, he said, 'Not yet, Jeanie. I'll have a bit of peace while I can.'

Andrew had set up a bird table in the garden in front of his window. He'd made the thing himself, with scraps of wood from the shed, and though it was a bit rickety Mother did her best to supply it with crumbs. 'Though what we're feeding birds for, when there's a war on, heaven only knows,' she said.

Whenever we had time to listen, Pa told us what the birds were doing, whether we'd had sparrows or robins or blackbirds. It was hard to bear, his simple enjoyment of these things, when I was caught up in such a tumult of emotion.

His innocent enjoyment threw my guilt into relief and made me restless. For I was in love with Matthew. It was all-consuming, like a burning sensation in my chest, as if my soul was screaming to get out. I would never have thought it possible to feel such a thing, this yearning. I thought it would break me apart.

Of course I had not written again to Peter, as if just ignoring his existence would make the whole problem go away. I knew it was wrong but every time I lifted up the pen I could not think how to tell him. At the same time, when I thought about breaking off our engagement and imagined a life with Matthew, I could not picture what sort of future that would mean. It was hazy, unformulated, shapeless. I'd always imagined a house in Carnforth and coming home to Peter. Matthew's life would be different, and I was scared of his well-educated parents, his Southern friends, the whole unfamiliar territory. It was as if I was tied down to Carnforth. Like Gulliver, there were a hundred different threads that kept me there and would not let me go.

On the day the film crew were leaving I passed the big wagon full of broken-up splintered wood from the set of the refreshment room, and the sight of it gave me a panicky feeling in my stomach. By lunchtime the wagon itself was gone, and now only the crew remained.

The actors had left the night before, in the first-class Pullman for London. What would it be like on the station without them? The film had glamorised the dreariness, made it seem like atmosphere. But the reality was that the town had been battered by five years of billeting, scrimping and neglect. I knew we'd soon be back to workers' overalls and railwayman's black and Matthew would be out of my life.

It didn't bear thinking about. Peter's engagement ring

touched my fingertips, deep in my pocket. It had been on and off so often with my changing state of mind. At home I wore it to prevent arguments with Mother, but on the station it was left rattling with my door key and loose change.

The stall was busy with rush-hour passengers, so I couldn't get away to say goodbye to the crew. I was on tenterhooks in case Matthew should go without me being able to speak to him. But he came puffing up to the counter just before his train and said, 'Can you spare five minutes to wave us off?'

Bob, a station porter, who was waiting at the counter with his paper, took pity on me. 'Go on, then. I'll cover for you if you like.'

I thanked Bob and handed him the key to the till. 'Five minutes,' I said, holding up five fingers. Matthew took my hand and as we went down the underpass we heard the train rumble in above.

'Come on,' I said, towing him along. 'You'll miss it.'

The platform was full of luggage; a porter's trolley was stacked high with the film crew's cases and bags. A crowd had assembled to see them off – the extras, the canteen girls, and George Farrer and his mate Alf who'd driven the engines. Matthew squeezed my hand, but then picked it up to look at it. 'You're not wearing your ring.'

'No. It didn't feel right, you know – not when we're—'

'Rhoda! Yoo-hoo!' It was Evelyn, approaching from the WVS canteen. She smiled at Matthew. I let go of his hand. 'Hello, Matthew. All set? What time will you get back home?'

'About six o'clock, I think.' He was being polite, but I just wished she'd go.

'Is there much filming left to do in London?' she asked him.

He cast me a glance, but answered her. 'A fair bit. There

are quite a few scenes in town, and one in a park, and then a few inside a cinema.'

She chatted on. 'You could have used the Roxy across the road – then we could have all been extras. Oh, look! Ed's shouting for you. It's time.'

The train was ready to go. I looked to Matthew hopelessly. It was clear we would only be able to make a public goodbye. I prepared myself for the disappointment. But he took hold of me by the shoulders and ignoring Evelyn and everyone on the platform, kissed me long and hard. I heard some of the crew wolf-whistle and whoop.

'I'll write,' he said, releasing me, 'soon as I can. Don't forget about the nice hotel.'

'I won't,' I said. The whistle blew and Matthew climbed on board. I watched him open the door to the compartment opposite me, and red-faced, put his hat and newspaper on the rack above his head. My heart felt as though it would burst.

49

1945 Rhoda

'Is IT FROM him again?' Mother asked. She said 'him' as if it was a dirty word.

I slid the paper knife under the flap, drew out the letter, and scanned it. 'If you mean Matthew, yes. He's asking if I can go down.'

'How? You've not the money for gallivanting. And where would you stay?'

I sighed. 'With his parents.' I did not dare mention the hotel.

'What about Peter's parents? I met Mrs Middleton at the WVS last Wednesday and she asked after you. I was so ashamed, I didn't know what to say. It's not just you it affects, you know, it's all of us.'

'When Peter's home I can explain. There's no point in upsetting him now. I need to speak to him face to face.'

I don't like what you're doing, Rhoda.' Mother took the breakfast plates into the scullery.

I put the letter in my pocket, followed her, keeping my voice low in case Pa should hear. 'I know. You've told me. But Mother, you'd like Matthew if you only gave him a chance.'

'You never brought him to meet us.'

'Because I was scared to bring him, that's why. You

made it quite clear he wouldn't be welcome. Mother, don't you remember courting? How it felt when you met Pa?'

'I wasn't already spoken for. And besides, look where it got me. Sometimes I wish I'd had more sense.'

'Pa was telling me how he was sorry for causing you all this trouble, with his hands and everything.'

She sighed. 'You're changing the subject. Your pa's daft. I don't mind having him here. It's good to know where he is. I used to look out of the window and wonder what the point was. Just cooking and cleaning for someone who barely said two words. It's brought him home to me. Do you know, we actually had a conversation?'

Sensing a little softening, I said, 'I didn't mean for it to happen, Matthew and me. I just need a bit more time to see if it will work out, that's all.'

'But it's not a steady job, is it, in films? Not like Peter with his teaching. They always need teachers. When Peter comes back he'll have a job for life.'

'But I'm not marrying a job, Mother.' Frustrated, I thrust more pots into the water in the sink. The cold water slopped up to my elbow, wet my cardigan sleeve. 'What's the point, if I want to be with someone else?'

She paused to look at me. 'Take my word for it, you can't live on love.'

But nothing Mother could say would dissuade me. I was determined to go to London despite her dire warnings of air raids and doodlebugs. A week later Matthew met me at Victoria and took me across London by bus to settle me into the 'nice hotel'. Travelling by bus in London gave me an unsteady feeling. The damage was worse than I had imagined, the jagged walls with the remnants of wallpaper and fireplaces still intact had once been homes; at night you used to be able to shut the door, keep everything out. Up until that time I hadn't really believed in the reality of war – I was both fascinated and appalled. Some places were untouched, others flattened, yet people were going about their business as if everything was still intact. It was peculiar.

Matthew checked me in at the hotel, and the receptionist looked me up and down as if assessing how much my clothes cost; the whole business of filling in the book with 'Miss' made me squirm, even though they were used to people like Matthew bringing actors for the film studios. Any other place would have looked askance at a young woman arriving like this on her own.

Matthew carried my luggage up to my room and I followed, taut with a mixture of trepidation and anticipation. He dumped the case by the single bed and whisked the curtains shut with a metallic rattle. The room became suffused with a red glow. He reached out for me and I stumbled into his arms unable to get there quickly enough. He slid his arms out of his raincoat whilst our lips were still touching.

I pushed my hand between the buttons of his shirt, felt the fine hairs on his chest. My knees were trembling with excitement. We made our way to the bed, mouths still exploring each other. One of his hands brushed over my breast, as if by accident, but I felt the nipple harden and my body press towards his. I fell backwards into the soft candlewick, and he fell on to me. I let out a groaning breath.

His weight was on top of me; one hand came round to my neck, while with his other his fingers fumbled to lift my frock. Suddenly I saw myself as if from the outside, as if I had just stepped into the room. I did not like the picture.

'No,' I said, sitting up, pulling my skirt down with my hand.

'What's the matter?' He pushed his hair back out of his eyes.

'I can't.'

'It's all right. I'm not going to press you if you're not ready.'

'I feel like somebody's watching us.' I was almost in tears.

'Silly, there's nobody here.' He stroked my cheek, then looked obviously over his shoulder. 'Nobody here but us chickens.'

I didn't really know what I meant, but it felt as though my mother, my pa and Peter were all there in the room, stifling me. I'd turned my head away, but when I turned back he was looking down at me. He was quite still, just looking. I was about to speak when he put his finger to my lips. It was a gentle touch; he traced the shape of my mouth.

'Rhoda King,' he said quietly, 'you are the most beautiful woman I have ever seen.' This time when his hand struggled to release the buttons of my dress I did not stop him.

I went every weekend to London to the same hotel, and my life was breathless, rushing through the week, hurtling towards the few precious hours spent with Matthew. I did not like the fact he had to loan me the money, but it was the only way we could manage it, with Pa out of work and me not able to work overtime at weekends. Matthew took me to the London Film Studios at Denham, a vast factory with sleek modern architecture, all white curved lines and glass windows.

It was another world. There were enormous queues at the gates — tradespeople and craftsmen in bibs and braces, come from all over London to get a day's work. I thought

Carnforth station employed a lot of people, but the scale of everything at Denham dwarfed my little world.

I was dazzled. Dazzled by the Londoners in their snazzy ties and the self-confident girls in baggy trousers or fox furs, their hair fixed into impossibly shiny patent waves. Nobody would know England was at war here.

Matthew shepherded me around the lots, and when we strode out I loved it that our footsteps were exactly in time. The site reminded me of an airfield, wide flat boulevards, everything spread out.

On the river close to the back lot was a galleon that had been used for *The Private Life of Henry VIII* just moored up, as if it was about to set sail. It looked like it was straight out of the Armada.

'Ship ahoy!' Matthew mimed, putting his hand over his brow.

'Andrew would die for that,' I told him. 'He's been doing the Armada at school, but this is much more exciting.'

We passed close to the colonnaded front of a Greek temple, but couldn't stop because they were filming there. From a distance it looked solid, with its painted marble frontage. On the steps before it a crowd of extras hugged their winter coats over their white robes, waiting for the cameramen to get set up. Around a corner and I was on a street made for an American Civil War film, its flimsy gingerbread frontage bright with pastel paint and hanging fabric foliage.

'Gosh, it's like walking through history,' I said, staring up at the blank windows. 'I need a big dress with a crinoline.'

'That's what I love about it. This street we're on is coming down next week, and into the skip. There's a row of Victorian villas going up in its place.'

'That's a shame, such a lot of work. Can't they save it?'

'I rather like the idea that it's so disposable. It's like real history, but just accelerated. One empire built over the next. That's what I love about filming on location – the world is vanishing every moment but we don't really appreciate it, and my job is to record it as it's going. Hard though, it's like trying to capture smoke.'

I squeezed his arm, loving his passion, his sense of purpose and vocation, but at the same time the fact that they were just going to throw the whole street away was too much to take in. More money must have been spent here to build these false houses than the real ones back home. I thought of Mother and Pa, scrimping to pay the doctor, and shivered.

'Oh, poor thing, let's get indoors,' Matthew said, thinking I was cold. He pulled me closer to him, put his arm across my shoulders.

'What do you think?' Matthew said.

'It's very good.' The recreation of the refreshment room at Carnforth was too clean and tidy. The walls were the wrong shade of green, and everything looked brand new, the tables and chairs all perfect, none of them mended like in the real refreshment room. There was something uncomfortable about seeing a fake version of a place that was so much a part of my life.

'You don't sound too impressed.'

'It's just, it feels strange to have our real life put here on a stage, as if …' I saw his disappointed face. 'It's lovely. They've done a wonderful job.' But something about taking it from its context and using it for a film made me angry, as if they might be laughing at it, at our way of life.

Matthew caught my mood. 'I know it doesn't look real yet. It only looks real once the lights are on it, and the actors are on set. You wait, it'll look just right once it's lit.' He put his arms around me for a hug. 'And I can't wait to take you to the film once it's out – I'll try and get you in to a preview.'

At Denham station we huddled under the glass roof at the far end of the platform, away from everyone else, waiting for the train back to London.

'I wanted to show it to you because I hope you'll soon be seeing a lot more of it. Soon as peace comes, we'll get ourselves a nice little house somewhere in the village,' Matthew said, pulling me closer. 'Something with a garden, a place for children to play. One with a nice new kitchen.'

'I didn't know you were a cook.'

'I'm not. I was rather hoping that would be your domain.'

'You mean you don't want to live on the leftovers I've scraped up from the pavement?'

'No, I want you waiting for me when I get home with my dinner ready on the table and my pipe and slippers warming by the fire.'

'You don't want much, do you?' I laughed, looking at him sideways, aware the conversation was sliding into dangerous territory.

'I want a quiet life. I'm ready to settle down – when I find the right girl.'

'Huh.' I turned away in mock anger.

He came and held me round the waist, spun me to face him. 'When I saw you'd taken off Peter's ring, I knew there would be room for mine.' His honesty unnerved me.

'So it's that straightforward, is it? What about asking me? I might say no.'

'You won't. You're mad about me.' He grinned.

'Try me.'

'Well, I had a more romantic place in mind, but I

suppose here is as good a place as any.' He knelt down on the platform and said, 'Dearest Rhoda, will you marry me?'

'Get up, you fool, your trousers are getting wet.'

'I'm not getting up until you say yes.'

'Ummm …' I pretended to consider it.

'Hurry up, my knees are freezing.'

'Course I will.'

He stood up and hugged me hard, lifting me off the ground and swinging me round. 'You see, I was right. I'm always right.'

'You're insufferable, that's all.' But we were laughing. I had the feeling that the world was moving too fast, that my mouth was speaking and the rest of me was being left somewhere far behind.

'We'd better go and buy a ring then.'

I stiffened.

'What's the matter?'

'Can we wait a while? I need to tell Peter. I can't keep two engagement rings – it wouldn't feel right, not until I've given him his back.'

'You are a very moral woman. But yes, I take your point. And you'll have to meet my parents. You'd better know what you're marrying into.'

'Are they that bad?'

'No, they'll adore you.'

I hugged him, but I was troubled. I loved him, yes, but I'd barely had time to think. If I married Matthew I'd be marrying this: the film studios, the London life. Did I want it? Of course I did, but it was like an illusion, as if I couldn't see myself here, as if the whole romance was not quite real. As if Matthew, the film, the whole of it was just a facade that would fall over if you blew too hard.

I'll get used to it, I thought, as we sat in the train leaning up against each other, watching the suburbs speed by.

'Ahh,' Matthew said contentedly, patting me on the knee. 'Glad that's all settled. I thought you might not have me.'

I looked at him and his candidness made me reach to kiss him again.

'You're wonderful,' he said. 'And it will be all right. I promise.'

50

1945 Rhoda

THERE WAS STILL no sign of Peter returning, though I was beginning to dread it. Mother must have told Pa about Matthew because after one of the visits he was waiting up for me.

'It's serious then, you and this Matthew,' he said.

'Yes, Pa,' I said. He was downstairs now, in his chair near the fireplace. I saw how he looked much less imposing without his railwayman's uniform.

'I thought it might fizzle out.'

'We're talking about getting married, Pa.'

'He hasn't asked my permission.'

'Oh, Pa, I'm too old for that now. And anyway, neither did Peter.'

Pa considered this a moment, sighed. 'Peter's different. He's a local lad. We know his family.' He rubbed a hand over his greying hair. 'Oh well, not much I can do, I suppose. Are you sure it's what you want, love?'

'I'm sure.' I leaned over to hug him.

'Hey, what's all this for?' he said, squirming away. 'Mind my hands.'

'Thanks, Pa,' I said. He smiled and nodded and it felt like a blessing.

Matthew always met me from the train under the station clock, and I would look out for his slim figure by the turnstile, his paisley scarf, or the rakish angle of his hat. It was March now and the bitter cold had lessened to be replaced with yet more rain.

Today the train had been full of airmen, on their way somewhere. You never asked where they were going these days, they were such a common sight. Besides, if you were a girl on your own you knew to avoid those carriages if you wanted any peace at all.

When I got off the train this time I could see no sign of him, but I reasoned he must have got held up, so I stood by the turnstile with my little overnight suitcase and waited. Another train came in and there was still no Matthew. The stream of people hurried past me, into the arms of those who had materialised just in time to meet the train.

Something must have happened. I weighed up what to do and looked at the station clock. I'd been there forty-five minutes. He wouldn't have forgotten, I knew that much. After an hour I thought I'd better go over to the hotel. Fortunately I remembered the way, though it was very different without Matthew beside me. I struggled to get out the pennies for the fare, clutching my umbrella in one hand and my case in the other. As the bus lurched away I hung on to the pole, and peered out anxiously into the drizzle, fearful in case I should miss the stop.

The hotel confirmed they had my usual reservation.

'Has Mr Baxter been in today?' I asked.

'I don't think so. I'll just ask.' The receptionist, a heavily made-up tabby blonde, went off into the little side room behind the mahogany reception desk, where I heard a muffled conversation before she reappeared. 'No,' she said. 'They say not.'

'When he arrives, can you tell him I've checked in, please?'

'Of course, miss.'

I took the key and went up. All of a sudden the hotel no longer felt modern and welcoming. I noticed the scuff marks on the stairs, the worn carpet beneath the dirty stair rods. When I went into the room the curtains were already drawn, but some of the hooks were hanging loose so they bagged at the top. I pulled them open, but there was only the movement of dimmed headlights outside. I drew them again. I had brought nothing with me to read, but found yesterday's paper stuffed in the drawer of the bedside cabinet. Some other guest must have left it there.

'*Prisoners of War on their way home*', it read. Peter would be coming home and I'd have to tell him about Matthew. I winced. I really should have written to Peter; it wouldn't be a very nice homecoming to find your girl was in love with someone else.

I read the paper cover to cover, but did not absorb the words. By now I was beginning to worry. I ate alone in the hotel dining room, but barely managed anything. I sat near the door and my heart leapt every time it opened. Afterwards I asked the girl at reception if she'd heard of any bombs or trouble in the city, but she said no, it had all been quiet, and threw me pitying looks.

I wondered if Matthew might have left a message for me at home, or at the station. He and Ed didn't have a telephone at their flat. In desperation I asked the hotel to get me a line to Carnforth station and spoke with Bob, the assistant station manager.

'No messages, love. Were you expecting something?'

'No, no. It's all right. But if a Mr Baxter rings, would you please ask him to call the Delamere Hotel. He'll know it.'

'Are you all right?'

'Yes, I'm fine. Just give him the message, would you, if he rings?'

I heard the click as the line went dead.

After that there was nothing for it but to go to my room and try to sleep. Matthew would know where I was, and be over in the morning. Some emergency at work perhaps, or an air raid.

Needless to say, I slept hardly at all. Every little noise woke me: sirens in the distance, a shout from the street, the sudden gurgle of the water pipes. In the morning I splashed my face with cold water and grimaced at the sight of the dark circles under my eyes.

No message at reception. Nothing. I'd have to go to his flat. I'd been once before and he'd cooked Ed and me dinner, so I knew where it was, and fortunately I had my London map in my bag. I hurried out of the hotel into the driving rain. What if I'd misunderstood him and got the wrong weekend? What if there'd been a bomb or something had happened to him? I waited a long time for a bus and then in my anxiety to get there, mistakenly got off too early and knew I had a long walk from the bus stop. I ran practically all the way, splashing through the puddles, my umbrella sluicing wet down the front of my coat.

His street was reassuringly quiet, the same as when I last left it: no bomb damage, just a peaceful Victorian street, quite down-at-heel, missing its railings as they all were. I stopped outside his house and checked the number. The curtains were open and the blinds up. His flat was on the middle floor, so I rang the bell and waited. I had no idea what I'd say to him if he was there. For a moment it crossed my mind that he might have deliberately stood me up.

But just then the door opened. It took me a moment to realise it was Ed. He looked different without a collar and tie.

As soon as he saw me I could sense something was wrong. As if he couldn't believe he was seeing me.

'Rhoda,' he said. He was rubbing his hand over his chin, waiting.

'Is he in?' I tried my cheerful voice, and put down my umbrella, shaking the droplets of water on to the path.

He seemed to be lost for words.

'He was supposed to be meeting me,' I said helpfully.

'Oh Lord. You don't know, do you?'

Behind me a car whooshed past and spray spattered up my legs, but I didn't take my eyes from his face.

His look had turned inward, away from me. 'He's dead.'

I still stood there, waiting as if he hadn't spoken.

Ed lurched into activity, threw open the door, stood aside. 'Sorry, sorry. You'd better come in.'

I followed him into the hall. There was some mistake, there had to be a mistake.

Ed sat me down in the living room. It was cold and it looked as if nobody had lived there for weeks. There were empty beer bottles and fag packets and an ashtray brimming over with ash and stubs. On the wall was a picture of Arsenal football team tacked up above a calendar showing a faded village green with Tudor houses. The back of the door still had Matthew's scarf hanging there. I could not even speak. I just waited for him to tell me.

'I thought they'd have let you know. His parents, I mean. I gave them your address. I did wonder why you weren't there. At the funeral. I thought perhaps you'd decided … oh Lord.' He shook his head. It seemed beyond him to explain. He shook a cigarette from the pack and lit up, dragging deeply on it. Then he sat down, his foot tapping restlessly on the blue lino.

'What happened?' My voice still worked.

'He was running for a bus, that's all. Saturday, on his way back from the library. They found his books in a bag next to him. An asthma attack. He forgot his puffer. You knew he had asthma, didn't you? An officer came round here. They'd found his address in his wallet and wanted someone to go down to identify him.'

My mind was making no sense of the information. It was as if everything was plugged in the wrong way round.

I sat dumbly as he continued. 'Of course I told the police where his parents lived and they telephoned them and his father drove them both up. So in the end I never saw him. I wish I had now. God, I'm sorry.'

But people don't die of asthma, I thought.

Ed jumped up then and opened a cupboard. 'I'm a jerk, I haven't offered you anything. Here –' He uncorked a bottle of brandy and sloshed a measure into a tumbler. 'Drink this. You look like you need it.'

I swallowed the burning liquid, and it brought me to my senses. Why hadn't he said asthma could be that serious? I didn't know what to do, didn't know what to say. I put down the glass, got up and said quite calmly, 'When was the funeral?'

As if to help me, he stood too. 'Thursday. I was sure they'd let you know. I told his mother. She was in a right old state though. Didn't seem to be able to take it in. Wait, I've got the order of service here.' He went to the clock on the mantelpiece and extracted a folded card from a sheaf of bills and passed it to me. On the front it said:

ORDER OF SERVICE
MATTHEW JAMES BAXTER
1919–1945

I didn't open it. Dare not.

'Please – may I keep this?' I asked. My hand did not even shake.

'Sure. Is there anything else … I mean, he'd have wanted you to have something.'

'No. I'd better be going.' It sounded so normal.

Ed seemed at a loss. 'Well, if you're sure. I could see you to the bus stop.'

'No, no, that's quite all right.'

I had to get out of there. Had to go. I tucked the black-edged card into my bag and slung the strap over my shoulder. 'Thanks for telling me, Ed. I'm staying at the Delamere. But I'll travel home tomorrow.'

'Will you be okay?'

'I'll be fine.' My voice was tight. 'I just haven't taken it in yet. I need some time on my own.'

'I'll be in touch, okay?'

I nodded and pulled open the door. Matthew's scarf dangled from the hook in front of me, but I did not stop. I plunged down the stairs and out of the door and walked briskly away, not caring where I was going. All around me people were going about their business with their stoical faces; nobody paid me any attention as I marched past through the rain, my umbrella hanging uselessly over my arm.

At one point I thought I saw him, Matthew, on the other side of the street. A great rush of electricity jolted through my chest and I called out 'Matthew!' but when the man turned it was not Matthew at all, but a stranger. And I realised in that one moment that from now on I'd be looking for him in strangers' faces all my life.

When I got to the hotel I asked again if there were any messages, but of course there were none.

Back in the room I was shivering so hard my teeth chattered, so I took off my sodden coat and switched on the electric fire. It buzzed and flickered and crackled with dust. Even crouched right next to it I could not get warm.

I tried to cry because that's what one is supposed to do, but I could not. I kept expecting his rat-a-tat-tat on the door, his voice calling 'Rhoda?' from outside. The room looked exactly the same as when I had left. There was the paper, its edges slightly curled, the same headline shouting out at me. How could it still be the same? It didn't seem right.

'Prisoners of War on their Way Home'. The irony struck me like a blow. I tore the paper slowly into pieces and let the bits drop to the floor. It felt phoney, like something in a play. This wasn't really happening. I was making a mess with my stupid gesture, but the idea of tidiness did not seem to matter any more. What was tidiness for? I couldn't make sense of why it was important. I climbed into bed fully dressed and stared at the lampshade with its faded row of red bobbles.

How little his parents knew him, I thought. Bloody stupid. They hadn't let me know. They never saw what was right in front of their noses. My own parents' faces loomed into my mind. How would I be able to tell them about Matthew at home? I couldn't bear it, their sympathy. They wouldn't understand and they'd try to comfort me, to tell me it would be all right, that grief fades with time. They wouldn't realise that I didn't want to ever get over it, that what we had was so perfect that I would never let myself get over it.

51

1945 Rhoda

PA WAS SITTING in a chair at the kitchen table, staring into the garden. His hands still had dressings on them, but the finger-ends poked out, pink and new. An 'I-Spy' book about birds was propped open in front of him.

'You've lost weight,' he accused.

'Have I?' I said.

'You need to look after yourself. I'm supposed to be the patient here, not you.'

His joke did not make me smile; these days very little did.

'Have you had your exercise today?' I asked, and went to join him at the window. Outside, the garden was a mess of brown twigs and faded daffodils.

'Yes. It's a struggle though, walking about without using my hands. I keep wanting to pick things up. Those daffs need deadheading, and the potatoes need sowing. Do you know, I can't wait to get myself working in that garden. I've watched the crows fly past with their little bits of twig for their nests and thought what a great feeling it must be to be building something. To be doing something useful. Providing for the next generation.'

'Don't be in too much of a hurry, Pa, you've to get your hands healed first.'

'I thought I might build a pigeon house. Sol Sykes has always kept pigeons. They're intelligent creatures, gentle. Did you know they've been using them to send messages to the front? Amazing that, they've trained them up and—'

A rush of hot anger came from nowhere. 'For God's sake, Pa, I don't want to know about pigeons. There are more important things to build than a bloody pigeon house.'

In earlier days he would have shouted back, tried to slap me and given me a piece of his mind for swearing. Now he just looked hurt.

Embarrassed, I made a show of folding his towel that was lying crumpled up at the end of the bed.

'I know it pains you, lass. But it doesn't make it hurt less by hurting other people.'

I put the towel down. He was right, but I wasn't ready to admit it. He could not know what I felt. There was a black chasm in my chest into which I dared not look. I had never realised memories could be so painful. The war had weakened us all, and despite the fact it looked as though we were fighting, the cracks were showing everywhere. We were tired of the beaches bristling with barbed wire, tired of patching and mending and never having quite enough. Matthew had given me new hope; he'd been my future. He was to have been my dancing days, my sunny kitchen, and my children. Now all those were wiped away.

And here was Pa talking of building pigeon houses.

These days Mother and Pa treated me with kid gloves. I'd told them the facts and they said very little. I couldn't help but think they must be privately relieved, which made me bitter. But I was finding it hard to anchor myself in anything. Nothing seemed to have any point. I'd wake up and it would be only a moment before a crater-like hole would burn in my solar plexus along with the sudden realisation that I couldn't bring Matthew back. That nothing I did would ever be able to change the fact that he was gone.

Patty was very good. I liked being with her because she had known him, and it was a comfort even though I never mentioned his name. After work she had got in the habit of talking me for coffee in the Belmont Tea Rooms. I still couldn't bear to go in the refreshment room; even the thought of it brought an almost physical pain.

Yesterday she'd brought over two scones with the coffee, treating me with her coupons. I saw her tap her nose as if to say 'Keep quiet' before she slipped a jar of jam to the grey-haired woman behind the counter. After bringing our tray she rummaged in her bag and brought out another pot of strawberry jam.

'I've been over to my sister's in Greenodd. She gave me four jars. Four! I'm not kidding, their pantry would feed the whole British Army. That's what living on a farm does for you. There now, I'll put it on good and thick,' she said. 'I'm feeding you up.'

My stomach had got used to its empty state and I couldn't face it. 'I don't think I can manage it,' I said.

She ignored me and slathered a good quantity of jam over all four halves of the scones and began to tuck in. I sipped my tea as my stomach protested.

'Have you heard anything from Ed?' she asked.

'No,' I said. 'Nor Alan. I would have thought they'd write. But there's nothing they can do anyway. I prefer it this way. It's better not to have to deal with them. I don't suppose we've that much in common any more.' I swallowed and my eyes prickled. 'It was Matthew that glued us all together.'

'Oh, love.' Patty came over and enveloped me in a hug. Hot tears leaked from my eyes but I brushed them away.

'I'm all right,' I said. 'You have the scones. I can't eat them.'

She sat and ploughed her way through three before admitting defeat. In between mouthfuls she told me about how her brother was on his way back from Japan and the preparations they were making for when he eventually got home.

'I've had a letter from Peter,' I said.

'What does he say? When's he coming home?'

'I don't know. Soon, I suppose. I daren't open it. Mother tried to ask me about it but I just got angry and told her to mind her own business. Sometimes I think I might be losing my mind. Oh, Patty, it's dreadful. I can't be civil any more, I just seem to fly off the handle. It's the pain. Nobody told me about the pain. When I think of all those grieving widows, all the mothers who've lost children. I never even really noticed them before, but now they're everywhere. And do you know what? I envy them. I bloody do. At least their men died for something – they can be proud. What was Matthew's death for?' I threw my napkin down on the table. The other customers were staring. 'Sorry Patty,' I said, pushing back my chair and hurriedly throwing on my coat, 'I'm not fit company today, I'll have to go.'

'But Rhoda—'

I didn't stop. I just hurried away down the High Street, all the way past the post office towards Millhead alongside the railway track. It was dusk and the trees stood out as black skeletons against the darkening sky. I paused next to the bridge and looked out on to the track, separated from the road by only a low wooden rail. It would be easy to walk out there, wait for a train to take me into oblivion. My mind butted in that I would have to check the train timetable first. The thought made me laugh, a hysterical laugh which forced me to cross my arms over my chest and hold myself tight in case it became tears.

The rusted track snaked away over its bed of cinders.

I had to survive this, but I didn't know how. The Church couldn't help – couldn't take away the picture I had of him lying on the pavement, gasping for breath, his books spilled out beside him. The imaginary memory I had of how it was. I hadn't been there to help him, and I was full of self-reproach. Mother seemed to think that because we hadn't known each other very long I'd get over it. As if somehow length of time equalled depth. But I couldn't haul myself up, back to life, and nobody could understand. I needed help. It was then that I made up my mind. I would go and see his parents.

What do you wear when you're meeting your fiancé's parents for the first time? Let alone in a situation like mine? The problem was to find something decent that was black. My wardrobe was full of worn-out, darned clothes. I had no clothing coupons left, and now that I'd lost weight even my work skirt hung off me. I could see my hipbones jutting out whenever I washed.

I was too impatient to write, and I feared they'd turn me away. I told nobody where I was going, except Patty, who was hard up as always and agreed she'd cover the bookstall for me whilst I had a couple of days off. The next day I crept down the gloomy stairs even before hearing the milk delivery. The only sound was that of Pa's uneven snores from upstairs. On my way out I glanced in the mirror to check my black skirt and dark blue polka-dot blouse – the best I could do. In passing, I propped a note against the cruet on the kitchen table where I knew Mother would find it, and was out of the back door and into the chill grey morning before anyone was awake.

I walked to the station because I didn't want to ladder my only decent pair of stockings by cycling. I'd already got my ticket, but I hurried into the Ladies' conveniences to brush my teeth and hair, and to put on some make-up. I wondered about mascara, and in the end I did scrub the little brush on to the paste and apply a touch of it, because I wanted his parents to think me pretty.

The early train was quiet, no troops – just the usual people on their way to work, nurses going to Lancaster to the Royal Infirmary, munitions girls, workers going to the parachute factory. A woman in an expensive-looking fur coat smiled at me as if to invite conversation, but I avoided her eyes. I didn't want to talk.

Watching the landscape slide past I saw fields with grey floodwater, dark plough sets, sheep huddling under the shelter of the hedges. We shot through several minor stations, empty but for birds that took off as we whistled through. It was drab, this England, the place we were all fighting for.

At the other end I had to change trains, get another from Marylebone to Ruislip. By six o'clock I was standing at Ruislip Manor station, its tubs and baskets empty of flowers, its walls covered in peeling posters and propaganda telling us to 'Dig for Victory' and 'Keep mum – she's not so dumb'. I asked at the counter how to get to North Park Road and was given precise directions and told it was twenty-five minutes' walk. I didn't mind. I walked fast – I needed to walk, to do something.

It was a bit out of town, suburban, the houses were larger, many of them stone built, detached or semi-detached with big front gardens and some even with cars in the drives. On the way I passed a hotel but didn't stop to drop off my holdall; it held not much more than a change of underwear and toothbrush and I was too impatient to get there before I lost the courage.

After several turnings, I was lost. I had to retrace my steps, the holdall dragging on my arm. I began to think I'd have to go back to where there was someone to ask, and I just couldn't bear it. It had taken such an effort to get here at all, to cope with the simplest of things. And now the whole idea of coming to see Matthew's parents seemed crazy. What if they simply refused to see me?

Just when I was almost in tears with frustration, in front of me was the left turn the man at the ticket office had told me about, with a sign for North Park Road. I sent up a silent prayer of thanks that the signs were going back up at last. I slowed and walked up until I saw a large old half-timbered house with 'Fir Tree House' on a painted board in the drive.

To my surprise there was someone in the garden. The whole front patch was divided into straggly rows for vegetables, and a man was there working. He was wearing a flat cap and a thick jersey and was digging. A pipe stuck out of his mouth though it wasn't lit. His spade kept getting stuck in the claggy earth but he still continued to dig. I baulked at interrupting him, yet I was fascinated to know if this was Matthew's father. He raised his head and glared, and I walked hurriedly past, heart beating hard in my chest.

At the end of the road I had to stop. The houses ran out; ahead was farmland and hedges for miles. I would have to turn round and pass him again. I screwed up my courage. After all, I'd come all the way from Carnforth. I edged into the drive.

'Mr Baxter?'

He stood, annoyed at the interruption, shoved the pipe into his pocket. 'Yes?'

'I'm Rhoda.' The name obviously rang no bells. 'A friend of Matthew's.'

He put down the spade.

'I've come from Carnforth. I wanted to talk to you …' Here words failed me. I swallowed back tears, gripped more tightly to my overnight bag.

He turned and went to the back door, leaving me standing on the drive. He pushed it open and shouted, 'Marion! We've got a visitor. Can you come?'

A small woman dressed in a black cardigan with a string of pearls around her neck put her head out of the door. Her eyes were rimmed red, her voice nasal. 'It's not very convenient. Can't they come back?'

I raised my voice a little so she could hear me. 'I'm sorry to barge in on you like this, but I had to come. I wanted to say how sorry I am. About Matthew.'

She looked at Mr Baxter with her eyes questioning. He said, 'She says she's a friend of Matthew's, from …?'

'Carnforth. We met whilst he was filming up there in January. And we got … close.'

Her eyebrows raised. 'You came all this way? You shouldn't have done that, you could have written …'

She paused. My eyes were wet. When I pressed the back of my hand to them, I made a black smear of mascara. 'Sorry. I'm sorry.'

'Oh dear. You'd better come in. The least we can do is give you a cup of tea. William, take … into the front room.'

'It's Rhoda,' I said, mopping my eyes. 'Rhoda King.'

Mr Baxter escorted me through the hall, past oak panelling hung with coats and into the sitting room, where a damped-down fire was settled in the hearth. 'If you'll excuse me a moment,' he said, 'I must get rid of my muddy boots. We weren't expecting any visitors.'

So there I was, in the house where Matthew grew up. I could hear them whispering in the hallway but I was tired, exhausted. I slumped on to the chintz-covered sofa. Next to me was a pair of needles pushed into a ball of wool and some rows of knitting in a hideous yellow. Above the fireplace hung a group of photographs and I automatically scanned them to see if Matthew was there.

There were photos of his sisters – girls in knitted knickerbockers and girls with giant hair-ribbons on the sides of their heads. A wedding photograph, very faded. I got up for a closer look and Matthew's face looked out at me, except of course it wasn't him, it was his father – much younger and his thick moustache not so grey. The ache in my chest grew.

Mrs Baxter brought the tea on a tray with a lace-edged tray cloth and a cream jug and sugar basin and tongs. Nobody quite knew what to say. I noticed Mr Baxter had put on leather slippers. Mrs Baxter had one button fastened the wrong way at the bottom of her cardigan. They looked worried and I realised I'd probably only added to their distress. 'Thank you,' I said as she offered me milk and sugar. 'Thank you.'

I knew I was thanking her too much but couldn't seem to stop. I wished I hadn't come. We sipped our tea, and they sat very stiffly in the two armchairs.

Eventually Mrs Baxter put down her cup with a clink on to the saucer. 'You said you were close to Matthew?'

'We wanted to get married,' I blurted. 'I loved him.'

I saw them look at each other for reassurance. Realised I did not look much like daughter-in-law material, that a few months didn't seem very long.

'He never said,' Mr Baxter frowned. 'Why didn't he tell us?'

'We were waiting … I mean, we wanted to do it properly, wait until the war was over. Have a proper wedding.'

'You're not …?'

'William!' Mrs Baxter reproached him.

'No, nothing like that.' I felt the heat rise to my face. 'I don't want anything from you. I didn't know he'd … not until after the funeral. Ed told me. I just needed to meet you. He talked of you all so much, and—' I couldn't go on. I just shook my head, afraid I'd cry again.

Mrs Baxter jumped to her feet. 'I'm sorry we weren't more welcoming. It's just we'd no idea. And he usually told us everything. Ed mentioned you, but we didn't know who you were, and it was just one more person to deal with …'

Next thing, she perched by me on the sofa and put her arms around me, and I felt myself crack and the tears came. I smelt her face powder and the tightness of her grip which made her pearls press into my chest. At some point Mr Baxter must have left and gone to get handkerchiefs because when we let go of each other they were there on the table, all nicely starched with his initials 'W.B.' embroidered in the corner.

We both blew our noses and after that we talked and talked. She wanted to know everything and I held nothing back. I even told her about Peter. During all this, his father said hardly a word, but went about closing curtains and putting on lamps, and supplying us with tea. He patted his wife on the shoulder as he passed, which was rather sweet.

'Matthew spent a lot of his childhood in hospital,' Mrs Baxter told me. 'He was severely asthmatic. On many occasions it was touch and go. I used to stay up with him at nights boiling kettles of water on the paraffin stove, trying to ease the pain of it. They told us he wouldn't live to grow up. But he always insisted on being treated just like the others. And as time went on, he just got on with it. We tried to get him to be careful, but he just wouldn't. You know what he was like. He'd say, "Live for the moment, Mother – none of us has a crystal ball.""

The clock ticked round to eight o'clock. 'I've made up the girls' room for Rhoda,' Mr Baxter said, after it had finished chiming. 'It's what he would have wanted. You'll stay, won't you?'

Mrs Baxter laughed. 'He's never made up a bed before – I hope it's all right.'

'I have too. In the army. Mitred corners and everything.'

After that they gave me instructions about the Anderson shelter in the garden in case there should be a raid, and I said goodnight. I think we were all exhausted. The girls' room had '*Betty and Evie*' on a little plaque on the door. I undressed and slid into one of the twin beds, between tight sheets and under the weight of several blankets. I could hear Mr and Mrs Baxter's low voices downstairs, and the murmur of it was soothing. For the first time I wondered if Matthew could see me here, whether he would be pleased. His parents were good to take me in, arriving like that out of the blue. I wanted more of Matthew. To see his house, to touch his things. There would be no more of him in the future. The only thing I could do now was to find some part of him where he used to be, in his past.

After I heard the Baxters come upstairs I went out on the landing. Matthew's room was opposite; there was a matching plaque with his name painted in blue. I took hold of the door knob and turned it, felt the door strain as I pushed against the lock. It wouldn't open. They'd locked it.

The loss of him made me catch my breath over. I wrapped my arms around my ribs, pressed hard to try to ease the ache. In the distance I heard the rattle of a train, thought of Pa, hoped they weren't worrying. Then I crept back to bed and wept.

The next morning it was pouring with rain so Mr Baxter drove me to the station. When I said he might be stopped and get into trouble, he said, 'It's an essential journey, as far as I'm concerned.'

They had accepted me, I realised. It felt good.

'Would you write?' he asked. 'It would mean so much to Marion if you would.'

I agreed and hugged him; he smelt of pipe tobacco. He kissed the air either side of my head, then he watched me board and waved me off, a tallish man with a greying sandy moustache and a lonely look about him. Matthew's words came back to me: 'He's not a bad old stick.' I was sad. I imagined this was what Matthew might have turned into, this polite, well-meaning man.

'Sis! A parcel for you!'

Andrew hung around hoping to see me open it, but to his obvious disappointment I retreated to my room. I had spotted the South London postmark. I had written to the Baxters to thank them for their hospitality, and I hoped it was from them.

I slit the string and opened the paper. Some loose photographs were on top, and a letter, along with an unstamped envelope marked 'Read later'. The photographs were all of Matthew, smiling his quirky lopsided smile. The first from when he was about seven, I'd guess, a school photograph perhaps. Our children would have looked like that, I thought wonderingly. Another one of him in what appeared to be a hospital bed, still grinning. How lovely of Mrs Baxter to send them.

I turned one over to look for a caption on the back and underneath was the picture of the packhorse bridge in Langdale, with a blurry photograph of Matthew and me standing there. His hat was about to blow off and he was reaching for it, and my hair was all over my face. It seemed a lifetime ago.

But the last one was a complete surprise. It was a close-up of a girl. At first I didn't recognise it, but then I saw. It was the photo Matthew took of me in the refreshment room with Patty and Evelyn. Except that he'd managed to enlarge my face and fade the others out altogether. There I was, mouth a little open, looking out through wide eyes, as if life was so startling I could scarcely believe it.

I read the letter.

Wednesday 18th April

Dear Rhoda,

I thought you would like these. We have been to Matthew's flat and begun to sort out his possessions. So sad. Edward gave us his camera and the letter I am enclosing. As you probably know he was a keen photographer and must have taken these shots of you. We recognised you straight away! You can see he was writing to us but hadn't had a chance to finish it or post it. I thought you'd like to have the letter as it speaks so highly of you and we have many others.

We still find it hard to believe he's gone. We keep expecting him to bound through our door. But I was so glad to hear he had found someone to love before he died. I know one thing, he would not want you to grieve. Get on with your

life, live it to the full. Let the past be what it is. Write
again soon.

With all good wishes,

Yours faithfully,

Marion Baxter

I opened the other envelope.

Dear Ma and Pa,

We're back in London now at last. It feels good to be back
in my familiar neck of the woods again. David Lean is
doing a marvellous job and though it's a bit of a funny
little film, Celia Johnson is terrific and it will be worth see-
ing just for her performance. They're filming in the studios
right now, but I'll be out and about looking at Beaconsfield
for night exterior shots. I might have the weekend free so I
wondered if I could come over. Will you make one of your
shepherd's pies?

Actually I want to bring someone with me. I've met the
most marvellous girl, and I want to show her off. Get out
your best china, Mother, because I want to impress her!
She's called Rhoda and I met her when we were filming
at a station up near the Lake District, we just sort of
'clicked'.

Our latest char has left us to go to war work again so our
flat is in a dreadful state and Ed and I are resolved to
try to sort it out by ourselves this weekend if we can't get
another. Do you still have Vera to do for you?

Here the letter stopped. He must have intended to finish it later. My heart was racing and I had a big smile on my face. *'The most marvellous girl'.* For a moment I had forgotten, but then it hit me again. He was gone. I would have to go on without him; we never would have the shepherd's pie on the best china. His parents would always remember me as the girl in the ill-matched clothes with the red eyes, not the marvellous girl in her best frock.

I'd have to bear it. Already it felt as if I had dreamt it, my life with Matthew. Even now I could not picture his face exactly; his features were fading too fast. In my mind's eye I was already only visualising his photograph. I took hold of his letter and pressed it hard against my heart, hoping it would hurt. Because the only way I would know I'd loved this much was to keep this pain.

52

1945 Rhoda

'UNDER THE CLOCK,' Peter had said.

I was so scared I could barely serve the customers. I hadn't seen him since I was eighteen, and I was twenty-four now, and he'd be nearly twenty-nine. It sounded so old. He'd been a young man when he left; I wasn't sure if I even remembered his face properly. And I wasn't ready, didn't know if I'd ever be ready. He must have kept me in mind all this time, and this made me ashamed. I hoped he would not be able to see what was inside me, the doubts, the lingering dark scent of grief. I couldn't tell him about Matthew, there was no point.

Would he even recognise me? I wore my hair up now, out of the way. The afternoon crept by, punctuated by my thoughts: *he'll be standing at Preston now, waiting to get on the Barrow train; now he'll be going through Lancaster.* I watched the station clock inch round. The memory of waiting for him there on our first date bloomed then faded in my mind. By the time the train chugged into the station I was a bundle of nerves, not sure whether to run away or wait.

The train doors swung open and the people waiting moved back to give the passengers space. I looked, but couldn't see anyone in uniform. A tall man limped towards

me in a dark grey overcoat, a hat on his head, a big suitcase.
Peter. Of course, he'd be in civvies now. His face was familiar and yet not quite. It was undeniably him, but a different
version from the one I'd remembered. He was thin, shadows hung under his eyes. He was scanning the huddle of us
standing under the clock. When he saw me he stopped dead,
as if he could not believe I was there.

I couldn't move. Other people from the train swarmed
past, then the next moment he was right in front of me. He
put his suitcase down on the ground and lifted his arms as if
he might embrace me, but I took an involuntary step back.
He let them fall.

'You're here,' he said. 'It's been a long time.'

'Let me take your case. How was your journey?' I
asked, flustered, rushing to do something, anything except
embrace him. His case was ridiculously light.

'No. I'll take it.' He pulled it from my hands. 'You look
wonderful. I can't believe I'm here.' His voice broke and a
tear leaked down his cheek.

I didn't know what to do. I'd closed myself off in case
he might intrude on my grief. I had no resources if he was
going to cry. I watched him wipe the tear away with the
sleeve of his overcoat.

'Are you going back to Crag Bank?' I asked.

'Yes, I rang home, just the other day ... when was it?
Tuesday I think, anyway I rang to say it would be any day
now, but Mother doesn't know I'm coming this afternoon. I
couldn't face too much fuss. And I thought I'd surprise her.
I've still got my key. I think so, somewhere. I kept it all the
way through the war.' He flashed a smile. 'I hope she hasn't
changed the lock.'

'I doubt it, not much ever changes round here.' I smiled
back, relieved we were on less intimate ground. 'I'll walk

with you. Mrs Illingworth's minding the bookstall. We can catch up.'

As we walked he exclaimed about all the changes that had happened on the High Street – the missing railings, the lack of food in Jenkinson's window, the general run-down look of the place. The sun was shining, the wind warm, but Peter looked pale, his manner hesitant; he kept his over-coat on as if he was cold. He was nothing like the confident young teacher I remembered. All the time I watched him, this familiar yet unfamiliar man, out of the sides of my eyes, wondering whether I still cared for him. He too cast quick embarrassed glances my way. Finally we fell to silence. The road to Crag Bank seemed longer than ever; I willed the walk to be over.

At the end of his road I stopped. 'I won't come up with you,' I said. 'I'll leave you and your mother to have your reunion in private.'

'She won't mind. Anyway, it was you I wanted to see.' He put down his case and reached out for me. I did not resist, but let him fold his long arms around me, pressed my cheek against the rough texture of his new woollen over-coat. He held me tentatively, and I moved into his arms, feeling his frame thin and bony under his clothes.

It was surprisingly good to be held by someone again, but I wasn't ready to let myself give in.

He was courteous, slightly formal. There was a struggle in his eyes, under the words, that I recognised in myself. 'I know it's been a long time,' he said, 'so things might have changed between us. And I know ... well, I've no right to expect anything of you. But I wanted to ask you – just to give me the benefit of the doubt for a little while. I might have forgotten what it's like, to be fit for a lady's company.'

His eyes searched mine. I shook my head, searched

for a response. He wasn't Matthew — every minute I was reminded he wasn't Matthew. But Matthew was dead, and here was Peter still wanting me. I would try, I thought. I'd try to put the past behind me.

'It's good to see you,' I said.

53
1945 Peter

AFTER HIS MOTHER'S hugs and tears, Peter barely had time to get through the door before she said, 'How do you like it? We had it decorated as soon as we knew you were coming home. Everything new. Isn't it lovely? We did your room, too.'

Peter looked around the brand new kitchen and hated it. It was like coming home to a stranger's house; it made him tetchy.

'It's all right. I suppose I liked the old one better.' He could not help himself. He had imagined being at home in their old kitchen for so long, and now it had shiny lemon-coloured kitchen cupboards and walls so bright it made him feel grubby just to be in there. He saw his mother's disappointed face, knew she must have gone to a lot of trouble, but he wanted the old kitchen back. It was unreasonable, he knew, but he was disorientated – still shocked at the colour and vibrancy of England in summer. It was as though he was looking at everything through a kaleidoscope. All the pieces were there, but wouldn't fit together.

So after Mother had exclaimed about his sudden arrival, after they'd hugged some more and she had brought in the obligatory tea and cake, she asked him if he'd walked from the station. 'You silly,' she fussed. 'Father would have fetched you in the car, if only he'd known,' she said. 'We can get a bit of petrol now, and he's gone out – gone to get a new spare tyre in honour of you coming, so he can take you about.'

'It's all right. Rhoda met me and walked up with me. She didn't want to come in, said she'd leave us to it.' He shifted uncomfortably on the newly repainted kitchen chair.

Mother frowned, and pushing a side plate towards him, said, 'I can well believe it. She's not been near us for six months.'

Peter went to dismiss this, to smooth it over, aware that his parents had never really liked Rhoda. 'She was probably busy … you know how it is.'

'No, not busy.' She folded a napkin on his plate very precisely, and placed a cake fork over it. 'I wasn't going to say anything, and I know it's not really any of my business, but you're my son, after all. And it's only right you should know …' She put her bony hand on his arm. 'I'm sorry, Peter, it's not good news. She's been seeing someone else.'

Peter felt his world crack and shift. 'She never mentioned anything.'

'Evelyn Biggs from the refreshment room told me. Someone from London. They came up here to make that film, *Brief Encounter*. Terrible little film. Anyway, apparently Rhoda started seeing this chap. She went down to stay with him at weekends and everything. I couldn't write and tell you, I only just found out. Anyway, probably best not to see her again – you're better off without her.'

Peter heard his voice come out calm and dry. 'Do you know, is she still seeing him?'

'No. Evelyn says he died. But even so, she can't just expect to carry on with you as if nothing's happened. I always thought she was a bit unreliable, not the girl for you.'

'She's not unreliable. How did he die? Was he in the army?'

'No, no. Some sort of seizure. Too much fast living, probably – you know what film stars are like.'

'How awful.' Peter knew what it was like to watch the life ebb out of someone. He hoped Rhoda hadn't had to see it happen.

'Aren't you going to say anything else? Aren't you at all upset that she's gone behind your back?'

'Mother, I've been away more than five years. In that time I've seen ... well, never mind. But things happen in war, things nobody plans. She was there to meet me at the station. As far as I'm concerned she's still my fiancée until one or other of us decides to change it.'

His mother's mouth opened and closed again. Then she shook her head. 'But she's made a fool of you.'

'Who else knows? Father?'

'No. I haven't told him yet. It could be all over Carnforth. Evelyn's not renowned for her tact now, is she?'

'Don't tell Father, will you?'

'But he—'

'Promise. Promise me you won't tell anyone else.' He gripped her wrist tight, squeezed. She pulled her arm away and rubbed it. He had hurt her. He didn't mean to.

'All right,' she said, her eyes wide. 'Though I can't see why you're so keen on her. She's only a railwayman's daughter – nothing special and—'

'For Christ's sake! She's special to me, Mother. I dreamt about her every day in that rotten camp. It was what kept me going, knowing I'd be coming home to her. Whatever happened while I'm away, it's nothing. Nothing, do you hear?' He was shouting, too big and too angry for the spindly chairs, the china cups, his mother's little lace collar. She was backing away. He took a ragged breath, calmed himself. 'We can make a fresh start. I know we can.'

His mother clung to the side of the sink, frail and tight-lipped.

'Look, if Evelyn says it's over, then let it be over. That's an end to it.' With that he mumbled, 'I'm going up.'

'But what about tea?'

He made a supreme effort. 'I'll come down for it later. Sorry if I'm grouchy. The journey made me tired, that's all.' He couldn't tell her anything. All that time he'd been away and he knew now he couldn't tell her anything, that the things he'd seen and the words that really mattered would just stick in his throat.

He mounted the stairs and turned in to his old room, now unrecognisably smart in pale grey and red, and still smelling of paint. He sat down on the bed. Everything had changed. His mother looked old, her face crisscrossed with worry lines. And she was more of a snob than he remembered, telling him a railwayman's daughter wasn't good enough for him. And Rhoda. She hadn't waited. He couldn't grasp it; the fact of it wouldn't register.

He needed Archie, his old buddy. He didn't like this real version of his life. He wanted to be back in his familiar bunk with Archie snoring above him, still dreaming of how it would be. It was all too bright, too blinding. Like a diver with the bends, he had surfaced too quickly from the murk of the depths, and the world above the water wasn't the one he had left. He wished Archie was here now. He'd give anything to hear Archie's voice, his reassurance, that they would get through this together. But he'd left Archie at the station in London. Both of them were wearing new suits and overcoats. It made Archie look different. When he'd last seen him at the barracks, in his new clothes, Peter did not recognise him.

'You look smart,' he'd said. His voice came out gruff – there was a lump in his throat.

'So do you. Rhoda will be knocked dead. You look like a film star.'

'From the horror studios, you mean.'

Archie ran his hand over his pinstriped jacket. 'It feels strange, though, doesn't it? I'm scared the man inside won't quite match up to what's on the outside.'

Peter was about to hug him, but something in their new status as civvies stopped him. 'You look fine. Your mother will be proud.' He held his hand out and Archie took it and pumped it up and down. 'You'll keep in touch?' he said.

'You promised me a pie and a pint. And I'm going to hold you to it.'

So they'd travelled together to Victoria and then gone their separate ways. Even the train journey north had felt odd without Archie.

Peter opened the wardrobe to hang up his coat, saw his schoolteacher's shirts and collars hanging there, the tweed jackets and polished shoes. He shut the door again, sat back down in his coat. Archie would be home by now. He wondered what he was doing, what he was thinking.

But Archie couldn't help him with Rhoda.

Rhoda had seemed like herself, and yet not like herself – it was hard to make sense of it. She looked just as pretty as he remembered, but her features were leaner, sadder, her hair different.

Damn. He hit his fist down on the quilt. Damn, damn, damn. Only now did he feel the sting of it, the hurt twisting, tightening in his chest like a tourniquet. He rolled over on the bed, grabbed hold of the pillow and pressed it to his chest. The loss of her was a physical pain that made him moan, despite the fact that his Mother could probably hear him below. He'd banked on getting home and starting from where he left off, everything just as it was. Now he was a stranger in his own life.

But he wouldn't give up. She'd come to the station, hadn't she? He was determined. No matter what had gone on, it was over, and he'd forgive her. After all, how could he preach? He, if anyone, needed forgiveness.

54

1945 Rhoda

IT WAS A September wedding. Not in St Oswald's but at Christ Church in the town, a hollow space so cold we could see our breath. Mother and I saved our coupons but we couldn't get any silk or satin. I'd managed to get a pale blue frock with a matching jacket from the second-hand exchange in Morecambe; fortunately it had three-quarter sleeves and Mother converted one of her felt hats with some pale blue veiling to match. It was not the sort of dress I'd dreamt of as a little girl, but then this was not the sort of wedding I'd dreamt of either.

Pa managed to walk me down the aisle with his hands still stiff and curled, but something like he used to be, proud and upright in his Sunday suit. And there was Peter looking serious and pale, his voice unsteady as he slid the ring on to my finger next to the diamond that he'd bought me so many years before. When the organ started to play the hymns he clung to the bottom of his jacket so tight his knuckles were white. *Please don't cry,* I willed him. I could not bear it, any emotion, in case it brought it up in me. I shut myself off so that as I said the vows back to him I could hardly believe I was saying the words. They seemed to possess no meaning, like smoke dissolving into an empty sky.

Down the aisle we walked, past Mrs Middleton who did not even look at us but kept her nose in her hanky, past Andrew, smartened up with his hair pressed flat, past Patty grinning like crazy, with Gordon, her littlest one, pressed to her chest. Out into the chilly grey day amid a patter of rice, and a chorus of shouts for us to smile for the camera.

The wedding breakfast passed in a blur of congratulations, well-wishers and brown-paper wrapped parcels. We hardly dared look at each other. Peter smiled politely, pleasing all the elderly relations. It was dark by the time we managed to get away, driven by Frank, Patty's husband, to Morecambe for the night of our honeymoon.

The Broadway Hotel was large and our window looked out over the front, but in September it was already too dark to see the view. We each had a small overnight case and when we went into the room we put them side by side on the stand at the foot of the bed. I heard Peter exhale.

'Well, we've done it,' he said.

I swallowed and nodded, unable to speak. Matthew would have lifted me up, swung me in circles. Peter looked at a loss, his hands hanging limply by his sides. For something to do, I unpinned my hair and dropped the Kirby grips one by one on to the dressing table, forcing the image of Matthew's bright face from my mind, marvelling how strange it was, that someone who was not there could still be so piercingly present.

I reminded myself he'd want me to be happy. I looked about me, at the imposing double bed with its walnut headboard and folded-down quilt. The window was shaded by heavy drapes. Gilt-framed pictures of grazing cattle and mountain landscapes hung on the walls. 'It looks like a nice room. Good big windows,' I said, walking over to look out.

'We might have a view of the sea in the morning.' Between us hung the idea of the night.

'Shall we unpack?' he said.

'I've not brought much, just a skirt and jersey.'

We hung our clothes in the big old wardrobe, which smelt of dust, and as the metal hangers chinked together I thought, this is what it is to be married, to see our empty clothes hanging up side by side.

I shut the door, went to the chest to put my change of underwear into one of the drawers, where it looked small and plain.

Neither of us knew what to do. Peter sat down on the bed, bounced a bit and said, 'Springs seem good,' but then he rubbed his hand over his face in an embarrassed way and stood up as if the bed might bite him. 'I'll draw the curtains, shall I? Keep the heat in?'

Someone had thought to put a paraffin heater in the room which had taken the edge off the chill. I went to warm my hands over it. Peter came up behind me and placed his hands on my shoulders.

'Hello, Mrs Middleton,' he said gently. 'I know it's early, but shall we get ready for bed?'

'If you like, it's been a long day.' I turned to kiss him, but missed his lips and caught him on the cheek.

'I'll turn the light out.'

'I'll need to put my nightdress out first, so I can find it.'

Both of us had left our nightclothes in our cases, unsure what to do with them. I watched Peter lay his pyjamas out carefully on one side of the bed, and followed suit. My night-dress was a flimsy silky thing, a present from Patty, not at all suitable for the weather, whereas his maroon-striped pyjamas looked solid and sensible. I saw Peter look at my nightdress and swallow, turn away.

When he switched the light out I could hear his breathing and the metallic click when he unfastened his belt buckle. I dropped my clothes on the floor in my hurry to cover myself up again, undressing the way I would at the swimming pool, arms crossed over my chest, hopping out of my underwear.

The springs creaked so I knew he'd got into bed. I reached out to feel for the edge of it and slid myself in next to him. Outside, the plaintive call of gulls spoke of the incoming tide. Peter reached for my hand and interlaced his fingers in mine, turned on his side so I could feel his breath on my face. I waited, but he did not move towards me.

'Thank you for marrying me,' he said, his fingers tightening. 'I don't deserve you.'

I could not move. It was I who did not deserve him. He was such a good man, lying there in his pyjamas that smelt of Fairy. Matthew never bothered to wear anything in bed; his limbs had slid over mine like water. The memory of Matthew rushed up to drown me. I pushed it away, sensed the edges of the howl inside that had never found its voice.

Peter moved over then to kiss me, a tentative dry kiss on the lips. I let him, but stayed still, did not encourage more. His other hand rested gently on my hip, and I prayed he would not move it. I did not make any attempt to embrace him.

He removed his hand, sighed. 'Goodnight,' he said. Then he turned his back to me, and left me lying facing the ceiling.

I had prepared myself to bear whatever it was he might decide to do, but I hadn't prepared myself for this. Didn't he want me? It was confusing. It was only just gone seven o'clock, and the night stretched out blankly before me. In the dark I could hear the September wind, the squeak and rumble of the trams, their lights streaking the curtains as they passed, footsteps and laughter on the pavement out-side. I lay still and tense, could not sleep, but after a while I heard Peter's breath deepen and slow. After an hour or so he moaned, pulled the sheets tighter into his fists.

At home Mother would be shovelling more coal on the fire and turning on the radio. But I would never be going back there. Peter had rented us a small terraced house in Carnforth and from now on it would be just me and him. And I had never felt so lonely in my life.

55

1955 Rhoda

I WAS IN the kitchen in my nightdress making the tea as usual, but this time I had gone to the bathroom first, brushed my hair, washed in our lovely new white suite and put on some make-up. I wanted to look attractive. Peter always waited in bed for me to bring the tea up to him, along with the morning copy of *The Times*. Later over breakfast he would tackle the crossword, and if I was lucky, I'd get the occasional clue thrown my way over the toast and Marmite.

But this morning was our wedding anniversary. Ten years. Usually Peter had to be prodded to remember, but this year I hadn't dropped the usual hints, I'd trusted him. I'd seen my husband in a new light since meeting Helen and finding out what a hero he was. I'd started to remember him as he used to be before the war.

Before we were married I used to watch him playing the cornet, hair flopping over his eyes, his serious expression as he rested it against his lips. When I served him tea I used to think of him as 'that posh boy'. I supposed he had made me posh too; I'd just absorbed his values over the years without even noticing. I was aware that Helen looked on me as slightly stiff and stand-offish by a dozen small things – the way she always asked me if the coffee was all right, the way she always waited for me to order first in Lewis's, the way she behaved slightly nervously around me.

I'd never had a friend like Helen since Patty, but Patty and Frank had moved to Canada now with all their children. I missed her. But I liked Helen, she was a good listener. Meeting her had caused me to look again at my marriage, to try to find out what was true about it, to sort the wheat from the chaff. I was restless. Since opening up to Helen I had a great urge to tell Peter the truth after all these years, to talk to him about Matthew. And the whole idea of keeping my meetings with Helen a secret was chafing me. I was changing, and I needed more change around me.

I made up a tray and propped up my card to Peter against his cup. I had spent a long time in the card shop trying to find something appropriate. Cards these days were all too lovey-dovey, or horrible cartoons of men with frothing pints of beer and women with too much hair. In the end I'd bought a card of a picture of France with cypress trees in a field, which was the only suitable thing I could find. Inside beneath the 'Happy Birthday' line I wrote the date and:

To Peter,

we survived another year!

Love from Rhoda

After I'd written it I wondered if I should have been more affectionate. But it was hard after this long to put anything real down. Too exposing somehow. I sighed. Was it foolish to hanker for a deeper connection after all this time?

I carried the tray up and opened the curtains to let in the meagre light. 'Tea's up.' I placed the tray next to Peter on the bedside table.

He struggled to sit upright in his pyjamas, propping a pillow at his back.

'What's this?' he said, smiling, holding up the card.

I climbed back into bed beside him, liking his delighted expression. 'Pour me one, while you're at it.'

I watched him put in the milk first, add the tea and then sugar his own cup. I'd watched him do it a thousand times, but today it seemed different; I noticed his slender forearms, how he was careful not to drip milk on the bedside table. He made my tea just the way I liked it.

He passed it to me, then leaned over the edge of the bed to retrieve something from underneath. 'You didn't think I'd forgotten, did you?' He handed me an oversized envelope. I smiled and rubbed him on the shoulder affectionately. The younger Peter smiled back. 'You look nice,' he said. 'You look just the same as the day we got married.'

'I hope not. That dress was awful. And it was so cold I think my nose was blue to match.' I opened the envelope to see one of the soppy cards I'd avoided in the shop, with embossed roses and a satin bow. But when it was coming my way it didn't seem soppy at all, just lovely. He'd always bought these, I realised, but I'd never let the sentiment in before today.

I watched him open my card, knowing he'd be disappointed.

'That's a nice picture,' he said. 'Is it Monet? I like Monet.'

Suddenly I couldn't bear it any more. 'I don't know, but whoever it's by, it doesn't tell you how I really feel. How I feel inside. You're a wonderful husband and a lovely man, and I've never really told you how much I care.'

He laughed nervously. 'What's brought this on? Is it something you've eaten?'

'No, Peter, I'm serious. I want us to be … closer.' I

reached out to hug him, and he let his arms fold around me. We stayed like that a few moments, whilst I felt the comfort of his arms round my back.

He kissed the top of my head the way he kissed our cat. 'Tea's going cold,' he said.

'I've got to tell you something.'

'What? What's all this about? It's too late to wish you hadn't married me, if that's what you're going to say.' He laughed.

I braced myself. 'I've been meeting Helen Foster.'

He sat up straighter, and edged away in the bed so he could look at my face. 'Helen?' He was looking at me very intently now. 'You don't mean Archie's wife?'

'Yes. We've been meeting for about six months.'

A pause. He scrutinised my face. 'She never mentioned it,' he said warily.

'But Peter, you never mentioned her to me! You've been friends with them for ten years, but you never once told me anything about them.'

He looked defensive, mulish. 'Archie was a wartime pal. I didn't think you'd be interested.'

'For God's sake! Why did you keep them a secret? Did you think I wouldn't approve, or something? I thought you were having an affair with her.' His eyebrows shot up. 'Don't look at me that way. Is it that ridiculous? When she told me you'd been friends for all that time I felt so stupid. So shut out.'

His face had flushed. 'No, it was you who shut me out. I would have told you about Archie as soon as I'd been demobbed, but you didn't want to look back. You kept saying, "Forget all that, let's look to the future."'

'It's what everyone did. And when you came back you

were so thin, and so morose, I couldn't seem to get through to you.'

Peter moved away, the hurt showing in his eyes. He got out of bed and began to take clothes out of his drawers.

Then he turned and said, 'It was you. You think I was morose? I kept thinking it must be me who'd changed, that the war had made me see things differently. I thought I was coming home to the happy girl who'd fall into my open arms, and instead you were hardly there. You used to look through me sometimes, and I'd wonder where you were, because you sure as hell weren't there with me. When I told Archie things weren't good between us he said I was probably imagining it because of what we'd been through in the camp. He thought I was paranoid.' He slammed a drawer shut. 'But it wasn't that, was it? Mother told me as soon as I got home. You'd been seeing someone else when I was over there.' He shot me a look. 'But he died, didn't he, so you had to make do with second best.'

My mind reeled. So he knew about Matthew. 'You've never been second best,' I heard myself say, the truth twisting and knotting. 'I wanted to get married, you know I did.'

Peter gathered up his clothes into his arms like a barrier between us. 'Yes, that's about it. You wanted to get married. Who I was, my feelings, never came into it.'

'You know that's not true.'

He stood before me still in his pyjamas and sighed. I saw the thirty-nine-year-old Peter again, the tired, harassed teacher. He looked defeated. The man who had survived such horrors in the war, defeated by his marriage. 'Yes, it is, Rhoda,' he said bitterly. 'I was always more in love with you than you were with me, I know that. I've always known it, right from the beginning. Do you have any idea what that feels like?'

He snatched up his clothes and went out of the door. On the landing he turned and said, 'At least I can talk to Helen. She listens to what I have to say. Unlike you, she's actually interested in my opinion.' And with that he went downstairs. Two minutes later the front door banged.

I didn't move for a moment. It was as if someone had thumped me hard in the chest. I leapt out of bed and went to the window, opened it, shouted, 'Peter! Peter?'

I watched him limp on to the driveway – yank open the car door, climb in, and slam it shut. The car pulled erratically over the kerb in a grind of gears, and away round the corner. I closed the window, sat down on the bed. My mind reeled. His mother. I cursed her, and then felt bad because she'd been dead two years now. She'd told him and yet he'd still married me, even though he'd known about me seeing Matthew from the very beginning. He must have loved me very much.

I closed the window, sat down. Had I really been as bad as he said? In the early days I was still so grief-stricken that sometimes I could barely get up in the mornings. So many nights in this same bed, a wedding present from my parents. I remembered a moment from the early days. It was a day when something must have woken us, because it was dawn, and the birds were singing away in their morning chorus. Peter looked at me tenderly. 'You look lovely, with your hair all wild,' he said, and he reached over to touch it.

'It's too early to get up,' I said. 'Go back to sleep.'

The light died in his eyes.

For six months or more, I could focus only on what was gone, what I'd lost, not on what was in front of me. I'd wanted to make the marriage seem right, silence my mother's expectations by getting pregnant, but even that we could not seem to do.

I picked up the mug of tea Peter had made and took a sip, hoping it might calm me. How naive and foolish I'd been, caught up in my own loss. Pa died four years ago of a bad heart, and I'd loved him, but the grief for him had faded naturally as it should. But losing Matthew was the loss of a dream. Somehow losing a dream was unbearable, more painful than losing the person.

I stood up and went to the window. The lawn was patchy with melting dew. The apple trees were already shedding their leaves and some windfalls lay on the ground. A pain like toothache sat just below my ribs. Peter had been there for me always, I realised; a quiet shadow at my elbow, and yet I hadn't seen him because I'd been too busy comparing him to Matthew.

At the side of the drive the dustbin waited to be brought back in. Peter had put it out the night before to be emptied just before he came to bed. My heart contracted. What would I do without him? A picture of Mother polishing Pa's shoes came to mind, the sound of the brush moving to and fro.

Downstairs the kitchen was quiet. No Radio 4 blaring from the Wilkinson radio, no kettle whistling or creak of the tin-opener as Peter opened food for the cat.

I didn't feel as though I wanted to cry, I just felt empty. I'd need to bring the bin in, so I pulled open the hall cupboard to get my coat. I saw he had taken his coat, his good overcoat. His gardening anorak still hung there where it always was. Would he come back? I wondered where he'd go.

Helen Foster.

I shut the cupboard door with a bang. After all, *she* listened to him.

I tottered to the sofa, my knees feeling as though they might give way. Of course a part of me had known all along. Why hadn't I admitted it to myself? I remembered that she had asked me all sorts of details about him, that she had made me vaguely uncomfortable with her questions, was sometimes a little too interested in our lives. And then there were those flowers when I was at her house. It had been Peter after all. My Peter.

I cursed my stupidity. I'd done just what she wanted and driven him straight into her arms. He'd be going there, I realised, to *her*.

A fierce rage of possessiveness took hold of me. I leapt up, ran to the phone, snatched the receiver off the hook, dialled her number. 'Come on, come on,' I said through gritted teeth as it rang.

Nobody answered.

'Answer it, you cow,' I said. Something cracked inside me. The buzz of the ringtone mocked me and I found myself shouting over it, 'Give him back to me, you bitch, give him back.' After five minutes I was hoarse, panting. I couldn't go on, I was ashamed of myself, ashamed of the woman I'd become, shouting and bawling like that. I slammed the receiver down and burst into tears. He was my life, I realised, and now I'd lost him.

He'd taken the car. There was nothing I could do. Only wait.

56

1955 Peter

HELEN WAS WEARING her nurse's uniform when she opened the door, and her face was pale and washed-out without the make-up she usually wore. Peter took the coffee that Helen offered him without speaking. His chest felt as though it had been cut open. He sipped, then took the spoon from the saucer and stirred mechanically to calm himself. 'Any sugar?' he asked, realising too late there was none in it.

'Oh, yes. Sorry, I forgot.' She hurried off to the kitchen.

Peter put his head in his hands and rubbed his forehead with his fingertips. This had seemed like a good idea when he set off, and he'd been boiling mad. It was odd how much it still ate away at him, the thought of Rhoda and that other man. Was this the same? Now he was here he just wanted to turn round and drive away. He didn't feel like trying to be attractive or charming to Helen any more, he just felt tired. He shouldn't have got angry; rowing never solved anything, and Rhoda was right really, he shouldn't have kept such a big secret from her. It was just that once he'd begun, and time rolled on, it had got harder and harder to tell her.

He looked around the living room; it was the same as it had always been, except that there was no Archie to talk about cars and music with. His old friend. He didn't know whether to be sad or happy he wasn't here. What would he have thought of him? He took a gulp of the coffee. He knew Helen was expecting something, for him to make a move, and he could feel himself sliding away from it, now it could be real.

Helen came back with the sugar bowl, plates and two slices of cake on a tray. 'It's home-made,' she said. 'Lemon.' She'd brushed her hair, he noticed. *It's no use,* he thought, with a sudden flash of sympathy; *I'm not going to try anything.* Helen passed him a plate with a generous slice.

'Oh, thanks,' he said. Automatically, his hand reached for the cake, and he took a bite. 'Mm, very good,' he said. He felt like crying. He didn't want to be here eating cake in this harsh bright daylight, but he couldn't think of a good excuse to leave.

Helen smiled nervously and took a small bite of hers, and then put it down, waiting for him to speak.

'So how've you been?' he asked, floundering. 'Flu better?'

'I'm fine. It's gone now. Sorry I couldn't make it for dinner. It's lovely to see you, I wasn't expecting to see you until Friday. Were you on your way somewhere?'

'No. It's Rhoda. I mean, she says you've been meeting.'

Helen stood up, her voice suddenly bright and forced. 'Yes. I wondered when that would come out.'

'She only told me this morning.'

'I know I should have said something to you, but she made me promise not to.'

'Getting her own back, I suppose.'

'No. It wasn't that.' Helen sat down again, her lips quivering as if she might cry. He stood up and walked over to comfort her, but then stopped. If he held her, then she might expect him to kiss her, and now, inexplicably, the idea had lost its appeal.

He stood behind her chair. 'What is it?'

Her head was bowed before him, the nape of her neck pale and vulnerable. 'I thought, maybe, you'd come to see me.'

'I have. I mean, I needed someone to talk to. We had a row.'

She turned. A crease had appeared between her eyebrows. 'I kept on at her to tell you,' she said, 'but she wasn't sure how you'd react. And Peter, you never told her about Archie and me. It seemed strange when she said you hadn't, like we were not really your friends or something. I was quite hurt, to be honest. Archie would have been upset to think you'd never told your wife about us.'

Peter went and sat down again, pressed his forehead into his hand. 'I didn't mean … I know, but—'

'And such a waste. We could have had such lovely four-somes through the years. Why didn't you tell her?'

'It was just too hard.' He looked at his knees, but Helen was silent, expecting more, so he tried to explain. 'After the war nobody wanted to know about men like me and Archie. We weren't heroes. We'd done nothing to win the war. All we'd done was work for the Germans all those years. We were the next best thing to traitors. It was demoralising.'

'But you survived life in a camp, and that horrendous march. Lots of men never even made it home.'

'I know. At first, I thought struggling through all that would count for something, but once the news broke about the fate of the Jews, of how they were starved and gassed, and rounded up in death camps, suddenly our story was dull in comparison, a story that didn't seem worth telling. And it made me livid when people gloated over our victory, not understanding. Having no idea of the human cost of it.

When I got home I couldn't even stand to think of it. I just wanted to put it all behind me. Except for Archie, of course. He was the only one who knew what it was like. I couldn't lose touch with him. Without him I'd have been finished.'

'You should have told her.' Helen said.

'How? Tell me that.' Peter let the words burst from his mouth. 'Should I have told her how the guards bludgeoned a man to death with a spade because he didn't dig fast enough? Should I tell her …'

Helen sat very still, clinging to the chair seat as if she dared not move.

Peter caught hold of himself again. 'Sorry. I'm sorry. She wasn't easy to talk to. I wanted to give her time, and we had all our future ahead of us. I thought I'd get round to it, but as time went by I just couldn't… I can't describe it in an easy way, not without feeling things I don't want to feel.' He closed his eyes; even now the memories threatened to burst into his head. The melted pavement of Dresden. A snatch of Harry's walk, the set of his shoulders as he pulled on the sledge. His hand open in the snow, the black bread just out of reach.

Peter opened his eyes, saw Helen sitting very upright. He forced himself to speak, to get it out. 'I didn't tell Rhoda because I was scared. I thought Archie might tell her about … something I did. Something I was ashamed of. Something I could be arrested and court-martialled for. Even hanged. There was a friend of ours, Harry Tyson, and I … I hit him.'

'No. Don't.' Helen put up her hand to ward off the confidence.

'You don't understand. I killed him. He never got up.'

'It was wartime. Lots of people were killed in the war.'

'But he was on our side.'

'Does that make a difference? Would it have been better if he was German?'

He thought of Annegret and Klara. 'No, of course not … it's just, I saw his face … I should have told his parents what happened, should have—'

'And deprive them of thinking their son died a courageous death? He's gone, Peter. It would only hurt them to dig it all up now.'

He was silent a moment, his head in his hands.

'Look Peter, Archie's dead, and whatever you did, it's over. Archie can't tell anyone now. Keep your secret.'

Peter looked up to see Helen watching him. 'You know, when I came home, Archie was my lifeline,' he said. 'When I got low, when things weren't working between me and Rhoda, then I'd talk to him. She had an affair, you know, whilst we were in the camp, and it didn't make things easy. I suppose I was trying to push that away too.'

'I knew about that, she told me.' Helen got up and piled up the empty cake plates. 'Look, Peter, what's going on? Is Rhoda all right?'

'She's fine. No, actually she's not. We had a blazing row and I stormed off. She told me she'd made friends with you behind my back and it made me feel like you were both conspiring against me. So we started arguing, then lots of other things came up and—'

'For heaven's sake! Isn't that exactly what you've done to her all this time? It seems to me you need to apologise. And you could apologise to me too, while you're at it, leading me on like that.' Helen seemed to have suddenly lost patience. He'd never seen her that way before. It took him aback. Her face was red and blotchy and she looked as though she might cry.

'I know, I'm sorry. I'm useless. I didn't mean to upset you.'

'I thought we ... never mind.' She clunked the plates down on to the coffee table, wiped a tear away with her sleeve.

'I've made a mess of everything, haven't I?'

'Peter, grow up.' It sounded as though she was telling off a child. 'I hate to say it but you never know what's round the corner. Look at Archie – it seemed one minute he was just a bit tired, had a sore throat, and the next it was cancer, then he was gone. So quick. You've no idea ...'

She picked up the plates again and turned away. Her voice came from the kitchen, brittle, as if she was throwing the words at him. 'You're lucky. Luckier than you know. You have each other. Don't be so bloody stupid. Don't waste your lives arguing.' A pause and a sigh. 'Go on home, make it up with her.'

He was a jerk. He'd let Rhoda down. She'd wanted to get close to him, she said and he'd pushed her away. It was ten years today, their wedding anniversary. And he'd let Archie down too, his pal. What would he think if he could see him now? He'd led Helen on with his invitations to dinner and long intimate phone calls.

Helen appeared in the doorway wiping her hands on a tea towel over and over. 'Go home,' she said.

He was aware that Helen was letting him off the hook. A wave of gratitude washed over him. 'It's today,' he said, 'our wedding anniversary.'

'Then what are you waiting for? Give her a call, tell her you're on your way home.' Her voice threatened tears. 'And stop and buy flowers on the way.'

Peter stood and would have spoken but Helen's eyes

had a warning look. He went to the phone in the hall. He dialled and Rhoda picked up straight away. 'It's me,' he said sheepishly. 'I'm on my way home. I'll be about an hour or so. Don't cook lunch. We'll go out.'

'But I've got some salmon—' He heard Rhoda's voice, just the same, objecting, not understanding.

'Never mind the salmon, I'm taking you out.'

'But—'

'We'll talk later. Get your glad rags on, okay?' He tried not to sound too desperate to get out of there.

'Okay. Where are you?'

Why wouldn't she shut up? 'Later, I'll see you later. Bye.'

He put the phone down. Helen was waiting in the lounge, twisting the tea towel in her hands. 'All set?' she asked.

'Yes.' He evaded her eyes but then changed his mind, lunged and hugged her tight. 'Thanks. You've been … thanks for listening.'

When he released her, her eyes were brimming. 'It's what Archie would have wanted after all. What friends are for,' she said.

As he climbed in the car to drive away, she waved at him with false cheerfulness and shouted, 'Give my love to Rhoda!'

He wound the window down. 'I will,' he called.

The engine drowned his goodbye. He put the car in gear and accelerated away. The wind was in his face and he felt like singing, as if he was a schoolboy again. Could Helen be right? Was it time to let go of all that, time to let go once and for all? He'd nearly made a fool of himself, but he was going home to Rhoda. If she'd have him. It had always been Rhoda, really. He glanced in his mirror to see Helen turn from the gate, go back towards her empty house.

57
1955 Rhoda

I WAS DRAINED. But he was coming home. He hadn't said he was leaving me, he'd said we were going out. I wasn't sure I wanted to go out; it felt like I'd lost a layer of skin, and I didn't know if I was ready to expose myself to the world just yet. And after what Peter had said about being second best, I'd a longing to do something special for him, to prove I cared. Maybe cook him a nice meal. But if Peter wanted to go out, we'd go out.

I went upstairs to change. When I opened up the double wardrobe my eyes fell on all his shoes. Some of them had been there for years, since he'd become headmaster at St Cuthbert's. Black lace-ups he'd worn to Speech Day, all covered in dust, quite a few pairs of similar leather brogues in mismatched pairs, all jumbled up with fallen belts and some of my stilettos that had strayed to his side of the wardrobe. His shoes reminded me of all the places we'd been to in our marriage, ten years of outings. I picked out his white cricket shoes, stained with grass, and a pair of brown suede shoes I'd always disliked, that he'd bought on a day out in Keswick.

I had an idea. I bundled the lot into carrier bags and took them downstairs. In the kitchen, I spread newspaper on the table and rolled up my sleeves. An hour later the shoes were all lined up by the kitchen door, the suede brushed and buffed, the white shoes Blanco-ed, the teacher's lace-ups gleaming with polish. It felt good to see them all clean and tidy like that in a long row, like putting the world in order.

The slam of a car door. He was here already. He must have driven fast. Nervous, I hurried upstairs and threw on a cherry-red jumper and navy skirt, pulled a brush through my hair, wished it wasn't so wild. Wished I'd had it styled the way Helen did.

I heard him push the key in the lock and his voice call 'Hello?' exactly the way he always had.

'Coming!' I called.

From the top of the stairs I heard him exclaim, 'What's all this?'

I hurried down, feeling foolish, an excuse ready, 'I just thought—'

He was crouched over the neat row of shoes. 'I'd forgotten I had these.' He stooped to pick up a pair of black lace-ups. 'They don't look so bad, do they? I might wear them again. With the drainpipe trousers I bought last year.' He held them out towards me with his familiar smile.

Something welled up inside me.

'You silly thing,' he said, holding out his arms.

His embrace was firm and reassuring. It felt exactly right, like something I'd grown into until it was the perfect fit.

'Don't suppose you washed my shirts as well, did you?' he said.

I moved away, grinned, brushed the tears from my eyes with my sleeve. 'Don't push it.'

'I'm sorry,' he said, and his eyes were glistening too. 'I've been an idiot. I should have told you about Archie and Helen. I wanted to keep you away from it all, to be the person I was before the war, away from the dirt and the mud and the whole bloody mess of it. And Helen is a lovely person, but she's not—'

I reached for him again, pressed my cheek to his chest. 'Ssh. It doesn't matter. None of it matters. You're home, with me, where you belong.'

He lifted my chin and kissed me gently on the lips. 'Are you ready?'

I nodded.

'Better go and celebrate that anniversary then.' He grinned with the sort of shy look he'd had when we first met, and my heart flooded with relief. 'Just got to go and get changed,' he said. 'Think I'll wear these.' He bent down to pick up the suede shoes I'd never liked, but I didn't say a word. 'Oh, and those flowers are for you.'

A bunch of carnations lay in cellophane on the kitchen table.

'They're beautiful,' I said.

He smiled again and bounded away up the stairs. Above I could hear him opening the wardrobe and then the gurgle of the sink running. Our ordinary life. What made me think I didn't know him? I knew him in all the small ways, the moment-by-moment getting by. Our ten years had finally gathered enough weight to outweigh the past. What was inside would always be inside. No matter how hard we tried we would never be able to turn each other inside out. And we'd have to learn to be tolerant, to let things that once grated slip by, to wear them smooth with the rub of the years.

Peter came down the stairs in his best blue suit and

tie. He had on the brown suede shoes that didn't go with it. 'Will I do?' he asked.

'You'll do,' I said.

As he opened the front door, the eighteen-year-old inside me was watching, full of the future.

Acknowledgements

Peter's experiences are fictional but constructed from the real-life ordeals of prisoners of war, based on their memoirs. I am indebted to the memoirs of Alec Barker, Charles Waite and Victor Gregg, whose books are listed in the Further Reading section. Thank you to John Adams and the staff of Carnforth Station Heritage Centre, in particular Win Hayhurst who agreed to be interviewed about her wartime memories. Margaret Barton was kind enough to write to me about her time filming *Brief Encounter*, and I would also like to thank Helen Burrow and George Coupe of the Carnforth Reminiscence Project who supplied me with fantastic photographs of old Carnforth station and transcripts of interviews made with railway workers and their families. A big thank you to Eliza Graham, Mary Chamberlain and Jenny Yates for their editorial advice, and special thanks as always to my husband John for his unflagging support.

Selected Further Reading

Anthony Beevor, *The Second World War*

Anne Bonney, *PoW to Lancashire Farmer: the remarkable life of Alec Barker*

Kevin Brownlow, *David Lean, a biography*

Kate Fleming, *Celia Johnson, a biography*

Victor Gregg, *Dresden: A Survivor's Story*

R. H. N Hardy, *A Life on the Lines: a railwayman's album*

Sheila Hardy, *A 1950s Housewife: marriage and homemaking in the 1950s*

Robert Malcolm, *The Diaries of Nella Last*

Patrick Mayhew, *One Family's War*

John Nicholl and Tony Rennell, *The Last Escape: the untold story of Allied prisoners of war in Germany 1944–45*

Virginia Nicholson, *Millions like us: women's lives during the Second World War*

Charles Waite, *Survivor of the Long March: five years as a PoW 1940–1945*

Sarah Wallis and Svetlana Palmer, *We Were Young and at War: the first-hand story of young lives lived and lost in World War II*

BBC WWII People's War Archive http://www.bbc.co.uk/history/ww2peopleswar/

Past Encounters

Reading Group Questions

1. Do you think that Peter's secret friendship with Archie is believable? Have you ever kept a big secret from someone close to you, and how did it make you feel?

2. Annegret and Klara are minor but important characters in the novel. What do they contribute to the plot and your understanding of the war?

3. Archie and Peter do not seem likely friends at the beginning, yet their friendship lasts for fifteen years. Is their relationship anything like a marriage? And if so, in what ways?

4. The novel mentions Ruth Ellis, who was hanged for murder in 1955. Discuss whether murder in wartime requires different moral considerations from a murder committed in peacetime. Should Peter have been punished for what happened to Harry?

5. How has Rhoda's father been affected by the First World War, and how does his later accident change him? Can Rhoda learn any lessons from her father?

6. Did Peter's experiences as a prisoner of war surprise you? What are the qualities that Peter found essential to survive life in a PoW camp?

7. Rhoda and Patty have a good friendship, but Peter and Archie's closeness takes time to develop. Is a friendship

between women based on different criteria than a friendship between men?

8. *Brief Encounter* is a classic film. How much reference does *Past Encounters* make to the film, and are there any themes which run through both? (The film can be found on Youtube.)

Praise for Deborah Swift

'Brilliant characterisation, scintillating dialogue and a thrilling narrative … a terrific historical novel.'

—*The Review Group*

'The past comes alive through impeccable research, layers of intriguing plotline, and the sheer power of descriptive prose … a classy, compelling adventure story and a true journey of discovery.'

—*Lancashire Evening Post*

'Filled with suspense, accuracy, real-to-life settings and characters, *A Divided Inheritance* will satisfy even the most discerning of history buffs.'

—*The Examiner*

www.davinablake.com

www.deborahswift.com

About Davina Blake

I used to be a set and costume designer for theatre and BBC TV, during which time I developed a love of research. I was inspired to write *Past Encounters* because I live in the north of England near Carnforth station, and I have often kept out of the cold in the *Brief Encounter* refreshment room whilst waiting for a train. I love a good cup of tea, preferably accompanied by a chocolate brownie! In Carnforth Station Heritage Centre *Brief Encounter* is showing on a video loop, and I was surprised to discover how powerful the film is, even seventy years later. I also enjoy writing historical fiction set in the seventeenth century under the pen name Deborah Swift, and run courses for writers from my home in a small village near the Lake District National Park.

www.davinablake.com
www.deborahswift.com

45672230R00265

Made in the USA
Charleston, SC
31 August 2015